The
Last
Hypothesis

The
Last
Hypothesis

L. C. Paoletti

A Novel

LCP

This novel is dedicated to those who already know.

Contents

The
Last
Hypothesis

Act Three

1

Most are forgotten but this day would remain with Dante Paolo forever.

It was early September in New England and although the leaves on the trees in Massachusetts were still green, there were a few sugar maples in the wetlands whose tops were tinged yellow, as if they were chosen by their kin to rise up and survey the status of the season. The cool, crisp morning air helped the professor relax as he began the first day of his second career, the opening of his life's act three.

Dr. Dante Paolo had an odd habit of labeling different parts of his life as if they were scenes in a grand play. He considered the period from birth to age five to be a wordless prologue. His endless imagination pictured a majestic burgundy curtain slowly rising on his life's stage accompanied by the rich orchestral melody of the *Intermezzo* from Mascagni's *Cavalleria Rusticana*—a tranquil beginning, a tribute to those who cared for him during those memory-less, completely dependent years as an infant and a toddler.

But by that early fall day his life had progressed well beyond the play's opening scene. Indeed, Dante Paolo felt the significance of the moment as he strolled across the neatly groomed campus of Wilmington College in the early morning light. For that simple but privately poignant moment marked the close of the first two acts that had consumed 51 years of his life. He knew that he was well beyond middle age and way past the potential for a mid-life crisis. And like the wild twist and turns that unfolded during acts one and two, act three was a surprise addition to the playbill; it was completely unscripted and for the most part, unrehearsed. Nevertheless he approached this new opening scene with a sense of self-confidence forged by a sound education and a solid family life in act one, and a very rewarding career and a stable, supportive marriage written in act two.

The brownstone buildings that dotted the campus of Wilmington College symbolized its New England puritanical roots. These stately structures serve as steadfast reminders of the college's high prestige as one of the first institutions of higher learning in America. This classic college landscape was a common theme in Dante Paolo's life as similarly beautiful buildings and rolling greens adorned with stately black willows, tall eastern pines, gray American beeches, white ash and red oaks also graced the New England universities he attended as an undergraduate and as a graduate student. And despite the fact that it was located in a busy city, in a crowded neighborhood on a bustling avenue, the medical school campus of Harvard University—where Dante had been a research scientist for 25 years—had it's own unique atmosphere. The cityscape of glistening marble buildings supported by solid pillars of stone housed scores upon scores of academics who, through pure brilliance and perseverance, sharpened the cutting edge of scientific and medical discovery daily.

But what separated Wilmington College from other institutions established in the 1800s was that it rejected the young country's call to only teach farming and agriculture for a less common path of offering a broad and more diverse education. The college founders sought to teach students how to gain knowledge. They wanted graduates to apply their newfound wisdom to benefit not only themselves but also all members of society. Indeed, the college's 137-year-old precept: *Scientia, Unum, Omnes* calls on every student to aggressively pursue knowledge simply to better oneself but then it also issues a direct challenge to apply this newfound knowledge to improve the lives and wellbeing of others. "Only when satisfying these three dictums will America prosper," reasoned the college's founders.

———•———

Although tenured and thus secure in their jobs, most members of the science faculty at Wilmington College were nonetheless cautious and partly suspicious of Dante Paolo. It wasn't because he was from Harvard, nor was it due to the fact that he was the first new hire in the department in five years, or that his course was the first new senior level addition in over a decade, but rather because of Dante's impressive research accomplishments and lengthy publication record—the highest badge of honor for an academic—that really made them envious. But only when they met and spoke with the modest professor, and especially after word spread that his position at the college was limited to one academic year with full-time status contingent on performance, course evaluation and approval by the President and the college's Board of Trustees, did they feel less threatened.

The science department was housed in Paine Hall, a relatively modern three-story red brick structure whose plain-faced architecture poorly matched the rounded-cornered brownstones common to Wilmington College. But as with all buildings on campus, Thomas Paine Hall was named after one of America's early leaders, a tradition started by the college's founders to provide examples to future generations of the value of education as a means to help others.

The classrooms in Paine Hall were moderately sized and outfitted with modern day teaching tools: white boards, LCD projectors and high-speed wireless Internet access. There was also a single lecture auditorium reserved for larger classes and special seminars. The laboratories were equipped with microscopes, pH meters, tissue culture hoods, chemicals, plaster models of animal organs, telescopes, electrophoresis equipment, computers, and cupboards filled with all sorts of chemicals, glassware and manuals. Faculty offices were plain but comfortable and the break room, where informal meetings and impromptu gossip sessions were often held, contained a small rectangular conference table, a refrigerator, a coffee maker and a microwave oven.

The small department offered a comprehensive list of courses that covered biology, botany, chemistry, comparative anatomy and physiology, and physics. The newly listed course, *Teach the Professor*, was advertised as a senior-level, general biology course. Its vague title matched its equally vague course description that simply "challenged students to learn more."

Dr. Paolo's heart sank as he strode towards the wooden podium at the front of the newly remodeled lecture auditorium. The number of students in attendance—five—was a complete letdown and an embarrassment. It also confirmed his closely guarded suspicions and worse fears that today's students were no longer interested in the biological sciences, not even the brightest of the bright enrolled at Wilmington College. Dr. Paolo noticed that the students—three males and two females—sat next to each other in the front row as if they were good friends that did not want to be separated.

"Good morning," he said to the impassive class. "I'm Dante Paolo and this course is called *Teach the Professor*."

Although he wasn't expecting a synchronized reply like parochial school fifth grade class, he did expect some sort of reaction. Even a purposely-dropped pencil would have been better than the absolute silence and blank stares that followed his greeting. He paused for a moment then recognized the great distance between where he was standing at the podium and where the students were seated in the front row. He walked to the side entrance of the large room where a folded metal chair leaned against the back wall. He carried the chair to the space between the podium and the front row of seats where he opened then sat in it; now he was no more that ten feet from the front row.

"Let's start again, shall we? My name is Dante Paolo and this course is called *Teach the Professor.*" This time he evoked a cordial greeting from each student.

Space did matter.

Dr. Paolo told them that he was born and raised in New Hampshire and that he graduated from that state's University with a Ph.D. in Biochemistry before any of them were born. Most of the students smiled and nodded at the age difference—he was starting to connect. He told them that he applied for, and was granted, "a special visa" to immigrate to the blue state of Massachusetts and the big city of Boston for postdoctoral training—a few more smiles from the small audience. He described how the next 20 years of his life were spent at a "small community college" known as Harvard Medical School—broader smiles and a few chuckles—where he pioneered painless ways to deliver vaccines. After describing the potential relevance of his research, Dr. Paolo told them about a course he had tutored at the medical school.

"First year medical students were automatically enrolled in a 10-week intensive course that covered pathology, microbiology, immunology and infectious diseases. This course—the last one of their freshman year—included labs and case study tutorials. At most universities each of these topics would require a minimum of 10-weeks. But this was not the case at the medical school where expectations were exceedingly high and where they often were met. Those freshmen rose to the challenge of the intensive course and that's exactly what I'm expecting from you in this course—a high level of intensity, drive and commitment, after all, this is a senior level course. And I'm also expecting that you demand the same from me. This course will be no less then a two-way learning street," he said in a stern voice that raised a few eyebrows.

"I've always wanted to teach this course, but, quite frankly, I thought that it would be taught at the graduate level. Since you're only a few months away from starting graduate school—assuming that all of you will continue on—and given that you've apparently received a top-notch education here at the college, I think this course will work. Actually, to be truthful, college officials aren't so sure. They view this course as an experiment in teaching, we're all a part of a grand experiment, an experiment in science education where we approach learning as a two-way street, a give and take. Are you ready for the challenge? I hope so because I am."

A hand shot up as soon as Dr. Paolo ended his sentence and a male student spoke without pause.

"My name is Ajay Adani. Could you tell us what this course is about? There was no real description in the syllabus along with just your name and the title. What will we be doing here?"

"Excellent question Ajay," Dr. Paolo replied. "But before I answer your question, I'd like to know each of you and what drew you to this class. Can we start with you Ajay?"

"Sure," replied the self-confident, dark-skinned young man. "Like I said, my name is Ajay Adani. I am interested in each and every aspect of computers and the world of computing. I intend to go to graduate school and to get an advanced degree in computer science. I was drawn here by the course title. But why would we teach the professor? Isn't it your job to teach us?"

"Are you a senior?" asked Dr. Paolo.

"Yes."

"Hang on to those questions Ajay, I'll answer them in a moment. All of you are seniors, right?"

All five students nodded.

"Great, that makes it easy. Who wants to go next?"

"My name is Amy Ito," said the pretty young lady with soft Asian features. "I've taken all of the biology courses that the college offers and I'm applying to medical school so I'll need some time to prepare applications and I've already met all of the requirement for graduation, so I thought to see what this course was all about," said Amy who instantly was not pleased with her convoluted response. She sank back in her seat knowing that her delivery was awkward and that it sounded somewhat pretentious.

"Hi, I'm Brad MacIntyre and I'm also applying to medical school," offered the well-groomed young man who looked and dressed the part of the all-American college preppie. "I've also taken all of the science courses except physical chemistry and I also don't need any more credits to graduate. I signed up because I'm looking for a challenge," he added for good measure as if he was jockeying for position at the starting line.

As if on cue, the casually dressed, sneaker-sporting young man sitting to Brad's left spoke. "I'm Phil Hess and I'm interested in physics and mathematics and I'm applying to graduate schools to continue my education in these fields. I was drawn to the course by its title."

The fifth student, a young lady who sat to Ajay's right at the far end of the row opposite Phil, struck Dante as a throwback hippie. When he was in graduate school, she would have been labeled a "crunchy-granola" for her apparently unpretentious, tree-hugging, free-loving ways. Abby's features were plain and common. She had a round, chubby face partially hidden by her brown shoulder-length hair; her baggy clothes hid most of her plump body. Dr. Paolo looked at her and extended his left hand to give the signal that it was her turn.

"I'm Abby Lark," she stated softly, almost apologetically as she looked down towards her well-worn blue denim backpack. "I've applied to some graduate schools but I'm not sure what I would like to study, maybe psychology," she said. "The title of your course caught my attention, that's why I'm here."

"Well then," said Dr. Paolo, "it looks like the name of the course worked. That's a pretty good start." He then returned to Ajay's question but instead of describing the course directly, he took a more complex and circuitous route. He reviewed a couple of common teaching methods and used his own experiences as examples of how these methods differed.

"All of us have been on the receiving end of a lecture. 'Lecture', a noun, a speech usually delivered in an educational setting, or 'lecture', a verb, as in a method, active, as in 'he lectures to the audience'. Since we were children we've been read to, we've been lectured. Sitting on our parent's lap, sitting on the floor in kindergarten, sitting at the one-piece metal desk in elementary school or sitting on a park bench with a grandparent, we've been lectured. In these cases, knowledge moved in one direction from the older to the younger, the learned to the learner, the teacher to the student. This pattern repeated itself constantly until one day, and perhaps quite abruptly, an inversion happened whereby the child becomes a parent, the student becomes the teacher. Inversions happen at different times in one's life for a variety of reasons. For me, an inversion happened when I became a teaching assistant, a TA, in graduate school. All of the sudden I was the teacher standing in front of a roomful of freshman biochemistry majors. I was expected to teach laboratory biochemistry to those who were only a year or so younger than me. I was the authority and I was very nervous. As a TA I had to learn and teach at the same time. Not only did I learn, or re-learn the material before class but I also had to consider other important aspects of teaching, like interpersonal behavior, like how to deal with various personalities and also to be cognizant of the audience's culturally diversity." Dr. Paolo rose slowly from his chair as if to emphasize the next point. "Good teachers can spot those in the class who will do well and those who will struggle; who will follow, and who will lead, those who will think inside the box or who will challenge the norm." He then paused for a moment to let the last point hang while making sure he still had their attention, which he did. In their own way, all five students were attentive and absorbing what the new professor was saying. Phil, Brad and Ajay were simply watching and listening while Amy listened and also jotted a few words in her notebook. Abby sat stoically with her eyes fixed on her backpack that was on the floor by her feet.

"The challenge in this class will not be the material itself," he said with conviction. "It will be your capacity to dig deeper, to forge new connections, and then to effectively communicate those new connections to others. Shortly you will choose a research topic that will consume your entire time in this class. At the end of the semester, you will deliver a lecture on your research topic that should be understood by everyone in attendance, regardless of his or her familiarity with the subject matter. Sound easy? Trust me, it's not. You're college seniors. Next year, when you receive your bachelor's degree you will surpass most of society in the level of education attained but you'll be like freshman again, at the beginning of a new starting line. You will become the next generation of teachers, of lecturers. But we're not going to wait, your inversion begins with this class," said Dr. Paolo.

He then launched into a synopsis on the teaching methods of the Greek philosopher Socrates. He spoke without notes, handouts or visual aids.

"Simply put, the Socratic method takes the 'profess' out of 'professor' and it's completely different from the didactic method I just described. Students learn by actively tackling problems in a give and take with the teacher who guides their reasoning instead of simply providing answers. First-year medical students at Harvard had to diagnose a patient's aliments with just a few clues. For example, a person arrives in the emergency room with a high fever, chills, total body malaise and she is in a state of delirium. The medical students dig for information on each and every symptom or piece of relevant data. Was the person who accompanied the patient to the hospital a friend, a spouse, or a lover? What did he or she know about the patient's health? What is the patient's age? Male. Female. Black. White. Hispanic. Asian. Diabetic. Obese. Anorexic? Do you have any prior condition? Did this person recently travel out of the country? If so, where and for how long? Did the patient have children or grandchildren, if so are they sick too? Does the patient have a documented immunodeficiency? Sometimes, a simple case of the common cold would take hours to diagnose because there are many illnesses that share the same clinical features as influenza that had to be ruled out. Professors who tutor the class follow the discussion very carefully. As needed they offer comments, or specifically pose questions, that could lead to new clues on how to reach the correct diagnosis. But the professors never answer student's questions directly; they made them think. At the end of the day, students exposed to this learning method have a deeper understanding of not only the patient, but also of the illness and the ultimate diagnosis; a more substantial understanding than what they would have gained if given the answer outright," he concluded.

Dr. Paolo then told his students that the Socratic method would be used in this class. They would teach him about their topic, and in doing so he should be led to think about an aspect of science that may be new to him, thus the course's title, *Teach the Professor*. His singular role was to guide their thinking by asking questions, period. The seniors were told that they were going to do the heavy lifting, that they would perform all of the research, and also that they would do most of the teaching.

The lesson plan was simple and straightforward: they were to choose a scientific topic, thoroughly research the topic, prepare and review reports with the class. Then they were going to refine and update their research and again present their findings to the class. There will be a great deal of interaction and discussion, so they had to arrive to every class prepared to participate, to ask questions and, most importantly, to find answers.

Class would meet from 8 to 11 a.m. on Tuesdays and Thursdays, and although there were no textbooks, a laptop or tablet was required to search the web for information. Dr. Paolo told them that attendance was mandatory and that their grade was a simple pass-fail that hinged solely on their individual projects and class involvement. There would be no midterm or final exams.

The first class ended with an hour to spare and with a simple assignment: to bring to their next class, on the following Tuesday, a research topic published within the past year from one of two high-level science journals, *Science* or *Nature*. Dr. Paolo told the students that both journals were accessible digitally online and also as hardcopies at the college's library. He suggested that they give a great deal of thought to their research topic; it should be something that captured their imagination, something that will hold their long-term interest.

After he described the first and only assignment of the course, Dr. Paolo dismissed the class then walked briskly down the hall to his office. The small rectangular room had a window that faced east-northeast with a view of a narrow asphalt path that paralleled the edge of thick, overgrown woods. Dr. Paolo wondered, as he stared at the steel-gray bark of the large beech tree near the edge of the woods, if he had made the right choice by taking on this responsibility.

His mind wandered, as it often did, to different times in his life. It darted from one time period to another until it settled on the not-so-long-ago days in his laboratory where he conducted experiments, reviewed results with others, planned the next set of experiments, or made on-the-spot adjustments to ongoing experiments. He was back in his orderly corner office with a grand view of the city where he spent most of his life applying for grants, reviewing experiments with post-docs, writing and editing manuscripts, reading journal articles, or simply thinking—it was a time that already seemed so distant, even a bit unreal. The soothing daydream ended abruptly by several sharp knocks on his office door, and since it was left ajar, the force of the knocks swung the door open to reveal Ajay standing at its threshold.

"Dr. Paolo?" started Ajay in a rapid, sharply punctuated cadence of his native Indian voice.

"Yes. Hi. Come in," replied Dr. Paolo who was a bit startled. "What can I do for you?"

"I wanted you to know that I'm going to drop your course. It's not what I had expected and frankly, I'm not interested in teaching you, my classmates or anyone else, I'm here to learn and, well, I'm also going to spend some time writing code for a small startup... my friend started a... and... well anyway, thanks." Ajay then turned and left the office giving Dr. Paolo no chance to reply.

Wonderful, Dr. Paolo thought. *Down to four, at least I think it's four; it may be fewer than that by the end of the day, I suppose. This is not good, not good at all. This will play right into Benedetti's hands. I can almost hear him now.*

2

"Don't even think about it. I have one of those, you can borrow mine," chided Rob as he sneaked up on Dr. Paolo in the tool section at Sears.

Robert Pierce and his family live in Dante Paolo's neighborhood in Andover, a sprawling suburb north of Boston and just ten miles from Wilmington College. Rob and his wife, Beverly have been neighbors and good friends of Dante and his wife Laura Kean since the two couples met decades ago at the opening of the new housing development where both couples settled. Over the years they spent quite a bit of time together to the extent that Dante and Laura were thought of as surrogate parents to the Pierce's twin boys, whom they first met as fuzzy gray images on a surprise ultrasound.

"Had I known you were heading here we could have driven together," offered Rob.

"Well I was at the liquor store and I decided to have a look at what was on sale."

"What have you been up to?"

"Not much, settling into a soft retirement while I look for some part-time work. I'm also starting to think more seriously about starting my own consulting business."

"How's Laura?"

"Fine, busy as ever. At least one of us is working. How about you, what's new?"

"Oh, not much. We're gearing up for finals and graduation exercises at the college. It's the usual end of the year crunch. Some of my kids are panicking about graduate school while others are simply preparing for finals. It's the same old, same old end-of-the-year routine. But who can complain? It's springtime in New England and it looks like we've survived another winter."

"True enough. This is my favorite time of the year, but soon we'll be moaning about the pollen, then the bugs and the heat..." His neighbor interrupted Dante in mid-sentence; he had to say something urgently as if the thought was about to expire.

"Hey, wait a minute," said Rob excitedly. "Didn't you just say that you were looking for part-time work?" And without waiting for his friend to answer he continued, "I have an idea, Dante—you should teach at the college."

"What?"

"Yeah, you'd be a great teacher, the kids would love you. C'mon, let's grab some coffee and talk about this."

———•———

Rob was a Biology teacher at Wilmington College, a seasoned veteran of fifteen years. It was not his first career choice but it was a job he grew to enjoy. When Rob was in graduate school working on a doctorate in Environmental Sciences, his father became ill and died suddenly. He was close to his dad and the shock of losing the central figure in his life affected him deeply. He was poorly prepared for the entire death scene from signing the next-of-kin form to meeting with the somber, swindler of a funeral director. After the trauma of the immediate grief, after the wake and the funeral, Rob lost his sense of purpose. He became depressed and discouraged to the extent that he could no longer focus on his research or his coursework. Eventually he had to abandon his pursuit of a Ph.D. but he did muster the will to complete the requirements for a Master's degree in Biology. Rob intended to tackle environmental problems by creating genetically engineered organisms to clean up oil spills, toxic waste and other pollutants that harmed the ecosystem; he called it molecular ecology. But without a doctorate degree Rob knew that he could not have a research program of his own so he abandoned the idea of being a laboratory scientist altogether. Along with the change in his graduate school program came a shift in career goals; he decided to become a science teacher.

Although he knew that teaching was a noble profession with many lasting personal and professional rewards, he didn't think it suited his potential; he thought it would be a poor utilization of his intellect. But he didn't want to leave the science field altogether. Besides he had just married Beverly, the love of his life, and with help from his in-laws, the newlyweds had also purchased a new house in the suburbs. They were also planning to start a family. In short, he needed a job, a solid, steady job.

By good fortune, Dr. Jean Holliday, the President of Wilmington College was a close childhood friend of Rob's mother. But unlike Rob's mother, young Jean decided to forgo the home economics and typing classes that were virtually forced on women at that time and instead applied herself to college-prep courses—desires that were not in line with those of her parents. They worried, "Jeanie dear, men do not find educated women attractive. You'll be condemned to an unmarried, childless and thus unfulfilled life, honey. Listen to us. See how well we've done?"

Undeterred, Jean not only became the first in her family to earn a college degree but she also was the first female to receive a doctorate from the Sociology Department at Harvard University. She sought to dedicate her life to higher education and after a decade of teaching at a small community college for women, she was installed as Wilmington College's first female President at the tender age of 35. It was Dr. Holliday who personally handled Rob's appointment to the science faculty at the prestigious college; a hire that no one dared to contest—for fear of looking sexist—and one she never regretted.

Students, parents and peers alike commented on how well Rob explained complicated scientific concepts and principles; his presentations were always clear and to the point. He also enjoyed helping others and freely shared his knowledge with anyone who sought it. In no time, Rob became President Holliday's model of a stellar faculty member.

———

"So, I'll say it again, you'd be a great teacher at Wilmington College," Rob said over a decaffeinated coffee and an almond-filled bear claw pastry. "Remember how well your lecture went when you came in to talk about the biochemistry of bacteria, like make their own magnets and how they can use oil for food, remember? They loved it, the kids ate it up!"

"Yeah, but it was just one lecture and I was a novelty. That was easy. I didn't have to deal with all the stuff you have to do like creating lesson plans, dealing with homework, dealing with parents, dealing with administration..."

"It's not that bad," interrupted Rob. "The kids are great, they're smart, they want to learn and the parents, most of them anyway, are quite supportive. I think you should try it. What do you have to lose? You've got a boatload of practical, real world experience. I'd build off of that platform."

"What would I teach?"

"Anything you want. Well almost anything."

"Actually, over the years I've been thinking about structuring a course in scientific inquiry following the same approach the medical school uses to teach future clinicians how to solve medical problems. The course requires highly-motivated students who are interested in digging up information, you know, good old-fashioned research like we did in grad school?"

"Do you mean bench research, like doing experiments in the lab?"

"No, not at all. The course could be structured in many different ways, but I'd have the students chose a scientific topic then spend the rest of the semester researching it in the literature, learning about it, then presenting what they learned to the class. I would guide and push. I'd guide them to make sure they don't stray off course and push them to learn more to dig deeper, to ask harder questions. If all goes well, by the end of the semester, each student will have an in-depth understanding of how the scientific method is used to ask questions, how to find the answers to those questions, and how to solve problems. Since there will be a great deal of exchange and interactions, each student will have a working knowledge of their classmate's topic as well."

"Has this approach been tried outside of the medical school?" asked Rob.

"I don't know," Dante replied. "Why?"

"Because I think you can make a great pitch to the college's curriculum committee to add this course. In fact, I think they meet next week to finalize the fall courses and if they approve, then you're in, you can teach your course. Hell, as far as I can tell, they rarely add new courses, so perhaps now's the time. Your idea is very interesting. They just might buy it."

"They might buy the course but do you think they'll buy me?"

"Why not?"

"Well for starters I'm not certified to teach in Massachusetts and secondly, I have no formal teaching experience."

"Dante, Wilmington College is private. It doesn't have to conform to State requirements and that includes teacher certification. And let me say it again, you have had what is arguably the best type of accreditation, it's called 'real world experience'."

"Yeah, I'm not sure."

"Look, hang tight until Monday afternoon. I'll chat with Jean and I'll get back to you."

"Jean? Who's Jean?"

"Jean Holliday, the President of the college. She's a longtime friend and the person who gave me a break when I was looking for a job. You'll love her, she holds a doctorate in Sociology from Harvard and has a ton of honorary degrees from other Universities for her teaching and administrative achievements. She loves innovation. Let me see if I can chat with her this weekend. I'll give you a call Monday night, okay?"

"Alright, sure that's fine with me," replied Dante with a slight degree of apprehension.

3

There was only one other faculty member at Wilmington College that could match the academic achievements of President Jean Holliday.

Dr. Lorenzo Benedetti was born and raised in a small Italian village just north of Florence in the cradle of great Renaissance thinkers, a fact he used often to demonstrate his elite pedigree as if intelligence itself was extracted directly from the Tuscan air. He earned a doctorate degree at the University of Bologna, and immigrated with his family to New York City where he accepted a postdoctoral position at the famed Rockefeller University. Dr. Benedetti's Italian upbringing prepared him well not only for the rigors and the politics of science in the big city but also for the terse, confrontational attitudes of native New Yorkers as most did not care for those who worked at the elitist "RockU". Lorenzo ignored those "small people" and others who disinterested him—which included most of the Rockefeller faculty—and cherished those precious few who provided intellectual challenges and sharp scientific discourse. He had no patience for mediocrity.

Dr. Benedetti's stellar career as a neuroscientist spanned exactly 40 years. During this time, he published over 500 scientific articles on his research findings, mentored 78 students, many who became leaders in academic departments across the world or heads of biotech companies during the boom of the 1970s and 1980s. Beyond the key advances, he was also widely credited with bringing order to an obscure and somewhat incoherent field of neurobiology, a discipline that was poised to mature, along with other areas of human biology, due to the availability of new visualization tools like the confocal microscope and brilliant imaging dyes.

His rise in academic stature paralleled his induction into several prestigious scientific societies including the New York College of Sciences, the National College of Sciences, the International Society of Neuroscience, and Society for Biological Imaging and Diagnosis. But the one accolade bestowed on Lorenzo Benedetti that was most treasured by his family was his induction into the New York branch of *L'Accademia dei Medici*, a broad-based intellectual society formed in Florence in 1525 in honor of their revered former ruler, Lorenzo de 'Medici.

Despite his achievements in the laboratory, most of Dr. Benedetti's last decade at RockU was devoted in large part to administrative assignments. These duties included five years as head of the Neuroscience Department, a task that was required of all full professors but one that was avoided at all cost because it detracted from the sacred time needed to conduct research. However, his ability to effectively manage a laboratory while expanding the Department by recruiting new young talent caught the attention of the RockU's President who persuaded him to accept a position as Associate Dean of Academic Affairs, a position that rapidly led to a promotion to the Dean of Academic Affairs.

Much to Dr. Benedetti's surprise—and to the disappointment of those in his laboratory—he actually enjoyed being in a more visible position of power, especially when he could make decisions without, as he would say to his confidant, "the tedious process of discussions or the need for consensus." Prestige and power suited Dr. Benedetti for his intellect was surpassed only by his ego. He had exceeded his childhood ambitions by becoming a successful scientist, a full Professor and now a Dean at a University in America, achievements that, at least in his mind, were on par with those of his Renaissance idols.

Lorenzo Benedetti resisted little when his long-time companion, an Italian-American woman he met at RockU, sought to move to New England to be closer to her aging parents. At 65 years of age, he was ready for a change, to leave the big city and to slow down a bit. Full retirement, however, was only a passing muse; he wanted his mind to earn a living until the day he died, so when his companion noticed a posting in the *Times* for a Dean of Academic Affairs at Wilmington College, she took it upon herself to update his *curriculum vitae*. She also drafted a letter on his behalf to the college's President effectively bypassing the instructions in the advertisement to send letters to the head of the search committee. The location of the college in Wilmington, Massachusetts, remarked Lorenzo's companion, "Was as perfect as it could be."

———•———

Dr. Holliday knew that there was a strong internal candidate vying to fill the open Dean position but she could not overlook the good fortune to have received an application from a widely published scholar.

"Dr. Benedetti," she stated simply and with conviction to the five-membered search committee composed of handpicked faculty, "is an accomplished scientist and a highly capable administrator. Without question, his presence would instantly raise the level of the college's prestige, both nationally and internationally. Alumni of all ages will immediately see the impact of having this man on our staff and our students will also benefit from his experiences at the Rockefeller." Her remaining comments to the small group began with a directive, "I expect that the committee will place Lorenzo Benedetti's application at the top of a short list of nominees accompanied with a strong letter of support. I also expect that the final list of applications will be forwarded to me for approval by close of business tomorrow as the Board of Trustees is scheduled to meet next week and the selection of a new Dean is at the top of their agenda."

The appointment of Dr. Benedetti as the new Dean of Academic Affairs at Wilmington College overshadowed the other faculty appointments Dr. Holliday announced that same day. In contrast to the swarm of publicity, complete with a full room of local news reporters that heralded Dr. Benedetti's arrival, the hiring of Robert Pierce as a new faculty in the Department of Biology was announced with an official press release of exactly 42 words:

Wilmington College announced today the hiring of New Hampshire native Robert Pierce as a new member of the Science Department. Mr. Pierce received a Master's degree in Science from the University of New England and currently lives in Andover with his wife.

4

Dr. Holliday wanted to be present for Dr. Paolo's interview, a request that came as a surprise to Dr. Benedetti especially given that the meeting was held a week after graduation, a time when most faculty, including the President, leave for the long-awaited summer recess. Because the faculty position would be filled only on a provisional basis, a search committee was not necessary and there was no overly formal vetting process. In essence, the decision whether or not to hire Dante Paolo resided solely with Dean Benedetti, with final approval by the President.

Washington Hall, named after the first president of the United States, was an attractive brownstone and granite structure with rounded corners and a majestic clock tower that chimed at the half and full hour marks. Situated near the center of campus, the original and once sole building now housed Wilmington College's Alumni center and Administration.

The interview was held in Dr. Benedetti's ornately decorated, wood paneled office in Washington Hall with a birds-eye-view of a central juncture on campus where students crisscrossed to and from classes. His chestnut wood desk was positioned majestically towards the back of the office facing the entrance to the room; the floor graced with a fine Persian rug. The built-in bookshelves held several neurobiology texts some of which were written or co-edited by the Dean. Conspicuously positioned on a single shelf just at eye level were ten thick, black leather-bound books containing original versions of his published research papers; in gold lettering on the spine of each volume was the time span when the research was conducted. Dante Paolo knew that Lorenzo Benedetti had published extensively but seeing them presented in a uniformed and organized manner was nonetheless quite impressive. The display served to drive home the point of how much of an impact the neuroscientist had on the field.

Dante Paolo arrived at Washington Hall punctually at 9 a.m. where the casually dressed Dean greeted him warmly. Although Dr. Paolo recognized the elder scientist from Internet images, what was not revealed in the computer search was the aura of superiority that complemented his strong Mediterranean features. The Dean's thick black hair appropriately accented with gray along the temples accentuated his wide forehead, full nose and brown sad eyes that deceitfully conveyed an even-tempered, compassionate demeanor.

The two scientists shook hands with eyes locked, focused on each other as if they were about to begin a chess match and each was trying to gauge the others opening move. And just as Dr. Paolo broke away to face an approaching woman he thought he noticed a slight narrowing of the Dean's eyes.

"You must be Professor Paolo," said Dr. Holliday warmly as she extended her right hand and delivered a firm, decisive handshake.

"Yes I am. Dante, please," responded Dr. Paolo who sought to do away with formalities as soon as possible.

"Jean, Jean Holliday, and you've already met Lorenzo?" she said turning towards Dr. Benedetti.

"Yes, we've just met."

The three academicians then settled around a round, glass topped mahogany table positioned in a corner of the office near two windows. Once seated, Dr. Holliday wasted no time in asking the applicant a series of direct questions.

"Dante, tell me. You've had a stellar research career. Over 200 publications, ten book chapters, two edited books, three issued patents, merit awards, a tenured position at Harvard Medical, why would you leave all that in the first place? Then why would you decide to teach undergraduates at a private college? Certainly, based on your experiences and expertise you could do anything. You can be an executive at any biopharmaceutical company in the world, or consult or serve on scientific advisory boards. Why Wilmington College and why now?"

Dr. Paolo was fully prepared to address these obvious questions. They were the same ones he'd asked himself many times since Robert proposed the idea weeks ago but he was a taken aback by the forceful nature of Dr. Holliday's delivery and how quickly these questions arose. *This woman is no nonsense*, Dante thought.

"Well, in short, research began to wind down when funding levels decreased, and although I still had a salary, my lab went from ten members to zero as I simply didn't have funds to support them. It was at that point—when the lab was empty—that I realized what I missed most about research. It was not the challenge of getting grants and writing manuscripts, nor the satisfaction of having papers published *per se*, nor was it the academic title, or travelling to meetings, or giving seminars, but what I really missed were the interactions with people who worked in my lab. I missed the students and their intellectual energy. Young people, who asked interesting questions, then answered them. I missed the students who worked through difficult problems, who were excited when they mastered new techniques or when they had a positive result or realized a new insight. I missed seeing them interact and support each other and I missed teaching them what I know. When they were gone I realized how much personal satisfaction I gained from watching them grow as scientists. That meant more to me than the discoveries, the prestige or the titles. It was all about them, after all."

Glancing at both Dr. Holliday and Dr. Benedetti whose attention he still held, Dr. Paolo continued his loosely rehearsed answer.

"I do not know when I transitioned from 'it's all about me' to 'it's all about them' but I must not have realized it at the time. And the more I thought about it, the more I realized that I had the same feelings of satisfaction when I was a TA in graduate school and also when I tutored medical students. So getting back to teaching seemed like something I should do. And as you both know, being a CEO or consulting or being a member of a scientific review board is not as rewarding as watching a young person grow."

It seemed that Dr. Paolo reached the end of his lengthy reply when he abruptly added, "And I've also had a longstanding desire to apply the Socratic method to teach the basic principles of scientific inquiry. The Socratic method is used at Harvard to teach first year medical students how to solve clinical cases. I think the same approach may be a perfect way to explain the rigors of the scientific method to college seniors, especially those who have a solid science base."

The silence that follows the end of a sentence during a discussion, especially during an interview, lingered a bit longer than usual. It wasn't that Drs. Holliday or Benedetti didn't have questions, but they wanted to make sure that Dr. Paolo did not inject another thought.

He didn't.

"The Socratic method is an uncommon form of teaching, especially in the sciences. Does precedent exist for the use of this method to teach science at any other university?" asked Dr. Benedetti. "In other words, do we know if it will work?"

"Not to my knowledge. I only know about Harvard Medical, and I really don't know if it will work in a nonmedical undergraduate setting," replied Dr. Paolo honestly.

"I can say that I've never heard of this technique discussed at any educator workshop or meeting," Dr. Holliday said. "Tell me more. Exactly how you would structure such a course." Dr. Holliday's use of "me" instead of "us" and her way of speaking directly to Dr. Paolo irked Dr. Benedetti who felt as though she was all but ignoring him.

Dr. Paolo described how he would design the advanced science course he'd titled *Teach the Professor*. The singular goal of the course would be to prepare seniors destined for graduate studies to face the rigors of original research, an absolute requirement for advanced degrees. With his voice rising in excitement he painted a virtually complete picture of the ideal student for this course, one who was driven to excel, passionate about learning and eager to share newfound knowledge.

"Once launched," he explained, "the class would have its own momentum. Students would learn from each other, they'd pose questions and supply ideas to each other's research. The instructor would simply provide the initial push, and then guide them to ensure that they didn't stray too far off course, to keep them on track. The teacher would essentially be in the background, almost like an observer."

Dr. Paolo added that he would alter the routine periodically with a lecture on a particular aspect of research such as details of the scientific process, the importance of controls, how to question published results or how to carefully mine the ever-expanding scientific literature. And he envisioned that this course would bring together all of the scientific principles and theories that they had learned in the prior three years at the college.

"By the end of the course," Dr. Paolo stated confidently, "the students would not only have been challenged to apply what they've already learned, but they will also be exposed to the discovery aspect of science. By the end of the course, he or she will be better prepared to begin their postgraduate career. That much I'll guarantee."

Their body language mirrored their respective interest.

Dr. Holliday's eyes were alert and focused, her face relaxed and she appeared genuinely interested in what Dante Paolo was saying whereas Dr. Benedetti often shifted in his seat, he appeared unsettled and distracted.

"While not completely without merit," the Dean began in a monotone voice that accompanied his condescending reply, "the course, as you described, may yield nothing more than a glorified science report interspersed with trivial details on the scientific method. While I agree that students who enter graduate school are ill prepared to face the challenges of research, without a laboratory part to your course that will allow students to gain hands-on experience—bench experience—your course will not reach your lofty expectations. Indeed, I predict that seniors will be thinking more about graduation then applying themselves to the high level of involvement that you think your course demands."

"With all due respect, the case study tutorials with medical school students were highly successful and instructive," countered Dr. Paolo.

"They were first year students, no?" asked Dr. Benedetti.

"Yes, but ..."

Dr. Holliday had sat through enough meetings with her handpicked Dean to know when he was about to launch into a belligerent offensive that was neither instructive nor constructive. Today, she simply wasn't in the mood.

"Dante, have you prepared lesson plans for this course?" Dr. Holliday asked as a way of deflecting the oncoming offensive from the Dean.

"No, I have not," he replied. "But I have an idea of how the course should proceed over the course of the semester."

"So you see this as a full semester course?" interrupted Dr. Benedetti. "Do you really think there is enough material to cover a full 16 weeks? Perhaps a mini, 8-week course would do, especially if you're not sure if this will work."

"Well, having not done this before in this type of setting I cannot say with absolute certainty how it will gel," countered Dr. Paolo. "But I think that it would require a full semester to initiate, then to complete the assignment."

Sensing Dr. Benedetti's discontent in his inability to mount an attack, Dr. Holliday seized the discussion, and effectively, the entire meeting.

"Dante, there is no better way to lose the attention of a room full of students than by meandering," declared Dr. Holliday. "That's why we develop lesson plans; they at least give you an idea of how the semester will flow. I am very interested in your course and I'm sure that Lorenzo would support me in asking you to generate a lesson plan so we can complete our evaluation and get back to you in time for it to be offered for the fall semester. If you can send me a plan by email say, by the end of next week, then we'll be able to move this process along. Is that acceptable to you?"

"Yes, fine. I've never generated a lesson plan before. Is there a standard form or..."

"Simply find a template online and use that," interrupted Dr. Benedetti who was doing all he could to contain his disapproval of his boss's end-game maneuver. "We do not have a standard template."

The meeting ended with Dr. Holliday rising from her chair and extending a hand to Dr. Paolo. She thanked him for reaching out to the college as she shook his hand.

"Thank you for taking the time to meet with me today. I'll get the lesson plan to you by the end of next week at the latest." Turning to shake Dr. Benedetti's hand, he added for good measure, "thank you as well for arranging this meeting and shall I copy you on the email as well?"

"Yes, that would be acceptable," replied Dr. Benedetti.

Dr. Paolo gathered his electronic notebook, turned and walked out the office through the door that had never been completely closed. As he walked down the hall to the exit, he wondered what was involved in generating a lesson plan.

"I hope this is the right move," he thought to himself as he suddenly ached for the comfort of his old lab at Harvard.

———•———

Jean Holliday closed the office door and returned to her seat at the table where Lorenzo Benedetti remained. The Dean knew that his boss had already made a decision.

"So what do you think?" she asked.

"Well frankly, I'm not convinced that he's thought this through. Evidently his heart is in the right place but he may not be prepared to tolerate a classroom full of students. It's one thing to tutor a few medical students at Harvard, *la crème de la crème*, but it's another thing to be engaged with a large number of students for a whole semester in a course that is poorly developed at best. Indeed, I'll go as far as to say that not only is he unfit temperamentally to do this job, but also that he is so narrow intellectually that it is doubtful that he is competent to teach such a broad-based course. He defined no limits to the scientific subjects the students can choose to research," ranted Dr. Benedetti using fingers of both hands to place quotation mark around the word "research". "Let's review the facts," he continued. "One, he has no formal training in teaching; two, he's never taught a lecture course and labs don't count, they're like playtime and three, he's has no lesson plan for this imaginary course that has no precedent in an undergraduate setting. I'll be surprised if he can generate a syllabus for two weeks let alone for an entire semester," he concluded.

Dr. Holliday fully predicted this negative response. She'd known Dr. Benedetti to have exceedingly high standards and to be unyielding in his lofty expectations when it came to the faculty, which he prided as being the best outside of Boston. And although she disapproved of his condescending manner, she never tried to change it; it was something she simply tolerated. Today however, Dr. Holliday noticed that not only did the Dean patronize Dr. Paolo but also he was unusually crass and aggressive, as if he felt threatened.

"Well then you've just articulated the basis for my decision," she replied. "If Dante produces a sound 16-week lesson plan, then I'll approve a senior-level, pass-fail, single-credit course with a limited class size of ten. If anyone asks, I'll say that we are experimenting with a new teaching method. How does that strike you?"

Dr. Benedetti contemplated her offer and formulated a retort in his mind that remained there for his pleasure only: *No clear minded senior would take a single credit course. No one will enroll and he'll be gone before he even arrives.*

"Fine," he said with a wry smile.

Dr. Holliday exited the Dean's office without saying another word.

———◆———

Dante Paolo left Washington Hall conflicted. On one hand, he knew he had clearly presented the concept and objectives of the course, but on the other hand, he thought he could have elaborated a bit more on how it would fit into a student's overall education. It would surely serve to tie together all that they had learned in the sciences and it would make them think critically. But what bothered him the most, what began to gnaw at his delicate ego, was that Dr. Holliday and especially Dr. Benedetti seemed to have doubted his ability to teach. On what basis did they cast their doubt? Was it because he didn't have a degree in teaching or because he hadn't prepared a lesson plan? Dr. Paolo felt as if his ability to convey information, teach and inspire young people—as he had done so many times before in many different settings—had been challenged. He could feel the anger grow and his shoulders tighten as he delved deeper in thought. It was negative energy at its best and he had to calm himself down so he could generate a plan. He also had to remind himself to concentrate on traffic during his short drive home.

"I'll give you a goddamn lesson plan that'll blow you away," he said aloud to the inside of the Volvo's windshield. "Holliday's reasonable but you Benedetti, you're a pompous ass! I know you. I know who you are and I know how you think. I've met people like you before, you self-serving arrogant ass. And I'll get the damn plan done before Friday, and it'll be the best-goddamned plan you've ever seen, asshole!"

Ironically, his anger brought clarity, determination and focus. His back was against the wall and he was eager to fight back. "I've proven them wrong before and I'll do it again. Watch, just watch."

Once home Dr. Paolo wasted no time in reaching out to his friend.

"Hi, Rob? It's me. I need your help."

"Hey, how'd it go?"

"Okay, Holliday's fine, Benedetti's an ass, and now..."

"Could've told you that but I wanted you find out for yourself," interrupted Robert.

"And now they want a lesson plan from me."

"They do? That's great!"

"What? Why's that great?"

"Because that means that they're interested."

"Yeah, well at least Holliday's interested but they said that they would make their decision based on the lesson plan."

"Standard procedure in teaching. You've got to have a plan or else they don't know what you're going to do. Everyone does one. Hell old timers like me have been recycling the same plan for decades. They have to have something in writing in case the Trustees come knocking."

"Trustees? What do they have to do with the curriculum?"

"Nothing. But if there's a complaint against the teacher, or someone decides to make an issue about something to do with what's covered in a course then they can refer to the lesson plan."

"Okay, fine," replied Dr. Paolo who was starting to relax. "Would you send me something to look at so I have an idea of what they expect? Do you follow a standard template? Is one available?"

"Sure, no problem, I'll send one by email. And no, there is no template but you may want to look online, maybe someone's posted something. You'd think the college would have standard forms, right? But they don't. Have a look at the one I send and rip one off. I'll be happy to look it over, just let me know."

"Thanks, Rob. I guess I should have anticipated this, I look forward to your email."

For once Dr. Paolo was not disappointed that Laura had a Friday night dinner meeting. With Robert's lesson plan as an example and with a template for science courses he found online, Dr. Paolo began to generate a weekly plan for *Teach the Professor*. The template had the basics: Learning Goals, Class Materials and Preparation, Teacher-Student Relations, Science Concepts, Integrated Work-and Study-Flows, Enrichment Experiences, and Evaluation of Mastered Concepts. He wasted no time in modifying the template to accentuate aspects of education that he thought were important: Integration of Skill Sets replaced Integrated Work- and Study-Flow, Problem Solving replaced Enrichment Experiences and Communication and Integration replaced Quantitative Performance Evaluation; improvements he thought better suited his course. What resulted after three uninterrupted hours and two glasses of red wine was a rough draft of not weekly but monthly lesson plans. The write-up detailed how the course would flow from month-to-month, from the beginning to the end of the semester. He also left room in his plan for flexibility so changes could be made without the need for a total rewrite. Each monthly plan was three to four pages of single-spaced type; the entire plan, including sources for reference materials, was fifteen pages in length.

Over the weekend Dr. Paolo tweaked the lesson plan to add or remove certain elements and by early Sunday morning he deemed it complete. Later that same day, Robert would comment in an email: It's the most detailed, complete and most thorough lesson plan I've ever seen.

———•———

Drs. Holliday and Benedetti were not expecting an email from Dante Paolo so soon; it was not even 7 a.m. Monday and it had already sat in their inbox for two hours. The subject line read: Lesson Plan, and the message was dated June 6, 2011 04:58:55 AM EST. It was a short, terse message:

> Dear Drs. Holliday and Benedetti,
>
> Attached please find the lesson plan for Teach the Professor.
> I look forward to your responses.
>
> Best,
> Dante

Dr. Paolo received a phone call at 5 p.m. that same day.

"Dante? Hello, it's Jean. Lorenzo and I reviewed and approved your lesson plan, and although we would have preferred the course outlined on a weekly basis, this will do." She then offered him a temporary position as a Lecturer to teach the course as he had designed with a credit of one. She also told him that she viewed the course as an "experiment in teaching" and that the future of the program depended on "the results of the experiment."

In truth, Dr. Paolo had no idea how credits were assigned to courses and although it seemed low, he was unfazed by the number or the concept of the course as an experiment. He was comfortable with experiments, whether he was designing them or even as a part of one.

He thanked Dr. Holliday for the opportunity to teach at the college and he assured her that he'd do his best.

Now, he knew, the real work began.

5

With an hour before their next class, Brad, Amy, Phil and Abby decided to head to the Student Union building for coffee. Ajay, who told the group that he decided to drop the course, headed straight to Dr. Paolo's office.

"Well he seems like a nice guy," offered Amy to start the initial assessment of Dr. Paolo. "But I think this course will be more of a challenge then we think."

"Finally," replied Phil. "It's about time Wilmington College has an intellectually demanding course in the sciences."

"Straight A's, Phil?" asked Amy wryly knowing full well that he hadn't aced all of the courses taught at Paine Hall.

"It seems like we're going to have more control of the content and assignments. Kind of makes me feel like an adult," said Brad. "But I hope it's not too demanding, these medical school applications take quite a bit of time."

"Tell me something I don't know," countered Amy. "I've sent out five med school applications and I'm only half-way through!"

"I didn't know you wanted to be a doctor," Brad said to Amy.

"A medical doctor, right Amy?" corrected Phil. "Which is quite different from a real doctor, a Ph.D., like I'll be someday."

"What are you talking about?" said Amy sharply. "Of course an M.D. is a real doctor."

But Phil, who always was ready to back up his statements with facts, was unfazed by Amy's challenge.

"In the 1800s," Phil countered, "physicians were addressed as 'mister' until a British journalist used 'doctor' to describe a surgeon in a newspaper article. The journalist didn't think it was right for someone as skilled with a sharp knife as the town's butcher should be called 'mister' and ever since the publication of that article anyone who practiced medicine was called 'doctor'. In those days, before anesthesia or antibiotics, a person who needed an amputation benefitted from having someone who was quick with a knife and a saw. A tourniquet was placed above the wound, a rapid back-to-front circular single slice was made on the arm or leg right down to the bone with a razor-sharp knife, then a little saw would cut through the bone in a couple of strokes and the stump dipped in hot oil to stop the bleeding. By this time, the patient had passed out from the trauma and although most died of infection, some did survive the procedure. So the journalist sought to distinguish the butcher from the healer by calling the healer 'doctor', which is too bad because until that time 'doctor' was reserved for those who earned a Ph.D.—a philosophy degree which is the highest degree conferred by a University."

"Get out!" cried Amy. "I never heard that. You made that up!"

"It's true. Check it out."

"I have to admit, I never heard of that either," interjected Brad. "Abby, are you buying any of this?"

Abby was listening to the conversation from a safe step behind the others. Although she knew her classmates well and felt comfortable in their presence, they were well outside of her third circle.

As a child Abby designed a way of grading relationships based almost exclusively on trust. She was at the center of three concentric rings. Her dad, once solidly in the innermost circle, was closest to her in an area that had also included her mother. But as she got older and no longer sought his attention nor approval, his position in this special circle became merely symbolic. Although over the years friends entered and exited the two outermost rings, no one steadily occupied either. As a consequence of these transient, and often shallow, friendships Abby became very protective of her intimate thoughts and emotions. Raised as an only child by a single parent she learned how to cope without the support of close friends or family. In essence, she was alone in the world.

"I know that to earn a Ph.D. one must unearth new knowledge, make a discovery. As far as I know, that's not a requirement for a medical degree," Abby stated.

"Right!" exclaimed Phil who practically jumped in the air in approval. "Abby's right on! It requires original research validated by publication and defended in front of experts. That's why it's the highest degree in the land and that's why physician-scientists with both degrees put the Ph.D. last, as in 'M.D., Ph.D.', the last degree is the highest one."

"Hey, maybe that could be your topic for Dr. Paolo's course 'The History of Suffixes' by Phillip Hess, Ph.D.-wannabe," chided Brad.

"Make that 'The History and Relevance of Professional Suffixes'," countered Phil.

When they reached the steps of the Student Union building, Abby split from the group and headed straight to the Library. She confessed to the others that she had never heard of the journals Dr. Paolo referred to in class and she wanted to check them out sooner rather than later. Unlike the others who lived on campus Abby needed to be efficient with time. She lived with her dad in a small house five miles north of Wilmington College and the last bus of the day that stopped a few blocks from her home left campus promptly at 6 p.m.

6

Disappointed that his class consisted of only four students, Dr. Paolo was not in the mood to hang out on campus after class ended. He needed time to reassess this whole teaching idea before it went any further; he needed to go for a run to clear his head and think. Did he have the passion to spend the next few months teaching only four students? Was this worth it?

After sending Robert a text message apologizing that he would not be able to meet him for lunch, Dante left Paine Hall, walked across campus to the parking lot where his 10-year old pearl white Volvo S80 awaited. The drive home was an easy ten miles along open secondary roads that abutted state parks and conservation land. It was a far cry from his usual take-your-life-in-your-hands commute to and from Boston on four-lane highways that seem more like the Indy 500 speedway that became more congested and more helter-skelter with each passing minute of each passing workday.

The problem at hand, the questions about his commitment to the students, and to teaching at all provided more than enough motivation to fuel that day's exercise. Towards the end of the five-mile run Dr. Paolo had finally settled on a plan, and it was a simple one at that. He decided that if all four students showed up on Tuesday with their assignment completed and if they were willing to stay with the course then he would fulfill his obligation for the semester. But if only one more student dropped out, then he would ask Dr. Benedetti if the course could be dissolved for lack of interest and, at least for now, he'd abandon the idea of teaching. He saw this as a reasonable plan and with it he defused the stress of the decision.

"It's up to the students," he said aloud to no one. "After all, it's their education, their future."

Take a walk

1

Dr. Paolo spent little time over the weekend worrying about his teaching career. *It's like nature, you can't control it so why worry about it, just adapt and move on,* he reasoned. The 'adapt and move on' motto was a relatively new addition to his way of thinking and one he sought to follow as he grew older. As a boy he worried about anything and everything including things that he couldn't control like the weather or the color of the harvest moon. As a scientist, his constant fretting combined with an ever-present attention to detail served him well especially when he was conducting an experiment and collecting data. But his careful and meticulous ways weren't without consequences. The increased pressures and the high and higher anxieties resulted in a great deal of stress and now, in his new career, he wanted to reverse course and "to chill" as he often was told by others to do.

So today, if he learned that the remaining students don't want to take his course, then fine, he'll move on, he'll find something else to do, he'll survive. Of course he understood that this *que sera, sera* attitude was directly attributable to the financial security he and his wife attained when their type A personalities were in high gear, a time that consumed decades but were now no more than dim memories.

He strolled into the large auditorium and immediately his heart sank; only three students were present. *So much for this experiment,* he thought. However, no sooner had he set his briefcase down next to the podium at the front of the auditorium than he heard the door to the upper level section of the room open.

"Sorry," was all Abby offered as she took her seat next to the others.

"Good morning everyone," Dr. Paolo said. "Since it's just the five of us, I thought it would be better if we relocate to a smaller room."

They gathered their items and followed Dr. Paolo out of the auditorium down the hall to a smaller room close to his office. According to Robert, the room was used for early-evening tutorial sessions but was otherwise unused. It had a rectangular table that easily accommodated six individuals and a 52-inch computer monitor mounted on the wall connected to a computer. The wireless keyboard and mouse were on the table with the passcode for the computer taped to the underside of the keyboard.

When everyone was settled in the more intimate setting, Dr. Paolo asked if anyone had chosen his or her research topic.

Amy launched into her presentation without hesitation or regard for her classmates. Her aggressive behavior matched her near perfect academic performance; after three years at Wilmington College she had compiled a 3.96 GPA having stumbled to a lowly A-minus in advanced physics. Amy's intellect matched her stunning looks. She was a beautiful woman with straight jet-black hair that highlighted her black-brown eyes. She was a first generation Asian American. Her father was a scientist who had been born in Japan and had immigrated to California with his family as a young child. And although her mother, a native

Californian, was also an attractive brunette, Amy's features were clearly Asian—less than average height with a thin, curvy body and a soft, smooth oval face with full perfectly formed lips. Because she was always serious and determined, few outside of her family saw the extent of her full beauty; she dressed simply, avoided eye contact unless confronted and only rarely did she show her warm and genuine smile. In spite of her attractive features, her body language declared a defiant attitude that kept young boys and older men alike firmly at bay; she neither sought their attention nor displayed interest in their subtle, often juvenile, advances. Skilled in the martial arts, Amy exhibited no fear. She had an unmistakable air of confidence in her ability to conquer whatever and whomever she sought to conquer.

Amy reported on an article found in *Nature* about the recent discovery of a gene that coded for a specific tumor in humans, an adenocarcinoma of the pancreas. The article described research findings that showed that the chances of dying from this type of cancer increased 300% in individuals that had this gene in their DNA. The article also showed that this particular gene was most prevalent among males of African-Americans descent; a finding that may explain the increase of this specific cancer in this population. The research article was accompanied by a Views and Implications piece written by experts in the cancer biology field not involved with the original research. They wrote on the importance of this study to the development of tests to screen for this gene in humans and the associated implications of having such a powerful tool for both diagnosing, and ultimately in curing, this type of cancer. The experts drove home their point by stating that this type of so called "translational research", that creates clinical benefits from basic research findings, is a clear example of "the potential and power of personalized medicine."

"Tailored, personalized medicine," explained Amy, "is now in its infancy. And it all began with sequencing of the human genome."

Digressing slightly, Amy told the class that her father was a mechanical and electrical engineer who works for a biotechnology company in California. She told Dr. Paolo and her classmates that he was the head of the team that created the instruments used to sequence the human genome.

"A lot of robots did the heavy lifting in preparing the 'blueprint of mankind,'" she explained. "And because of my interests in medicine, and because of my father's contribution in designing robotics used in the human genome project, I've decided to do my report on the human genome and personalized medicine.

Amy then looked across the table at Dr. Paolo who was seated between Brad and Abby. She wasn't sure if Dr. Paolo had to give approval for her chosen topic but she had made a conscious decision to state clearly that it was her one and only choice. If Dr. Paolo disapproved of her topic she was ready to drop the course; it was DNA or the door she decided, although deep down she really didn't want to leave.

"That sounds like an interesting and timely topic Amy," commented Dr. Paolo. "And without a doubt, you will find a great deal of information on both the human genome and the future of personalized medicine."

Outwardly, Amy showed no reaction—as if she expected nothing less—but internally she was relieved to hear the decision. She passed the first test of the class and thought she was off the hook until Dr. Paolo asked a follow-up question.

"Amy, you said that you were applying to medical school. What type of doctor would you like to be?" Dr. Paolo asked in an attempt to learn more about her ambitions.

"Umm, a pediatrician," she responded quickly. "In fact, I'm interested in learning if the personalized medicine movement has considered infants. It seems to me that if personalized medicine is going to have an impact, it'll have to start at the earliest age possible, probably just after the baby is born."

"Okay Amy, good point. I think you're right. A complete lifetime of medical monitoring should probably begin at birth," commented Dr. Paolo clearly impressed with Amy's complete response. "I'll look forward hear to what you learn. Who wants to go next?"

Phil Hess volunteered.

To his friends and family, Phil described himself as an archetypal college guy. His sandy blonde hair was slightly overgrown and partly covered his eyes; a look that relayed a relaxed, laid back style that reflected poorly his intense intellect. Slightly taller than most men his age at just under six feet tall, his body was neither lanky nor awkward; Phil carried his solid athletic build with ease. With a wrinkled pale blue button down shirt tucked into faded jeans and with well-worn sneakers, Phil portrayed the appearance of someone determined to make it on his own.

He told the class that he'd always been a math nerd ever since his mother gave him her well-used Texas Instruments calculator that used reverse-Polish logic, which at first he thought was some kind of a joke, but was an efficient way to use a calculator. He explained that he liked math because an elementary school teacher once told him to think about math as a tool, like any other tool, to explain or to fix things, like to explain gravity or how to launch a space probe to intersect with a meteor. After the brief introduction of who he was, Phil reached in his backpack and retrieved a glossy color print of the April cover of *Science* that showed a picture of the deep universe taken by the Hubble telescope. He held the image out so it faced the others in the room. Across the magnificent image were big bold red letters that read: "Quantum Physics Comes of Age."

"This is me," he told the class. "Quantum physics is so cool, but I have to confess that I know very little about it. I only know that it uses high-order mathematics to explain the universe."

Phil knew from experience that speaking with others about his interest in mathematics usually resulted in a lonely one-way conversation. No one, except for a teacher here and there, wanted to discuss mathematics. If someone asked about his career interests he'd simply say engineering—electrical or mechanical—depending on his mood. So, based on history, he didn't expect an enthusiastic response to quantum physics but Dr. Paolo surprised him.

"Phil, I'm delighted you chose this topic. It has intrigued me for quite some time and I'll admit, I just don't get it. So, I'll leave it up to you to teach me about quantum physics and the universe in a way that is intuitive or shall I say that makes sense. Over the years I've watched NOVA specials on this topic but the concepts just don't click with me, so I'm looking forward to learning about this topic." Dr. Paolo then paused for a moment before asking a question. "Phil, why do most people find mathematics difficult to master? Most folk I've met, from professors to interns, college, high school, male, females, young, old, most of them have difficulty with math. Why is that?"

While Phil really hadn't given too much thought as to why people struggled with math. He thought to take a wild stab at the question but he knew that his answer would be more fabrication than fact.

"I have no idea," Phil replied honestly. "Maybe it has something to do with how it's presented to us when we're young. For some reason, math to me as a kid was fun. It all seemed so logical, it just clicked, but I know it's not that way for everyone."

———•———

Brad politely listened to the discussion but he could care less about quantum physics or mathematics for that matter. Since he was sitting next to Phil, he was up next and although eager to present his topic he wanted to give Abby the option to go ahead of him because that's the way he was raised, to be thoughtful and respectful. He glanced at Dr. Paolo then at Abby then waited for a green light. After an approving nod from Abby and a return stare from Dr. Paolo, Brad began his delivery.

Brad's entire appearance—from his neatly cropped dark brown hair to his polo shirt emblazed with a country club's insignia to his creased tan khaki pants and dark brown leather boat shoes—reflected his privileged upbringing. His father was the head of a law firm that was started by Brad's great-great-grandfather and his mother was the chairwoman of the board of directors for The MacIntyre Foundation, the family's philanthropic organization. The MacIntyre family lived in a well-kept Victorian overlooking Sandy Bay on the north shore of Massachusetts. It was a stunningly situated and meticulously groomed estate with well-terraced, ocean-taming retaining walls made of natural stone. The grounds were landscaped to rival those of the famous Newport mansions complete with a carefully manicured putting green, working water fountains and meditative garden paths.

Brad was the most recent member of the fifth generation of MacIntyre's to attend Wilmington College—one of the longest family lineages at the college—and one of its founding benefactors. "Education is the foundation of an individual's character," his grandfather was fond of saying to his heirs as they headed off to school. The oft-recited declaration served to instill a sense of purpose to school and it also garnered respect for their educators. And while Brad did not shun his family's high social status or wealth, he did not eagerly embrace it either. He recognized and appreciated both its power and its perils. Before leaving for college, he announced to his family that he was not going to become a lawyer; a burden thankfully deflected by his older brother who had earned a degree from Harvard and who just passed the bar exam. Instead of law, Brad was interested in biology and medicine. He thought that he'd like to become a physician and to apply his skills to help those who were less fortunate and in need of care.

Brad calmly began his report to the class with a story he recounted from memory. It was a true story of a terrific accident that happened long ago when workers laid the first railroad lines in New England.

"A foreman named Phineas Gage was a boss's dream. Not only was he strong with a solid work ethic but also smart with impeccable manners. Phineas was a handsome yet rugged individual who earned the respect of men, from furloughed prisoners to young Irish immigrants, who labored under him. Joke and he'd laugh, cross him and he'd respond with complete resolve.

One day Phineas was at the center of a most bizarre accident. A drill hole used to blast bedrock was filled with explosive powder and, as he had done many times before, Phineas gently inserted a large, tapered iron rod about three and one-half feet long and weighing about thirteen pounds into the hole to compress the powder. But this time something went wrong and the powder exploded violently. The tamping iron fired out of the hole like a rocket. The tamping iron entered Phineas' face here," Brad explained pointing to his left cheek below his eye, "and it exited here," he said pointing to the top left part of his head. "The blast threw him backwards a good ten yards. When his team saw that a part of his skull was missing and brains were splattered about the ground they thought Phineas was dead."

The group sat silently, transfixed by Brad's gripping story.

"But he wasn't dead." Brad continued.

Phil accurately visualized the accident and opined: "I hope this was the first recorded mercy killing! He must've been in a lot of pain. Man, can you imagine the pain?"

Brad looked directly at his friend and said, "Wrong on both counts Phil. He wasn't killed nor was he in pain. In fact, he was fully awake and conscious right after the blast. He recognized the doctor on the scene and after being tended to by this doctor, Phineas was seen writing in his diary. Everyone at the site thought that their eyes were playing tricks on them. Here was a man who was walking and talking missing a part of his head and a good chunk of his frontal lobe. How could that be? Was this some sort of miracle?"

Amy could no longer contain herself. "Did he survive beyond the day, the week? Didn't he lose a lot of blood? Did they have antibiotics?"

"Yes, no and no," replied Brad obviously pleased with the questions and of his ability to remember details. "He survived the episode and he lost some but not a lot of blood although a nasty infection almost killed him because, to answer your last question, the accident happened before the discovery of antibiotics. Actually, he was very lucky to have recovered from the infection."

Brad went on to explain, "Phineas indeed lost his left eye but he did recover most all of his strength. However, something else happened to Phineas that was not as obvious as a lost eye. As it turned out this mild-mannered man became moody, mean and he was often irrational. Some doctors reasoned that the part of Phineas' brain that was lost forever was somehow responsible for his personality traits. This remarkable incident, and equally remarkable insight, marked the beginning of studies that linked the human brain to behavior. Studies of the brain were very crude in the 1800s. But today, neurobiology in general, and structure-function studies of the brain specifically, are yielding some amazing things. Dr. Paolo, you asked us to bring an article from *Science* or *Nature* and while I did find an article relating to a specific neurotransmitter in *Science*, it was a review article in the *Journal of Neuroimaging and Neuroprocessing* that caught my attention. The title of the article is *Advances in Structure-Function Studies of the Human Brain.* What I told you about Phineas Gage was a story I read as a child and it stuck with me for all these years. I have a feeling that this review article will be with me for a long time too. Dr. Paolo, I'd like to learn more about neurology and about the human brain," Brad concluded.

"That's a great story and it's a great topic but you may want to narrow your topic a bit or you'll spend forever just trying to grasp the breadth of neurology or neurobiology," replied Dr. Paolo. "It's a huge field that has exploded over the past decade. But before I ask you another question, Brad, I want to ask all of you what other take home message is related by the story of Phineas Gage?"

"The ability of the body to fight infection without antibiotics?" asked Amy.

"That's true, but I'm thinking more broadly," responded Dr. Paolo.

"The improbability of this type of accident?" offered Phil.

"Hmm, well that's not what I was thinking but that's true, the story does lend itself to statistical analysis of how often unscripted events can occur in the course of one's day or lifetime," said Dr. Paolo.

"It might have to do with the observation itself," stated Abby in a soft, tentative voice.

"What about it?" Dr. Paolo asked.

"The doctors recognized something beyond the initial injury, infection and recovery. They made a new connection between a specific part of the brain and personality."

"Exactly!" exclaimed Dr. Paolo who was relieved that Abby joined the discussion. Until that point she'd been silent. "Louis Pasteur said 'Chance favors only the prepared mind', and those doctors happened upon a patient who presented with significant personality traits following a specific injury. Their 'prepared minds' were not only open to new ways of solving problems, but they had the right type of information necessary to design testable hypotheses. Scientific discovery is often unscripted and serendipitous and what affords the individual the ability to make a discovery is a working knowledge of different aspects of science and nature. Making connections is key to making discoveries, and possessing a broad knowledge base and being observant increases the odds that these connections will be meaningful."

Dr. Paolo glanced at his notepad to see that it was close to 11 a.m. and the class was nearly over. "Abby, given the hour I think we'll start the next class with your presentation, okay? Would you like to give us a preview?"

All eyes turned to Abby and all she could do was to look down at her notepad where she had scribbled a few notes.

"I haven't settled on a topic yet," she replied. "But I'll be ready on Thursday."

"Okay then," replied Dr. Paolo. "Any questions before we break?"

There were no replies, just shaking of heads to affirm that there were no questions. As they started to gather their books and jackets Dr. Paolo added, "To those of you who presented today, nice job. I approve everyone's research topic. Start developing a plan, an outline of what you will research. Remember to keep it focused. Okay, I'll see you in this room on Thursday."

Dr. Paolo knew that Thursdays were mixed blessings for students. They were either one-day away from a big exam and they needed to cram or they were cruising to the weekend. In either case, the students around campus as well as in Dr. Paolo's class seemed more energized towards the end, than at the beginning, of the school week and this particular Thursday was no different. Amy, Brad and Phil were ready to sit back, relax and listen to Abby's project proposal.

Abigail Lark was what Dr. Benedetti would later label a "hardy"—someone admitted to the college on a hardship tuition waiver due to the poor financial status of her family. Although she was a solid B student in high school Abby often struggled to maintain the required minimum B-minus grade average during the first three years at Wilmington College. Her long-term goal was to obtain a Masters degree in psychology and to teach at the high school level.

Unlike her classmates, Abby's physical presence did not attract notice. She dressed plainly in loose-fitting, pattern-less clothes resembling more the college "gal" than the college "preppie". Her brown hair was straight and lacked style; her body was, as Phil would privately comment to Brad, "closer to Rubens then Venus." Her chubby round face still retained some teenage blemishes but her hazel-brown eyes were soft and nonthreatening.

Abby began her presentation tenuously. She'd found a topic to research but it was in an issue of *Discover*, the science magazine aimed at the general public. *Discover* was not even close to the caliber of *Science* or *Nature*, and although Dr. Paolo knew that Abby had already broken a guideline of the assignment, he said nothing.

In a voice that was more apologetic than declarative, Abby told the class that she'd always had a deep interest in parapsychology especially telepathy and precognition or the ability to see things before they happen. She knew that parapsychology fell outside of mainstream science and that it was often grouped with the bizarre and unusual pseudoscience—the UFO-type, laughable and impossible-to-explain weird things. But after reading many books related to the various aspects of parapsychology Abby began to develop her own questions, thoughts and ideas.

Her presentation was low key and uninspiring until suddenly, and with little warning, it became deeply personal. Her words stemmed not from her head but directly from her heart and what Abby said next took the class, including Dr. Paolo, by surprise.

"My mother died in a car accident when I was 15 years old," began Abby who seemed to be in a trance, her gaze downward, her voice solemn as if the event occurred just moments ago. "It was a typical day. I got up, dressed for school, yelled goodbye upstairs to my parents and walked out the front door to catch the bus. About an hour later, the principal and a police officer came to my classroom. They asked me to follow them. We went to the principal's office where the police officer told me that he was instructed to take me to the hospital where my father was waiting. When I asked why, he said he didn't know. It was the principal who told me that there was an accident and that my Dad had asked for them to arrange transportation for me to the hospital. They had no other information. When I saw my father at the hospital, standing in the busy hallway, he looked dazed and confused like he was unsure of what to do next. It was then that I knew. Before that moment I had never seen my father cry. But now he was broken, in shock. He told me that she died instantly, no pain, no suffering. The accident had apparently been horrific; another driver— who they said was probably drunk—slammed into her car at high speed. I was not allowed to see the car or my mother."

With the exception of the low continuous hum of the ventilation system, the intimate classroom was dead silent. Dr. Paolo, remembering the recent passing of his own father, gazed at the electronic notepad on the table. Abby glanced at Dr. Paolo but he did not look at her.

Abby continued. "A grief counselor met with me that same day. She told me about the different stages of grieving and that the feeling of total devastation I was experiencing was normal. She told me that I'd get through this but that it would take a lot of time. She was wrong. I was over it the next day."

The room was still silent as the last statement hovered in mid-air like a helium balloon that lost its desire to play with the ceiling. Abby's face looked tormented. Her eyebrows furled. She had never told anyone what she was about to say and she was still unsure if she wanted to say it. Then, after taking a deep breath, she continued, her gaze focused on a random spot on the table in front of her.

"My mother appeared to me on the night she died. I was asleep alone in my room. The room was dark and silent. I recognized her despite her youthful appearance; she was much younger than she was when I last saw her, she was like, twenty-something. She looked beautiful. I was calm. I was not scared. No words were spoken. It was clear that she came to deliver a message." Abby paused again for a long moment and after taking another deep breath she continued. "Without words my mother told me not to be afraid to develop my gift but I should know that it comes with responsibilities and that sometimes it can be very unpleasant. She also told me that someday I would help everyone. Then she left. She disappeared as quickly as she had appeared. Afterwards I awoke, sat on my bed and looked around my room. It was just after ten o'clock. I slept peacefully that night and the next morning I no longer felt sad, nor alone, nor did I feel sorry for myself."

Then, as if a fog had lifted, Abby's voice lightened. Blank looks met her gaze as she admitted that she'd never told anyone about this before, not even her dad because she knew that no one would believe her—not even her dad. Without waiting for comments, she opened a folder and lifted out an article from *Discover* titled, "Confirmed Paranormal—The New Normal?"

"This article," she told the class "discusses ways of measuring paranormal activities. It not the smoke and mirrors used to create illusions, no trick photography, no magic like those on the Ghost Story channel but real instruments, real labs, real science done by real scientists in real universities. I'd like to learn more about the current tools available to accurately measure these types of activities."

The room was dead silent. There was no response from her classmates. Everyone's attention turned to Dr. Paolo who was unsure where to start after having heard the profoundly personal story.

"Well, Abby," he began. "Needless to say, I'm sorry for your loss. I don't think we are ever ready to lose someone but I think it's even worse when it's sudden and totally unexpected. What you experienced after your loss is not uncommon. What I mean to say, is...is that although it doesn't happen to everyone I have heard of apparitions, but not many, and none that deliver a message or at least a message like you just described." Dr. Paolo was grasping to connect his thoughts. He knew he was heading down a potential slippery slope in discussing the supernatural because, as Abby correctly mentioned, it is outside the realm of sound science. He wasn't sure where he was heading but just as Dr. Paolo was about to continue Amy asked a probing question.

"Abby, what was meant by a 'gift'?" asked Amy sincerely.

Abby looked directly at Amy and said, "Ever since I could remember I communicated with my mother telepathically. In fact, because I did not speak until a late age I was taken to therapists to learn how to make sounds, then words. I guess I didn't see a need for language as my mother was always with me and we just communicated non-verbally. Obviously, she knew that I needed to learn how to talk and, once I started, I picked it up easily. So, one of my gifts from birth is telepathy."

"Are you still telepathic?" asked Brad.

"Yes."

"Do you use it often?"

"No. Not really."

"Why not?" Amy asked.

"Because, just like it takes two to communicate verbally, it takes two to have a two-way nonverbal discussion and there are few who are, like transmitters, I guess you'd call them transmitters."

"Transmitters? What are transmitters? I mean, I know what electrical transmitters are but are you referring to something else?" questioned Phil whose body language appeared to be cold and indifferent to Abby's entire presentation.

"That's my label for those who can send messages telepathically..." started Abby.

"Wait, let me guess...and a receiver is someone who can receive messages, right?" Phil interjected in an overtly sarcastic tone of voice.

"That's right."

"No, that's bullshit!" said Phil forcefully and without hesitation. This made the short exchange between the two students sound like a scene from an overly melodramatic tragedy.

Phil's outburst took almost everyone by surprise.

Although she was not surprised, Abby was taken aback by Phil's defiant tone rather than by his disbelief. She immediately regretted having told the class about her telepathy and, like a newly hatched painted turtle caught in the tight grasp of wide-eyed toddlers, she wanted nothing more than to return to the safety of her protective shell. But then she suddenly realized that the moment was an opportunity, a golden opportunity. Having quickly assembled a response Abby looked directly across the table at her classmate and said with eyes focused, "Phil, you are absolutely right. Thank you for being so honest. Telepathy is complete bullshit. It is not real. It does not exist. It's a trick and it's a joke. It is bullshit to most everyone but it's not bullshit to me. Imagine Phil, just imagine for just a moment, what your life would be like if you were blind from birth, if you never saw a damn thing in your entire life. Then imagine that day when someone tells you that the sky is blue and the ocean is blue too, that the grass is green and that leaves are green too. And that white is made up of all colors. Imagine your response, Phil. Imagine your goddamned response. No doubt you'd say 'that's bullshit!' and you'd be right again, it would be bullshit because you have no frame of reference, not even the slightest concept of color, so to you it would all be crap. Meaningless. Nothing. Get it? And that's why I chose this topic, and if Dr. Paolo approves, I'll try to find out if scientists are getting any closer to actually quantifying the so-called sixth sense, ESP, extrasensory perception. To me telepathy is real, but I know that to you and to most everyone I've met, it's not real. How do I make the blind see?"

It was Phil's turn to be startled and initially he wasn't sure how much he wanted to push back. In the three years since he's known her, Phil could not recall a time when meek Abby had so much to say or when she showed so much emotion. And while he did not dislike her, he was never attracted to her either. His view of her was neutral—she was harmless and of little significance. But he challenged her, she responded and now it was his turn to reply or to back down. Phil rarely backed down.

"Look Abby, I've read about telepathy, telekinesis, ESP, communicating with the dead and all that, and frankly, it just doesn't add up. It's inconsistent. Sometimes it works, sometimes it doesn't, some can, and others can't. Your analogy about the blind is a good one in that it's probably true that blind don't understand the concept of color, but it's a bad one because we know there are reasons why they are blind, like a genetic defect or something, right? Personally, I hope Dr. Paolo allows you to work on this topic, because maybe there's something new about this all this stuff. I gave up on it a long time ago."

"Me too," said Brad. "I'd like to know more about this topic. Our house is over 200 years old and I'm convinced that it's haunted. When I was young I think I saw a ghost but I keep telling myself that it wasn't real. Most of my family has had similar experiences but we really don't talk about it. There are stories of people who lived in that house many years ago and of their untimely death but I never know what to believe. I think Hollywood made it difficult for me to come to grips with the paranormal."

"Dr. Paolo, will you allow Abby to study this topic?" asked Amy who always liked to get to the point.

Dr. Paolo enjoyed the lively exchange because it told him that each student had an interest in Abby's topic.

"Here's what I'm thinking," the professor began. "Without a doubt, this entire area is at the far edges of mainstream science. It falls squarely under the umbrella of 'pseudoscience' mainly because of the exact issues Phil raised. Observations or events are not easy to reproduce, they're hard to quantify, they're vague, uncertain, sporadic, embellished, over-sold, all of these shortcomings have kept the study of paranormal activities at the fringe and opposite from the true cutting edge. Discoveries in science are made with new tools and fresh hypotheses that are grounded in previously determined fact. That said, the question becomes: Should efforts be made to better understand paranormal activities or should it be left to wallow forever in mediocrity? That's the main question. There are many examples of how science is pushed forward without knowing exactly how things work, and then it's figured out later. A good example is Edward Jenner's famous vaccine. As I'm sure you all know by now, Jenner observed that women and farmers who milked cows got mildly sick with a cowpox infection. When they recovered from the infection they had these ugly looking pockmarks on their body, on their hands and on their face but they did not get the deadly smallpox infection. So he put some of the material from the pockmarks, that is, cowpox into a cut on the skin of a healthy person and he found that that person was then protected from smallpox. Jenner had no clue how or why this worked but this simple observation, and this simple procedure, saved millions of lives. It was much, much later when new tools were developed to study viruses, as well as the immune system, that we understood that Jenner was priming the immune cells to cross-protect against a deadly virus with one that was closely related, but not deadly. Well maybe now, in the twenty-first century, we have tools to study paranormal activity. Is that what interests you Abby?"

Abby had said enough—perhaps too much—for one day so she simply nodded.

"Alright, here's what I'd like to do. Each of you will have a week to generate an outline of the research. As a part of the outline, I'd like to see a list of credible references that you will use in your research. While there is little doubt that there is ample data on the human genome, the human brain, and quantum physics, I simply don't know if there is enough information on the paranormal to make it a viable research topic. Abby, if by next Thursday you don't have enough references, then you'll have to choose a new topic. How's that sound?"

Again Abby simply nodded in agreement.

"Great," continued Dr. Paolo. "On Tuesday, we'll meet here then take a leisurely walk around the reservoir, so check the weather and dress appropriately. It's about five miles round trip. Any questions? If not have a great weekend."

There were no questions. They all left the room except Abby who lingered behind.

"Abby," said Dr. Paolo, "thank you for sharing your story today. I hope you find some good information for your research."

"Thanks. But I kind of wished I had kept my secret a secret. Now I have to prepare for the fallout."

"The fallout? What fallout?"

"I'm sure my story will make its way around certain cliques soon enough, if it hasn't already. I'll hear about it. For sure someone will say something dumb and I'll…

"Who Abby?" interrupted Dr. Paolo.

"Could be anyone Dr. Paolo. You know I'm like a fish out of water here. I've never really been a part of this scene. These guys have it better than I do and they let me know about it when they have the chance. It's quite subtle. That's why I don't spend any more time on campus then I have to. The only reason I'm still here is because it's free. I wanted to go elsewhere but my dad said that he couldn't afford it. He says that he'd get me anything as long as it was free, so I just tolerate it here." And with that Abby picked up her backpack and headed for the door. Dr. Paolo did not respond but thought, *poor kid.*

Abby stopped at the door, turned to Dr. Paolo and said, "Sympathy strengthens my resolve."

———————

"Man, I never sat through a class like that before," Phil said to Brad and Amy as they left Paine Hall. First Abby bares her heart about her mother, then she tells us she's had apparitions and 'oh by the way, I'm telepathic too,'" he continues in a poor imitation of Abby's voice.

"Why are you so down on her?" asked Amy.

Phil ignored Amy question. "And what about Dr. Paolo? Allowing this crap of a topic to...

"Hang on," said Brad. "Dr. Paolo did not give Abby a clean pass. The stipulation is that she find enough references to continue."

"C'mon, he's going to let her do it and Amy, I'm not down on Abby, I'm just into level playing fields and that topic, ESP or whatever it is, is as soft as her body," replied Phil chuckling at his sharp sarcasm.

"Phil, don't be an ass. What's wrong with you today? You're being a jerk," said Amy.

They walked together in silence before Amy veered down the path to the right that led to the cafeteria while Phil and Brad continued straight ahead towards the library. Amy was relieved to have left Phil; she had little tolerance for those who insult and ridicule others.

"Do you believe that crap?" Phil asked Brad.

"You know, honestly I don't know. I think there's something to it and I also think that Abby might be onto something when she said that we haven't developed the tools. So I'm keeping an open mind, plus I swear our house is haunted!"

"Oh, I see what's happening. It's 'Phil the antagonist-skeptic-asshole' against the rest of the class. If that's the game, then fine, I'll play. The world spins on the energy of us skeptics."

2

Dr. Paolo didn't immediately comprehend Abby's outburst but he vowed to analyze it during his afternoon run. Overall, he was pleased with the verbal jousting and he was also starting to get a clearer picture of the personalities of the four seniors. He could tell that they were motivated, but now the challenge was to keep them interested in the course. He also hoped that they were immune from senioritis: a ritualistic, reversible condition that can make any scholar coast to the finish. One way to prevent the dreaded illness was to apply the proper preventative measure and he thought that mixing up the routine was one such measure. Next Tuesday's walk in the woods would be the first of many unorthodox events that will hopefully keep senioritis at bay, or at least lessen its symptoms.

Dr. Paolo was in a good mood after completing a solid first full week of classes, even if it was only two classes; it was a start, and not a bad start at that. But as he was heading towards the exit of Paine Hall, his demeanor dimmed significantly when he spotted Dr. Benedetti walking directly towards him.

"Dante, do you have a moment?"

"Sure. How are you?"

"Fine. Let's go to my office," replied Dr. Benedetti.

The two men left Paine Hall and strolled across campus to Washington Hall.

They sat across from each other at the table where he had first met the Dean and Dr. Holliday earlier in the year.

"Dante, I've just completed an initial review of our fall courses. This review tells me the number of students enrolled in each course and the makeup of those students. We use this information to ensure that we're offering the best for our students and it also serves to provide valuable feedback to the Trustees and to the alumni as well. The challenge with any school is to keep the courses current while maintaining the core curriculum. It's a delicate balancing act and one that becomes more of a challenge with upperclassmen because they've already taken many courses and they begin to focus on what interests them. Your course was attractive to us because it provided something different, even if it was experimental."

Dr. Paolo listened attentively and showed no emotion. It was clear that Dr. Benedetti was delivering a setup or at least he was attempting to soften a potential blow, like a boxer throwing soft jabs to make his opponent underestimate the power of the knockout punch.

"Your course enrolled only four students, down from a total of five that attended the first class."

"That's correct."

"To be frank Dante, I'm surprised you have that many. It is the lowest number of students we've ever had in any class at the college since I've been here."

"They're good students, they seem to be interested in the..."

"It's not about whether or not they're interested in the course, it about the bottom line, Dante. The costs associated with your course are not covered by tuition and is doesn't help that one of your students is a hardy."

"A what?" Dr. Paolo asked.

"A hardy, replied Dr. Benedetti. "A hardy; also known as a hardship case. Someone who made the grades in high school but is from a family who can't afford tuition so it's waived. Abby is one of two hardies in the senior class; there are only seven of them at the entire college. They are local kids and the Trustees think they're good PR for the college. They're nothing more than political pawns used to demonstrate goodwill to Town officials when they come around and try to squeeze us for more free money.

"Abby appears to be a good student with a great deal of potential," Dr. Paolo stated with a less-than-convincing voice. Indeed he was not sure whether she was on the same intellectual level as the others. Abby was quite reserved in class and she chose a questionable research topic. Nevertheless Dr. Paolo wanted to give those like Abby—those who persevered—a chance. He did not like the degrading "hardy" moniker placed on Abby but since he wasn't sure where Dr. Benedetti was going with the conversation so he let it slide.

"They all have potential now don't they Dante?"

"Yes, but she seems..."

"Forget her Dante, what I wanted to let you know is that I'm going to bring the issue of your enrollment size to Jean. We have until Wednesday to close down the course then we can give the students until the end of the week to enroll in a new course before the enrollment period closes."

Dr. Paolo felt the uppercut land squarely on his jaw.

"But what if the students want to continue? What if I want this course to continue? Do I have any say here?"

"I'm afraid not. This is strictly business, nothing personal, I assure you."

There was nothing more to say, the round was over and the score was tallied.

"Is that it?" asked Dr. Paolo outwardly disturbed by the news and how it was delivered.

Dr. Benedetti simply nodded without saying another word. Dr. Paolo rose, left the ornate office, exited Washington Hall and headed directly to his Volvo.

———◆———

Abby stepped off the bus approximately one-half mile from her home. Not once in the three years since she started at Wilmington College did her father pick her up, not even when New England weather was dishing out all it could muster for that particular season. Drenching rains in the fall and spring, biting cold temperatures with dangerous wind chills along with wild Nor'easters in the winter. Brutal weather tested her love of the region. But the weather on this Thursday was quite pleasant, sunny and dry and the walk was used to reflect on her day and to organize plans for the evening.

She knew that the front door to the small, single story ranch would be unlocked because she saw the light coming from her father's room.

"Hello. I'm home," Abby announced to no one in particular. As usual, the first to greet her was Woodson, a middle-aged and quite timid orange tiger cat. Judging by his aggressive rubbing against her legs, the cat apparently was happy Abby was home. Her father, a gruff, unrefined man of medium build, came out of his room and without as much as a glance in her direction announced that he was leaving for the pub. Although not formally diagnosed as an alcoholic, her father leaned strongly in that direction. His free time was spent with his bar pals, who apparently loved to be with each other because they had not one difference among them. And they all wanted the same thing and that was to be as far away as possible from having anything to do with parenting. Since the death of his wife, Abby's father lost his bearings and his common good sense of purpose. He never spoke to Abby about the tragedy and, perhaps as a consequence of that silence, they drifted apart to the point where each knew that neither cared much for the other. He held a job as the manager of several parking garages in town and supplemented his meager income by lending a hand doing odd jobs with his pals on the weekends. He was nonthreatening to her and she was, for the most part, nonexistent to him.

Without a mother and with a mostly absent father, Abby learned to be content being by herself although, as she wrote in her personal journal:

> Someday I'd like to start my real life away from him and far
> from this place. Soon (hopefully) I'll be in graduate school.

But it was after a day like this one, when things were not great, that she missed her mother the most. She needed someone to talk with, someone who cared about her, someone she could trust and reassure her. On this Thursday night she needed more than Woodson to keep her company. It was not the kind of day that led to lengthy journal entries, as she was not happy about what had transpired in class nor was she happy about her exchange with Dr. Paolo afterwards. She spared no detail in recounting the events of the day in her journal with most sentences dedicated to her presentation, and her contentious give and take with Phil:

> I made a mistake today. It was a big mistake that I'm going to have to live with forever. But there's no turning back now, I'm going to have to live with it and move on. Perhaps it's a new beginning? Actually, I'm looking forward to doing the research. I want to prove Phil wrong. I want to make him squirm.

The journal entry for that day ended with a question:

Do you think he knows?

———◦———

"That bastard!" Dr. Paolo said aloud in the Volvo. "He's out to get me! 'Nothing personal' my ass! I'll have to figure out what to do next; perhaps a preemptive strike, an offensive," and with that he decided to take this dilemma on a run as soon as he got home. He knew better than to be agitated while driving and so, to divert his anger, he turned on National Public Radio and listened to someone who wrote a book about how the Internet, instant messaging, and email have contributed to the creation of a less civil society. Upon hearing the author describe her findings, Dr. Paolo smiled and thought to himself, *Benedetti is too old to blame his behavior on the Internet. Clearly, he was born a bastard.*

Dr. Paolo's workouts alternated between resistance training and outdoor jogging, a pattern he had maintained for over two decades. When he started jogging it was music that served as a companion but over time he learned that the only thing he needed was a problem to solve and Dr. Benedetti was the problem *du jour*. He started his run slowly in order to stretch and to bring his heart rate up to a good steady level and it was during this first half-mile stage that he reviewed in his mind the past three classes with his students, including the very short discussion he had with the young man who dropped the class. *I'm not interested in teaching you or anyone else*, he recalled Ajay saying. At first it seemed like Ajay didn't care for the course format but about ten strides later Dr. Paolo deduced that it was laziness more than anything else that made him drop the course. His thoughts then turned to the remaining four students. Amy, a no-nonsense over achiever is destined to do well as an M.D., no problem there. Brad, mostly self-assured, not as forceful as Amy, but he too will succeed. Phil, an outspoken thinker, a lover of math, sees the world as more black and white than gray; he'll do well. And then there was Abby.

What to make of Abby, he wondered as he approached a slight up-hill grade. *Unlike the others, Abby was from a lower class family. She's also endured a sudden loss. I wonder how that will affect her in the long run.*

The next thought almost made Dante Paolo stop dead in his tracks.

Abby told the class that's she's telepathic. I bet she's already read my mind, he thought. *The last thing Abby said to me today was 'sympathy strengthens my resolve'. I bet it was her response to my thought of her as a poor kid. Man, that hasn't happened to me in a long, long time.*

Although Dante was stunned by the real possibility that Abby read his mind he had to focus on Lorenzo Benedetti and face the other real possibility—that the course could very well be terminated. But the professor wasn't about to throw in the towel, especially now that the course was finally off the ground. He devised a plan to save the course but he was going to need help and it was during the last two miles of his run when he decided to take the case directly to the students. On Tuesday he was going to take them for a walk in the woods to demonstrate the power of observation and although he would follow through as planned he also decided to tell the students directly and unequivocally that it might be his last day as their teacher because the course may be terminated. He would keep this to himself until they had almost completed the walk so the entire day would not be ruined. Then he hoped that the seniors would be disappointed and ask for guidance on how to save the course.

Dante panted heavily after sprinting the final two hundred yards of his run. It was during the recovery period, when his heart decelerated at a healthy rate, that he concluded that if there was no such action from the students then the entire teaching experiment failed. He would teach no longer, he would move on and live with the result. *Que sera, sera.*

3

Rob's idea to celebrate Dante's first full week as a teacher at college was well intended but ill timed. He was about to learn that it might also have been the scientist's first and last full week at the college. Nevertheless, Dante looked forward to a Friday night out with Rob and Beverly and they decided to explore a newly renovated bistro located within a walking distance of the college and a short drive from Laura's practice.

It was a pleasantly warm evening and everyone was in good spirits including Dante who had, by this point, not only developed a plan but was also quite confident that the outcome would be to his liking. He was also thrilled to finally have the opportunity to let everyone in on what was happening at the college and especially happy to chat with his wife whom he rarely saw during the week given her late work schedule combined with his desire to turn in early in the evening.

Toast of the Town was different than most eating establishments. It was opened from 5 a.m. to 9 a.m. for tea, coffee, and toast made from hand-made bread prepared the previous evening by the baker who was also the chef as well as the owner. Creamy, hand-whipped butter, a variety of locally produced homemade jams, seasonal honey, organic peanut butter, and fine olive oils were the only items offered as toppings. For Christmas and for Valentine's Day, the owner would add a hazel-nut-chocolate spread to the menu, an instant favorite with children. The doors to the bistro were closed from 9 a.m. to 5 p.m. when they reopened for drinks and light entrees that changed with the season or at the whim of the baker-chef-owner.

"You see?" exclaimed the baker-chef-owner to everyone who walked through the door, "A toast to the day ahead and a toast to the great day you just had!"

The light entrees were larger than most appetizers but small enough so that the customer had plenty of room left for the desserts made by the baker-chef-owner's wife. Given that *Toast of the Town* seated only fifty-two and had a limited, ever-changing menu only added to its comfortable and relaxed ambiance; it truly was a local treasure.

Dante was excited to see an empty table for four towards the back where it would be relatively quiet and away from the chatter of the small bar located towards the front of the bistro. Once drinks were served, Rob grabbed his cold beer and declared a toast. True to the waitresses' instructions, Rob stood, turned to the patrons, raised is glass and said in a loud voice while pointing to Dante, "I'd like to propose that my friend be the 'Toast of the Town' for having completed his first full week at his new career as a teacher!" And with that, the crowd, most of whom were well versed in such announcements cheered in unison, "Hear, hear!" And for the next five minutes or until the next toast was motioned and approved by the friendly crowd, Dante was the *de facto* toast of the town. The bistro's baker-chef-owner could be spotted behind the bar grinning broadly with satisfaction in the spontaneous toasts—his innovation that made patrons feel a bit more connected, a lot less inhibited and thus more willing to stay and spend longer.

"So doctor toast of the town, how'd it go?" asked Beverly. "Was it what you thought it would be?"

Beverly Pierce, a brunette with a provocative smile, was inwardly fond of Dante. She was a non-practicing Catholic of Irish heritage, an accountant and a caring mother to her twin boys. Beverly kept her body in shape by jogging and her mind clear with yoga that she practiced alone in a small room that faced the morning sun. Dante found Beverly to be seductive and mysterious in ways that he could not quite understand but that he definitely enjoyed contemplating. She was the type of woman who became more alluring as she aged.

"Well," replied Dante, "it has it's ups and downs, but on the whole, its been quite balanced, that is, until I met with Dean Benedetti yesterday."

"What'd that idiot want?" asked Rob who had nearly finished his first beer.

"Well, after class on Thursday he called me in his office, which, by the way is quite impressive with wood paneling and high ceilings, and he essentially told me that there weren't enough students enrolled in the course and that it may be terminated along with my position. Turning to Beverly, Dante added, "By the way, there are only four students in my class, down from five on day one."

Beverly nodded.

"Enough for what?" Rob asked while gulping the last of his beer.

"Enough to pay the bills, I guess. Benedetti said that the cost of the course is not covered by tuition and so he was going to talk with the president about terminating it possibly as early as next Wednesday. So, ladies and gentleman, we may be back here next week to celebrate the beginning of my second retirement!"

To appease the young waitress who had asked twice if they were ready to order, Beverly and Laura chose fried calamari, shrimp and scallop medley and Buffalo tenders with fried jalapeños. Rob ordered a second beer.

"No way!" cried Rob. "I've never heard of such crap. The college has more money than they know what to do with and your course is only a single credit and you're just part-time. What the hell? That just doesn't add up. Something else is going on here."

"Rob, what's the smallest class size at the College?" asked Dante.

"Probably around ten or so in senior level advanced..."

"Any smaller than ten?"

"Not that I remember."

"Well then, Benedetti has a point, doesn't he?"

"Yeah, but..."

"What will the students do if the class is canceled?" interrupted Laura who was listening intently while assessing her husband's state of mind.

"Good point Laura," said Beverly. "They must have an opinion, don't they?"

Dante took a sip of his gin and tonic while he waited for Rob to chime in.

"Yeah, good point!" added Rob who by now was half way through his second beer and feeling the effects while eyeing the tantalizing appetizers that had just arrived.

"Some of those kids have parents who could influence..."

"One's a 'hardy'," said Dante.

"A what?" asked Laura who turned to Beverly puzzled.

"Oh, that's not good," offered Rob as he filled his plate with a sampling of all three entrees. "Who are the others?"

Dante defined a 'hardy' to Laura and Beverly and without hesitation they agreed that it was inappropriate and offensive label that should not be used anywhere but especially not in the halls of higher education. Rob had heard the label tossed around in the past at faculty meetings and, although he suspected that it was derogatory, he never bothered to learn what it meant. To address Rob's question, Dante presented his own brief character sketch of each student starting with Amy and ending with Abby. He mentioned that they all shared a common drive to excel and to continue their education beyond the college. Dante did not fail to describe what he perceived to be social class differences between the four students but he did not say who was in which class.

Later, while the four friends were sampling each other's desserts, Dante shared his plan to engage the students during Tuesday's walk in the woods. He explained that he would tell the four students what was happening with the course then he'd leave the next step up to them. Rob, along with Beverly and Laura, agreed that Dante's plan was a good one but they wondered whether the seniors would make the extra effort to save a demanding course taught by a professor they hardly knew, a potential double whammy, according to Rob. Dante did not disagree. He knew that he had one chance during the three-hour walk to win them over. He wondered aloud if he could do it.

To himself he wondered if he *wanted* to do it.

———◦———

Two years ago it wasn't easy, but now Lorenzo Benedetti had progressed beyond the disappointing loss of his longtime companion; she simply left him for "a younger man of lesser intellect" with little rhyme or reason.

But as it turned out, the aging Dean realized that bachelorhood suited him just fine. He grew to enjoy the solitude of his secluded house in the woods and the freedom to do as he pleased.

On this Friday evening after the first full week of classes, he relaxed with a glass of Chianti; *La Bohème* played softly in the background. He was seated comfortably in the leather chaise lounge in his closed-in porch that faced west. As the last rays of the setting sun filtered through the trunks of the trees and the evening skies darkened, his mind grew more alive. For Lorenzo, evenings were the best time of the day to think critically.

It was just after midnight when he logged onto his computer and opened a new word document to draft a letter to Dr. Holliday regarding Dante and his course. He knew the points he needed to make. He typed:

> Dante accepted the ultimate fate of the course with a clear understanding of the issues and with the highest degree of professionalism. I wish Dr. Paolo well and hope that he would again consider, at some future date, rejoining the faculty at Wilmington College.

He leaned back in his chair and reread the letter. He was satisfied with what he had written. The rhythm and clarity of the prose matched the sharp overtones and clean finish of the Chianti. After making a few minor edits he saved and labeled the file as the final version, he wouldn't need to edit it again. It was ready to be printed on his personal stationary, signed then hand-delivered to Jean's personal inbox first thing Monday morning.

His weekend was now unencumbered.

———•———

Brad's Saturday morning drive to his hometown of Rockport, Massachusetts was nothing short of boring. He was thankful for the news and entertainment of National Public Radio that diverted his attention as he maneuvered the open and rather scenic roads that wound eastward towards the ocean. But on this day, Brad not only wished he had gotten an earlier start, but he was also aware of how often he had made this trip alone. In his sporty Audi A4 Quattro—a high school graduation present from his grandparents who used any occasion to again spoil their already spoiled grandchildren—Brad glanced at the empty passenger seat and wished someone occupied it.

Abruptly, he thought of Amy.

He wasn't sure how she got in his head, but there she was and Brad simply smiled and ran with it. He switched off the radio and spent the rest of the short ride thinking about the smart and quite foxy classmate.

Brad's day home was like many he had endured over the past three years. "What's new? How are classes? Is there anything we can do for you? Anything you need?" These were common questions from his parents that he usually answered with the usual, "Not much. Fine. No, I'm good. No, thanks." But on this day, with thoughts of Amy fresh in his mind, Brad told his parents about the class taught by a new professor at Wilmington College named Dante Paolo. His parents were delighted almost to the point of being shocked that their usually reserved son had something of substance to share with them. Brad described in detail the demands of the one-credit course with the unusual title. He told them about Dr. Paolo and how the course differed than any other he had previously taken. Brad explained how each student had to chose and study one topic, and then they had to deliver several presentations on that topic to the professor and to the entire class over the course of the semester. "In many ways," he explained, "the teacher-student roles are reversed. I'm looking forward to that challenge." Brad also liked the fact that the class size was small and intimate. He enthusiastically told his parents about his own research topic and those chosen by his classmates, leaving the overview of Amy's project for last. Brad let his parents know that Amy Ito was also applying to medical school, a fact that seemed completely out of context with the rest of the discussion but one that was appreciated by his parents nonetheless.

Joan and Livingston MacIntyre were beside themselves with glee. They had not heard this much about their son's experiences at the college in the past three years combined. It was readily apparent that this new course struck a chord with Brad; they knew that it took only one spark to ignite a lifelong fire. Perhaps this course was what Brad needed to become impassioned about medical school. They had quietly harbored concerns that their son was not really interested in becoming a doctor and, as such, they refrained from putting undo pressure on him to pursue one particular career path over another.

Like his father and grandfather before him, Livingston MacIntyre was an alumnus of Wilmington College and one of its current Trustees. He had been on a leave of absence from the board since the day his son enrolled at the college; a move designed to eliminate any potential conflict of interest. Brad's enthusiasm for the *Teach the Professor* course, and the refreshingly new approach to teaching, compelled Livingston MacIntyre to write an email to his longtime friend, Dr. Jean Holliday.

4

Dr. Paolo would have loved to climb an entire mountain in this weather—partly sunny skies with highs in the mid-60s—but on this Tuesday the short hike with this class was the call of the day. Besides a few mental notes Dante did not have a specific lesson plan for the walk in the woods he simply sought to learn more about each student in a setting that differed from the classroom. No one was late for this class and with the morning sun still low in the fall sky, Dr. Paolo and the four students—each with no more than a bottle of water and a snack bar—started on the well-worn and well-marked path that headed east, looped to the north around a small reservoir, then back around to the start point close to Paine Hall.

"Have any of you hiked in the White Mountains of New Hampshire?" Dr. Paolo asked.

"No, not me," replied Amy.

"Me neither," said Phil.

"I've hiked some trails in New Hampshire but not a mountain," Abby said.

"I've climbed Washington to Tuckerman's Ravine with my snowboard one spring," Brad said.

"You've skied Tuckerman's?" asked Dr. Paolo.

"Yup, several times with my dad and uncle. Funny though, I've never climbed it in the summer. I have no idea what it looks like without snow."

"It's awesome. It's a glacier-carved amphitheater. You should...you all should see it someday," replied Dr. Paolo. "It's well worth the effort."

Dr. Paolo then told the students, who could hear him easily as they were walking in a tight formation in a quiet mixed woods forest, that he's always sought the wilderness as a way to refresh his mind, especially when problems arose or when he had something very difficult to solve. He told them about a particular time as a graduate student when things weren't going well. The equipment he was using malfunctioned, he was making simple mistakes in calculations and overall experiments just weren't working; nothing was going right. He was exasperated and discouraged. Upon noticing the growing aggravations, his advisor suggested that all lab members go for a day hike to climb Mount LaFayette, a five thousand foot peak in the White Mountains.

"We hiked the following day, a Saturday," Dr. Paolo began. "I remember it like it happened yesterday. It was a miserable, gray day. It was rainy with a cold raw wind from the north that sliced through my thin, faded fleece. Before long we all were drenched but we trudged onwards and upwards towards the top of this mountain. We couldn't see a damn thing because we were in a dense cloud but we persevered and made it to the rocky summit. We were soaked, muddy and sweaty. There was absolutely no view because we were immersed in a cloud. After a few moments at the peak, we turned and headed back down the trail, a path that was becoming a small stream. We made it back safely despite the slippery ledges and moss-covered rocks. I returned from that hike completely exhausted, physically beat. That night I slept like a baby and I spent Sunday nursing muscles that hadn't been used in some time. By Monday morning I felt reinvigorated. I remember sitting at the desk in my office and designing a whole new set of experiments. Things in the lab were back on track. That hike helped me break away from the problems. It gave me time to clear my head and to look at those problems from a new angle. That hike taught me a life-long lesson and perhaps one that you could use someday. There are times when one needs to let go of a situation, to take a break, to let your mind refuel by allowing it not only to wander but also by giving it other challenges. Although we were never in real danger, my mind treated that hike as if it was a matter of life and death. I was in a survival mode of sorts that led to a way of thinking that differed greatly from the problems back in the laboratory. Exercising these different brain modes can only help keep the mind agile, and an agile mind can think fluidly, creatively and with clarity."

While the four students listened to Dr. Paolo's story and while they understood his message their anxieties dealt more with their own future than with the professor's past. They all were well into the process of applying to graduate schools and their concerns were related not only to the application procedures and the inevitable interviews, but also to the entire adventure that lay ahead.

"Dr. Paolo, did you like graduate school?" asked Phil. "I want to go but I have to admit, I'm not sure of what I'm getting into."

"And I heard that getting into medical school is the toughest part," offered Amy. "Is that true?"

"I heard the same thing about med school. Once you're in, they make sure you succeed," added Brad.

"What? No one fails out of medical school?" Phil asked aloud. "That can't be true."

"Yes, essentially it's true," responded Dr. Paolo as they walked virtually in unison. "For many reasons, a medical school can't afford to have a student drop out. Every student is a part of a revenue stream that the school cannot afford to lose. So they'll work very hard to make sure you're keeping up with the material, that you can handle the workload and if necessary, they'll assign a tutor for the entire four years. So, in some ways, yes, the hardest part is getting in. Graduate school is a bit different. You have to maintain a high GPA, get involved with a research project, and also you'll probably be asked to teach a course or two, mainly lab courses."

"That sounds like a recipe for failure," opined Phil.

"Well, it's certainly a challenge, but it's also a lot of fun," continued Dr. Paolo as he launched into another story. "I was working as an intern at a State Lab when I received the acceptance letter. I was thrilled beyond belief. I shared the good news with others in the building including an established investigator with a small but highly productive lab. I'll never forget his response, he said: 'Congratulations. I am so happy for you. I'm envious. My years as a graduate student were the best years of my life.' I instantly recognized the irony. What I wanted was to be where he was, a well-established scientist with lots of publications and doing great research while he wanted to be where I was, back at the beginning. It wasn't until I reached his age, with my own lab and list of publications, that I completely appreciated his statement. Graduate school is a time of great exploration. A time when you push yourself to new heights intellectually by performing research, discovering new things, and interacting with others who share your passion to learn. It's awesome. And if you do end up teaching and you enjoy it, then there are fewer rewards in life that surpass that of transferring knowledge and watching students grow intellectually. But be forewarned. Graduate school is also a selfish period. It's all about you, your studies, your research, your students, and your grades. There is little time for anything or anyone else. It's almost impossible to begin a lasting relationship or to keep up with family obligations. There is simply no time for anything else but school and study."

"But medical school is different, right?" challenged Amy. "It's not about you but about the patient too, right?"

"So," began Dr. Paolo who was enjoying the discussion. "I lived the medical student life vicariously through my wife who entered medical school when I started my postdoc training. There's no doubt that the medical school curriculum is demanding and that a solid understanding of biology and chemistry is essential. You're right, Amy. At the end of the day, it's less about you and more about the patient, but don't be misled, the time demands on you are great and there is little room for others. It's well known that most medical students who marry while in school are divorcees by the end of their residency. It's simply too demanding."

"And research?" asked Brad.

"That depends on your program," replied Dr. Paolo. "There are M.D.-Ph.D. programs that combine the rigors of both medicine and research, and there's also the M.D. who chooses to do more clinical-type research, more population-based studies, like making connections on lifestyle and cancer, or testing new drugs or vaccines on a specific patient population. And another thing, a common thread among all of these career paths is the ability to solve problems. In some cases, like the emergency room doc, you must solve problems quickly while others, like the Ph.D.-researcher, the problem could take a lifetime to crack. In fact, your ability to solve problems, big or small, life threatening or non-life threatening, instantly or over a considerable amount of time, will ultimately define you."

Dr. Paolo looked up from the forest floor and realized that they were about half way through their walk as they reached the edge of the vast reservoir that served as the source of water for the local communities. Yellow and orange signs warned of the penalties associated with polluting or swimming in the pristine, spring-fed water that rippled easily on the sandy man-made shore; a lone trail marker pointed the way back to the college. As the group paused to take in the scene, Dr. Paolo wondered exactly what he was going to say to his students towards the end of this hike. He wasn't sure if he was connecting with them or pontificating pointlessly. And he did note that Abby hadn't said a word over the past hour and he worried that she was losing interest and may drop the course thus sealing his fate. But his concern was short-lived, as it was Abby who started the discussion on the return leg of their hike.

"So is that why you left the lab and came to teach?" She began. "Is this a new problem for you to solve or is this a problem-solving course?"

"Yeah, why did you leave the lab Dr. Paolo?" asked Phil.

Dr. Paolo smiled at the line of questions. He considered all three to be challenging and genuine and he responded by answering the last question first.

"The ability for me or for anyone else to do research depended on having available funding. When I started my career, I spent about a quarter of my time raising money by writing grants and the rest of the time was spent doing research and teaching too, but mostly research. Gradually, that changed to the point where I was spending most of my time writing grants that did not get funded due to, among other things, government cutbacks in funding levels. I was spending less and less time doing research. It wasn't fun anymore. So I decided to do something different with my interest in science. And to answer your question Abby, yes to both. This course could be considered a new problem for me to solve and, hopefully along the way I can help you hone your ability to solve problems. Creating problems for you to solve is my job."

"Do you miss research or the lab?" asked Brad.

"Both," replied Dr. Paolo without skipping a beat. "The part I miss the most relates to what I was saying earlier about teaching and its rewards. I miss teaching someone how to do research. I miss sharing in their excitement when they get a great result." Dr. Paolo was pensive, as his mind filled with images of those who had passed through his lab on their way to their own careers.

They walked along the wooded path cautiously but with ease and some in the group were starting to think about lunch when suddenly and without an apparent reason, Dr. Paolo stopped walking and by association so did the others.

"Has anyone heard the expression, 'You only see what you know'?" he asked.

"Yeah, I've heard that," answered Brad who recognized the phrase uttered many times by his grandfather.

"Look around you. Tell me what you see," said Dr. Paolo who had hoped that this exact opportunity would arise.

They responded in rapid fire. Trees, leaves, branches, poison ivy, rocks, pebbles, poison oak, clouds, sky, the list went on as they all were somewhat amused to participate in this childish game. But when they had exhausted their accounting of the surroundings Dr. Paolo asked the obvious question.

"What else? You missed something."

"Something big?" asked Amy.

"That's relative," remarked Phil.

"Okay then, something obvious?" countered Amy.

"Yes. To me it's very obvious," answered Dr. Paolo.

After a few more additions to the list, Dr. Paolo informed the students that the time was up and that they had missed something that was not only obvious, but something that he had spotted ten yards away. Dr. Paolo was careful to avoid the poison ivy as he walked off the path and towards an old oak tree. At the base of that rather large tree he knelt next to a light brown mass that had several leafy rosette-type outgrowths.

"Does anyone know what this is?" he asked looking up at the students.

They all shook their heads.

"The common name of this mushroom is 'hen of the woods'", Dr. Paolo stated. "Asians know it as 'maitake' and mycologists call it *Grifola frondosa*. It is an edible mushroom associated with specific hardwood trees including this red oak. This mushroom is parasitic for the tree; it saps energy from the tree's roots to grow."

"Maitake! Yes, my grandmother mentioned maitake and when she spoke of it she and my grandfather became very animated," recalled Amy. "Apparently she used to find this mushroom when she was a child. Do I remember that she said it had healing powers?"

"Yes," Dr. Paolo said with a chuckle. "There are as many folktales on the benefits of mushrooms as there are varieties of them, but these claims have not been rigorously verified. There's no denying the nutritional value of mushrooms—edible ones, that is."

The students watched intently as Dr. Paolo harvested the young hen of the woods by tugging on it gently from its base. He then placed it in a plastic bag that he had retrieved from his back pocket. Dr. Paolo started to study and catalog local mushrooms only a few years ago and now, after many hours in the woods, his eyes could spot most species amid the wooded background that virtually camouflaged their existence.

"And by the way," the professor added, "there's a ten-dollar reward for the first person to spot a Black Trumpet of Death. It's a cone-shaped, small mushroom that is jet black and grows in clumps, sometimes in mossy areas. It's a prized, choice mushroom and it's not poisonous despite its name. I've had no luck spotting them but I know they're in New England. I'll be damned if I can find one."

In character, Dr. Paolo drove home the 'you see only what you know' message by saying that before he started this new hobby he was like them—blind to the presence of this strange-looking maitake.

"The opportunities each of you have to continue your education without preconceived notions or biases will open your eyes and let you see more. Perhaps your work will also allow others to see more too," he concluded. The value of the big picture message was not lost on the four seniors as years later they would personify those very words.

The trail evened out and became more worn as they approached its end; they could see the college through the tall pines and bulky beech trees.

Dr. Paolo stopped next to a large rock and turned to face his students.

"I want to thank you for joining me on this hike today," the professor said knowing this statement of gratitude was completely unnecessary. "And you should also know that this might be our last class."

This blunt statement hung lazily in the mild September air while it's meaning was processed by the four hikers. As Dr. Paolo expected it was Amy who spoke first.

"What do you mean? Why would this be our last class? Are you going back to the lab?" she asked.

"No," replied Dr. Paolo who then answered two more questions—one from Brad and the other from Phil—before he told them about his little chat with Dean Benedetti. The mood of the small group quickly dampened. They were quiet with eyes focused on the smooth ground ahead of them; the pace of their walk during the last few hundred yards had quickened, fueled by consternation and concern.

It was eleven o'clock when they reached the front of Paine Hall.

"I wanted to tell you about the course myself. I didn't want you to find out from anyone else," Dr. Paolo said. "If this is our last class I want to wish you all the best in your future endeavors. It was my pleasure to have met you." Dr. Paolo then made sure he looked into their eyes as he shook their hands and wished them well individually. Dante knew that there was a better than even chance he'd never see them again, at least not as their teacher.

The moment was awkward for everyone; even Amy was at a loss for words.

————•————

The biannual meeting between Dr. Benedetti and Dr. Holliday to review the current semester's courses had always been a predicable *pro forma* event. It was held in the morning, on the Wednesday after the first full week of classes, the last day students could change courses for the semester. Dean Benedetti reported on the number of students enrolled in each course and the distribution of students per class. He also touched on any staff issues as well as any concerns with the physical space where the classes were held.

But on this Wednesday Dr. Benedetti had not even settled into the chair across the president's oversized desk when he realized that there was a problem. The look in her eyes gave it away.

"So," began Dr. Holliday in a troubled voice, "would you tell me why I've received no fewer than six emails in the past four days raving about Dr. Paolo's course? Then this morning I read your letter telling me that the class is over? I just don't get it! Four students took the time to send me separate emails and they also felt the need to show unity by sending a separate email cosigned by each of them to emphasize the point that they did not want Paolo's course to end."

"Yes. I can explain," said Dr. Benedetti calmly. Over the next few minutes, he reported not only on the course loads and space usage, but this year, he also added a new twist by producing a spreadsheet on the economics of the each course. He called it the 'value factor' and it was simply the gain or loss of each course based on the cost of salary and overhead divided by the tuition rate per student enrolled in that course. The data clearly showed that the only course at the college that was losing money was *Teach the Professor*. He also described the recent meeting with Dr. Paolo and reiterated that it was the new hire's own recommendation that *Teach the Professor* be terminated immediately so the students would have the time to join another course.

"Lorenzo, Dr. Paolo has held only four sessions. Based on these emails he's already had an impact on these four students," she replied waving printouts of each email in the air.

"Yes, but it's not profitable, it's a financial drag. What will you tell the Trustees, Jean?" Dr. Benedetti asked the President.

"Funny you should mention the Trustees. Let me read this email from Livingston MacIntyre, you remember Livingston don't you Lorenzo?" asked Dr. Holliday who had the email printout in her hand.

Dr. Benedetti nodded, as he knew all too well the stature of Mr. Mac-Intyre among the college's Trustees. Dr. Holliday read directly from the printout, "'Based on my son's enthusiastic description of the course *Teach the Professor*, it seems like you've hit a home run, Jean. Providing a senior-level course that allows students to think critically seems firmly in line with the type of course that results in highly educated individuals that the United States sorely needs. I will be interested to hear how this course progresses as it may become a model not only for those majoring in the sciences, but also for those who major in other fields of study as well. Congratulations to you and to your staff for having the wisdom and foresight to provide a progressive and innovative course to the students. Best, Livingston.' And I'd like you to recall that we both understood that this was an experimental course. As such, this course will continue and I will be more than happy to defend the cost deficit if such defense is ever needed. Experiments require capital investment, Lorenzo," she said. "You of all people should know this." Dr. Holliday concluded the meeting by adding, "And, I'd like for you to respond to the students, copy me and Dr. Paolo, and tell them the course will not be eliminated as they had feared and that class will continue as scheduled. That's all for now."

Dr. Benedetti left Dr. Holliday's office calmly, but inwardly he was seething with anger. He wondered exactly how many lives this Dante Paolo has.

The Projects

1

The students applauded as their Professor entered the classroom the day after they received the email from Dr. Benedetti stating that their class would not be canceled. Dr. Paolo's broad smile accompanied his mind's ear where Puccini's Calaf asserted in his high-timbered voice, *Vincerò, vincerò, vincerò!* The victory was both his and theirs and to show his approval he joined in on the fun and clapped along with them.

"This is your class now," declared Dr. Paolo who was obviously in a good mood. "Let's see if we can learn something together and maybe in the process we'll teach a few people around here a thing or two about the learning process." For the first time Dr. Paolo felt like he belonged at Wilmington College. The class felt right, the students were perfect and his role was clear. He'd finally arrived. And now with all of the uncertainties aside, Dr. Paolo focused on the student's projects.

Over the ensuing months, *Teach the Professor* found its weekly rhythm. During class each student spent about 30 minutes describing what he or she learned about their research topic since the prior class and with each passing session the information became more complete.

At each turn, Dr. Paolo challenged them to dig deeper, to learn more, to question what they had read, to determine what they were going to accept and what they were going to challenge. He asked them to consider the source of the information and also to consider that the data may be incomplete or the results misinterpreted. He wanted them to be aware of who funded the research and to consider whether or not the sponsor could have influenced the study in any way. Dr. Paolo simply wanted them to question anything and everything. The more questions the professor asked the more answers the students provided. The four seniors were maturing right in front of Dante Paolo's eyes.

With no advanced warning Dr. Paolo would deviate from the routine and lecture to the class. He would discuss details of the scientific inquiry; provide definition on key elements of the process or pointers on other facets of being a scientist.

"Clear your mind," Dr. Paolo told the attentive students. "Let it be free, open. Have no preconceived ideas on how something that is unexplained should be. Then propose a hypothesis, a potential solution to what is not known. Take time to design clever experiments to support or to disprove your hypothesis. Carefully observe, record, and analyze the results. Think critically about what you've learned."

He would describe the importance of both positive and negative controls and how to interpret results, re-evaluate the hypothesis then review the approach based on what was learned. What made his lectures so unique was that Dr. Paolo used both textbook definitions as well as his own real-life experiences. His lessons were a blend of practical information and tested wisdom.

In one succinct lecture he delivered a primer on how to speak publically and how to organize an oral presentation. He discussed the most important aspects of public speaking—make sure you know the topic inside and out, know your audience so you can tailor the presentation to their level especially if the audience is young and not at all familiar with your topic. And he'd emphasized how one must rehearse the presentation in front of a mirror then, if possible, in the exact room where it will be delivered.

"A key to success in many different fields, and even in everyday life, is having solid communication skills. The ability to clearly convey information, ideas or thoughts is important for everyone but especially critical for those who want to be leaders," emphasized Dr. Paolo. "Historically, effective leaders are often gifted orators. That's why I'll get on your case if you use poor grammar and incorrect word usage in this class. I will be ultra critical so you will become clear, effective communicators. My goal is for all of you to excel."

Before long it was October and the cool winds from the north not only tore at the few autumn leaves that stubbornly clung to arched branches but they also forebode of the long winter months that lay ahead. The school year, it appeared, was trying to match Mother Nature's rapid seasonal transformation. Classes raced on at an accelerated rate accentuated by the skimping of the day's ration of natural light. But the change of season with its negative effects on sun-loving adults had no affect on the demeanor of Dr. Paolo's dedicated students. Indeed, as the daily temperature in New England dropped, the confidence of his four students rose to new heights, to the point where they were confident with their progress and ready to present their research findings to each other.

The format was simple. Students would present their research findings in two parts, the length of which was limited to one hour per day. The remaining time was dedicated to discussion and critique. They were instructed to end their presentation with no more than two slides that speculated on the future direction of the chosen field because Dr. Paolo wanted them to take any potential advance to the extreme. He wanted them to push the boundaries of their imagination.

2

It was a foregone conclusion that Amy would be the first presenter. She had led the discussion in almost every class over the past ten weeks but she did so in a manner that did not overpower anyone. Dr. Paolo wrote in his personal notebook,

> Amy Ito possesses a clever way of drawing her classmates into a discussion by tapping their unique intellectual strengths to empha-size her point. She cleverly used them to her advantage and no one seemed to notice or mind.

Amy started her presentation by projecting two bold numbers on the large screen. A black number four was positioned above a black number ten against a bright yellow background. This image hung for a moment as the class silently stared at the two seemingly unrelated numbers.

"Four," started Amy in a declarative, decisive voice as she stood behind the podium wearing a plain black dress and a white sweater. "Only four. Four nucleotides. Four nitrogen-based molecules."

She paused to let that simple message sink in.

"Four nucleotides, some phosphate and a few sugars provide all the code necessary to produce over ten trillion cells in the human body," she continued with an emphasis on 'trillion'. "Think about that. Over ten tril-lion cells organize into specialized tissues that form unique organs that comprise complex systems that function collectively as the human body is orchestrated by only four nucleotides."

Amy had hooked her audience with a single slide, two numbers and a clever delivery. The well-rehearsed opening accomplished the first and most important part of public speaking: she captured their attention. They were in her control and despite the fact that her classmates and Dr. Paolo had learned a great deal about the human genome from Amy over the past couple of months, they found themselves hungry for more. Her presentation presented facts, followed by a series of questions followed by answers to those questions. Amy systematically explained the discovery of the genetic elements including a brief overview of scientists who isolated, purified and solved the simple structure of DNA. She recounted the timeline from the initial discoveries to the advent of molecular biology and its impact on medicine. The first hour of her presentation passed quickly and it ended with a slide outlining the second hour that was scheduled for the next class. Like a teaser trailer to a movie, Abby first highlighted the enormous effort that led to sequencing the entire human genome then posted a question in bold black lettering against a white background that read: Will this change your life?

The small audience erupted in applause. Amy, who appeared to be pleased with her performance, shot a quick glance at Brad who was both clapping and nodding in approval. He was spellbound by her presentation. She was brilliant and at the very moment that their eyes met he felt more attracted to her than ever before. It remained a mystery why he had not noticed Amy in the past. She was beautiful and smart and, unlike many other women he met, she had a solid career goal. The only other person in the room who noticed the spark between the future medical students was Abby Lark.

Dr. Paolo rose, turned to the audience and asked if there were any questions for Amy. Weeks ago he spent an entire class discussing effective ways to answer questions following a formal presentation, and to get the ball rolling he asked the first question.

"Amy, there is no doubt that human life is encoded in our DNA but is DNA required for all organisms to replicate?"

"Yes," responded Amy without hesitation. She wanted to give a more complete answer but the question was so simple and obvious that she could think of little else to add.

"Is she correct?" Dr. Paolo asked the audience shifting his role from moderator to professor. The three-seated students had no answer.

"Yeah, I think so," offered Brad tentatively.

"I think so too," said Phil as he looked over at Abby who shrugged her shoulders and nodded in agreement.

Dr. Paolo noticed that Amy was taking notes while the others were responding. Taking notes during a question and answer session was something the professor passed along to his students after watching presidential debates on television; it not only ensured that the candidate focused on the question but it's also a clever move that provided a few precious seconds to generate a more thoughtful response. Amy was jotting down the provocative question; it needed to be researched before her presentation on Thursday. Dr. Paolo let Amy's answer stand and pointed at Brad who had his hand raised.

"I've always been interested in the scientists who discovered the structure of DNA," said Brad who realized that he simply enjoyed looking at Amy. "What did you learn about Watson, Crick, Franklin, and others that you didn't know before you started this project?"

It was a soft question that Amy had no trouble answering. Like the others, she had heard about James Watson and Francis Crick before her taking this class but she knew little about the others involved with this discovery. She learned about Rosalind Franklin who became an instant role model for Amy because Dr. Franklin was a trailblazer, a true pioneer. She was a top female scientist in a time when women were greatly outnumbered in the sciences and, in most cases, shunned by their amply-arrogant, condescending and self-serving male counterparts. It irritated Amy to no end that Dr. Franklin was not a co-author on the original Watson and Crick publication that described the double helix structure of DNA despite the fact that it was Rosalind Franklin who took the X-ray image of DNA—an image that was absolutely critical to the paradigm-shifting discovery.

Abby, who had taken several notes during the presentation raised her hand and asked, "Before your presentation I was not aware of the number—ten trillion cells—I mean, this is an extremely large number. Does that mean that the entire length of our DNA is used to create a human being? Is there any DNA to spare?"

"I have to admit," added Phil speaking out of place. "I never thought about it either. I associate numbers that large with the cosmos or bits of computer data that zip across the Internet, but not with things in my own body."

Dr. Paolo allowed the conversation to continue unchecked. He also kept the answer to himself because it was more important to see how Amy responded. She paused for a moment, and then recalling Dr. Paolo's advice said, "That's a very thoughtful question. Let me do more research and get back to you."

It was this kind of progress that made Dante Paolo's day. Unlike most politicians and cable news pundits, Amy didn't simply answer the question for the sake of saying something; instead she softly admitted that she did not know the answer while providing assurance that it would be addressed.

Previously, Dr. Paolo told the class, "An educated person can admit his or her shortcomings. One becomes more learned by then closing that gap in knowledge."

The forty-five hours between the time Amy ended the first part of her presentation to the beginning of the second part seemed more like forty-five minutes as she rushed to improve her presentation. She sought nothing more than perfection. Having laid the groundwork on DNA in the first hour, she was now ready to describe the human genome sequencing effort and how the enormous amount of information would be applied to benefit mankind. She was careful not to exaggerate the accomplishment and she used simple analogies sparingly.

"Before the human genome project, molecular biologists only had the equivalent of the alphabet to work with, in other words, not much," Amy told the class. "Now, with the entire human genome sequenced, they have a complete dictionary of the code of life. The logical next step is to compile the encyclopedia, a task that will be completed by our generation. But it will be our children's generation that will reap the full benefits and confront the downsides of these collective efforts. What I'm referring to is nothing short of 'individual personalized medicine' or iPM." Using a series of slides Amy described iPM, an abbreviation she coined, in terms of what it means using today's criteria and level of understanding.

"There are at least fifty genes that have already been identified and linked to diseases ranging from cancer to diabetes. Understanding what controls the function of these genes, what turns them on, what turns them off, is the key to better overall health and prevention."

She ended the formal part of her presentation as Dr. Paolo had instructed. Amy speculated on the future of personalized medicine using her new acronym as a launch point. She envisioned iPM would logically lead to cPM, which stood for 'community-wide personalized medicine' and ultimately to wPM or 'world-wide personalized medicine'. "cPM," she explained, "will be a collection of genomic data from an entire community. These data will allow molecular epidemiologists—those that track disease outbreaks and trends—to then use a larger, broader dataset to study a single individual's genetic information. It would directly address nature versus nurture influences, that is, it would determine if a given disease or a disease outbreak is associated specifically with genes or the environment or both. Sets of statewide cPM could be combined to form a medical collage of a country. And with the involvement of several other countries and with the help of international groups like the World Health Organization, a global view of personalized medicine could be derived. Condensation of billion bits of genomic and health data would provide a health profile that could lead to targeted preventative strategies anywhere in the world for an emerging infection or it could provide therapy for a specific disease that erupts in a tiny village before it became a larger problem. It could be used reductively starting at a worldwide or countrywide level, then down to the community and individual level. This type of tailored prevention, or intervention, will lead to healthier lives, stronger more productive communities, states and countries. It brings today's 'One Medicine—One World' initiative to the highest level possible," concluded Amy.

Amy was indifferent to the applause of the small audience as she closed the cover of the laptop that made the projection screen turn blue. She walked across the room to the projector, switched it off, and then returned to the small podium in front of the class.

"I want to tell you what I learned after I researched the questions that Dr. Paolo and Abby asked the other day. I didn't include these details in my presentation because I'm still trying to understand what they mean. In fact, I find them both interesting and troubling. Dr. Paolo asked if DNA was required for all organisms to replicate. I answered 'yes' but I was wrong. As strange as it sounds, there are malformed proteins called prions that can replicate on their own; they cause neurological diseases in humans and other animals. No DNA, no RNA. It's unbelievable."

Glancing down at her notecard Amy continued, "Then Abby asked if there was any DNA to spare. As you know, segments of DNA code for genes that are then transcribed to RNA, then translated into proteins that create cells, tissues, organs, and systems. But there also exists non-coding DNA; it doesn't code for anything, well, at least anything that's been described. It's also called junk DNA. Not a big deal, right? I mean it's just a few base pairs out of three billion, right? Well, get this," said Amy who paused briefly before continuing. "Non-encoding DNA comprises over ninety-seven percent of the human genome, ninety-seven percent!" her voice rising in disbelief. "And this amount of junk DNA has been with us for a long time. It's evolutionarily conserved. We've been inheriting DNA from our parents that is ninety-seven percent useless."

Her classmates were dumbstruck.

After listening to Amy's entire presentation on how our DNA is the essence of our being and of how sequencing it will lead to a golden age of personalized medicine only to be told that only three percent of it is relevant was inconceivable to the young audience. The rest of the time was spent with the class asking Amy, and each other, a series of probing questions: "How did this junk DNA get there? Does it really code for nothing? Can a human be cloned with only three percent of the DNA? Can bases be added to the nonsense DNA to make it useful?"

Dr. Paolo thought after the students had left the class, *this might just be working. It might just be working.*

After class, Brad looked at Amy's weary face and saw an opportunity.

"Hey, nice job this week. You set a hell of a standard."

"Thanks. It was harder than I thought it would be especially when I learned about prions. That sent me for a loop. And I'm really glad Dr. Paolo didn't ask questions about them. There's really a lot more to learn."

"Listen, I was wondering if I could take you out to dinner Friday evening. We'll celebrate the completion of your project."

Although the offer took Amy by surprise it only took her a brief moment to accept the harmless invitation.

"Yeah, okay. Dinner sounds wonderful. I have an exam tomorrow but then I'll be ready for a break."

They exchanged cell phone numbers, agreed on a time and a place to meet then parted ways. Brad was elated. Amy's use of the word "wonderful" played and replayed in his mind for the rest of the day. He felt like a smitten high school sophomore as he wondered if her "wonderful" matched the poetic nature of his definition of "wonderful". *Time will tell,* he thought.

The slow bumper-to-bumper traffic didn't faze Brad during this Friday's rush hour. In fact, the drive to the Massachusetts seacoast was a delight with Amy in the Audi's passenger seat. She looked absolutely adorable in plain black slacks and a simple white top with a light lavender sweater that highlighted her dark features. Brad was also dressed casually for the fall evening forgoing a tie for a blue button down shirt, dark pants and a light tan blazer.

They arrived at the *Ship-to-Shore* a few minutes after six-thirty. The salty cedar-shingled exterior of the restaurant in Gloucester, a coastal town just south of Rockport, did not reflect its elegant interior décor; an intimate ambiance with its famed view of the rugged, rocky seacoast. It was a local favorite with a comfortable, casual bar where oysters on the half shell were the best bargain in town and the menu offered the right blend of fresh seafood paired with tender beef and locally grown vegetables. Brad was well familiar with *Ship-to-Shore* as it was frequented by his parents who often sought the restaurant as a venue to entertain out of town guests and business associates. During those long, often boring evenings, young Brad's role was to simply to be charming.

By sheer luck, they were seated at the last table for two by the large array of windows overlooking the dark ocean below. The waves were as calm as the two seniors on this October evening. Although this was their first date, they were quite comfortable with each other mainly because they were comfortable with themselves; they knew who they were, what they wanted and where they were going.

They ordered a bottle of Californian merlot and agreed to split a focaccia with fresh tomatoes, olive oil, and a blend of herbs and clams casino as appetizers. The evening's special—beef tenderloin topped with pan-seared ocean scallops—sealed the choice of entrée. That Amy chose to have her tenderloin rare brought a smile to Brad's face, because according to his father, it was the only way a fine cut of beef should be cooked.

Amy spoke openly and freely. It had been a long time since she shared so much about herself with someone. What would become apparent to her later, when she was alone, was how much she missed her childhood friend and sole confidant who chose to attend a school in California when Amy came east. Over the past few years, including long summers when she worked as a receptionist at a doctor's office, Amy put no effort in making new friends. She had no patience with "foo-foo girls" whose lives hinged on every contrived episode of the latest television reality show or the next high-end make-up fad, nor could she be bothered with adolescent men who tried to hit on her every now and again.

But Brad seemed different. He was smart and courteous with impeccably perfect manners. He listened to what she had to say and when he spoke, his words were well chosen, his sentences complete, and his thoughts sound.

Could he become my new confidant? She wondered.

Amy also took note of all of Brad's mannerisms from how he addressed the valet parking attendant to his actions at the table. As a child Amy's parents stressed the importance of proper table etiquette, "You can tell a great deal about a person's upbringing by the way they conduct themselves at the dinner table," they'd say repeatedly. And even in this category, Brad shined. Amy was relieved to see that her date knew how to properly use a knife and fork. According to her parents, there was only one way to use dinner utensils. Her parents taught her to place the fork in her left hand and the knife in her right when the knife was used to slice. The fork was held at a shallow angle between the forefinger and thumb, while the knife was held in a similar angle in the opposite hand. Both instruments were used delicately and with purpose. Once a slice was made, the knife was then placed on the dish and the fork, with its content, is transferred to the right hand and brought slowly to the mouth. Any other pattern of use revealed a lack of etiquette, education and sophistication; those who gripped their fork like it was a stake about to be plunged violently into Dracula's heart were, according to her parents, "Uncultured barbarians to be avoided at all costs."

The conversation between the seniors flowed easily through the appetizers and the entrée and by the end of the two-hour meal they'd covered a great deal of their young lives. Amy was born and raised in a small town in coastal California; she was an only child. Brad, the younger of two boys, was born and raised in Massachusetts. Amy's grandparents emigrated from Japan in 1952, less than a decade after the end of the Second World War whereas Brad's ancestors were among America's original settlers with paternal roots that led back to the first New England settlers. Middle class, academically driven parents for Amy, upper class, financially minded lawyers and philanthropists for Brad. Yet despite the cultural and social differences Amy and Brad discovered that they each felt a firm, yet silent, expectation from their respective parents to excel, to lead. Also, and perhaps most importantly, both harbored a deep-rooted desire to help others.

Of the many stories they shared about their lives and family, Brad was keen to learn that Amy's father, Jainbin Ito, earned a doctorate in engineering from MIT in the first half of the 1980s. It was also during his time in Cambridge when Jainbin learned about Wilmington College and of its high academic standards. After earning his degree, Dr. Ito returned to California and joined a biotech company as lead engineer to design a robotics system to sequence the human genome. Amy told the class that her father was involved with the human genome project but she hadn't revealed his exact role. Brad appreciated the importance of an automated system to the success of the human genome project and as the evening progressed he also appreciated Jainbin's decision to send his only daughter to school in Massachusetts.

It was obvious to anyone who glanced in the young couple's direction that they were genuinely content to be in each other's company. The only person who was bothered with their deliberate disregard for time was the waiter who sought to flip the table with its spectacular view of the dark seacoast as often as possible. But once Brad told the young man that they were there for a good while and that he'd take good care of him, the waiter relaxed and gave them space, a tact Amy appreciated.

Over a rather large helping of tiramisù that complemented the last of the merlot, they discussed the anxieties of applying to medical school and the high demands of the medical profession. Amy thought that she'd like to be a pediatrician or an obstetrician, but that she was leaving all options open until she learned more about medicine in general. Brad was interested in neurology but he wasn't sure if he'd become a neurobiologist performing research in a laboratory or a neurosurgeon. He admitted that the research he'd done on the human brain for Dr. Paolo's class galvanized his interest in the field.

Brad was allowed to pay the dinner bill only after agreeing to Amy's condition; she would pick up the next tab. They left the crowded restaurant and stepped into the cool New England evening for a walk along the dimly lit boardwalk that led to the well-preserved Cape Ann lighthouse with its lantern aglow. Brad interrupted the sounds of the gently lapping waves and softly asked, "Would you mind if I held your hand?" Amy's left hand silently found Brad's right hand and the two instantly drew closer to each other. They walked in silence and savored the tenderly romantic moment that they'd vividly recall decades later.

With little traffic, the Audi purred its way back to the college in a fraction of the time it took to get to Gloucester. Brad smiled to himself as he thought about a scene from his favorite movie, *Annie Hall*, when on their first date, a young Woody Allen abruptly kissed a younger Diane Keaton before dinner to ensure proper digestion. Amy noticed Brad's smile and she forced him to confess his thoughts.

"Well, la-di-da, la-di-da, la-la," Amy responded in imitation of the smitten Annie Hall in a classic early scene as she laughed and confessed that it too was one of her all-time favorite movies. Then she asked him what other scenes from that movie were his favorite and without hesitation Brad conjured up a white lie which, according to his mother was permissible so long as it did no harm, to say that he was thinking about the movie as a whole and the great messages about love and relationships.

"Relationships are like sharks, they always need to move forward in order to survive," said Amy paraphrasing another line from the famous movie.

Brad parked the Audi and walked Amy to her dorm. Back in the cold night air, the two hugged just a bit longer then what would be considered a casual hug. Then Brad gave Amy a soft kiss on her left cheek then took a moment to look deeply in her dark brown eyes. She thanked him for a lovely evening, turned and entered her dorm.

In Brad's mind, the evening was absolutely delightful that ended perfectly. Amy thought that the evening might just be a beginning.

3

Brad MacIntyre began his presentation to the class with a sobering fact. Standing next to a projection of a slowly spinning three-dimensional image that looked more like a helmeted, monopod creature from outer space then a multicolored model of the brain stem of a human, Brad told Dr. Paolo and the class that this simple, primitive structure perched at the top of our spinal cord controlled our autonomic functions.

"Without it we would not be alive," he stated staring directly at the audience. "The brain stem controls our heart rate, our breathing, our sleep pattern and even when we eat. In size and in function, it is similar to the entire brain of a modern reptile. Structures like the brain stem that regulated your first and last heart beat and your first and last breath appeared in animals about 500 million years ago." With a tap of the laptop's keyboard, the brainstem stopped spinning; another tap produced the entire human brain and a third tap made the new image rotate about its central axis.

"This three pound mass of very delicate tissue with the consistency of a poorly made flan located above and around the stem is what makes us human," continued Brad who spent the next few minutes describing the various regions of the brain and the body function they controlled. With each tap of the keyboard, different regions were highlighted: the occipital lobe where vision is processed, the temporal lobe where sound is analyzed, the relatively smaller somatosensory cortex where touch signals are relayed, and the interconnected prefrontal lobe positioned at the front with the olfactory bulb that process smell and taste that was safely tucked deep inside the brain. Brad aptly explained that more complex, higher order social and behavioral functions such as decision making, social interactions, emotions, and problem solving were mapped to various parts of the right and left side of the brain and named after neurologists who described them such as Wernicke's area, critical for the comprehension of speech, and Broca's area that was responsible for verbal communication.

"With its two hundred billion specialized cells called neurons, the brain handles each and every process of the human body, every second of every living day. In essence, the brain is the body's central processing unit complete with a motherboard, and an apparently endless amount of random and long term memory, storage and access," said Brad who deftly transitioned from the lesson in basic anatomy to a brief history of brain exploration. "Early civilizations were somewhat puzzled by this mostly amorphous structure securely encased in their heads. The brain, along with every other organ except the heart, was removed in the process of mummification widely practiced by ancient Egyptians. The heart, however, was left intact because it was considered the source of intellect and wisdom and therefore needed in the next life. And acupuncture, a therapy that originated over two thousand years ago, that had more to do with interrupting electrical circuits in the body then it did with direct studies on the brain, inspired others to think about how specific body functions were controlled and interconnected."

After describing other milestones in our understanding of the brain, Brad introduced the audience to Dr. Thomas Willis. Widely considered the 'father of clinical neuroscience', Dr. Willis was a British physician and the first to publish complete details of the brain in 1664. Brad then continued to discuss the advances in understanding how different regions of the brain communicated with each other and how the newly invented microscope advanced our understanding of neurological tissues and cells. He continued the background segment of his presentation with a little known story.

"The history of science and medicine is full of stories of how unplanned often accidental events, when critically analyzed with open minds, led to profound insights and groundbreaking discoveries. Phineas Gage suffered an unbelievable injury while on the job in 1848 that damaged his left frontal lobe and resulted in a permanent change to his personality. Before this event, little was known about the connection between the brain and behavioral traits but Phineas' accident changed all that," Brad continued with the help of two slides that described details of the accident including a picture of the actual tamping rod and the path that bored through a model of Gage's skull. "The concept that the brain controlled every aspect of our system—including our very personality—was so profound that it could be considered the beginning of modern neurology," he concluded thus ending the first hour of his presentation with a slide that foreshadowed the next segment. It was a simple title in bold yellow letters on a solid blue background that read: The Second Millennium—The Brain Optimized. Brad closed his laptop as the small audience clapped politely.

This time it was Phil, not Amy, who got the jump on asking the first set of questions. "In the mummification process, how were the brains removed? Weren't holes drilled in the skull? And also doesn't MRI give us a better understanding of what part of the brain is active when we experience different emotions?"

Brad jotted down keywords to Phil's question despite the fact that they were straightforward and easy to address.

"I'll address modern imaging technology on Thursday and with regards to the mummification process, the brain was removed through the nasal cavity. The brain like other parts of the body starts to decompose immediately after a person dies. Because the brain is like jelly it was easily removed by suction with a tube through the nasal cavity thus preserving the structure of the skull."

Amy's hand shot up. Brad acknowledged her while keeping his thoughts about their first date in check.

"Phil may be thinking about an old method to relieve pain by drilling holes in the skull of a living person," Amy offered.

"Right," Brad said glancing at note cards positioned to the left of the lit podium. "I didn't discuss that ancient process called trephining, and I probably should have because drilling holes in the skull has been used throughout our existence and especially on the battlefield to alleviate brain swelling. It has also been used in witchcraft to expel evil spirits. Surgical techniques, as crude or unusual as they may seem today, were not always in the best long-term interest of the sufferer."

Abby winced when she heard the word 'witchcraft'. She was well aware of the associations, as weak and as untrue as they were, between that crazy practice and her own gifts. She jotted the word in her notebook and underlined it twice.

Dr. Paolo asked the next question mindful of the limited time left in class.

"You spoke of the reptile-like brain stem and showed how our brain cavity and brain size has increased as we evolved, so my question is: Is our brain still getting larger?"

Brad went back to his slides and found the one that displayed the series of skulls and brains of primates to hominids over time. With a red laser pointer Brad highlighted the part of the curve that showed a sharp increase in the mass of the brain over that last million years ending with the present. He explained that while there is some debate among evolutionary scientists as to whether or not the brain size will still increase, the graph clearly does not show a change in the positive slope of the line over the past five hundred thousand years, suggesting that the brain is still increasing in size. Glancing down at notecards, he added that the body dedicates a significant amount of energy to keep the brain healthy. Brad speculated that with today's increase in caloric intake by those with ready access to food could lead to increased brain size and development. He also wondered if areas of the brain that currently controlled specific functions could evolve to perform additional or different functions in the future.

"Our sense of smell, for example, is much less sensitive than those of other mammals, even New World monkeys who depend on this sense to reproduce," said Brad. "Perhaps the decrease in our ability to smell, or at least to rely on it less and less, is making way for other senses to develop," he added.

Abby made note of this point.

"Well done," said Dr. Paolo as he started a second round of applause noting that class time had expired. "We look forward to part two, Brad. Well done."

Other than a quick call on Saturday to thank him for a wonderful dinner, Amy had not spoken to Brad nor had she seen him until she arrived at Dr. Paolo's class on Tuesday. Although both were being coy it was a bit easier for Brad because he had to focus on his presentation. While he was calm, she was anxious. Amy wanted to be with him again yet she knew that she had to be patient and wait until class ended, and even then they might not be alone.

Only Abby noticed Amy's angst.

As they left Paine Hall the four classmates were met by a gray overcast November sky. Together they started down the same walkway as they had done most of the semester but this time Brad, who was quite happy with his presentation, stopped and asked if anyone was interested in joining him for a cup of coffee downtown. Phil and Abby declined but Amy, after a quick glance at her watch, agreed.

"Nice job this morning," Amy said as she wrapped her chilled hands around the plain white mug full of hot coffee.

"Thanks," Brad replied. "You set a pretty high bar so I had a lot of work to do this weekend just to get through today's presentation and I still have a ton to do before Thursday."

"It's paying off. I thought your presentation went well, you were clear and the slides were great. You had good questions, a good discussion and I'm sure that the next part will be interesting too. The brain is remarkable. And thanks again for dinner the other night, I had a great time. The weekend seems so much longer when Friday night is fun."

"It was my pleasure. I hope we do it again soon."

"Actually, I was hoping you'd say that. How about Friday? We'll celebrate the completion of your project, except this time, dinner's on me."

"Well Friday works for me, but you won't need to treat..."

"Then forget it."

"Okay, okay fine," replied Brad who really loved her firm resolve.

"That's more like it. How about this as a compromise? I'll pick out the place but since I don't have a car, I'll let you drive, okay?"

"That's fine with me," said Brad with a smile.

It was obvious to anyone in the small diner who took notice that Amy and Brad were infatuated with each other. And if they could read each others mind, they would know that they both harbored the same thought of putting life on hold for a moment longer, to ignore the next item on their busy schedule and to simply spend the entire day together, cuddled and snuggled in a warm bed, just to take time to enjoy their youth. But, in a pattern that they would ultimately follow for the rest of their adult lives, they did no such thing. They had full schedules to keep, deadlines to meet and above all, they were in the process of arranging interviews at medical schools. Now wasn't the time, not at this exact moment.

It was the time of year when seniors realized, with some trepidation, that their lives were entering a new phase. But what they did not realize as they looked beyond graduation was that their most rewarding days at Wilmington College, at least for Dr. Paolo's students, still lay ahead.

Brad was making final edits to his presentation as Dr. Paolo joined the rest of the class in the small room. It was not that Thursday arrived quicker than expected or that he had procrastinated to the point of having to pull an all-nighter to wrap up the second half of his presentation but it was rather that Brad had an idea as he awoke that morning; he thought of a better way to end his presentation. Fortunately he found a few minutes before class to incorporate those final edits.

He began part two with a slide depicting a simple yet complete pencil and caulk drawing of the human brain as sketched by the hand of an inquisitive Renaissance artist.

"For hundreds of years before the discovery and perfection of the microscope, this is the way we viewed the anatomy of the brain," Brad explained referring to the detailed drawing. "It's not bad, actually. The anatomy is quite accurate and the exterior, as well as most interior sections are representative of an intact brain. But we've come a long way since then. Here's where we are today." And with a twitch of his thumb on the small remote control, the image morphed into a neuroscientist's proverbial Land of Oz. A stunningly bright, beautifully multicolored image of the brain with each specialized section labeled with a different color highlighting its distinct morphology and architecture.

"High powered electron microscopes and new imaging technology developed in the past 50 years have changed the way we visualize different parts of the brain. We now can study, in fine detail, what these different parts actually do," said Brad who then moved into high gear by describing the newer cutting edge fields of neuroscience—computational neurobiology, neuronal intranet, neuronalomics, cognitive neuroscience, the study of continuous grid structure, descriptive hierarchal processing nodes, comparative interspecies neural morphology and evolutionary, and genetic construction of human brain—all relatively new fields that seek to understand the immense circuitry that operate silently within our skull. He succinctly described the power of each new technique and provided stunning examples of how each one is applied beginning with pictures of relatively simple magnetic resonance images then progressing to functional MRI, diffusion MRI, real-time MRI and finally, interventional MRI used in specific types of surgeries. Brad had a firm understanding of how each different technique was applied in both experimental and applied medicine.

Brad's interest in neurology had become obvious and infectious. And as he stood before the small class to present the last segment of his talk, Brad realized that he had found his lifelong passion.

In the closing segment of his presentation Brad projected a slide of Dr. Jin Sukawa, a family friend and a professor emeritus in the Integrative Biology department at MIT. The picture showed Dr. Sukawa in the laboratory wearing a white laboratory coat with his name and affiliation stitched neatly above the left pocket. A slight, wiry man now in his early seventies, Dr. Sukawa first met the entire MacIntyre family, including Brad who was only ten years old at the time, at an MIT capital fundraiser.

"Dr. Sukawa is a pioneer in mapping human brain function under different emotional and environmental conditions," Brad stated. "His research combines three fields: neuroscience, computer science, and mathematical models of high order communication, to study the vast untapped power of the human brain. Dr. Sukawa is someone who doesn't speculate on the future, he develops it." And with a simple example, Brad explained the type of research Dr. Sukawa was performing at MIT.

"Let's say you construct an email, attach a picture to it, and then send that email to your friend. Done every day, right? Now imagine that you do that while walking down the street with nothing in your hands. No computer, no cell phone, no tablet, and no mobile device. Just you and your personal brain implant. And now imagine that while you are doing that little activity, you also solved a problem that's been nagging at you all day. You instantly take the solution and back it up to the implant so that later you can download the stored information to your personal computer. This is the future Dr. Sukawa is developing. It's nothing short of the optimization of our brain," he said as the final slide—a transparent image of the human brain superimposed on a picture of the universe—appeared on the screen.

And with the provocative photomontage positioned to his right Brad thanked the audience for their attention. His presentation ended to a round of applause and a steady stream of questions.

"Are you saying that Dr. Sukawa's research will lead to some form of electronic telepathy?" asked Phil; a bold question that made Abby shift nervously in her seat.

"Yes," replied Brad. "Dr. Sukawa told me just last week when I visited his lab that he is studying individuals with telepathic tendencies to understand what part of their brain is active during telepathy."

"Brad, do you know if Dr. Sukawa has published any of this work relating to brain implants or studies of telepathic individuals?" asked Dr. Paolo who sensed that Brad may have revealed information that was not yet public knowledge.

"Um...I'm not sure," replied Brad.

"Or do you know if he's presented this work at a meeting? In other words, is this information public knowledge or is it confidential?"

Brad froze and his heart rate jumped.

He didn't need to hear the stern tone of Dr. Paolo's voice to comprehend the gravity of the question. Within seconds the palms of his hands became moist and he became uneasy on his feet.

"I don't know. I don't think he said anything about it," Brad said nervously just as he recalled the placard on the door to Dr. Sukawa's laboratory:

Absolute Rules. Discussions that occur inside of this room are to remain CONFIDENTIAL. Nothing is allowed out of this room unless authorized by Dr. Sukawa. Violation of these rules will result in immediate dismissal from the laboratory.

The laminated placard was signed and dated by Dr. Sukawa. With his heart pounding, Brad also recalled the special card reader placed immediately to the left of the door for added security. Brad made the mistake of saying too much. He was unsure of how to handle the predicament or what he should say.

Dr. Paolo knew exactly what to say. The professor launched into a ten-minute lecture on the importance of confidentiality, intellectual property rights, securing data and findings, as well as the arduous process of submitting manuscripts for publication. He explained that even after a research paper was accepted for publication, the journal or the funding agency could impose an embargo on disclosing the findings until there was sufficient time to prepare a proper press release. In some cases, manuscripts were not submitted until patent applications were filed. In other words, Dr. Paolo explained, once something is in the public domain it is free for everyone to use. For most scientists and their inventions, this was not a big deal, while for others it could be the difference between fame and perceived failure. Dr. Paolo stressed that everyone, not only scientists, deserves credit for his or her invention, original thought or idea.

"Until Brad asks Dr. Sukawa about the confidential nature of his work, I ask all of you to keep this information to yourself. I ask you to do this in the name of common decency," Dr. Paolo pleaded. Then, in an effort to preserve the bulk of Brad's presentation he quickly asked if there were any other questions.

Amy who was eager to help her new friend asked, "Is the brain the largest organ in the body? I think so, but I'm not sure if it's the brain or the liver."

"Yes, well that's an interesting question," said Brad who was relieved to be moving on. While the liver is larger than the brain the largest organ in, or rather on our body is the skin."

"How much does an adult brain weigh?" asked Abby.

"About three pounds," replied Brad.

"That's not that much when you think about what it does," added Phil.

"True enough. Well, get this. Remember how Amy told us that most of our DNA does not code for anything?" asked Brad. The class and Dr. Paolo nodded.

"Even with all of our modern methods and instruments, the function of ninety-eight percent of the brain is unknown," Brad stated from memory. "Can you believe it? Ninety-eight percent."

Despite the positive feedback, Brad was still upset with himself over disclosing Dr. Sukawa's research. Brad always thought of himself as the ultimate confidant and now that core pillar of his being suffered a serious blow. Why hadn't he been told? How could he have been so careless? Why hadn't he paid more attention to the message on the MIT lab door? Was it completely his fault or did Dr. Sukawa share some of the blame too? Brad couldn't shake the mistake that nagged at him like a brewing migraine. As he showered and dressed for his date with Amy, he desperately wanted to let it go so he could enjoy the evening but the more he tried, the more the problem plagued him.

Brad picked up Amy on time. Once inside the Audi and after a quick look at his face Amy could tell that Brad was not himself. And as she would do for the rest of their lives together, Amy cut to the chase and addressed Brad's problem head on.

"You're bothered about Sukawa's data, right?"

"Yeah, that and the fact that I was sloppy with the information. I should have been more aware of the sensitive nature of his work..."

"Wait a minute," she interrupted. Let's review the facts. One, he escorted you into the lab, right?"

"Yes."

"Two, did he or did he not give you any specific information about the sensitivity of his research?"

"No he didn't, but I..."

"Three, did you tell others besides the four of us in class?"

"No."

"Four, Dr. Paolo asked us to keep the information confidential, right?"

"Yes, that's true but I still feel as though I let Dr. Sukawa down."

"Okay then that's what you're going to need to resolve. That's what you're going to focus on. I think it's simple. I suggest you meet in person with Dr. Sukawa and tell him exactly what happened. Tell him about Dr. Paolo's lecture on confidentiality and how you are feeling about it."

"He'll be very disappointed."

"Doubt it."

"How do you know? You've never even met him."

"I checked him out on the MIT website and at the USPTO. He's a highly accomplished scientist with about three hundred papers and eighty issued patents. He's on the scientific board of several companies. I doubt you're going to ruin his career. Just go visit him. Thank him for spending time with you and tell him how your presentation went. In fact, give him a copy. He might like to see it. Then tell him about how you ended your presentation and how Dr. Paolo was sensitive to protecting the unpublished information."

"Yeah, you're probably right. I'll send him an email this weekend and set up a visit."

"Great, now let's go. I'm starving and I know just the place. Take the highway and head south," Amy said with a smile. Brad felt as though the clouds had finally lifted and glancing over at Amy, who was looking at something on her cellphone, made him feel better. Actually, she made him feel great.

———◦———

Abby spent that same Friday evening alone and anxious. She was scheduled to give her presentation after Phil who was up next week and she wondered how she was going to come even close to matching

Amy and Brad's presentations. Although she had received quite a bit of guidance from Dr. Paolo during the semester, her research was not coming together at all. It lacked, among other things, a firm beginning. In fact, none of it—beginning, middle or end—was gelling into a cohesive report. To do well she would need to do something different. She would need to think outside of the proverbial box. And she needed to do it soon.

———

The Audi exited the highway and snaked its way along Reservation Parkway towards the center of Winchester, a sleepy Boston suburb that was a natural boundary between the urban and seashore landscapes to the south and rural, hilly terrain to the north.

Brad was shocked when Amy instructed him to pull into the narrow residential driveway at 2657 Landscomb Lane; the car idled until Amy told him that they had arrived.

"We're here."

"What's this?" Brad asked.

"Actually, it's a classic Victorian. I should say, a recently renovated, classic Victorian."

"Am I missing something here?"

"No, I don't think so. The restaurant is just down the road by the center of town, about a half-mile walk. I'm staying here this evening. I'm housesitting and taking care of the cats for the weekend while the Kelly's are out of town. The Kelly's are old friends of my father and I've done this many times since I've been at the college. See, they left the porch light on for me."

Brad was trying to suppress his thoughts but his brain stem—the primitive structure inside his head—took over and his pulse naturally increased.

The young couple held hands as they made their way downhill to *Mia Toscana*, a cozy restaurant nestled in an old brick building just one block from the center of town. They were seated at a small table for two in a corner of the restaurant with most of the light emitted by a honey wax candle placed in the center of the square wooden table.

Brad noted the flickering candlelight dancing on Amy's lovely face that was momentarily turned downward as she studied the short wine list. Her tan skin tones, symmetrical features and long black eyelashes were even more beautiful in the soft natural light. Amy ordered a Chianti Classico, which as she explained, would complement the homemade fusilli in a rich marinara sauce that they would order as the *primi*. As it did a week ago in Gloucester, the discussion between the two students flowed easily. Their conversation was stress free, even when the agnostic and the atheist stumbled onto religion, a subject discussed over the *secondi* that consisted of grilled lamb with roasted potatoes and a *contorno* of zucchini wedges. The young, left-leaning couple also lampooned national politics over *dolci*—a sampler plate of mini cannoli. Their common ground made for amiable, often humorous, exchanges. They also learned that each had at least one parent who did not share in their religious or political views and they discussed how they dealt with this very real challenge throughout their youth.

Until this evening, threats of a hard frost had not materialized in this part of New England, but given that the temperature was already thirty-five degrees and the stars were visible at 8:45 p.m. ensured that this clear evening would mark the official end of the growing season. Brad's left arm easily covered Amy's narrow shoulders and she responded by holding his waist as they walked in stride to the Kelly's residence. On the Victorian's oversized front porch, Amy reached inside the mailbox and pulled out a key, slipped it in the lock and opened the heavy walnut door. In the foyer, illuminated only by the dim outdoor porch light, Amy reached up with her right hand and gently pulled Brad's face to hers. But instead of meeting her lips, Brad cupped Amy's slender face with both hands and drew her nearer. He then did something he'd never done with anyone before. Spontaneously, and ever so slowly, he gently positioned his left eye into Amy's left cheekbone. Remarkably, their young smooth faces slipped into perfect position like well-worn pieces of a three-dimensional puzzle. With her left eye in his cheekbone Brad felt her left hand touch his face. They held the position for just a few seconds but it easily could have been a lifetime.

"We match," he said *sotto voce*. Amy did not reply, she simply gave him a kiss unlike any she had given anyone before; it was passionate, soft yet intense. The two students drew closer to each other as the embrace and the kiss deepened in purpose and passion.

Moments later, under the flannel sheets of the queen size bed in the guest bedroom with its vaulted ceiling located on the second floor of the old Victorian, the entire world of the two seniors consisted solely of each other. Amy aggressively explored Brad's lean, muscular body beginning with his neck and ever so slowly working her way to his hard, rippled abdomen. Once there she drove him wild by slithering her slender body upwards, her small breasts straddling his right leg, to again kiss him on his lips. Each time she repeated these sensual moves Amy made her way lower on him until after the third time, when he thought he would explode, Brad grabbed her narrow waist and flipped her under him, much to her delight. He looked deeply into her dark eyes then kissed her with a force that at first he thought seemed too hard, but one that Amy readily matched. During the kiss she reached down and slowly guided him into her. Brad froze and looked at her with wide, inquisitive eyes. He started to say that he had no protection but she whispered that she was on the pill, and that she loved him very much and with another deep kiss, she arched up and met his gentle thrust.

Because Amy had not bothered to turn up the heat in the room where the new lovers slept, the morning temperature hovered around sixty degrees. The quality of sunlight filtering into the room suggested that the time was well past eight o'clock but their late evening of passionate exploration left them both weary and hungry. Each made a feeble attempt at getting up out of bed only to dive back under the covers and into the other's open arms. Their morning was filled with impassioned lovemaking punctuated by short spells of sated sleep. It wasn't until noon when they had showered, dressed and decided to start their Saturday with a hearty brunch in town. Afterwards they followed the red-bricked sidewalks of this old New England town and explored the antique stores and boutiques before returning to the Victorian for a lazy afternoon of lying in bed and learning more about each other's dreams, desires and passions.

That evening, as luck would have it, Annie Hall was featured on one of the many movie channels. It was the first of many Woody Allen movies they would watch together over the years. They identified their favorite segments and laughed anew at the scenes they had seen many times but seemed fresh when shared with each other. At the end of the film, they vowed to forego the shark and to keep their relationship moving forward at all costs. And, as if they needed to punctuate their commitment to each other, they began a second long evening of lovemaking.

Years later they would consider those two carefree days as the launch of their relationship. It would be known as "The Victorian" and over time, they would apply those memories to renew their love for one another, to rekindle the fire, to strengthen their commitment when they drifted apart which they did once or twice during their forty-five years together.

And it was impossible for Amy to have known on that brisk November weekend as they explored each other and the little town of Winchester, that those two days would be played and replayed in her aged mind melancholically—the smells, the excitement, the anticipation, the warmth, the tears, the touch, the laughter, the dreams—like an endless loop on a distant, equally cool October day when she buried the remains of her husband, the father of her two children, her sole love and soul mate.

4

The image filled the large screen. The stunning oval image with its horizontal pink-white midline and blue-purple clouds framed by pillows of red and orange looked more like abstract artwork than the electromagnetic spectrum of the entire Universe. Within seconds, the words *The Quantum Universe* in bold yellow letters appeared from the center of the slide followed by the name of the presenter, Phillip Hess.

Phil stood behind the podium, looked down at the screen of his laptop that mirrored the projected image and then up at the audience. Unlike Amy or Brad, Phil had not prepared opening lines nor had he given a great deal of thought to what he was going to say. He decided to carefully prepare the slides then improvise the rest.

"I'll admit," he started, "I'm overwhelmed by the sheer magnitude of our universe and I am equally overwhelmed by the field of quantum physics. So I don't really know where to begin but I'm in good company because astrophysicists who study the universe don't know where to begin either. Some start with the Big Bang while others start with what existed before that monumental event. Either way, it was one-hell-of-a-blast that caused a great deal of chaos over a long period of time, at least as we define time and over a lot of space, at least as we define space."

Before he knew it, Phil smoothly and effectively launched his presentation. He next described a timeline of events; something he sought to avoid because it seemed like that's what everyone else did who spoke of our universe and he wanted to be different.

"Without sounding like Spock," Phil continued in a more casual voice, "a cosmic timeline is the only logical way to discuss quantum physics. Quantum physics is the study of very tiny objects—matter and energy—at the molecular, atomic, nuclear and microscopic levels. But before we can measure matter, it first has to be born and that takes us back to the beginning of the universe and to the so called Big Bang."

The next slide was a short video that showed a beautiful computer generated artist's rendering of the formation of the universe starting fourteen billion years ago with a massive explosion that formed the entire universe, followed by galaxies, progressing to planetary systems, then the planets and ending with the formation of Earth about five billion years ago. And with the next slide Phil said, "I'd like to impress on you that the universe that eventually will house galaxies, stars, planets, suns, moons everything, the entire thing as we know it today, was shaped within one millionth, that's one millionth, of a second after the Big Bang." He paused briefly for emphasis then continued, "And by one second, the fundamental building blocks of particles and energy like quarks, electrons, photons and neutrinos formed and by two whole seconds later, or the exact time it took for me to say the last six words, basic elements like hydrogen and helium, were beginning to form."

In a more rapid pace he spoke of the early events of the universe, the formation of radiation and matter moving on to stars and galaxies. Slide after slide Phil systematically deconstructed matter, and then energy to their most simple forms. He admitted that the names of particles, like photons, gluons, quarks, bosons, fermions and nucleons, sounded like they came from a *Star Trek* episode rather than a physics text, but he cleverly kept the definitions both simple and orderly. He had learned from Dr. Paolo's classroom lectures that it's easy to lose your audience if they are overwhelmed with a list of facts and with this topic of quantum physics, Phil's challenge was to strike the right balance between necessary information and technical overload.

"Now what's cool about quantum physics is that the simple act of observation alters the physical nature of what is being observed. It's sort of like trying to determine the shape of a blob of jelly at zero gravity where just touching it changes its shape. In the world of quantum physics physical interactions are not allowed. So how can you study these interactions? It would seem impossible, right? Well physicists not only take measurements of energies left over from early events, like microwaves and other forms of energy, but they also use mathematical probabilities to define events that occurred in the quantum universe. Specifically, physicists use non-classical probability calculus along with non-classical propositional logic," said Phil enthusiastically as if everyone in the room had a natural understanding of these types of higher mathematics. And with his voice quickening in excitement, Phil used the last thirty minutes to derive six of the most important mathematical equations used to describe the current condition and content of the universe. To some the equations were elegant but to most, including the small audience in attendance, they were nothing but gibberish. The look in the eyes of the captive members of the audience who tried in vain to comprehend how "...the value of the unknown variable A is well within the limitations of the range B within a non-distributive non-Boolean structure..." remained distant until finally after six slides of dense equations Phil abruptly ended day one of his presentation. The final slide of the day read: Next. String Theory and the Multiverse.

The class clapped half-heartedly, more in relief then in approval. They had enjoyed the first segment but barely survived the second that was heavily laden with abstract concepts and mathematical equations, and given the title of the last slide, it seemed like they would be in for more of the same on Thursday.

"Any questions?" asked Phil who was so thrilled with his delivery that he was eager to pounce on any question. Knowing full well that most of the class did not follow the latter half of the presentation, Dr. Paolo raised his hand to start the discussion in an attempt to avoid what would have been lengthy and awkward silence.

"Phil," began Dr. Paolo, "you said that elements formed three seconds after the Big Bang. Does that mean that all of the roughly one hundred natural elements on the Periodic Table were formed at that time?"

Phil scrolled through a series of slides in a separate file that were not a part of his presentation and found the information he was seeking.

"The very beginning of the formation of neutral atoms occurred in the so-called 'Matter Domination Era' that took place about one hundred thousand years after the Big Bang. So Dr. Paolo, no, not all of the natural elements were formed three seconds after the Big Bang."

"I remember my father wondering if theoretical physicists ever verify their mathematical models," said Amy. "My father thought that their calculations needed to be confirmed with actual measurement, actual data. Does that happen?"

"Yes from what I've read, yes, in some cases," replied Phil. "But it can take quite a bit of time and, in most cases, technology needs to catch up with the models. For example, the ability of the Hubble space telescope to capture and record light energy in different wavelengths has been used to confirm calculations and hypotheses proposed decades earlier. It's been used to further support Einstein's theory of general relativity and to show that the universe continues to expand. Data gathered with new technologies not only strengthen or weaken existing theories but in most cases they create new ones too."

Dr. Paolo made a note of Phil's ability to answer questions completely and concisely, a rare trait even among seasoned scientists let alone undergraduates. He also made a note about Phil's enthusiasm. To Dr. Paolo, this level of passion and engagement was absolutely necessary in order to excel in graduate school.

Total darkness surrounded Amy, Brad, Abby and Dr. Paolo as they sat in the small classroom on Thursday. The only light came from the glow of the projected bold yellow words 'The String Theory and Variants Thereof' that contrasted sharply against the title slide's black background. A piece of tape was placed over the light switch to keep it in the off position in case anyone tried to turn on the lights, and the room was silent except for the low hum of the projector positioned towards the back wall.

With dramatic flair, Phil entered the room and swiftly closed the door behind him to minimize light exposure from the hallway.

"There are forces in our world we cannot ignore," Phil said to no one in particular as he stared straight ahead in the dark room. He then slid his hand against the wall and located the string he had taped there earlier that morning. He pulled the string off the wall and gave it a firm tug. The string released a simple mechanism that untied netting placed above the classroom. Thirty small balloons that had been placed in the net by Phil earlier in the morning made their way haphazardly to the floor of the classroom with many bouncing off of the heads of the attendees.

"And gravity is one of them," Phil said before he turned on one bank of room lights. The dramatic effect definitely worked. The different colored balloons were scattered across the floor of the classroom, some still wobbling in place. Each person thought the same obvious question, *who would ignore gravity?*

"I think we can all accept the fact," started Phil, "that each of us occupy space and that we occupy this particular space at this particular time." All nodded in agreement. "Now, if we add gravity to that interwoven meshwork of space-time, then the forces of both space and time can be influenced. We observe this every month when we watch the moon come and go as it orbits our planet. Our moon is affected by the Earth's gravitational force, that much is known."

Phil then highlighted the works of Galileo, Newton, Einstein, and Eddington. He spoke with vigor about their common interest in the movement of objects and also of their common purpose to define energies that cannot be seen, touched, readily measured or even comprehended by many outside of the exclusive circle of particle physicists.

"In many ways," opined Phil, "they must have been lonely men for few in their day, especially in Galileo's time, could grasp the exceptionally high value of their remarkable observations, careful measurements and profound insights. And in many ways, history is repeating itself with a new breed of physicists who today are using high-speed particle accelerators to describe and to provide evidence for the 'String Theory', an all-encompassing 'Theory of Everything'." With excitement, Phil switched, somewhat haphazardly, from describing Strings as the one-dimensional tiniest particle that forms the substructure of all matter with all of its different vibrational patterns, to the complex multi-dimensional, inter-cosmic landscapes known simply as 'Parallel Universes'.

"Imagine," Phil said using his hands to accentuate the point of the message, "that space is infinite and that it is still expanding. An infinite number of universes occupy this space. One multiverse hypothesis predicts that within one or more of these universes exist galaxies, each with it's own set of solar systems that contain a countless number of stars and planets. The laws of probability then predict that on at least one of these planets, in one of these solar systems, in one of these galaxies, in one of these universes, events unfold precisely as they do here on Earth along the identical space-time continuum. In other words, at this very moment of space-time, multiple Phils are uttering these exact words to multiple Amys, Brads, Abbys, and multiple Dr. Paolos. And that these occurrences may be happening at a dozen different places simultaneously. Actually the more I think about it, the more I'm convinced that the defining accomplishment of our species may be in providing absolute proof of the existence of multiverses."

Phil's wild, rambling statements left the class speechless. The very idea of multiple universes was so provocative, so outrageous, and so inconceivable that there was a momentary delay in applause as the audience tried to grasp the take-home message. The last projected image was a spectacularly clear photomontage of the universe—with small spiral galaxies, mysterious black holes, bright gaseous nebulae and countless stars dramatically frozen in a powerfully explosive supernova—captured with the Hubble telescope's crystal clear eye.

Following the brief applause, each person in the room asked a question.

"Brad?" said Phil pointing to his buddy.

"Phil, I've always heard and read that the universe is expanding, but isn't it also possible that it could contract? Or if the concept of multiverses is correct, can they all implode at the same time, something opposite of the Big Bang, like the Big Compression?"

"Some have called it the 'Big Crunch' so yes, to answer your question directly. At some point the immense expansion is expected to cease and given the gravitational forces that each celestial body exerts on the other, like Earth's pull on the moon, a contraction is a real possibility. And such an event would be as defining as the Big Bang," said Phil.

"And if the Big Bang began with a high rate of speed but then slowed..." continued Brad

"Then the contraction will start slowly and speed up to the final spectacular implosion," said Phil completing Brad's thought.

No sooner had Phil answered the last question when Amy stated, "It took billions of years of evolution with unique atmospheric conditions to support the formation of simple cells that led all the way to complex life forms, and you're telling me that this exact set of events happened elsewhere in the exact same way and at the exact same rate as it did here on Earth and not only that, but complex beings exactly like us, same DNA and everything, exists elsewhere?"

"The conceptualization of multiverses is limited by our brain's ability to comprehend and appreciate such information. During our lifetime our brain absorbs ten thousand trillion bits of information but how we process and organize this information is a mystery. So while we have the potential to conceive and derive extremely large numbers, including the number of universes that exist, what we do—or at least what most of us do—is disregard it as meaningless. But get this, theoretical physicists have calculated that there are ten to the power ten to the power ten to the power seven universes, and with that figure come the high probability that the formation of our Earth as we know it today with the exact events that unfolded here also unfolded elsewhere in direct parallel," explained Phil.

"Exponentials of exponentials?" asked Amy. "I've never heard of that."

"Me neither," said Brad.

"They're commonly used in astrophysics. We're talking about a huge number of objects in a vast sea of space," responded Phil who had moved on from the question and pointed at Abby to ensure that she got to ask the next question.

"The idea that there are identical multiples of us is wild," said Abby who paused momentarily. "So, well..." she started then paused to consider whether the question she had in mind should be asked at all. To avoid embarrassment over the simplicity of her proposed question she decided to ask a different one instead. "When theoretical physicists develop these mathematical models, do others physicists review them to make sure they're correct, or even plausible?"

Phil spent a few minutes discussing the scientific process and how it applied to all field of science, including the theoretical sciences. He spoke about different institutions around the world with teams of physicists and mathematicians working on similar, if not identical, problems just as botanists or behavioral scientists would do in their respective fields.

"Because the quantum field is so specialized, everyone seems to know everyone else no matter where they are in the world. It's essentially one big club, so yes, they are always checking each other's work. In this field, verifying someone else's findings is itself considered an important accomplishment."

Dr. Paolo asked the final series of questions of the day. "So Phil, do you think that in the world of astrophysics the best is yet to come? And if so, will we enter a lull in discoveries until the next set of instruments are built? Like more powerful telescopes or particle colliders?"

"Dr. Paolo," replied Phil with an air of confidence that even caught him by surprise, "the best is yet to come and, if all goes well, I'll be right in the middle of it."

And with that audacious response, the audience gave Phil a hardy second round of applause just as the class ended.

5

The Tuesday before Thanksgiving at Wilmington College was filled with trepidation as students scrambled to complete their assignments or to take the last poorly scheduled test before making their way home for the brief holiday break. But for Abby this Tuesday arrived sooner than expected despite the fact that it had been highlighted in yellow on her desk calendar since Dr. Paolo made the assignments in September. She was the last in the class to present her research and she often wondered if Dr. Paolo had purposely placed the best students before her as a way of providing motivation. Alone with her thoughts, a pen and her journal, Abby often pondered what others in the *Teach the Professor* course expected of her. What exactly did she expect from herself? And given that her topic was "not real science" perhaps she would be considered "not real serious", the sole underachiever amongst a crowd of overachievers. "A typical hardy," as Dr. Benedetti might have said. The introspective and quite honest analysis of her situation provided the fuel needed to ignite a new fire. Over the weekend Abby developed a bold idea, a plan she wasn't sure would work. However, Abby knew that if her idea worked as planned she would set a new course for herself.

The plan must work, she confided to her journal as well as to her current and future self.

———•———

The Abby who walked into Dr. Paolo's classroom on the Tuesday before Thanksgiving was not the same Abby who had left class after Phil's presentation a few days ago. Her hair was pulled back to reveal more of her wide, full face. Her unassuming eyes and thin lips were highlighted with carefully applied makeup. And instead of loose fitting clothes, Abby wore a beautiful black skirt patterned with tall ivory colored orchids, and a tight-fitting sheer black sleeveless top with a low neckline. The black pushup bra created a deep, inviting cleavage that drew attention to her ample, firm breasts; the mid-heeled pumps added a few inches to her height and accentuated her full but shapely backside. Abby had never looked nor had she ever felt sexier in her life.

With the audience seated and the projector off, Abby sauntered into the classroom with a purposeful bounce in her step. She clearly had everyone's attention. At the podium and without a word, she retrieved the pen planted there an hour earlier along with four white envelopes. On the outside of one envelope Abby wrote Phil's name then opened it and pulled out a small blank piece of paper that was tucked inside. Under the curious gaze of the audience, she swiftly wrote a few words, placed the paper back inside and sealed the envelope. Abby repeated the process three more times creating a small envelope with a note for each member of the class, including Dr. Paolo. Abby then handed the envelopes to the rightful addressee and asked that they remain sealed.

Abby began her presentation knowing that her topic lacked the hard facts and solid history of the human genome, the brain and quantum physics that served her classmates well. But this same understanding gave her a clear shot at a new angle. She introduced the topic of the paranormal as a pseudoscience, a study in limbo because it lacked the rigors of proof that defined a true scientific field. As a vivid example, Abby compared and contrasted the false world of astrology with the true science of astronomy. She also spent considerable time describing the many aspects of metaphysics, and how this philosophy—with an Aristotelian branch and a supernatural branch—raised more suspicions than provided answers. She also explained how Brad's powerful brain and Phil's quantum mechanics had their roots in metaphysics. "Our perceived existence could be considered a simple interaction of our mind with all types of matter," she declared.

The first segment of her presentation went smoothly.

So far, so good, she thought as she glanced at the clock on the upper right of the computer screen. With one hour left, Abby began to elaborate on the passing of her mother and how she developed her sixth sense.

In essence it was the same story she told the class earlier in the semester but this time with more vivid details. Abby said that the thoughts of those in her presence were always accessible to her but before her mother passed she had never felt the presence of someone who had died. Using just a few slides that highlighted key words she gave examples of her experiences. Some of the stories she shared were light and non-threatening, some were surprising and seemingly coincidental, and one was simply scary. Then after a long pause, she told the attentive class that telepathy was just one simple aspect of her abilities that had been honed over time. Abby then walked across the room and turned off the projector. The room was silent.

Abby, who had returned to the podium, asked the class to find the envelope she had given them an hour earlier.

"Open the envelope and read to yourself what is written on each piece of paper. Then put the paper back in the envelope. Don't show the paper to anyone."

The class did as they were told. Abby watched intently as each read their personal message.

> Thank you Phil for noticing my tits (as you call them). And yes, they've been here all along.

Phil glanced up at Abby without saying a word only to see her staring back at him expressionless.

> Amy, I like the print on this skirt too, and yes I have worn my hair like this before.

Amy looked up at Abby and smiled.

> You're right again Brad! I'm a C/D cup depending on my

cycle and Amy is a B, as are breasts of many women of Asian descent.

Brad instantly made sure Amy wasn't trying to sneak a peek; Abby shot him a wry smile.

Dr. Paolo's message confirmed his earlier suspicion about Abby. And it also confirmed that his ailments were more on his mind then he acknowledged. Abby's simple note rang true.

Make an appointment with your doctor soon.

Abby collected the envelopes containing the notes and promised to destroy them. She also said that what was written on the notes would remain confidential. Abby then asked for a show of hand on whether or not the notes accurately reflected their thoughts and she reminded everyone that she wrote them about an hour ago.

All four hands went up.

Quietly, Abby turned on the projector and waited patiently for it to recognize the computer's input. She concluded the first part of her presentation with a slide containing three simple words: Need More Data?

"Questions?" she asked.

The audience—still stunned by having had their thoughts read so accurately—clapped politely, and for the most part, they were perplexed by the question posed by Abby's last slide.

Amy's hand shot up.

"The message you wrote to me could have been a guess. How would I know if you actually read my mind or simply guessed at what I was thinking?"

"You can't know," replied Abby who thought quickly, then posed a question to both Phil and Brad. "But let me ask the guys. Did I provide enough detail to convince you that I did not guess?"

Brad knew that he was in a tight spot but thankfully Phil's reply defused the situation.

"Yes, without a doubt you read my mind clearly and accurately. I'm convinced." Brad simply nodded in agreement. "But what I'd like to know," continued Phil, "is how do you cope with all the noise? I mean you can hear folks speak their minds...well...that must be a lot of information to process. How do you deal with it?"

"Well, it's not like I'm tuned into everyone," replied Abby. "It's like walking down a crowded street. There could be many people chatting with other people, or talking with someone on their cell, but you're not really tuned in to what they are saying, right? In fact, you may not even hear them because you're focused on something else. Your mind is elsewhere. That's what it's like for me too. For the most part, I don't read others. Actually, it's rare that I do."

"But you can read them when you want too?" asked Phil.

"Well, kind of. Yeah. Like when you want to eavesdrop on someone's conversation, you tune in and focus," replied Abby.

"Abby," said Dr. Paolo, "I find your talent to be most interesting. I've often wondered if this sense is lost for most of us, such as our relatively insensitive sense of smell as we discussed before. Did your research reveal anything about methods of nonverbal communication as a part of our evolution? I recall that the development of language is a relatively recent event in our evolution but how did we communicate before language evolved?"

"Dr. Paolo, thank you for those questions. My research revealed absolutely nothing about the earliest descriptions of the sixth sense or telepathy. It simply appeared in the literature in the mid-1800s as voodoo or associated with witchcraft or the supernatural and the authors of these works had mainly a religious angle that led to nothing substantial. The authors danced around the possibility that this could be a naturally occurring sense. Even today, there is little mentioned about it in the scientific literature. As someone with this ability, I find this very frustrating," replied Abby.

"So where does that leave us?" asked Dr. Paolo who was pleased with the first part of Abby's presentation.

"That, Dr. Paolo, I'll try to address after the holiday," Abby replied knowing that the class had run over by a full ten minutes. Each member rose and clapped in approval. Brad was the first one to approach Abby. He told her that she did a great job although what he really wanted to tell her that he was embarrassed, but then he thought better of it as the others were within earshot. Abby simply smiled and said in a low voice so only he could hear, "Don't worry about it."

Amy told Abby that she was looking forward to part two next week and Phil said the same thing along with a subtle thumbs up gesture before he left the classroom along with Brad and Amy.

"Well, Abby," said Dr. Paolo as he slowly rose from his chair, "you certainly got everyone's attention, including mine. I can hardly wait to see what you have in store for us next week. You're off to a good start."

Although she simply said "Thanks," she really wanted to ask Dr. Paolo about his ailments but at the same time she did not want to be intrusive. She also sensed he was not in the mood for questions about his health.

"Have a nice holiday," he said as he left the room.

"You too," she replied.

6

The much-maligned New England meteorologists were right-on-the-money in forecasting the weather for the mid-November holiday. Gray skies with freezing rain in the morning that turned to raw driving rain in the afternoon created a less than ideal way to spend Thanksgiving especially if you were one of the thousands who had registered to run in an early morning Turkey Trot. In past years, such weather would not have deterred Dante Paolo from participating in the local 5K run but this year instead of lacing up his sneakers and donning his running cap he laid in bed with flu-like pains that radiated from all corners of his body. Laura was on call at the hospital which meant that he would be spending most of the dark day alone, a common occurrence since Laura's mother, who had lived with them, passed away one year ago. With no parents, siblings or extended family, events like birthdays, graduations, weddings, and holidays like Thanksgiving either didn't exist or they were empty experiences for Dante and Laura. The occasional invitation to a neighbor's party to watch the Superbowl or to celebrate one thing or another was plenty of entertainment for the professional couple, especially after they'd listen to the endless before-during-and after-complaints of those who organized such gatherings.

Given the inclement weather with its associated travel delays and hazards, it was sheer luck that Dr. Paolo's four students had planned to stay close to campus this holiday. At Brad's apartment, pre-dawn sleet bounced off the south-facing bedroom window as he and Amy melded their young naked bodies together under the covers of his twin bed. Despite the comfort of being wrapped in Brad arms, Amy was feeling uncharacteristically apprehensive about the day that lay ahead. She'd spent the past few Thanksgivings with the Kelly family in Winchester but on this dreary day Amy would meet not only Brad's immediate family but several members of his extended family as well. For his part, Brad tried to prepare her the best he could by describing the Rockwellesque Thanksgiving Day scene at the MacIntyre homestead complete with a review of the strengths and weaknesses of every family member likely to attend the traditional meal of stuffed turkey with all of the trimmings. The simple fact that the entire menu, including dessert, was going to be catered suggested that the MacIntyre's definition of "traditional" differed dramatically from the definition Amy's family practiced.

"Thanksgiving at my house meant time in the kitchen to help my mother and my grandmother prepare an Asian meal. We made everything from scratch, even dessert. It was just my parents, my grandparents, and me. It was just like another Sunday, really. We were all together. Two Sundays in one week; it was great."

————•————

Abby loathed Thanksgiving. She thought the day should be recast as a national day of fasting as a way of making people appreciate their daily bread as opposed to the game show-like competition of who can gorge themselves with the greatest amount of food and drink the highest volume of alcohol before passing out like a bunch of inebriated sows. And she didn't care much for New Years Eve, or the overly commercialized Christmas season either. She despised the endless advertising that starts around Halloween to persuade people to buy things with money they didn't have for people they've all but completely ignored the rest of the year. She also despised the spell of hypocrisy that most every holiday, especially the religious ones, cast on society.

But, in fact, it wasn't as much the holiday itself as much as it was being forced to be with her father's family and their relentless insistence of consoling her year after year over the loss of her mother as if the poor woman had passed away that very day. In their naïve and simple way, they thought they were being helpful when actually they were being nothing but annoying.

On this dreary day, Abby was determined to work on her *Teach the Professor* project. She needed time to prepare for the second half of her presentation and so she faked a migraine and nausea to successfully escape the torture of spending the day with her father's family. The ploy worked perfectly. Her father left at eleven so he could be at his sister's house for the holiday gathering by noon, when the football games and the real drinking began in earnest.

An ecstatic Abby was home alone.

Phil rose early and drove his reliable Honda Civic hybrid west on the Massachusetts Turnpike to Rivers Bend, a working class town on the east side of the Berkshires. He arrived home by six o'clock on Thanksgiving morning just ahead of the stormy weather and without the company of the frenzied holiday travellers. He was greeted by his parents with open arms and freshly brewed coffee. His younger sister Judy would sleep until ten then laze around most of the day in her comfy pajamas. Phil would spend a calm day with his family. They'd prepare the traditional turkey dinner complete with gravy, mashed potatoes and peas. Afterwards he and his father would watch some of the football on television while others would cozy up by the Vermont Castings wood stove and read. Without drama, they all would retire the holiday by nine that evening.

———◆———

For most college students, the final push of the semester—the four weeks following the Thanksgiving break—was a time when every test, quiz or paper could mean the difference between an A and a C. For some seniors, this is the swansong of their undergraduate career and the end of structured learning. While for other seniors it was just the last part of this academic chapter in their lives.

Having made her point in the last class, Abby had no reason to again draw attention to herself. Phil was somewhat disappointed that Abby was not dressed as provocatively as she was the prior Tuesday. She wore a tailored white blouse accented with a loose fitting purple scarf and black pants with matching colored flats. Abby was all business as she re-projected the slide that read: Need more data?

"There is little doubt that modern scientific techniques and methods need to be applied to understand the mechanisms that drive metaphysical events," Abby said convincingly. And with that all-encompassing sentence, Abby launched into a series of slides on The Scientific Method, beginning with The Observation.

"You've all experienced telepathy first hand, right?" she asked the class who all nodded in agreement. So it's clear that we've satisfied this stage. Moving on to the next slide Abby said, "Now then, next we have to 'Define the Problem', and for the most part, this is simple. As Amy suggested, you may have thought that what I wrote on your piece of paper could have been deduced without the need to read your mind. Therefore, the problem is that each of you requires more proof, not just a single observation but repeated observations, repeated measures. That's a highly acceptable and commonly applied aspect of any study—to ensure the observation is real, that it's repeatable. So that we aren't just making measurements and observations without a proper scientific framework, one needed to 'Propose a Hypothesis', as shown in this slide. Thus, I'd like to propose a hypothesis," she continued by reading directly from the projector screen. "I hypothesize that my telepathic abilities are statistically superior to those of someone else matched to me by age and gender." With an eye on the clock and a great deal more material to cover, Abby quickly moved on; it was twenty past ten.

"To test my hypothesis I've designed the following experiment and I'll need everyone's help."

No one was prepared to actively participate in an experiment, but that's exactly what was about to happen. Abby rapidly and thoroughly reviewed the entire design including everyone's role in the experiment, the methods that will be used and also a way to statistically analyze the findings.

Dr. Paolo, still a bit weakened from last weekend's cold, was momentarily caught off guard by what Abby was about to do but he recovered and remarked, "Abby, before you continue, I want you to call the experiment an exercise for reasons I'll explain later, agreed?"

Abby agreed and launched into the exercise by describing the rest of the elements of the Scientific Method. "At the end, we will develop a theory based on the data whether or not the data supported or rejected the proposed hypothesis," she said. "Is everyone ready?"

And when he heard the word 'ready', Abby's friend Ajay opened the door to the classroom carrying an ultraportable laptop. It was exactly eleven o'clock.

Dr. Paolo, Ajay and Brad were sent into the adjoining classroom while Amy and Phil remained in the main classroom. Abby gave Phil her cell phone number and walked down the hall, down one flight of stairs to the unoccupied chemistry lab that was on the same wing of the building but opposite the classrooms. She relaxed and waited patiently.

Each person followed his or her respective assignment in the elegantly simple telepathy exercise. About six feet directly across from Dr. Paolo sat Ajay with his laptop opened. At Abby's request, Ajay had created a small program over the holiday weekend that randomly displayed one of fifty images of everyday objects colored in one of the four primary colors. Brad sat next to Ajay but faced away from Dr. Paolo so he could not see Dr. Paolo or Ajay's computer screen.

The exercise began when Ajay pressed the enter key on his computer.

"Go," Ajay said as the screen displayed a simple image of a blue train along with a twenty-five second digital countdown timer positioned in the upper right hand corner. Ajay's command prompted Brad to send a "go" text message to Phil's cell phone. In the adjacent room, Phil read the instantly transferred text and said to Amy, "Go, and twenty seconds." Amy had twenty seconds to receive the simple computer image sent telepathically by Dr. Paolo who continually but silently repeated *blue train... blue train...blue train* in his mind. Amy was to announce the answer within the twenty-second time limit or be marked "wrong".

"Ten seconds," said Phil with clipboard and cellphone in hand. Amy said nothing as Phil pronounced, "end" indicating that time had expired and that Dr. Paolo would be sending her the next image. Phil jotted down "wrong" next to the number one on Amy's tally sheet. Ajay again hit the keyboard's enter key and a white baseball appeared with the countdown timer reset to twenty-five. Brad again sent the "go" text to Phil who then said "Go, and twenty seconds." This time, Amy closed her eyes as if she was trying to channel all of her energy to her mind.

When all ten images were shown to Dr. Paolo and after Amy had time to respond, Phil dutifully placed the results in a envelope marked "Amy", sealed it and placed it on the desk in the front of the room as instructed earlier. Amy then left the room and, as instructed, made her way to the study lounge down the hall and waited to be called back to class. Phil then called Abby on her cell phone and told her that she could come to the classroom. Moments later Abby was seated across from Phil and he texted back to Brad that he was ready.

The experiment was designed so that Dr. Paolo did not know if he was sending telepathic messages to Amy or to Abby. By eleven-twenty, Abby was seated across from Phil and within moments of texting Phil "ok" he received the first "go" text.

Five seconds after Phil's command Abby said, "Yellow triangle". Phil jotted Abby's reply on the tally sheet. Just over fifteen seconds later, Phil said, "Go, and twenty seconds." Almost instantly Abby replied, "red car" and Phil again jotted down her response. Over the next few minutes, Abby announced the next eight different objects. She hesitated momentarily only once but gave her answer well within the twenty second time window; Phil never had to say, "ten seconds" with Abby. After the last answer, Phil folded the tally sheet and placed it in the envelope labeled "Abby" and sealed it closed.

By eleven thirty-five everyone was reunited in the main classroom and, as requested by Abby, Ajay attached his computer to the projector. He stood at the lecture podium and addressed the class, including Abby who was seated next to Phil.

"I want you all to know that no one, not even me, knows exactly the type of image the program will generate. In fact, I don't even know why we're doing this. I just did what Abby asked me to do. The program contained images of fifty simple objects what could be generated in one of four different primary colors red, yellow, blue or black that resulted in exactly two hundred and eighty possible combinations. Not only do I not know what types of images will be generated, I don't even know why I showed them to Dr. Paolo. I just did as my friend Abby asked me to do."

"Thank you Ajay," said Abby. "And have you shown me this program or any of the images?"

"No," replied Ajay.

"As I recall, you were able to save, in order of appearance the twenty objects generated by your program. Is that correct?"

"Yes."

"Great," said Abby. "Would you pull up the file and project the first image? And Brad, would you be so kind as to open the envelope labeled

"Amy" and let's see if Amy received the image Dr. Paolo saw on Ajay's computer screen."

The image on the screen was a blue train.

"This was the first of twenty images," said Ajay.

"Next to image one "wrong" is written," said Brad, a response that led Amy to add, "I didn't sense anything!"

"Let's move along," said Abby who kept a sharp eye on the clock.

Image number 2 was a white baseball.

"Wrong," said Brad.

The third image was a yellow car

"Wrong," repeated Brad.

The fourth image was a black camera.

"Next to image four is written 'truck'," said Brad who followed up by proclaiming the obvious, "wrong."

"I took a stab," replied Amy, "I wanted to answer so badly I needed to say something."

Abby asked Ajay to stop after the tenth image was shown.

Amy was zero for ten.

"Brad, would you open the envelope with my name on it?"

Brad complied.

Ajay, please continue," said Abby.

Ajay projected the eleventh image. It was a yellow triangle.

"Right!" exclaimed Brad.

The twelfth image was a simple red car.

"Right again!" said Brad who repeated this answer six more times until the eighteenth image was shown. It was a black trophy, complete with a base, and handles on both sides of the cup.

"Wrong!" Brad said in a surprised voice. "Black cup is written next to the number eighteen. "I think this one's wrong."

No one argued Brad's scoring for they knew it would be a moot point. Abby got the last two images correct for a total of nine correct and one wrong.

"Thank you Brad," said Abby. "Ajay," she said looking in his direction "is there an online program to do a two-by-two contingency table?" In a matter of seconds, such a website was found and Ajay needed no help in inserting the results to the intuitive, and powerful online statistical program which was being displayed onto the screen for all to see.

"The two-tailed Fisher's exact test shows a highly statistically significant P value of 0.0001 between the two sets of results. In other words, it is highly improbable that these results occurred by chance," concluded Ajay.

"I'd agree with that," opined Phil who watched Ajay closely. "This was a slam dunk, Abby," Phil continued, "I'm convinced. You're a real telepathist."

"I'll second that," said Amy. "I sensed nothing, not a thing. I just sat there wondering if anything was actually happening. These results are amazing Abby. I mean, what you did last week was cool, but this is all the proof I'll ever need. You have an additional, and a quite special sense that others, well, at least I, don't have."

"Well done Abby. I think you proved your point with a well-designed and carefully controlled, straightforward exercise," said Dr. Paolo. "As I said earlier this year, I knew that I was a good transmitter, but before today I never knew for sure. I guess a transmitter is only as good as the receiver."

"Thanks everyone for participating and a special thanks to Ajay for doing me a huge favor. I thought of it on Thanksgiving Day and Ajay was nice enough to hear me out and to write the program. He had no clue what this was all about. I just asked him to play along today, and man, did he ever," said Abby who then led a round of applause for Ajay.

"And one last thing," continued Abby as she plugged in her computer to the projector. "I think the data we collected supported my hypothesis. However, I think this experiment, or rather exercise was just the beginning." Abby's last slide showed three words with a question mark that morphed into an exclamation point. It was her new slogan: Need more data!

As the class clapped in hardy approval Abby knew that at this moment, on this day, in this classroom she too found her lifelong passion.

It was exactly twelve o'clock noon, the end of class.

"Abby, everyone, wait just a moment," said Dr. Paolo waving his arms to get everyone's attention. "Abby, I'd like to have time for questions. Can we continue this on Thursday?"

"Sure," said Abby.

"Great. And one more thing, I'd like to ask all of you to keep this information, the results from this study, everything from today's class confidential. I'll explain Thursday, okay?"

Everyone nodded in agreement.

"Okay, great. See you then."

As the others were leaving the classroom, Ajay approached the professor.

"Dr. Paolo, I have something to ask of you. From what Abby's told me about the class, and also from what I witnessed today, I think I made a mistake leaving after day one." Dr. Paolo listened as Ajay continued. "I have Tuesdays from ten to twelve free and I was wondering if you'd let me sit in on the class for the rest of the semester."

"That's fine with me but there are only three more Tuesdays in the semester, I'm not sure you'll learn much of anything at this point," replied Dr. Paolo.

"Somehow, I think I will. Thanks Dr. Paolo, see you next week," said Ajay as he left the room.

For the first time in five weeks, Dr. Paolo's class convened without a projector. In fact, they weren't even in their usual classroom in Paine Hall. Everyone sat around a small roundtable in a small, carpeted room in the library usually reserved for committee meetings. Dr. Paolo relocated the class because he thought that a change of scenery and a more intimate setting was necessary for the final few weeks of class. According to the course's lesson plan these last few weeks were critical in evaluating the progress and accomplishments of each student. When Dr. Paolo wrote the lesson plan, he actually had no idea how he was going to evaluate each student. He still had no idea, but he did know that he wanted to let the course forge its own path.

"Okay everyone, let's start by asking Abby questions since we ran out of time to do so on Tuesday, okay?" asked Dr. Paolo. "Who wants to start?"

"Abby," said Amy. "Now that I've had some time to think about what happened during the exercise, I was wondering if Dr. Paolo could have known to whom he was transmitting? Perhaps he was a uncontrolled variable in the exercise."

Abby thought for a moment then replied, "Dr. Paolo, would you like to comment? I'll just say that the exercise was designed for as much randomness as possible."

"I had no idea who was next door. I just tried as hard as I could to stay focused on the image on the screen. It's not like I was thinking 'I have to send this image to Abby or to Amy', I just kept on describing the image over and over again in my mind."

"The more Amy and I discussed the exercise, the more I began to wonder what you were experiencing, Abby," said Brad who was still surprised that Abby had read his mind so accurately last week. "Did the images just appear in your mind like they do on a screen? Did you have to focus on Dr. Paolo?"

"No, the images were not like flash cards, they were just thoughts. For example, I think 'turkey' with a classic image in my mind of a tom with all of its tail feathers out in full display. You all have an immediate thought of a turkey too but it came from memory and it may look similar to my classic turkey. Then, a few milliseconds later my mind imagines the frozen version wrapped in plastic, but you're either stuck on the live tom or, if you can receive my signal, then you'll envision the frozen turkey. I can sense the change in thought signal. Last week, when I received messages from each of you, they didn't come across like voices in my head, just thoughts. Pure thoughts. I really don't know how else to describe it."

"Energy?" asked Phil. "Is it like energy? Like, some sort of an electrical charge, a slight shock?"

"No, nothing like that at all. I've just learned how to realize my thoughts. In fact, the hardest part was the color. If I say 'ball', you think of a ball with no specific color. Now I say 'green ball' and you think of a ball with that color. Thoughts are color blind. We add details later, if and when they become available."

"Abby, what's the worst part of having this ability?" asked Dr. Paolo.

"What bothers me the most is how others perceive this ability. They think I have some magical power but I'm really no different than anyone else. I think I know how to use this sense, and I think with practice others could develop their ability to communicate this way too."

"So, you think we all have the ability, we just don't use it?" asked Phil.

"Yeah, I think so. Why should you develop this sense when your other senses serve you so well? It wasn't until my mother passed away that I developed this ability. I really wanted to communicate with her; to send her a message."

"So it's used mainly to communicate with the dead?" interrupted Phil who immediately wondered if "dead" was too blunt a word to describe her mother, perhaps "deceased" would have been a better choice.

"No, not necessarily. It's just their way of communicating," responded Abby emphatically, almost impatiently as if she wasn't getting her point across.

"Whose way?" said Phil who was becoming more and more intrigued with Abby's intellectual, as well her physical attributes.

"Those who are no longer with us physically. They're dead, yes, but... I don't know... their spirit... their energy is still around. They communicate nonverbally."

"Perhaps this is like our walk in the woods," said Amy who wasn't quite listening to the exchange between Abby and Phil because she was focusing on making a connection between a few different concepts. "Remember how Dr. Paolo spotted that brown mushroom?"

"The maitake," said Dr. Paolo who recalled the mushroom clearly.

"Right, that's it, the maitake," continued Amy. "We didn't see it. None of us saw it. But there it was at the base of that tree. We all have good vision and we're all smart but we just didn't see it. Only Dr. Paolo did. Why did he see it when we didn't? I'll tell you why. It was because he sharpened his visual sense to spot that brown thing growing among other things that looked like it in the woods. He trained and tuned his sense of sight. And I bet that's what Abby's done. She sharpened her ability to communicate nonverbally, right Abby? Am I right?"

Abby always wanted to give thoughtful replies, especially when it came to this particular topic. And although she'd already stated that everyone had the potential to communicate telepathically, she really wasn't one hundred percent sure if this was really true. On one hand, she wanted to appear knowledgeable about telepathy, but on the other hand she didn't want to say something that was unproven. It was time to use the last analogy she had stored in her mind.

"You may be right, Amy. It may be as simple as honing a skill or uncovering a sense and with practice anyone can do it. However, it may also be like playing the piano. We all have the ability to learn how to play the piano. However, not many of us have the innate ability to actually play it well. Technical proficiency does not equal artistic mastery. And this may be true for telepathy but I really don't know for sure. This field needs to be developed like other fields in science. It needs to come into the twenty-first century. That's the entire point of my presentation," Abby concluded.

"Abby," Dr. Paolo said, '"that was great. I really enjoyed your presentation and thanks for giving us the opportunity to ask you more questions and for sharing more of your personal experiences." He paused momentarily in an attempt to shake off fatigue, glanced down at his notes, and then described the difference between an experiment and an exercise before discussing the last item of the day.

7

Dr. Paolo was very pleased with the quality of the presentations. Each student accepted the challenge and, in friendly competition, tried to outdo each other with their unique presentation style and mastery of the topic. It had gone much better than he thought it would and, perhaps the greatest surprise of all was how much he enjoyed the experience.

Over the weekend he dedicated a great deal of time to thinking about the last few weeks of the semester. It was a pass or fail course, so that part was easy, they all were going to pass. But the challenge was how to convince Dr. Holliday and Dean Benedetti that this *Teach the Professor* course should be extended into next semester and perhaps to next year as well. What could be done to convince them? Dr. Paolo wanted to show them how well it went, how much progress each student made, and the value of this teaching approach. The more he wrangled with the problem, the more the solution eluded him. Then towards the end of a restless night's sleep, the solution presented itself unexpectedly like a thunderclap in the middle of a blizzard.

"So, as you recall," Dr. Paolo told his students, "this class was very close to being cut. Frankly, I was surprised that it was allowed to continue given the pushback I encountered when I first proposed the course to Dean Benedetti and President Holliday last summer. I asked them to consider this course as an experiment, a way to evaluate a different way of teaching—an approach that could only be appreciated by advanced, motivated students. Dr. Holliday more than Dr. Benedetti bought the argument and it was because of her will, because of her desire to try something different, that this course existed at all. So, here we are. After a rocky start, we're here, it's the first of December and there are only a few weeks left in the semester. Tell me honestly, would any of you like to do this again next semester or have you had enough?"

Without hesitation Amy replied, "Yes I would. Definitely."

"Me too," Brad and Phil replied in unison.

"Are you kidding? Of course I would. And I bet Ajay would jump at the chance too," said Abby.

"Great, then we're going to have to show them that we've made progress, real progress. And here's what I think we should do. I propose that you each present your research topic to the college in a mini-symposium format. You would have twenty minutes to present your topic. At the end of the symposium, you all would be on stage to entertain questions from the audience. We'd be sure to have the symposium when the faculty could attend with a special invite to President Holliday and Dean Benedetti."

"How will we put two hours worth of material into twenty minutes?" Phil asked. "That's impossible!"

"Well, yes and no," Dr. Paolo replied. "Yes, you'll have to trim your presentation back dramatically and no, it's not impossible. We'll work on it together. I'll show you how to focus on the take home points. How about I propose this symposium idea to Drs. Benedetti and Holliday and we'll try to schedule it two weeks from tomorrow, Friday the sixteenth. That'll give us plenty of time to get it together, right?"

They nodded in agreement while trying to gauge the amount of work needed to get their presentation down to the short time frame. And while they were thinking about this hurdle they were also concerned about taking their public speaking skills to a larger audience. Speaking in a small classroom setting to familiar faces was one thing but delivering a talk to a large group of strangers in an auditorium was another challenge altogether. But they trusted that Dr. Paolo would provide the right type of guidance; he hadn't let them down yet, and they doubted he'd let them down now. The first class of December adjourned with a plan. Dr. Paolo would meet with the Dean and the President as soon as he could and then he would let them know by email whether or not the symposium was approved. In the meantime, they were instructed to start trimming their presentation.

They had only one practice session in the newly renovated Anderson Auditorium, a bowl-shaped room with seating capacity of one thousand and ten persons. It was a multi-use venue that served as the site for freshman orientation, concerts, and general assemblies and for special seminars by in-house or visiting scholars. The teak-floored auditorium boasted a crisp sound system. The stage featured a large screen and a wooden podium set off to the right. The projector was perched in a small, soundproof room in the back of the auditorium and the controls to advance the computer-generated slides were integrated into the high tech podium. Although a small adjustable microphone was built into the podium, Dr. Paolo recommended that they wear a wireless microphone that would be clipped to their lapel, along with a transmitter that would allow the speaker a greater freedom of movement.

The only time that the Auditorium was available on December sixteenth was at ten o'clock in the morning. Fortunately, both Jean Holliday and Lorenzo Benedetti had openings in their schedules from ten to noon that day in a week that was otherwise packed with end of the semester meetings during the day and holiday events in the evening.

The *Teach the Professor* seminar program was open to the entire college and surprisingly, many of the science department's upperclassmen were in attendance as were most of the science faculty including Robert Pierce who's self appointed job was to keep an eye on Dean Benedetti. Rob positioned himself off to one side of the auditorium with a direct line view of Dr. Benedetti who sat in the front row next to Dr. Holliday. Other college professors who considered themselves worthy enough to be seated with the President also occupied the front row. Unbeknownst to Rob, Brad's parents, Livingston and Joan MacIntyre, sat in the row behind him to his right. The MacIntyre's insisted on attending the seminar despite weak objections from their son. Ever considerate, Brad thought it would be odd to have them in attendance when parents of the other class members were unavailable. Abby, in fact, hadn't even bothered telling her father about the event.

It was the first time in their college lives that Abby, Amy, Brad, and Phil took center stage. They were nervous but did their best to comfort and encourage each other as they watched Dr. Paolo on stage introduce himself then welcome the audience to the program. After he thanked Drs. Holliday and Benedetti for taking the time out of their busy schedule to attend, he described the concept and goals of the course, *Teach the Professor*. He informed the audience that what they were about to hear was the work of the students who chose their own subject, developed their own questions, did their own research and wrote their own presentations. Finally, Dr. Paolo described the format of the program.

"After the presentations, which will not exceed twenty minutes, all speakers will be invited back onstage and take a seat at the table. Questions will be asked at this point in a press conference-style manner. I'll serve as the moderator. The first speaker is Amy Ito and the title of her presentation is 'Your Genome: Your Code. Your Health.'"

Amy rose from the front row, climbed the steps and strode across the stage to the podium as if she owned it, along with the room and the entire building. Her delivery was smooth and sure. She had memorized the order of the slides and the information presented on those slides. DNA never sounded so exciting and the future of medicine, with therapies and treatments tailored to an individual's need based on their unique genetic makeup, never sounded so promising. At the end of her nineteen-minute presentation the audience, that Robert had judged to be just over one hundred, applauded in unison.

Amy's solid performance instilled confidence and purpose in her classmates. As the applause waned, Amy turned off her transmitter, removed the microphone clip and handed both parts to Brad who had already made his way onto the stage.

"Just do it," she told him in a voice that was all business. Brad slipped the transmitter in his right pocket, turned it back on, and then clipped the microphone on the lapel of his sports coat. Brad's parent's straightened in their chairs. They had never heard him speak in public before, however, since they expected him to be a leader in his chosen field—which would entail giving speeches all around the world—his parents were excited to be at their son's speaking debut.

Brad captured the attention of his parents, the college's teachers, and the entire audience by starting his short lecture with a large slide that read "2%" and a sobering fact.

"Two percent," Brad declared in a concrete voice. "Despite centuries of research, we can only assign function to only two percent of the human brain." His delivery was quick, crisp and polished, as if he's delivered it a hundred times before. In fact, he had Amy listen to the entire presentation so many times over the past few days that they both committed most of it to memory.

After Brad's final slide, the MacIntyre's led the applause in a proud display of approval. Rob overheard Mrs. MacIntyre tell her husband, "that was his best moment at Wilmington." Mr. MacIntyre nodded in agreement as he kept his gaze firmly on the stage where Phil was clipping the microphone onto his lapel. Rob, who by this time had figured out their identities, realized immediately the value of Mrs. MacIntyre's comment.

Phil and Dr. Paolo worked together to develop clear examples to explain quantum physics, string theory, multiverses and the meaning of very large numbers to a general audience. Deleted from his original two-hour presentation were the laborious mathematical formulas, intricate details and over-explanations. They were replaced with vivid visuals and animations of the cosmos that convey the complicated message that we may not be alone in the universe. And despite the revised material, Phil stayed on course and on time.

The shortened applause may have reflected the audience's hesitation to accept Phil's premise or perhaps it was a function of the length of the program, in any case, Phil was happy to help Abby position the microphone on her blouse. Abby, ever perceptive, simply smiled.

"I have a unique sense," Abby declared publically for the first time in her life. "I am telepathic. I can communicate without the use of my eyes, or ears, or any other commonly used human senses."

It was also the first time in her life that she'd wish her father was a different person. She would have wanted him to appreciate her intellect, to hear her story and to tell her how much he loved her. Abby also knew that these were childish, unrealistic thoughts; he would never be someone else.

"We conducted a simple exercise to test my abilities in a controlled fashion using the standard scientific method of inquiry," she continued.

Rob noticed Dr. Benedetti stiffen in his seat as Abby began to explain the design and then the results of the telepathy exercise. Dr. Paolo made sure that Abby omitted the names of the participants in her presentation; "aged and gender-matched" was how she referred to the control subject. Data were presented with brightly colored bar graphs; the results of the in-class exercise were crystal clear. The audience sat mesmerized. Abby ended her presentation with a prediction, which sounded more like a challenge.

"We ought to use every modern mathematical and molecular tool available to understand this and other quiescent senses that humans either have lost through evolution or through their environment. By doing this, we will learn more about our past and perhaps even our very existence," she boldly concluded.

As they had rehearsed earlier in the week, Abby's three classmates joined her on the stage during the applause. They sat at a long rectangular table behind their respective name placard. Dr. Paolo, who was still, along with the audience, clapping for Abby, made his way to the podium to preside over the question and answer session. Rob noticed Dr. Benedetti make a note on a small index card he had retrieved from his shirt pocket.

With less then twenty minutes remaining in the program Dr. Paolo was sure to start the questioning with the most important person in the audience.

"Yes, Dr. Holliday," said Dr. Paolo gesturing to the President seated just off to his right. Dr. Holliday rose with her back straight and with an unmistakable air of command as she asked Dr. Paolo for the wireless microphone and transmitter. She held the transmitter in her left hand and the tiny clip microphone in her right then activated the transmitter.

"I would like to commend you, Dr. Paolo, and your students on a truly remarkable series of presentations," Dr. Holliday stated with the authority of a worldly scholar. "While I knew something about each field, I can now say that I've been brought up to speed and I've perhaps been given a glimpse into the future especially with respects to the mapping of the brain and the potential importance of the quiescent senses, as you called them. My single question is directed at each of you. Besides the subject matter presented, what was the single most important lesson you learned from this course?"

Amy, of course, seized the tabletop microphone and turned it on with one smooth motion.

"Thank you for asking this important question Dr. Holliday," said Amy in a manner that sounded a bit too rehearsed. "The most important lessons I learned from Dr. Paolo's course was how to mine information from various sources, critically assess the information, and how to effectively package and communicate it in a concise and clear fashion. No other course at the college offered this opportunity, and in the process, this course made me realize how much I want to study medicine, individualized medicine." Amy's answer was not lost on the MacIntyre's who were becoming more and more impressed with this young lady friend of their son. It also was not lost on Brad who felt his love for Amy grow with each passing day and especially when she took control of situations as she has just done.

Brad told Dr. Holliday that he most enjoyed the freedom to explore a topic of his choice. "Whereas other classes target a single topic, this class allowed each of us to find our own interest."

Phil echoed Brad's answer then added that he was also enjoyed the teaching style. "It made me feel like an adult, like I was beyond the structure of the other classes. I was allowed to take charge of my own destiny and I now feel like I'm ready for grad school because Dr. Paolo told us that we'd be doing quite a bit of data gathering, analysis and presenting in graduate school."

Abby was handed the mike from Phil and said that she too has found her passion. "This course not only gave me the opportunity to come forward with my telepathy, to make it known to others, but it also showed me that there is a great deal of research, solid control-based, research that needs to be done in this field. The exercise and results that I shared with you are just the beginning. I want to do more in this field; it's what I want to do for the rest of my life. I guess you can say that this course also set me on my life's course."

Dr. Holliday's question consumed most of the allotted time for the Q&A segment of the program but Dr. Paolo made sure to get some questions from the students in the audience. A junior psychology major asked Amy about individual counseling when a genetic screen showed that he or she possessed a high-risk for a particular disease. Although a bit outside the scope of her presentation, Amy nonetheless answered the question clearly and with ease.

The other question had two parts that were answered rapidly by Abby.

"Do you think most of us have additional senses than the ones we know of?" asked a young lady seated towards the back of the auditorium.

"I do."

"Why?"

"Because over the years I have heard people say that they've known something was going to happen before actually did, or they knew what the other person was going to say before it was spoken, or that they had a strong premonition, felt a presence or had an event that they couldn't explain logically. These events suggest, but do not prove, that we have additional senses but they are mostly hearsay, not hard data and that's why I want to study telepathy further."

After Abby completed her answer, Dr. Paolo addressed the audience.

"I'd like to thank everyone for their attention and a special thanks to our panel of speakers. You all did a fine job. Thank you."

Livingston MacIntyre wasted no time. He leapt out of his seat, leaving his wife behind, and rushed up to the front of the auditorium to see Dr. Holliday who had just stood up along side Dr. Benedetti.

"Jean," said Livingston MacIntyre who placed his right hand on Dr. Holliday's left shoulder and all but ignored Dr. Benedetti. "That was absolutely wonderful, congratulations! It's the best thing I've seen in years. Kudos all around."

"Livingston," replied a surprised Dr. Holliday, "I didn't know you were here! How nice that you were able to come. Is Joan with you?" As the question was posed, Dr. Holliday spotted her good friend who was just few feet behind her husband. "Joan, how wonderful to see you and how nice it was for the two of you to attend this seminar. Brad did a wonderful job, don't you think?"

"And so did Amy, the Asian student. She and Brad have been dating for about a month now," Joan said softly and in a guarded manner.

"You both remember Dante?" asked Dr. Holliday who realized that neither had paid a moments worth of attention to him. "As you recall, Dr. Benedetti is the Dean of Academic Affairs. He helped recruit Dante Paolo to the college and he has been monitoring the progress of this new senior-level course from the beginning."

"Pleasure to see you again," said Dr. Benedetti as he shook their hands. "This course is on a trial basis. We'll need to assess the impact on the Department, review feedback and evaluate whether or not to continue it after the semester ends," said Dr. Benedetti in a tone that seemed to challenge the MacIntyre's exuberance.

Rob passed Drs. Holliday, Benedetti and the MacIntyre's as he made his way to the stage where Dante was surrounded by his four students, as well as other students from the Science Department. He arrived in time to hear a senior ask if the course would be offered in the spring. "I'm not sure," replied Dr. Paolo who felt satisfied that he had at least piqued the interest of a few students and that he'd fulfilled the minimum of expectations for the new course.

The next group to use the auditorium was making their way into the building as Dante and Rob departed. The skies were steel gray and a few scattered snow flurries swirled around the professors as they made their way back to their offices.

Rob was preparing for the last few days of the semester that were quite busy as final exams needed to be scored and grades issued in short order. Spreadsheet programs provided the numerical scores but the subjective score for promptness and participation that Rob stressed at the start of the semester would account for fifteen percent of the grade awaited his attention.

Finals week came with it's own twisted schedule. *Teach the Professor* would meet one more time—one hour on Thursday—then the semester would be over. Dr. Paolo's temporary position at Wilmington College was perhaps winding down.

Later, over a couple of beers at Toast of the Town, Dr. Paolo told Rob how much he enjoyed teaching the course, and that he was proud of his students. He also thanked Rob for dragging him to the College. Rob shrugged off the acknowledgment but he did tell his neighbor that he was surprised that Laura was not present.

"Did you invite her?" Rob asked.

"No. She really has no idea what I do and she's so straight out busy and beat by the end of the day that I didn't even bother to tell her. I just go on my way to the next day."

"Dante, sometimes I think that we goal-oriented, over-achieving, be-better-than-your-parents baby boomers who leave no time for anything else but work create our own demise. It's a real downfall. You probably should have told her about the seminar."

"You're probably right. I should have given her the option to opt out. And I agree completely with you. Most of us are on a free fall to the grave and we don't even realize it. We haven't a clue do we? Not a single clue."

Dr. Paolo arrived home at six-thirty in the dark. The Volvo's headlights accentuated the snow-filled cracks in the asphalt as he headed up the driveway and into the attached garage. He was glad that the squalls didn't leave appreciable snow accumulation, as he wasn't in any mood to shovel. In fact, the Irish red beer, spicy Buffalo wings, and deep fried calamari he enjoyed with Rob at *Toast of the Town* weren't settling well at all. In general, he wasn't feeling himself these past few days. Beside the sharp cramps that shot through his belly he felt tired and achier then usual. As he headed straight to the shower he vowed to tell Laura about his ailments the next day although he could predict her curt and direct response: "Make an appointment with your primary," she'd say. And the discussion would end before he even had a chance to describe a single symptom.

The hot shower was soothing and soon his thoughts drifted to the events of the day. He was pleased with himself for completing a semester of teaching, of having done something different and he was especially proud of his students.

They all are high achievers and they'll do well in graduate school, he thought. He recalled their presentations, their unique styles and he thought about their take home messages—the most important part—the one or two points they wanted members of the audience to keep forever.

With the hot water streaming down the back of his neck, he thought of Amy and DNA and of Brad and the mysteries of the brain. The steam of the hot water mixed with thoughts of Phil and the wacky multiverses, and Abby's clever use of the experimental design. And as he turned to the right towards the water's source, his eyes closed and his left arm upstretched in preparation for the soapy washcloth held in his right hand, it came to him.

It was fuzzy at first, but then slowly, ever so slowly it became sharper and sharper, until suddenly it gelled.

He froze in place.

He knew this feeling. It was one he had to capture before it vanished.

He'd experienced these fleeting moments only rarely when he was trying to solve a problem, a convoluted research problem that would ultimately result in a discovery. But this time he wasn't trying to solve a problem in the laboratory, at home or anywhere else for that matter. It just came to him for no apparent reason.

Holy cow, he thought to himself. *I better write this down now.* He finished his shower, dried himself quickly, slipped into his oversized bathrobe and went into the home office he shared with Laura. In the bound laboratory notebook that contained about five year's worth of his ideas and thoughts he quickly sketched pictures to capture the big aspects of his idea. Then, with labels assigned to each part, Dante Paolo began to create and develop the connections to the various parts. He tempered the exhilarating moments with caution. He had to give them time to mature. He had to evaluate each piece from every possible angle. He needed time to learn more about it, to research it and to find its strengths and to anticipate its flaws.

It must have a fatal flaw. It must have one, right? It must.

The slow grind of the garage door opener signaled Laura's arrival. Dante looked up and glanced at the silent clock that sat on the desk. It was eight-sixteen. He had been scribbling notes for the better part of an hour when he closed the soft-covered notebook satisfied that he had captured the essence of the idea. He would spend the rest of the calendar year, refining, rethinking and reformulating the hypothesis. But on this Friday evening his fatigued mind recalled his aching body. The short-lived adrenalin rush had run its course and with a vow to keep his idea to himself, Dr. Paolo crawled into bed and quickly fell into a deep sleep completely unaware that he failed to greet his equally exhausted wife.

Sometime in the early morning hours, when Dante was close to waking, the idea he had written in his notebook entered his subconscious mind. His heart rate quickened as parts of the idea came to life like animated objects floating aimlessly on a multidimensional game board.

An invisible prompt beckoned the player to start the game. Dr. Paolo watched himself enter the space. He was both the spectator and the sole player. He watched himself move his right hand in front of his head as if manipulating an invisible touchpad that brought together four element that were floating aimlessly in space; four distinct elements that formed his hypothesis. Dr. Paolo watched as he rearranged the elements one in front of, or behind, the other to understand how they fit together. It was a complex puzzle with only four simple pieces that were constantly changing shape.

Keep working the pieces. They'll fit. They will. It's not impossible, encouraged the observing Dr. Paolo to his self that was manipulating the pieces. *They will, you'll see.* And just as the four forms started to coalesce, started to make sense, a large hatchet appeared from the darkness from the left hurling itself end-over-end towards the manipulating Dr. Paolo. There was no time to move nor was there time to pull down his right hand that had tried in vain to position the final element with the other three, when the hatched sliced through his body. The observing Dr. Paolo tried to warn his image of the pending impact but it was too late. The observer watched helplessly as the burgundy red hatchet, which had increased in size and speed as it approached then pierced his unassuming frail likeness.

Dr. Paolo tentatively opened his eyes. The green numbers on the digital clock read four eighteen. He heard Laura breathing deeply and felt the warmth of her slender body beside him. He could feel his heart racing. His body was covered in a thin layer of perspiration under the warmth of the flannel sheets.

What was that all about? He wondered. *I'll be sure to remember it in the morning.* He then willed himself back to sleep and within seconds he was somewhere else.

He was nowhere in particular, the scenery nondescript. The place was both new and familiar to him. There was no sound. Had he been there before or had he just heard about this place? He saw an image, an icon, and a symbol of sorts. The symbol of sorts was what the manipulating Dr. Paolo was trying to create in the previous dream. The symbol of sorts was not on a signpost nor emblazed in neon. It just existed in space.

Quietly, and without warning, a presence appeared. This presence was familiar to Dr. Paolo, very familiar. Yet strangely enough it felt as though he had never seen him before. At least not like this. Or had he? The presence was a young boy with curly light brown-red hair. He was dressed simply and wore no shoes. In his right hand he held a slingshot. Dr. Paolo knew without asking that the little boy had whittled the slingshot himself from a branch of a live chestnut tree. He also knew that it was the boy's treasured possession. Without speaking the boy told Dr. Paolo not to be afraid, that he should follow his heart and that they were making preparations. Silently, effortlessly Dr. Paolo asked the boy where he was going. The boy looked down at his slingshot, tugged at the crude rubber band cut from a discarded inner tube, then back up at Dr. Paolo and as they locked eyes, the boy mutely replied, Anywhere. Dr. Paolo sensing that the time with the boy was only transient asked with his mind, do I know you? The boy's simple reply was rapid, terse yet tender, as if the intonation of the thought would expose the obvious answer, Si. And no sooner had the thought been sent than the little barefoot boy with the handmade slingshot disappeared as mysteriously as he had appeared. The symbol of sorts was also gone and Dr. Paolo found himself alone in the void.

Dante rose from bed in a daze; it was four-twenty a.m. and still very dark in the room. Several hours later he would recall the details of the two interrelated dreams but it would take him much longer to comprehend them.

———◆———

Weekend call meant that Laura was the sole physician responsible for close to twenty thousand individuals, the collective patient population of the six doctors in the call group. At any given time over the two days and nights someone was being admitted to the hospital, experiencing complications from a recent surgery, or was close to death or had some medical issue that required Laura's attention. During call weekends, the dedicated physician practically lived at the hospital. On call doctors were rarely home and when they were they were spent on the phone with the hospital's nursing staff. On this particular call weekend, as the young winter was making its presence known with temperatures in the mid-thirties and a threat of freezing rain looming, Dante had little to do other than to work on his newly developed hypothesis. His focus was interrupted only by more pronounced episodes of nausea and stomach pains that he still blamed on an overindulgence of fried food and beer.

The calamari was bad, he thought as he gazed at the sick man in the mirror. *If I could just puke and get it over with then maybe I'd look less jaundiced and feel better.* But, unlike his mother who had been a pro at vomiting at will, he absolutely hated the unnatural process of sticking your finger down your throat to induce another unnatural process. So he suffered with his ailments for most of the gray weekend subsisting mainly on green tea and a few crackers as he sat at the computer and researched his new project.

By the time the last day of finals arrived at Wilmington College, Dante had spent well over fifty hours refining what he simply called *The Hypothesis*. He woke early that day feeling physically weak but mentally energized by the thought of sharing *The Hypothesis* with his students. He strode into the classroom for the last time that semester like he'd won the lottery but hadn't yet told anyone. Despite the weekend ailments, Dr. Paolo's energy level was high—quite opposite that of the four exam-weary students who were ready to complete the semester and enjoy the long holiday break.

"Good morning," Dr. Paolo said quickly as if time was in short supply. "This course is pass or fail and clearly you've all passed. If I were able to give letter grades, you all would have A's. You've exceeded my expectations, well done. Now, I have something important to share with you. Over the weekend I had a moment of profound clarity. An idea based on your research topics, an idea that seems too obvious to be true.

I've formulated this idea into a testable hypothesis that I think you will find very interesting but since this will not affect your grade, I will not require you to stay. If you have a plane to catch or something else to do, then you may leave."

Not one senior moved.

The Last Hypothesis

1

Dr. Paolo was animated yet serious. His eyebrows were knitted together, his eyes focused. "What came to me in an instant may take generations to understand," he proclaimed as he paced uncharacteristically in front of the class. "As I thought about your presentations, I realized that each of you said something that was new to me. I heard you, Amy," he said pointing to her with the knuckle of his right hand index finger, "say that 'most of our DNA is non-encoding', right?"

"That's correct," answered Amy.

"Then I recalled that Brad said that we only understand a small percentage of what the brain does, right Brad?"

"Yes sir," replied Brad shocked at his use of the word "sir" that he'd used only when he addressed his grandfather, the family's patriarch. "Most of the brain is uncharacterized, greater than ninety-five percent or more," he added not recalling the exact amount.

"Okay," Dr. Paolo said as he walked over to the whiteboard and picked up several dry markers. "Let say that all of our DNA is contained within this rectangle. Now let's draw an oval inside the rectangle so that the resulting four small corners represent DNA that codes for something so now inside the oval is non-coding DNA," he said. "With me so far?"

They all nodded.

"Okay, good." Dr. Paolo then drew a rhombus inside the oval such that the corners roughly bisected the horizontal and vertical lines of the rectangle. "Inside the rhombus are the unknown functions of our brain, and the small wedges between the oval and the rhombus are the parts of the brain that we understand. Are we still good? Still with me?"

Another silent nod from the class as Dr. Paolo drew lines with the marker that connected the rhombus corner to opposite corner and again from the mid-point of each of its sides to create a center point in the middle of the image that now resembled an old fashioned, black and white television test-pattern.

"Okay, here's where you come in Phil," said Dr. Paolo who turned to face the class. "These eight segments," said the professor as he pointed to the spaces created with the four lines inside the rhombus, "these represent the multiverses you told us about. This could be eight, eighty, eighty thousand or whatever number you want as you keep bisecting the segments.

And this center point?" he asked tapping the whiteboard at the intersection of the lines within the rhombus on the drawing, "Would anyone like to take a stab at what's at this center?"

"Us! We are at the center," exclaimed Abby who was as certain of this answer as she was about anything in her life.

"Right!" replied Dr. Paolo matching her excitement. "The center is you, the individual. Each of us occupies our own center of this world, of this universe."

Although they were following Dr. Paolo's reasoning, it was not obvious to them what it all meant. Selfish children, conceited teenagers, and self-promoting adults have always been the center of the universe—or at least of their own universe—so that concept was not new. But they sensed that the professor was trying to convey something larger than the minuscule world that exists in the mind of vain individuals.

"So let me see if I understand what you're saying," said Amy in a quizzical and pensive voice. "An individual exists in the center of your diagram, but can also exist in each of the eight worlds following the laws of probability on the existence of multiverses."

"There could be way more than eight," Phil added.

"Right," said Dr. Paolo, we could bisect these eight spaces an infinite number of times."

"And that the ability to exist with our other selves, is…" continued Amy who suddenly and uncharacteristically was at a loss for words.

"Not 'exist' but interact or communicate," said Abby who was then interrupted by Brad who practically jumped off his seat and added, "Using the unchartered parts of our brain!"

"Right, with instructions stored in our junk DNA!" exclaimed Amy.

"Exactly!" said Dr. Paolo. "The hypothesis I formulated states that the great majority of our brain serves to interact with our other selves in other worlds and that the ability to perform these high-ordered functions is encoded in our DNA. I'll say it again in another way. Most of our brain is dedicated to interacting with our other selves in other worlds and that these high-ordered functions are encoded in our DNA."

The room was silent as they tried to absorb Dr. Paolo's hypothesis.

After a long moment Phil broke the silence. "This seems a bit farfetched."

"Thank you Phil. That's what I need, a skeptic. But tell me why you think this is implausible?"

"Because, it doesn't follow the evolutionary pattern of higher order gain of function over time. Wouldn't this form of communication be more advanced than what we use today?"

"Okay, your point is valid," replied Dr. Paolo. "And it's a conundrum that occurred to me too. I can theorize that as our cranium expanded and our brain size increased along with it, we began to construct more complicated ways of communicating verbally. Drawings turned into symbols that led to simple alphabets that eventually led to words and so on to the point where sounds, words, sentences became more widely used and accepted. As a consequence of these apparent advances and adaptations, nonverbal communication—that may have been the first way we interacted with each other—was displaced. As such we also lost the ability to communicate with others and our other selves."

"So are you saying that telepathy could be a remnant sense from an earlier timepoint in our evolution?" asked Abby.

"Yes, definitely," replied Dr. Paolo. "It's a sub-theory that is a part of the entire hypothesis. And I think it can be tested, here's how."

Dr. Paolo did not need to review the notes on the elaborate experiments he had written in his bound notebook. He had the details memorized. Experiments were designed to test whether or not unchartered areas of the brain are active during telepathic episodes and whether or not there is concurrent DNA activation that would lead to the production of signaling proteins involved with telepathic episodes. He theorized that specific DNA activation would be temporally aligned with the telepathic episodes in a binary all-or-none, on-off manner. He spoke in less detail on exactly how the experiments were to be conducted but he did lay out, in broad strokes, the experimental design.

A group of four to six persons, including telepaths, were needed for the experiment. Brains needed to be imaged and cell samples collected from all participants. DNA needed to be extracted from the cells then sequenced and analyzed. Dr. Paolo knew that none of this would be simple, easy or inexpensive. And because this type of research was outside his area of expertise he would have to rely on others for help and advice, a tough task in these days of tightly regulated research and low funding levels.

All of these experimental and technical hurdles were predictable. However, what Dr. Paolo had not anticipated was the high level of enthusiasm from the students—who were only twenty minutes away from being his former students.

"Dr. Paolo," Brad offered. "I bet Dr. Sukawa, the MIT professor who does the brain imaging research I spoke of in my presentation would help with the experiment. Maybe we could use his lab for a couple of hours on weekends or something?"

"And I'll chat with my dad over break. Maybe he can find someone to isolate the DNA and do the sequencing. How many samples do you think you'll have?" asked Amy before Dr. Paolo had a chance to address Brad's input.

"I'll volunteer myself as the test subject. I want to learn more about this and I bet I can recruit Ajay to help analyze the data," said Abby.

"Count me in," said Phil. "I think this stuff is wild. Dr. Paolo, if your hypothesis is correct then there will be a whole new line of research that will need people like me to place the findings into mathematical models."

Dr. Paolo wasted little time in seizing the student's interest and energy.

"Wow, that's great, it's all great. Okay, Brad, see what you can learn about the availability of Dr. Sukawa's lab but don't tell them any details, just say that we'd like to do some simple tests on areas of the brain involved with communication without giving out details, and ask if it would be possible to use their equipment. Amy, I think we can do this with about twenty samples total, ten for the test and ten for the control. Abby, thanks for volunteering, this couldn't happen without you and the experiment you did earlier would serve as a guide, like preliminary data. Phil, we'll need you and Ajay as well. Let's keep in touch by email over break and we'll reconvene in January."

"Do you think the experiment will work?" asked Amy.

"Do you mean, will we discover what we're hoping to discover?" replied Dr. Paolo.

"Yeah, that's what I meant."

"I don't know but that's the exciting part about research. It's doing something that no one else has done before. What we learn could be very exciting or it could be nothing. That's the promise and the perils of research. Most of the time the hypothesis doesn't pan out but we continue to be driven by the unknown, to do the experiment to the best of our ability in the hope that we'll learn something useful. In fact, no matter how the experiment ends up, we always learn something. In many ways, this has already been a success because it captured your interest. To me that's a palpable achievement."

"Are you teaching the course next semester?" asked Phil.

"I'm not sure. No one has said anything to me about next semester. I hope I'm still here but one never knows. I'll keep you posted." And with that promise, the shortened class session ended.

As they left the room for the final time that semester Dr. Paolo told them, "Thanks for a great semester, I learned more from this course than you realize."

———•———

As he erased the diagram of the hypothesis from the white board Dr. Paolo was in his own world. He was reliving past enthusiastic interactions with students in doing the experiments. Alone in the small classroom he thought to himself, *Am I sane? Is The Hypothesis really testable? I have no research money, no lab, and no real connections to anyone in these other fields. What am I thinking? And what about this teaching career? Would I be invited back or is this my last day at Wilmington College?*

His mind bounced from one topic to another as he reflected on the entire semester. He was thankful that his regular class was two-hours long because one hour was simply too short as today's class had shown. Yet despite the shortened class he felt tired, physically worn as if he had just finished a grueling half marathon. He was looking forward to heading home and crawling into bed when Dean Benedetti entered the classroom.

"Dante, I'm glad you're still here. Jean and I would like to meet with you for a few minutes if you have time," said Dr. Benedetti rather curtly.

"Sure, when?" said Dr. Paolo who was clearly caught off guard.

"Fifteen minutes. In the President's office."

Dante was irritated not by the fact that Drs. Holliday and Benedetti wanted to meet with him, but rather that they gave him no advanced notice. It was just plain rude and it served as yet another example of the lack of civility by members of our current society. Dante observed that personal electronic devices created a culture of instant gratification, abbreviated, often terse, interpersonal exchanges and outright discourteous behavior. He often thought that *Technology and the Erosion of Human Civility* would be a dynamic topic for a sociology student's masters thesis with the byline: *Less patience, more arrogance, less class.*

I'm probably being fired, he thought as he gathered his wits before heading across campus to President Holliday's office.

Dr. Holliday's affable assistant, Ann Tremont, who has held the position for the better part of two decades, escorted Dr. Paolo into the large office. Dr. Benedetti was already present at the small solid mahogany conference table alongside Dr. Holliday. Dr. Paolo seated himself across from the President.

"Dante, thank you for coming on such short notice," said Dr. Holliday. Her honest intonation defused Dr. Paolo's tense demeanor and it also made him wonder who exactly had proposed the impromptu gathering. Dr. Holliday continued, "As you recall, your course was an experiment, and based on what Dr. Benedetti has told me, there were aspects that were good, some that were not so good, and truthfully, some things that are, or can get, quite ugly."

Dr. Paolo's mind raced to determine what aspects of his course would fall into the last two categories. What could possibly be labeled "ugly"?

The President continued, "The good part is obvious to anyone who attended the seminar. The students did an excellent job presenting their research and the audience was captivated by what they had to say. Without doubt, they learned a great deal from taking your course and you should be commended for that achievement. The bad is that there were only four students enrolled. This is hardly a blockbuster course but I will say that your idea of holding a seminar was brilliant for many reasons but it also served to market the course to other students so I would expect that these initial four students were trailblazers of sorts and that there will be greater interest should the course be offered again."

Dr. Paolo had little time to reflect on her use of the word "should" before Jean Holliday moved on to the final, and most damning point.

"The ugly, Dante, may or may not have been discovered yet. What I mean is that so far, we have not received any formal complaints, but it may happen and we need to be prepared."

Dr. Paolo still had no idea what the President was insinuating. The well-known academic evils of plagiarism, cheating, and sexual affairs with students scrolled though his mind but none of these applied to him or to his class.

"The last student to present at the seminar, a young lady, Abigail Lark, spoke of a telepathy experiment, that she performed in your class. Is that true Dante? Was a telepathy experiment performed in your class?"

"Well sort of, yes. Abby applied the scientific method to investigate telepathy. She would like to pursue graduate studies in the paranormal senses. She believes that modern molecular tools and rigorous experimentation will reveal the true power of additional senses other than the five we currently use. She's quite passionate..."

"So, you admit that an experiment involving your students took place in your class?" interrupted Dr. Benedetti.

"Sort of," replied a visibly annoyed Dr. Paolo.

Dr. Holliday made some notes on her yellow legal pad as Dean Benedetti launched into a heated reprimand that lasted a full three minutes. He reminded Dr. Paolo that Wilmington College was an undergraduate institution with no state or federal approvals to conduct research of any sort, including humans. He lectured the professor that even if Wilmington College had a true research program that there would be regulatory hurdles that needed to be in place in order to perform the study including a panel of experts to ensure the protection of an individual's rights.

"Have you ever heard of informed consent?" Dr. Benedetti asked Dr. Paolo rhetorically, in a tone that was clearly condescending.

Dr. Paolo was outwardly calm but internally livid. Due to the decades spent with pompous, oversized egos at Harvard, Dante was immune to the transparent powers of authority, especially those who were unable to understand the limits of such power. In addition he had spent endless days over his research career completing all necessary paperwork required to gain approval to do a simple experiment with animals and complex clinical trials with humans; needless to say, Dante Paolo was well versed on the rules of the regulatory road.

The vast room was silent for several moments after Dr. Benedetti completed his tirade. Dr. Paolo allowed time to drift for a moment while he sharpened his response.

"Well Lorenzo," began Dr. Paolo who addressed the overheated Dean by his first name to make his retort just that much more personal. "While what you said is correct in that experimentation on animals and humans require institutional, local, state and federal approvals you are technically incorrect on one key point." Dr. Paolo moved forward in his chair, rested both arms on the table and folded his hands together. With eyes locked on Dr. Benedetti he said, "Abby conducted an exercise, not an experiment. If you were listening you would have heard her say as much. Experiments require approvals exercises do not. That's a fact. If it did, there would be no labs in chemistry, no dissections in biology, no water sampling in environmental sciences and no marbles rolling down hallways in physics. Every science class at the college would be in violation and as the Dean, you would be held accountable. What Abby did was no more than a simple undergraduate exercise. Don't create a chasm when there isn't even a fissure."

Dr. Holliday's shoulders dropped. She then leaned forward and crossed out something on her legal pad. The roller coaster ride was leveling off, along with Dr. Paolo's blood pressure.

"Dr. Paolo," the President said in a steady sure voice. "The feedback to your course was outstanding. We have also received several inquiries from students on the availability of your course next semester and based on these inquiries, we predict that the class size could grow as much as ten-fold. We'd like you to remain at the college to develop a lesson plan to accommodate at least twenty, perhaps forty, students for the fall semester. We'll pay you a part-time salary to work over the spring to develop the course. You'll have access to your office, as well as the resources at the college. I sincerely hope you will accept my offer."

Dean Benedetti was silent.

Dante Paolo really wasn't in the mood to discuss a job offer but he decided to accept the offer immediately knowing full well that he could quit at any time.

"Thank you Dr. Holliday. I accept your offer," he replied stoically.

The meeting ended as abruptly as it was called. Wearily, Dante left the President's office without as much as a glance in Dr. Benedetti's direction. He also did not extend holiday wishes to anyone because he knew they would ring hallow.

Dr. Paolo walked to Paine Hall, retrieved a few items from his office, and then left the already deserted science building for the last time that year. In this disjointed season of prepackaged love and joy, he was beginning to downright hate Lorenzo Benedetti. He tried to clear his mind of the negative thoughts and focus on the positive as he drove his Volvo home to start the long holiday break. But the overcast day only enhanced his dour mood.

The glass is half-full, he thought. *Things could be worse. At least I wasn't fired and it looks like the course survived. Things could have definitely been worse.*

2

With good reason Dante and Laura didn't get caught up in the frantic, consumer-driven frenzy of the end-of-the-year extended holiday season marketed heavily to children and adults alike. At this point in their lives they had accepted their fate as a childless couple, but it wasn't supposed to be that way.

It was early in their marriage when Laura miscarried late in her pregnancy. The event was so sudden, so unexpected, and so devastating that they, especially Laura, lost all desire to have children; she did not want to risk the heartache of another devastating loss.

That tumultuous time in their lives affected both of them profoundly but Dante took the loss particularly hard. His Italian heart held a deeply engrained passion to nurture children; even as a child he was drawn to babies and toddlers. And as a young man he imagined himself teaching his son how to catch brown trout in a shallow stream not with tackle and bait, but with nothing more than their bare hands. His mind foresaw taking a photograph of his young daughter as she held the taunt end of a string attached to a high-flying kite, the string held firmly in her little chubby hands, her eyes focused upwards with eyebrows knotted in concentration. And he imagined the festivities of the holidays too. He had thought of ways to make Santa Claus more real than ever by placing magic sparkly oats on the snow in front of the house to attract the sled-pulling reindeer, and making boot prints by the fireplace, or by quietly assembling a shiny new desk in their bedroom on Christmas Eve as they slept. Young Dante stored these ideas in his mind only to have them sit forever idle like ancient files on an old hard drive that eventually become inaccessible and superfluous.

And with the death of their respective parents, the traditional holiday meals for Dante and Laura became more or less an intimate dinner for two. It wasn't a particularly happy time nor was it a sad time but it was just a time near the end of a long year when most everyone agreed that it was okay to slow down for a moment, to stop and experience life without regard to deadlines, details or drama.

But something was different. Dante felt odd this holiday season.

For starters, he had little to no appetite, which was remarkable because he always found food enjoyable to prepare, to share and to consume. He didn't consider himself a foodie but more of an amateur chef molded after his paternal grandmother who was able to create an unforgettable meal for twelve with only a few eggs, some flour, and a couple of tomatoes. And despite having taken a week off from running, the annoying pain in his back persisted. For the first time in his life, he felt old and mentioning it resulted in only passing sympathy from his wife. "Welcome to old age, sweetheart," she'd say dismissively. However, Laura did show concern when her husband welcomed the dark Christmas morning by vomiting the sparse meal he had eaten the previous evening.

"What's wrong?" she asked wearily.

"I don't know, probably food poisoning or something. I feel like crap and my back is killing me too."

Laura looked at her husband's reflection in the mirror as he leaned against the sink in their bright bathroom to brush his teeth in a desperate attempt to rid his mouth of the displaced bile.

That's when she noticed his eyes.

"Come here," said Laura. "Look at me." Dante rinsed his mouth then turned to face his wife. He looked at Laura's eyes as the freezing rain pelted the outside of the small bathroom window.

"How long have they been like this?"

"Like what?" he asked as he turned to again face the mirror. It was the first time he noticed that the whites of his eyes were not exactly white.

"Dante, face me and look to the right."

"Now to the left." Again, Dante did as instructed. "I think your eyes have a yellow tint. You could be jaundiced," said Laura.

"What? Jaundice? No. They're just off white, probably because I've been puking my guts out for the past five minutes."

"You should see Kincade this week. I can talk to him if you'd like but I think you should call his office tomorrow and tell the receptionist that you haven't been feeling well and that you may be jaundiced," said Laura in her declarative, no nonsense voice as she left him alone in the bathroom to ponder his not-so-white eyes.

"What could this mean?" he asked in a voice loud enough so his wife could hear him as she made her way down the stairs to the kitchen.

"I don't know," she lied. "Ask Tom. I'm not your physician and guessing won't do anyone any good," she added for good measure.

The rest of Dante Paolo's Christmas day was spent watching the progression of the nasty New England weather and mining the web for information on *jaundice*. The amount of material was so overwhelming and he felt so weak that he decided that Laura was right not to speculate and that he should simply call Dr. Kincade's office in the morning.

Although Dr. Thomas Kincade has been Dante's primary care physician for about two decades, they barely knew each other. When it came to his health Dante always practiced prudence and prevention. He received vaccinations—usually courtesy of Laura—on time, never skimped on sleep and he kept his weight and blood pressure under control. He drank only moderately, never smoked and exercised as often as possible. For her part, Laura kept an inconspicuous eye on her husband. She readily handled any minor health issue that arose over the years, which, fortunately, amounted to only a nasty case of influenza when he was in his thirties. Dante was lucky to be in good health because he really didn't care to be bothered with the effort of scheduling an appointment and then dealing with the entire medical exam routine. He found Dr. Kincade to be competent but overly chatty, which was a problem because Dante did not want to have a social relationship with his doctor or with his dentist, for that matter. He preferred to have his medical and dental experiences to be like a trip to an old fashioned gas station—you pulled up to the pump, the attendant filled your tank, washed the windows, you paid him and off you went. No dilly-dallying. In and out, done.

But Dante's visit to Dr. Kincade's office on this sunny New Year's Eve morning was anything but in and out, done.

Dr. Kincade's usually good spirits were decidedly sour as he shook Dante's hand and glanced into his patient's eyes. Both doctors suspected that this was not going to be a short visit. And both were right.

The exam room was just large enough to accommodate an exam table, a chair, a small utility cabinet, and a computer with a monitor, mouse and keyboard. It also had a small sink for hand washing and assorted literature for the patient to read while waiting for the doctor to arrive. Dr. Kincade made his way to the small black stool by the computer and entered his access key. He then pulled up Dr. Paolo's electronic medical file that was quite sparse compared to the files of most of his patients.

"Okay Dante," started Dr. Kincade. "Let's get some history on you and get your chart up to date. It says here that you do not have any siblings, but I have nothing on your parents. Tell me about them."

"Well they're both deceased. My mother died five years ago of a heart attack. She was sixty-nine."

"Is there a history of heart disease in her family?"

"As far as I can recall, yes."

"And your Dad?"

"He died of lung cancer that had metastasized to his bones. He was a two pack a day smoker. What a disgusting, vile habit."

"How old was he when he died?" asked Dr. Kincade as he typed information into the database.

"He was seventy."

"Both young," commented Dr. Kincade. "Unfortunately that's not uncommon, especially among smokers."

"Yeah, both of them never really took good care of themselves, but the smoking was a constant presence during my childhood. I couldn't wait to leave the house just to get some fresh air. It's probably why I spent most of my childhood outdoors."

"Do you know anything else about your father's family?"

"No, not really. Just stories of how they used to take care of sick people in the homes. I think my father's mother also died of cancer but I'm not one hundred percent sure of this. I was a little kid when she died."

"Okay," said Dr. Kincade pivoting from his stool to face Dante. "Tell me what's going on with you."

Dante told Dr. Kincade that he had not felt right for about a month or so. He told him that he'd lost his appetite and he was tiring easily. He confessed that there were other nagging things like his transient back pain and occasional bouts of nausea and vomiting.

Dr. Kincade pulled out a small penlight from his lab coat pocket and aimed the beam into Dante's eyes.

"Your eyes have a tinge of yellow to them. How long have they been like this?"

"Laura noticed them on Christmas Day. I didn't see them until she pointed it out. That's why I'm here. She insisted."

Dr. Kincade had Dante lie down on the exam table then palpated his abdomen and along his sides. Although his thrusts were deep they were not painful.

"Have you noticed any change in the color of your stool?"

"No, why?"

"Just curious," Dr. Kincade said. "You can sit up now."

With Dr. Paolo sitting on the exam table, he told him that he agreed with Laura; his eyes looked jaundiced. Dr. Kincade explained that elevated levels of a chemical called bilirubin in the blood causes jaundice and that bilirubin is a result of the normal breakdown of the oxygen-carrying heme in red blood cells. "That's why there is a yellow color around a bruise," he added. "It is usually excreted by bile and urine but when it's not excreted we have to find out why. I'd like to take some blood to do a full workup. I'll send the nurse in to draw a few tubes. I'll give you a call when I get the results. Anything else?"

"No. That's it," said Dante.

Over the next few weeks, simple blood tests led to more involved and sophisticated tests with acronyms like ERCP and CT scan, the results of which ultimately led to the diagnosis that Laura had already reached on her own using a combination of experience and acute observations. She just didn't want to believe it. For once she wanted to be wrong.

———•———

As a young reader, *all the world's a stage* was about all the Shakespeare Dante could tolerate and yet this short, awkward phrase echoed in his mind when Dr. Kincade delivered the diagnosis.

As it was, the cancer, that is, Dante Paolo's pancreatic cancer also had a stage.

All the world's a stage, and not just any stage, mind you, but *the* stage. Dr. Paolo's cancer couldn't just be a lowly stage one, or a tolerable two, or even a borderline three. No, it had to be the lofty stage four, the highest allowed. It was the most feared of all; the mighty and mature, Roman numeral type IV.

All the world's a stage, he thought and even his cancer agreed. Stage IV pancreatic cancer meant that the evil cells had traveled to other parts of Dante Paolo's body. It took not only center stage, but also the orchestra pit, the balcony and in fact, the entire theater including the two-bit bar in the lobby and the marquee; it even held top and final billing.

All the world's a cancer is more appropriate, Dante wildly thought as he measured the immense gravity of the moment.

Throughout his life, Dr. Paolo was intrigued by human responses to death. When he attended wakes and funerals he'd study the reactions of mourners and noted whether or not they were related to the deceased or merely acquaintances. And on television, during the news report of a shooting, he watched not the person being interviewed but the neighbors who had gathered in the background. He studied the face of a mother whose son was innocently killed in gang crossfire, and the athletic pals of a cyclist who had been struck by a car and killed. He studied them all; he tried to decipher and catalog their grief. For those Dante observed first hand—at his grandparent's funerals, his parent's funerals, and those of his aunts and uncles—he noticed a particularly interesting pattern. Dante realized that the closer in age the survivors were to the deceased, the greater their sadness. He reasoned that folks were overcome with grief not only because they had lost someone they loved—which was certainly true—but also because they were now one step closer to the grave themselves as if everyone was standing on a chronologically-driven conveyor belt to the abyss. *Could it be that the realization of their own mortality was the main reason people grieve?* He pondered.

So when they arrived home carrying the news of his ever-expanding stage IV cancer, Dante could only think that Laura was subconsciously acknowledging her own death when she buried her face in his shoulder, hugged him tightly and sobbed uncontrollably. The last time she'd shown so much sorrow—or any emotion for that matter—was when she lost the baby so many years ago. Because of its naked cruelty, the pain that parents endure over the loss of a child is absolute. A child, Dante reasoned, was not supposed to be on the conveyor belt—offspring should not skip line.

And now with his own death looming as sure as Orion's presence in the clear winter night's sky, Dante Paolo found himself in silent awe of his own absolute existence. He was stunned-dumb. Despite his lifelong interest in death and dying, the profound weight of the diagnosis, the first and last diagnosis he would ever experience, paralyzed his mind.

It was not only the end of a long day in a New Year; it was, by all odds, one of his last days of his final year. And thus, just like that, the curtain rose on the last act of Dr. Dante Paolo's life, and it did so with no musical accompaniment—a foreshadowed dead silence.

3

Dr. Paolo's last class gave Abby a way to survive the pathetic December holiday season that she loathed even more than Thanksgiving. Abby immersed herself in her favorite professor's wildly fantastic hypothesis as a way to distance herself from the memories of her youth and of her mother who loved everything there was to love about Christmas—from the sappy songs about cold, snow and chestnuts to the messy, gooey gingerbread houses.

From the notes she frantically scribbled in class, Abby examined all of the components of the hypothesis and tried to find flawed logic, or more importantly, details of Dr. Paolo's hypothesis that could not be tested experimentally.

She found none.

On New Year's Eve, Abby sent emails to Phil, Amy and Brad that described her analysis of Dr. Paolo's hypothesis as well as an outline of experiments that she thought were needed to put it to the test. To her surprise and delight, she received a reply from Phil within a few hours of midnight. He confirmed her analyses and suggested ways to perform the experiments; tests that required expensive equipment. He ended his response by telling Abby what she already knew, that for these experiments to see the light of day, they were going to need Brad and Amy's help.

As luck would have it, Amy was once again house sitting for the Kelly family who had decided to spend another New Year holiday at a ski resort in northern New Hampshire. Brad and Amy had been virtually inseparable since the semester ended and they viewed the opportunity to spend time in the Victorian as a sign that they were indeed destined to be with each other for the rest of their lives. They both turned down invitations to attend New Years Eve parties opting instead for an early evening dinner for two at their new favorite restaurant in downtown Winchester followed by an extended evening of pure lovemaking. Over dinner they agreed to tempt and tease each other right up to the stroke of midnight when they would try to climax together under the warm comfort of the goose-down filled duvet. Their planned synchronous bliss would be in stark contrast with lovers shivering outside in sub-freezing temperatures at First Night Celebrations in Boston or at Times Square in New York City, or anywhere else in the northeast for that matter.

Amy and Brad knew that they were in the throes of the infatuation stage of a new relationship, but they also knew that their passion ran deep. Their love was heartfelt and true and they were certain that it would endure the hard test of time.

The starlit New Year's Eve sky gave way to dark morning clouds that created the perfect atmosphere to sleep in the extra hour. The combination of wine with dinner, champagne toasts and adventurous lovemaking, combined with no commitments until noon made the decision to cuddle an extra hour effortless. After a visit to the bathroom, Amy leapt back to bed and reached for her laptop that was leaning against the bottom of the nightstand. Amy scrolled through the dozen or so emails she had received from friends and family wishing her a Happy New Year when she came across the two emails from her classmates.

"Brad, look," Amy said to her lightly sleeping companion. "Abby and Phil have been discussing Dr. Paolo's hypothesis and they have some ideas on what needs to be done to put them to the test. Phil says that they'll need our help."

"What kind of help?" Brad replied as he lightly stroked Amy's leg under the sheets.

Amy closed the laptop, set it on the nightstand and positioned herself under the sheets facing Brad. She studied the fine features of his face as his hand explored the smooth curve of her lower back. The thoughts of discussing the hypothesis were overpowered by her desires to continue their First Morning after their First Night with each other. She reached up and gently pushed Brad's shoulder so he was laying flat on his back.

He allowed her to straddle his left leg, her pelvis grinding into his knee. She reached up and kissed him as passionately as she had done at the stroke of the prior day's midnight.

A short while later, in the steaming heat of the shower Amy asked Brad if he was intrigued by Dr. Paolo's hypothesis and if he was willing to help out as he had done for Abby's experiments. Brad replied that he wasn't sure how much spare time he would have this semester because he anticipated a great deal of travel to meet with admissions officers at some of the medical school where he'd applied. Amy told him that she was willing to help out as much as possible even though she too expected to be meeting with admission officers.

"I think we should stay involved. After all, the hypothesis is based on our reports and I do think it's quite clever and different."

"Oh it's different alright," said Brad who thought about Abby's written comment on the size of Asian women's breasts as he playfully lathered Amy's chest. "Perhaps a bit too different."

———•———

New England's unpredictable January weather lived up to everyone's expectations. The region received heavy snow to the north, rain to the south and the dreaded mix of freezing rain and its evil twin, sleet, sandwiched in the middle. It was the type of winter weather that created chaos with every aspect of normal everyday life. And if the day wasn't stormy, it was clear, windy and bitterly cold. Some days were filled with bright blinding sunlight that temporarily thawed some of the snow only to lead to dangerous driving and walking conditions at night when the temperatures retreated to the teens.

During these days of sparse light, Dr. Paolo worked deep into the night and sometimes even into the early morning hours in his well-lit home office. He wanted to do as much research as possible on what he

knew would be his last hypothesis before his body's immune system sur-
rendered to the aggressive cancer.

After reviewing the literature on radiation and chemotherapy used to
treat pancreatic cancer, he opted to forego all treatments. He exchanged
time for mental acuity. At stage IV, the nonspecific, debilitating poison
would sap his strength along with his spirit in return for only a bit more
time on Earth; a poor tradeoff. He wanted his mind to remain clear as
long as possible. Since the cancer wouldn't disclose an exact timetable,
Dante had to guess at the endpoint as best as he could, a situation that
was, ironically, motivational.

Despite the fact that he had no idea how, or even if, he would be able
to do them, Dante nonetheless outlined key experiments to be conducted
to test the hypothesis. He anticipated the results and made special note
of potential pitfalls and hurdles. He sketched an outline of how the presumptive results could be interpreted and he made sure to leave room
for alternative interpretations because he knew that the actual data could
modify or sharpen the hypothesis. Finally, he discussed the anticipated
results in a concise and succinct way. Utterly unorthodox among scientists, he wrote the entire manuscript without having performed a single
experiment. He felt that he had no choice. Time was no longer a luxury.

The manuscript was written for the scientific community because
the burden of proof, the need to replicate and to verify the findings, fell
squarely on the shoulders of other scientists. With each revision of the
manuscript, the significance of the results—that eventually would be validated by others—became sharper.

The need to clearly communicate the impact of the results to the
general public did not escape Dante either. He knew that the findings
would be highly controversial and that they would lead to bold, telling headlines. And given that the Internet spawned a society whereby
distortions and defamation overpower definitive data and truths, he

wanted to be the first to frame the public discussion on his hypothesis and to place the presumptive findings in the right light and in the proper context. So after the draft of the scientific manuscript was in hand, he penned an article for *The Atlantic*. In *The Atlantic* piece he reached back in time and described Galileo's interests, inventions and observations. He wrote about the persecution Galileo received from intellectual infants of his day who were emphatically driven to prejudge what they could not comprehend or what did not fit neatly into their wildly flawed view of the world.

Dr. Paolo used unambiguous terms to describe the anticipated research results and the implications of the data that, on the surface, appeared to be more science fiction than science fact. He wrote:

> These findings will not cure all diseases, prevent plagues or end famine; they cannot ensure peace nor save our planet from destruction. But as sure as the sun is the center of our solar system they will, one day, relieve us of our profound cognitive limitations.

Drafting a manuscript and writing an article for *The Atlantic* were easy compared to solving the problem of how to actually publish the eventual findings. Dante thought that while he expected to live long enough to perform at least some of the experiments, odds were high that he would die before the project was completed.

Research took time, and time was a commodity in short supply for Dante. He needed a plan, one that was foolproof and sure to work. After careful deliberation he decided that he needed a specific person to be involved, someone with the right connections, someone who knew how to manipulate the system. The wily Dante Paolo knew exactly who that person was. He also knew that he only had one shot at getting it right.

The twenty-third of January was the first day of the new spring semester at Wilmington College but the cold and gray weather was not spring-like at all. And while the campus was bustling with activity Dante Paolo was not. His appetite was nonexistent, he was rapidly losing weight and his face looked decidedly pale and more gaunt than it did even a week ago. He had given up on exercise and the cold weather did little to convince him otherwise. He marveled at how quickly he had lost muscle tone. *Hard to build, easy to lose except when you have cancer then it's easier than ever to lose,* he thought.

The house was silent by nine on that cold morning. Laura's morning breakfast meeting left Dante with a pot of coffee and an Internet worth of news articles complete with unsolicited, mostly thoughtless comments from those who yearn to be heard but not seen, like the man behind the curtain in Oz. He clicked from one site to another—*The Boston Globe, The New York Times, The LA Times, CNN, BBC*—scanning the headlines to get a snapshot of what had happened in his state, in the country and the world since the last time he checked it not more than nine hours ago. He was reading an opinion piece on the shortsightedness of mankind when a computer tone signaled the arrival of a new email.

It was from Abby whose username "onalark" made Dr. Paolo smile. Subject: The Hypothesis. Date: January 23, 2012 09:11:01 AM EST. It was sent to the professor's college email address and copied to Amy, Brad and Phil.

Dear Dr. Paolo,

Happy New Year! I hope you had a nice holiday. Over the break, I gave a great deal of thought on ways to test your hypothesis. Together, Amy, Brad, Phil and I outlined three different experiments that could provide some important clues. I would like to arrange a time to meet with you to discuss our ideas. Would this be possible? If so, please send some dates and times. As this is our last semester at Wilmington College, our schedules are quite flexible and open.

Sincerely,

Abby

Dr. Paolo read the email three times then stared at it for a long while in complete disbelief. While he could have predicted all of the events that headlined the day's news—a killing here, an economic slump there, a celebrity spoof and a political goof—this email was as unexpected as a winning lottery ticket. Abby's email instantly lifted his sagging spirits and energized him like a combination shot of espresso and adrenaline so much so that he immediately noted this event, this one short email, as a key moment in the Final Act, the new and brutally realistic title he had given this time, the last chapter, of his life.

His mind raced. What experiments did they have in mind? Did they really want to work on this? Where could they meet? He poured himself another cup of coffee and typed a short reply to all.

Subject:re:The Hypothesis. Date:January 23, 2012 09:45:11 AM EST

Happy New Year to you all!
I hope this year brings each of you the rewards you've so rightfully earned. Please give me a call to discuss your ideas. My contact information is on the Wilmington College web-site.

Best,

Dante

His mind raced.

Without parents or siblings, Dante discussed his cancer only with his doctors and with Laura. He hadn't bothered to tell Rob or anyone else in the neighborhood, as he didn't want to get them down during the holidays nor did he seek sympathy. But with the real possibility of reuniting with his students, Dante would have little choice but to tell them about his cancer and of the dire prognosis. He wanted to put everything on the table so if they went ahead with any experiments, or if they spent any time together over the next few months then they would be prepared to witness cancer's dramatic effects. He decided that the best place to speak openly and frankly with them would be his home, away from the eyes and ears of the college.

He was still deep in thought when the ringing of his cell phone startled him.

"Hello."

"Hi Dr. Paolo? This is Abby. Happy New Year!"

"Thanks, and the same to you. How have you been? It seems like you've been busy over the holiday."

"I'm fine and well yeah, I would say that your last lecture in fact, made my holiday because it gave me plenty to think about."

"Um, well wonderful," replied Dr. Paolo who was momentarily shaken by Abby's use of the phrase "your last lecture". "What were you thinking about exactly?"

"Your hypothesis and, well, specifically I was thinking about ways of testing some parts of it."

"Such as?"

"Well, like our telepathy experiment, for example," said Abby meekly; unsure of how the next part would be received. "I think we could do a more interesting experiment and perhaps a more complete experiment too. And the others are interested, I mean, Amy, Brad, Phil and I drew up some experiments and we'd like to show them to you. We'd like to do these experiment and we want you to be involved since it's your hypothesis."

Dr. Paolo was momentarily silent as he thought about the series of experiments that he had sketched and wondered to himself how they might differ from those that the students designed.

"Yeah, sure, I'd love to hear what you've done."

"Great. We were hoping you'd say that."

"How about I invite the four of you over to my house for dinner, say this Friday night, at six? Then we could meet informally. It would give me a reason to practice my culinary skills."

"Sounds good to me. Let me check with the others and get back to you, say by Wednesday?"

"Great."

"Could I just text?"

"Sure. Text or call or email, it's up to you. All work for me."

"Okay...um Dr. Paolo, just so you know. We're keeping this project private as you recommended."

"Wonderful. Have a good week and I'll hear from you soon."

"You too. Okay. Bye now."

"Bye."

The First Experiment

1

Dr. Paolo's home was modest compared to the newer construction in adjacent developments that featured enormous and pretentious mini-mansions. The raised ranch contained three average sized bedrooms and one-and-a-half baths. It was plain, simple and efficient. Other than the few paintings by local artists that hung on the off-white walls, the décor was nondescript and boring, yet the house was warm and inviting despite its plain features. It was clean and extremely tidy for they both shared a strong distaste for utterly useless knickknacks of any sort, even those that may have short-term sentimental value. Dr. Paolo's two favorite items in the house were the burgundy-enameled Vermont Castings wood stove in the living room and the professional grade Viking gas stove in the kitchen. While the woodstove required only the lining of a chimney, the choice of the massive Viking required a complete overhaul and expansion of the original kitchen. Dante and Laura joked that upgrading the kitchen was proof that they were having a mid-life crisis, when in fact, it was a project they'd discussed on and off for over a decade. It was their first, and what would turn out to be their last, significant home improvement; they could not have been more pleased with the final result. The kitchen was stylish but practical, with clean lines and clear paths from the stainless steel Sub Zero refrigerator to the deep, two-tub ceramic sink to the stove to the cherry table with ample seating and effective lighting. The modern style cherry cabinets with soft close doors extended to the ceiling left no space unused.

Ironically, while they both enjoyed cooking and the company of close friends, they rarely entertained; they opted to dine out, or to be alone, after a hectic workweek so Friday night's dinner party with the students was a great diversion for both Dante and Laura. Indeed, when they thought about it, they hadn't hosted a dinner in well over a year when Dante's lab gathered for grilled hamburgers, chicken, and pork ribs to celebrate the acceptance of a manuscript, the first publication for one of the graduate students.

Dante developed the Friday night menu and, as usual, took the lead in the kitchen. An oven-roasted sirloin strip seasoned with olive oil, sea salt, coarsely ground pepper and garlic powder, complemented with steamed asparagus and a spinach salad. He also prepared a wild mushroom risotto with the hen of the woods harvested with the students on their fall hike. The combination of pungent dried porcini with the highly textured maitake created an earthy, aromatic creamy risotto that was an instant hit.

Laura reduced her patient load for that Friday and arrived home an hour earlier than usual to set the table with white square dishes, utensils, cloth napkins, water and wineglasses. The last few weeks had been hard on her too. Dante's refusal to be treated was a decision she disapproved of yet understood completely. Instinctively, she wanted him to fight, to seek treatment. It would be the course of action chosen by most patients without hesitation, even by those with no real hope of being cured. Over her years in practice, Laura had seen the debilitating effects of aggressive cancer therapy. Even when diagnosed at an early stage, the chemical poisons meant to destroy the rapidly growing cancer cells also killed healthy ones too. It was known as collateral damage, a situation that may be acceptable at early stages, but at stage IV the treatment would be worse than the disease itself; Dante would be weakened to the point of mental, as well as, physical surrender. On balance and with a stiff upper lip, Laura accepted the inevitable and vowed to let him do as he pleased. "It's been your life," she told her husband. "And it'll be your death."

The students arrived together promptly at six. Their youthful exuberances instantly converted the usually silent, reserved home into a boisterous atmosphere of greetings and introductions. While the students noticed Dr. Paolo's pale appearance it was not overly obvious and his physical presence went without being mentioned. They all were, however, quite eager to meet Laura whom they'd only heard of in passing, and in return, Laura was interested to meet them. Dante felt his spirits rise from the moment the four seniors entered the house from the dark winter's night. Technically they were no longer his students but figuratively he was still their teacher and mentor, and as of that moment, he became their friend—a rare triple play.

Despite the fancy tableware, the dinner was informal and relaxed. The menu pleased everyone's palate. They were all fond of beef and completely thrilled with the inclusion of the maitake in the perfectly prepared risotto. It delighted the host that Abby accepted a second serving of risotto and both Brad and Phil helped themselves to another slice of the sirloin strip. Interactions during the meal were quite pleasant and for the most part only one conversation ensued at a time. Amy and Brad peppered Laura with questions about the world of medicine that ultimately and predictably led to questions about how she met her husband which, in turn, led to separate, entertaining versions of their awkward first dates that really weren't dates in the formal sense but more like "planned spontaneous events" as described by Dr. Paolo.

The professor was not surprised to see his wife at ease with their young guests. She was uncharacteristically chatty that, together with her natural social charm, resulted in a pleasant atmosphere. The meal ended with a simple vanilla custard dessert prepared by Dr. Paolo served alongside the blueberry pie—a gift from the students.

It was at the dining room table over dessert, coffee and tea that the discussion turned to science. Dr. Paolo was glad that Laura stayed and listened to the discussion, as he had not told her about his hypothesis—it never occurred to him that she would find it interesting. And although she knew something about the telepathy experiments she did not know the results nor that Abby was the telepath. Moreover, she was unaware of her husband's ability to transmit thoughts telepathically. In fact, Laura would learn more about her husband's scientific passion and expertise in the next hour then what she had gathered over the past two decades combined.

With the dinner coming to a close it was time to discuss the plan. Amy glanced across the table, locked eyes with Abby and gave her a silent nod, although the nod itself was unnecessary.

"Dr. Paolo, we'd like to discuss a set of experiments to test your hypothesis," Abby said simply. Everyone around the table knew what Abby meant except Laura who looked quizzically at her husband.

Dr. Paolo saw his wife's knitted eyebrows and offered, "Abby is referring to a hypothesis I shared with them on the last day of class last semester. A hypothesis that was based on their collective research projects. It's kind of wild, but most of the elements are testable. Over break they came up with a plan to test one or more of these elements. That's one of the reasons we're here tonight."

"In fact Dr. Paolo, it was Abby who wrote the first draft of the experiments," said Amy who wanted to be sure to keep the record set straight right from the beginning.

"With help from Phil," added Abby as she looked at Phil sitting to her left.

For most of the evening Phil was quite reserved. From the moment he entered the house, he was strongly attracted to Dr. Paolo's wife and he was concerned that Abby would read his mind and roundly disapprove. As it was, ever since he saw her in the provocative outfit in class last November, Phil had also developed an attraction to Abby. So Phil spent most of the evening trying not to think about Abby, or now Laura, or anyone else's cleavage, which was quite a task given that both women wore enticingly loose fitting, low cut blouses. To put it mildly, it was a very challenging night for Phil.

"In fact," Abby continued, "I've incorporated everyone's comments in this proposal." Abby reached into her bag and produced a manila envelope. She opened it and gave the ten-page proposal to Phil who passed it along to Dr. Paolo. Turning to her right to face Laura, Abby said, "Sorry I only brought one copy."

"That's fine," said Laura who watched her husband flip through the pages.

"So would someone like to go over it and that way, we could all be included in the discussion?" asked Dr. Paolo.

Brad, Amy and Phil turned to Abby who described the experiments in details. Sounding like a seasoned researcher, Abby outlined the goals of two major experiments. She explained how the second experiment might need to be refined depending on the outcome of the first one and as such, they focused their energies on the initial key experiment.

Dr. Paolo couldn't believe what he was hearing.

The first experiment Abby described was related to mapping the area of the brain active during telepathic episodes. She discussed the latest brain imaging technology and the type of setup needed to perform the experiment. This experiment would be conducted similarly to the one designed for her class project but with the inclusion of brain imaging.

"I've sent Dr. Sukawa an email to ask if it was possible for us to use the equipment at his lab at MIT," said Brad who followed Abby's overview. "I sent it out yesterday and he hasn't responded yet but I'm hopeful that he will soon. The equipment he's developed would be perfect for this study."

"It's not invasive," added Amy, "so I don't see why he would object."

"Right," concurred Phil who chimed in mainly to steal another look at Laura.

Much to Dr. Paolo's surprise Laura was intently listening to the discussion and he could tell that she was eager to join in.

"Let me see if I have this right," began Laura. "You want to do a telepathy experiment and try to visualize brain activity as it's occurring?" she asked if it was a tossup question on a quiz show.

"That's correct," replied Amy.

"Whose brain?" Laura asked.

"Ideally, we would like image the brains of both the transmitter and the receiver at the same time," said Abby.

"That would be the best way," added Brad.

"What I meant to ask was who will be in the study?" asked Laura.

"Me and your husband," said Abby turning towards the professor.

"I see," continued Laura who was then briefed by her husband on what had transpired during the initial telepathy exercise. Having digested the information Laura continued, "So you want to repeat your first experiment and expand the project by adding the imaging aspect."

"Right," said Abby.

"Are you telling me that with all the recent studies on the brain including the mapping of neural pathways, and with all of the drugs available to control Parkinson's, AVMs, the delay of dementia—all this research and no one has done this exact experiment?" Laura continued.

"I didn't find anything remotely close to this when I did my research on the brain," Brad replied.

"Nor did I," added Abby.

"You'll need a control group," said Laura.

"Right. We thought to have Brad and Amy be the controls, although we really don't know what to expect," said Phil who couldn't shake Laura's seductive allure. He daydreamed a romantic scene where Dr. Paolo's wife made a strong move on him—he Ben, she Mrs. Robinson—a temporary spell broken by the sound of Mr. Robinson's voice.

"That's not a good idea," interjected Dr. Paolo. "Because then you change two variables. Each person is a variable. And before you suggest it, Amy, you're out all together as you would present a bias to the experiment because it's known that you are not telepathic. We'll have to have someone else take your place, either Brad or Phil...."

"Or Ajay," interrupted Abby. "He wants to be involved." Abby explained that she had discussed the experiments with Ajay over the break only after he vowed secrecy. He agreed to be discreet and he wanted to help with the data analysis aspects of the experiments.

"Okay, fine," said Dr. Paolo. "Brad, would you be willing to be the other test person?"

"Sure, that's fine with me."

"Alright, so now we wait to hear back from Dr. Sukawa and take it from there, right?" asked Dr. Paolo.

"Yes, okay. Do we want to review the second part of the experiment?" asked Abby.

"No, let me read it over and we'll reconvene again when we hear what Dr. Sukawa has to say. It would be moot to discuss more before we know if we can even do the experiment at all," said Dr. Paolo. "Okay? Is everyone okay with that?"

Everyone nodded in agreement.

"Good because I have something to tell you."

Abby looked down at her empty dessert plate as the others, including Laura, were looking directly at Dr. Paolo.

"I'm not sure how to say this, so I'll just say it simply. I have pancreatic cancer. I was diagnosed a few weeks ago and it's at an advanced stage, it's metastasized. I'm foregoing treatment because I don't want to be incapacitated during my remaining days. The length of time I have left is based on odds alone and treatment will do nothing more than to prolong the agony and rob me of some quality time. Cancers are on their own timetable and my body will do only what it can do to alter that timetable."

The room was absolutely silent as Dante continued. "Since the diagnosis I have dedicated all of my energies to the hypothesis. You've matched the design of my first experiment almost exactly, I just wasn't sure how it was going to be done. You've provided a great plan. Let's hope we can carry it out."

The students were stunned; no one but Abby suspected anything. She knew something was troubling Dr. Paolo all evening but she wasn't exactly sure what it was. She hoped that it was something minor but now she knew what everyone else knew, that it was quite serious. Inside she was devastated. Outwardly Abby didn't quite know how to respond. Neither did the others.

After a long moment, it was Amy who, in character, was able to quickly assess the situation and deliver a proper response on everyone's behalf. "Dr. Paolo, Laura, as you can see, we're all in shock. I don't think any of us can imagine what you two have been going through. We're very sorry, and," Amy paused to gain her composure, "thank you for telling us. For me, anyway, you have done more to solidify my career path than any other teacher at the college and because of that I am thankful. I'm ready to help out as much as I can with the hypothesis and with anything else you might need."

"Me too, Dr. Paolo," said Brad.

"And me," added Phil.

Abby looked at Laura and then turned to Dr. Paolo; she simply nodded in agreement. Her feelings for Dr. Paolo were more than she cared to share with everyone. She was afraid to speak for she knew that one word would expose her heart.

Dr. Paolo understood.

With the house once again silent Laura and Dante cleared the dining room table and straightened up the kitchen.

"I don't think they took that very well, do you?" Laura asked.

"As well as could be expected, I suppose. I had to tell them sooner or later."

"I guess there is never a good time. I've had many patients who refuse to talk about their illness even though they're on their deathbed. No one wants to admit it. You certainly are different that way."

"I think it was the right thing to do. When Amy and Brad get to medical school they'll learn how to handle dying people."

"And hopefully how to deal with the families of dying people. Sometimes they're harder to deal with then the patient." Laura's voice trailed off as, without prelude, a torrent of tears raced down her face. "Honey, I have to admit that I'm not dealing well with this. I'm just ignoring it. Pretending like it's not real. But it's real and..."

Dante rinsed his hands of soap, dried them with paper towels and he gave his wife a tender hug in the soft glow of the under cabinet lights. He was scared too but he didn't want to admit it, and he refused to show it. He tried to assure her that he had accepted his fate. He told her that their life together was wonderful and that he held no regrets.

The one part of his life that he did regret, however, went unspoken.

She knew. She knew that they were very close to having a family; that he came so close to being a father only to see it slip away at the last moment. It was their only disappointment as a couple, the only sorrow that they thought about daily and one that he would think about on the last day of his life.

With his wife swaying softly in his arms he again replayed the imaginary scenes, the snapshots of how it would have been, how it should have been. His mind saw the first clumsy steps, the one-year old birthday party with colorful balloons and a messy ice cream cake, the little body wrapped in a bulky snowsuit as unyielding as a straightjacket. Hot chocolate with toast made with his homemade bread and those ever-revolving joyous holidays. Halloween costumes that changed like the seasons over the ages. Thanksgiving. The nerve-wracking proms with dreaded boyfriends and expensive gowns; polite girlfriends, tentative sleepovers, expensive driving lessons, a new license and a used car, SATs, college, the empty nest; the wedding with the tear-jerking father-daughter dance; the first grandchild. Individual photos strung side-by-side on a clothesline like movie clips that played again and again and again, over and over and over they'd turn in his mind so relentless, so real that some nights, when his body flared in pain, he simply wanted it to end; he wanted to die.

"What the fuck!" Phil exclaimed from the backseat of the Audi. "We plow through three years with no issues then this guy shows up out of nowhere, takes us for a walk in the woods, teaches this wild class on how to do a science literature review and a presentation, comes up with this far-out hypothesis and we're all in—hook, line and sinker. Then he has us over for dinner, we come up with a great plan and then, to top it all off, he tells us that he's fucking dying. What the hell? Is this fucked or what?"

"It is kind of crazy when you add it all up," said Brad from the driver's seat.

"I agree with you Phil, but can you tell me who else at Wilmington has impacted you as much as Dr. Paolo?" asked Amy who kept an eye on the merging highway traffic from the front seat.

"I mean, why am I so interested in this? I should be more worried about getting into grad school, not some freaking bizarre hypothesis," continued Phil who was clearly agitated.

"Why do I keep thinking that this will get more and more interesting?" asked Amy.

"Because it probably will," replied Abby who was still reeling from Dr. Paolo's bombshell.

"Yeah, you're probably right," said Phil with a heavy sigh. "It probably will."

The email arrived from: Sukawa, Jin. Subject: re: Request. Date: January 31, 2012 06:08:11 PM EST. It was addressed to: McIntyre, Brad at his college address and it was copied to: Wyle, Robert. It read:

Brad,

Greetings from Japan and Happy New Year. I am here at the Neuroimaging Institute of Japan on sabbatical in the laboratory of a former graduate student. I'll be here for all of 2012. The experiment you described is very interesting and I think it should be done. I've cc'd Bob Wyle on this email. Bob is a scientist in my laboratory and a HHMI investigator working on new ways to label neural cells *in vivo*.

Bob, Brad is a lifelong friend and a senior at Wilmington College who would like to do a simple experiment as described below. Please contact him and make arrangements. Could be very interesting.

Best,

Jin

Continued below Dr. Sukawa's email was Brad's initial message. On Jan 21, 2012, at 7:43 PM, Brad MacIntyre wrote:

Dear Dr. Sukawa,

I hope this message finds you well as we enter this New Year. Do you recall my visit to your lab last fall as a part of the course I took at Wilmington College called Teach the Professor? Well a classmate in that class demonstrated her ability to send messages telepathically in a simple, yet convincing exercise. As you might expect, our professor, Dr. Dante Paolo (formerly of Harvard University) and the rest of the class (four total) wondered if the active part(s) of the brain during telepathic events has (have) been mapped. A review of the literature did not reveal any article that addressed that question specifically so I am writing to ask if you would be interested in helping us perform a telepathy experiment in your laboratory to visualize the area(s) of the brain that are active during telepathy. I look forward to your response and the very best to your family.

Sincerely,

Brad MacIntyre

2

An emotionally spent Laura went upstairs to bed and left her husband to fuss over the final wipe down of the kitchen. Dr. Paolo was physically exhausted but mentally he was wide-awake. It was a combination that usually led to a restless night so instead of going to bed and risk bothering Laura, he laid down on the cool leather sofa in the living room and covered himself with the tan colored wool blanket his mother knitted for the newlyweds twenty-six years ago; in less than a minute he was lulled into a deep sleep by the low grinding hum of the dishwasher.

It was his mother he recognized first. She appeared from the left part of the darkness. But something about her was different, strangely different. The person he recognized as his mother did not resemble the woman he knew as a child, nor when he was a young man, nor was she as he remembered her at any time in his life. She was not the well-worn old lady who died only four short years ago; she was younger, much younger. She looked like the little girl with ponytails in the old, small and partially faded black and white pictures with the wavy borders. She was perhaps twelve or thirteen years old. She was neither clothed nor naked; her features were soft, subtle and through direct eye-to-eye contact they instantly knew each other and of their perpetual relationship and, without a word uttered and with no gestures, she beckoned him to come to her. What did she want? Then without fanfare his father emerged from the darkness behind his child-mother. He appeared as a young man in his early twenties; his hair a tad wild yet befitting for his round full face. His child-mother and twenty-something father appeared to know each other although they did not interact nor did they utter a word. The child-mother looked concerned while the twenty-something father seemed content and showed no signs of the effects of the lung cancer that killed him. The once proud two-pack-a-day chain smoker suffered greatly but he was now carefree, his vile addiction mattered no longer, the pain absent.

Abruptly his oddly aged parents disappeared and his treasured auntie Kay, deceased for over a decade but never forgotten, appeared from the right. She presented herself as he remembered her when they would spend time together at the art museums, or at the ice cream parlors, or at the movies. She was appropriately aged; it matched his memories directly and with such clarity came memories so vivid, so real that he instantly longed for her; asleep he wept. Auntie Kay's face lacked expression. She was neither happy nor sad as she faced him and, as with his oddly aged parents, no words were exchanged yet Dante knew that she too coveted him. Then, like a dove released from a magician's empty satin gloves a young man emerged from behind auntie Kay. He stood to her left and faced Dr. Paolo. He too was expressionless and seemingly without want or need. Then, auntie Kay and the young man vanished.

Dante's eyes popped wide open. He could feel his heart thump-thump, thump-thump in his chest. He felt flush, strange, stupefied. Slowly his hearing returned and sounds were processed just in time for him to receive the long solitary beep that signaled the end of the dishwasher's power scrub cycle. A confused tear rolled down his right cheek and onto the corner of the damp pillow. He awoke exhausted.

3

As instructed by email, Brad called Bob's cell phone to announce their arrival at the entrance of Building 6, which was secured by a card swipe. Dressed in worn blue jeans and an old black and white checkered flannel shirt with a torn right elbow over a gray Red Sox tee shirt, Bob Wyle with his thick black curly hair looked like a genius to Amy, Brad, Abby, Phil and Ajay but to Dr. Paolo he was a typical high-achieving, pretentious slob.

Bob kept a disheveled office adjacent to Dr. Sukawa's laboratory packed with all sorts of electronics.

Building 6 was built in 1904 when red bricks ruled the landscape and before anyone had the cunning idea to allow wealthy donors the opportunity to adhere their names on buildings in return for even greater donations. The design of the plain, five-story rectangular building on a narrow street named Milky Way stood in sharp contrast to the newest MIT building—The Dr. and Mrs. Oliver St. James Hall—which stood directly across the street from Building 6. St. James Hall, with its gravity-defying corners protruding off-angle to the building's main stainless steel and aluminum façade and oddly shaped windows, looked like it was modeled after remnants of Lego pieces that survived a toddler's temper tantrum.

"I love it here on the weekends, especially Saturday morning when everyone's still hung over from Friday night, no one's around," stated Bob as he led the visitors to the stairs for the climb to the second floor.

"No party for you?" asked Dr. Paolo.

"No way," responded Bob. "We're nearing the end of our pregnancy, or rather, my wife is nearing the end of her pregnancy. I'm sort of just watching at this point. There's no way I can leave her to be miserable alone. We're pretty much home bodies anyway."

"That's great," said Dr. Paolo who was feeling a bit winded as they reached the door labeled 6-2 on landing to the floor as if everyone needed a reminder of which building they were in. "When's your due date?"

"A couple of weeks, thirteen days or so. I guess it's tough to predict the first one, at least that's what they told us, who knows," rambled Bob to the group that was larger in number then he had expected. They walked down the empty corridor; past Bob's cluttered office through the laboratory and into an adjacent room that was furnished only with a small wood table, three chairs, and a computer table with a keyboard, mouse and monitor.

"We call this the *Subject Room*. It's where test subjects are placed, and this room," said Bob as he walked through the subject room and into a smaller room that was connected by a heavily padded door, "is what we call the *Control Room* also known as the 'crazy cube' because of the padded walls."

"Padding?" asked Amy.

"Insulation. The *Control Room* is insulated so the subject doesn't hear us. We can see them through this one-way mirror and we can hear them because the room is wired with microphones but the subject can't see or hear us."

"What if you have to leave during the experiment?" asked Phil who was surveying all the high tech equipment and devices in the *Control Room*.

"Someone is always present during an experiment. Everything is monitored but if someone has to leave while the experiment is in progress we can use this small door," Bob replied pointing a small, virtually invisible pad-covered door at the far end of the room.

The *Control Room* had a console that manipulated cameras and audio equipment hidden in the *Subject Room*. It also had a computer with side-by-side monitors and a small refrigerator. The one-way mirror, located in front of the console, provided a clear view of the well-lit *Subject Room*.

"So how does this all work?" Dr. Paolo asked.

"Okay, so let's say we're studying the difference in brain activity from olfactory stimulation like when someone smells something like vanilla or cigarette smoke," said Bob who went into the *Subject Room* carrying what appeared to be a blue ski hat. "The subject is seated here," he explained pointing to one of the chairs or we can bring in a couch or a bed or a recliner or whatever we think is necessary for the particular experiment and then we simply ask the subject to relax and to put on this hat." Bob explained that the unassuming blue hat was, in fact, a fourth generation prototype combination detector and transmitter of brain activity. Inside the hat was a rubber liner embedded with two hundred and fifty sets of micro probes and transmitters spaced evenly and symmetrically. Each probe is able to detect the electrical moment created when a cluster of neurons are activated. The entire hat could measure the electrical moment created by approximately one hundred million neurons or one thousandth of the total potential activity of all one hundred billion neurons in the brain. The measurement from each probe was transmitted wirelessly to a small receiver that looked like a mini satellite dish perched next to the computer inside the *Control Room*.

"I've been working on this baby for ten years," said Bob as he held out the blue hat for all to see. "This is only the second one ever made that sends data wirelessly to a computer, and not only that but it's about four-times as sensitive as its predecessor which means that, for the first time, we can get clear images without asking the subject to shave their hair! Only two like this in the world," he chuckled. "Patent pending, of course."

"Subjects had to shave off all of their hair?" asked Amy.

"Yeah, well we had to with the wired hats and going bald was a deal breaker for most recruits. Hell, I've shaved my head so many times I've gotten used to it. Being bald is more efficient, actually. Me and the monkeys, neither of us cared."

"Monkeys?" asked Abby. "You can do experiments on monkeys?"

"Yeah, this hat has made it much easier to study the activity of nonhuman primates. Before, when the hats had all sorts of wires, they would tear them apart and essentially destroy them. Now we just have to train them not to take it off and that part's not too bad. It's actually works."

"How many monkeys do you have?" asked Abby who knew as soon as she completed the sentence that Bob was not comfortable with the question. For some reason he did not want to talk about monkeys and Phil's question, which overlapped Abby's question, gave Bob the clear way out.

"So two hundred fifty measurements are sent to the computer and then what?" asked Phil.

"Then what is right," echoed Bob as he placed the blue hat on the small table and made his way back to the *Control Room*. Sitting in front of the computer Bob entered a passcode and logged on. He moved the cursor to the star-like icon in the left side of the screen labeled *JSImage* and clicked on it.

"Imaging software?" asked Ajay who was positioned to Bob's right.

"Yup, Dr. Sukawa wrote it himself," said Bob. "It's awesome and it allows for ... well here, I'll show you." With a few targeted clicks Bob opened a dataset labeled Cookie and tiles of small images filled the large monitor. Bob explained that each tile contained fifteen minutes of data received from the hat during an experiment. He then clicked on a tile with a label positioned on the bottom center in tiny print *2012.01.02. Cookie.00:00:30*. The tile sprang open and produced a grid of images that filled the entire monitor.

"Each image is a composite of all of the data transmitted by the two hundred fifty sensors taken at that one timepoint," said Bob staring at the image on the screen. "A reading was taken every ten seconds."

"So," said Phil thinking aloud, "that's two hundred fifty images, ten seconds times six is fifteen hundred data points a minute times fifteen minutes is...um...twenty-two...um...two-two-five...twenty two thousand five hundred every fifteen minutes or um...ninety thousand data points per hour. Holy cow! That's incredible."

"And if you take four consecutive fifteen minute blocks," said Bob as he highlighted *2012.01.02.Cookie.00:00:30*, *2012.01.02.Cookie.00:00:45*, *2012.01.02.Cookie.00:00:60*, and *2012.01.02.Cookie.00:01:15* and opened them all together, "you can see a one-minute time lapse of the signals in three dimensions."

The monitor displayed a small brain in gray tones. When Bob clicked on the right arrow, a progress bar made its way from left to right momentarily flashing the exact time in ten-second intervals. Different areas of the small brain flashed white then receded back to gray while other areas flashed white as still other areas remained dark.

"Here's where Sukawa's program is better than all of the others." And with a slight click of the mouse, the pointer turned into a small hand and Bob was able to rotate the brain in every direction as the time lapse continued. "These white explosions are where the brain activity is greatest at that instant."

"This is amazing! The clarity is stunning," exclaimed Dr. Paolo who was standing towards the back of the tightly packed students.

"It's the balls," replied Bob.

"So, these white explosions are activity on the surface of the brain, right? And that's not a human brain, right?" asked Brad.

"Exactly," replied Bob. "In fact, this experiment was done on a monkey, a rhesus macaque named Cookie after the *Cookie Monster* because we trained him to keep the hat on by rewarding him with cookies. We usually use M&Ms but we ran out so we used chocolate chip cookies we found in someone's lunch and, well Cookie didn't mind the change. And yes, this is surface activity. Part of the experiment was to test a new combination small molecule tracer to visualize activity inside the brain, and we also modified the software to allow the sensors to scan horizontally across and through the brain instead of just scanning in the inward direction. I haven't had much of a chance to look at these data but at the fifteen-minute mark, the handler gave Cookie the tracer through a PICC line, you know a peripherally inserted central catheter, that we, or I should say the vet, inserted in Cookie's arm earlier in the day so we didn't have to jab the monkey during the experiment."

"Direct access to the heart. Instant dispersal of the tracer," commented Amy.

"Exactly," replied Bob without taking his eyes off the monitor as he highlighted panels 2012.01.02.Cookie.00:15:00, 2012.01.02.Cookie.00:15:15, 2012.01.02.Cookie.00:15:30, and 2012.01.02.Cookie.00:15:45.

Instantly, an image of Cookie's small brain appeared on the screen. Bob hit the play button to start the clip and, like fanning through a deck of cards, the images of Cookie's brain were seen as a progression of top-to-bottom slices. But instead of the small white explosions seen earlier on the surface of the monkey's brain, the internal scans showed explosions that looked more like diffuse lightning that stretched across a stormy night's sky.

"Holy cow!" was all Bob said as he stopped the progression freezing an image that showed a large amount of diffuse light. With everyone watching his every move, he then pulled down a menu on upper part of the computer screen and activated a set of tools. The icons resembled photo-editing tools but they seemed to be slightly different. Bob chose a dampening tool and used the pop-up slide bar to adjust the image brightness.

"Lowering the pixel intensity?" asked Ajay.

"Yeah, except this tool also enhances the distribution of light on each pixel so the data are actually sharpened." And with that simple adjustment, the diffuse lightning honed in on individual strands that stretched mostly to the right with just a few strands extended towards the base of the brain. Bob sat back in his chair, stared at the screen and folded his arms and with a smile stretching across his face calmly said, "Look at those signals. Would you look at those signals? No one else in the world has seen synaptic activity like that before, no one. This is Nobel Prize stuff, this is beautiful, just look at that! *RW88*, you're almost perfect, baby."

Dr. Paolo couldn't believe his luck. In less than an hour he and his students had not only been exposed to the latest advances in brain imaging technology but they also witnessed a scientific discovery—that rare moment in research when something actually worked, when experiments turned out as planned, when the study revealed something new. Dr. Paolo, more than anyone else in the room, appreciated these scarce and fleeting moments in a scientist's life.

"What do you mean 'almost perfect'," asked Abby. "Why wasn't it perfect?"

Bob spun his chair around to face Abby and his small audience. "*RW88* is the eighty-eighth version of the tracer I've been developing. Most all of our studies on *RW88* have been done *in vitro* on cultured monkey neuroglial cells. But those are mostly tox studies. We test the toxicity of the tracer on the cells before we administer it to animals. *RW88* looked good with cultured cells and it even passed studies in mice so we went ahead and got approval to use it in this experiment with Cookie."

"Well it looked like it worked," said Phil.

"That it did," replied Bob who stood up, opened a cabinet above the computer and retrieved a vial labeled *RW88*. "The images look beautiful, but there is just one hitch," he said as he placed the vial next to the keyboard and spun his chair back to the computer. He then moved a new window and opened Cookie's entire dataset. "Here," he said pointing to the file positioned to the far right of the screen labeled 2012.01.02.Cookie.

00:16:15, "at the sixteen minute mark, or about one minute after *RW88* was administered, Cookie had a seizure and died. It happened so fast, so violently, that the handler didn't even have time to euthanize him. We're lucky the vet wasn't physically injured, but mentally she's a wreck. She was very close to Cookie."

The sound of Bob's cellphone chiming the first ten seconds of the *William Tell Overture* interrupted the short discussion that followed the description of Cookie's unfortunate death. The call was a sharp reminder from his wife of their appointment with the OB/GYN at eleven-thirty. Bob told his expectant wife one of those "white lies" that his mother said was permissible as long as no one gets in serious trouble. He lied that he was well aware of the time and that he'd be there to pick her up shortly. In fact, the appointment had completely slipped his mind. He would have to scramble to arrive home within his usual ten-minute tardiness window.

Bob grabbed his backpack and apologized for having to leave so abruptly. He promised to get in touch with Brad so that they could schedule a time to do their experiment. On their way out of the Building 6, Dr. Paolo and the students thanked him for his time, for giving them a tour and for showing them the equipment. Standing outside in the bright, late morning sunlight on Milky Way, Bob waved goodbye to the visitors, glanced at his watch then broke into a light jog.

Dr. Paolo and his students walked a short way up Milky Way to one of Cambridge's original coffee and donut shops. There, among the sweet atmosphere of sugar and oils, and the sounds of clanking plates, the small group discussed what they had just experienced.

"That was really exciting stuff," commented Phil. "But man, it seems like such a long way from where I am now to being a scientist like Bob."

"I agree," Ajay added. "And what about that program? It must be so complex to be able to gather and analyze so much data. I wouldn't know where to begin. It's amazing."

"My dad has shown me some of the stuff he worked on when they were developing the genome sequencers. I remember a team of about six people who worked on computer programs just to run the robotics and another team that did nothing but design software to read the sequences."

"Was he a programmer?" asked Ajay.

"No, not really. He knew some programming but he's a mechanical engineer and he was the head of a group that made the automated DNA sequencers."

"You know, not to change the subject, but I think we experienced a 'eureka moment' when Bob saw the results of the tracer," said Brad.

"Oh, that's for sure," Phil said as he reached for another glazed donut, "that was really cool."

"And what about poor Cookie?" asked Abby who had been a bit anxious all morning with the thought of doing another telepathy experiment. "Dr. Paolo, what do you think she died of?"

"He," corrected Amy, "Cookie was a male."

"Right," said Abby, "what do you think he died of?"

Dr. Paolo calmly looked around the coffee shop to see who might be in earshot of their discussion. He knew that their topic could draw the attention of any busybody, but he was particularly worried about the rabid animal lover who was opposed to the use of animals in research. Fortunately, the place was mostly empty and their corner booth provided sufficient privacy against the two old men seated at the counter in their familiar daily stools, and the young couple seated at a booth at the far end of the shop.

"I have no idea," said Dr. Paolo's honestly. "It could be anything, but the tracer must be able to cross the blood-brain barrier in order to get to the brain from the peripheral blood, right?"

"Yeah that's right," Brad said. "The BBB is a highly selective gateway that does not allow most things to get to the brain. Sugar, oxygen, water, and amino acids, I think, are the only things that can cross this barrier. It's a cool way of protecting the brain from toxic substances in our blood. So if Cookie seized, it would make sense that it was the tracer... well, right the tracer would have crossed the BBB in order to see the images, so perhaps it was the wrong dose? Could it have been a dosing problem?"

"Who knows," said Dr. Paolo. "We could speculate on this all day but it won't solve the problem. They'll probably need to do a post-mortem so they'll know exactly what happened."

"Didn't Bob say that the tracer was safe in mice?" asked Amy.

"Yeah, he did say that," Brad replied.

"But remember," added Dr. Paolo, "mice are rodents and monkeys are primates, like us, and although we are primates too, monkeys are different. They're only animal models and sometimes the model accurately predicts what will happen in humans, and well, sometimes it doesn't."

"But those images were awesome," said Phil who was not interested in discussing the pros and cons of using animals as research tools.

"You can say that again," said Brad. "I wonder what else they learned from that experiment."

"Cookie paid the ultimate price," said Abby softly who had mixed feelings about the use of animals in research.

"Well Abby," said Dr. Paolo, "think of it this way. Cookie probably did more to advance our knowledge of science than most of us ever will. You can rest assured that he did not die in vain and what they learned from that experiment may one day lead to discoveries that could benefit everyone."

"Or the experiment could simply have shown that beautiful images of the brain can be obtained with a lethal tracer," retorted Abby whose words hung heavily in the sugary atmosphere of the donut shop for a few lengthy seconds.

"True enough," replied Dr. Paolo sullenly. "True enough."

The clear moonlit evening was wild at 1:37 a.m. Dante could almost feel the house bending against the strong, persistent winds that rush down unabated from the Canadian Arctic permafrost. From the warmth of his bed he visualized the tall pines on the knoll above the wetlands surrounding his home arching and bending back and forth, begging for mercy. Branches of the near frozen pines could be heard snapping off, in essence sacrificing themselves for the sake of the entire tree. He remembered that the temperature was forecasted to be around zero and he guessed that the wind was gusting at close to fifty mile per hour; the wind chill would be near something he didn't want to experience. He thought about his remaining days as he turned onto his left side and backed himself into Laura's warmth. He could tell that the cancer was taking over his body but he was determined not to let it invade his mind. He knew that he was slowing down, his energy lagging despite his self-prescribed intake of fortified green juices, and vitamins with essential minerals prepared specifically for silver-haired men. He thought about Abby and Bob and the laboratory on Milky Way. And with his eyes closed in a vague sleep, Dante thought about his hypothesis, the experiment that he wanted to do with his students, and the experiment with Cookie and the monkey's final moments. His thoughts were screaming like the wind, bounding from topic to topic. He thought about his cancer, then he imagined the veterinarian's shock as Cookie with his head covered with the strange blue cap went into a wild, thrashing seizure; his final brain activity captured electronically for all to see, his final...

Suddenly his eyes opened and darted across the moon lit room like they were tracking a lone pinball bouncing off bumpers, kickers and flippers. Then, like the absolute truth of placing the final oddly shaped piece of a jigsaw puzzle into it's now obvious space—a space that had been there all along—Dante Paolo unequivocally and completely reconciled his hypothesis. With the revelation firmly cemented in his mind, he rose out of bed, slipped on his sweatpants and sweater, and made his way downstairs to the small study. In front of the computer, to the sounds of the howling winds, he typed nonstop for four hours until the very faintest light from the sun could be seen peering from behind the weary pines to the east.

4

Dr. Bob Wyle reached up and pulled a black three-ring binder from the shelf above the computer cluster in the *Control Room*. In the two weeks since he first met Dr. Paolo and his students Bob worked feverishly to meet grant deadlines and put the finishing touches on a manuscript. He also reviewed experiments with the younger members of the laboratory before his wife's regularly spaced contractions turned into regularly spaced contractions with real meaning. The long days and sleepless nights were taking a toll on Bob; he looked physically more disheveled then ever and he had significantly less energy.

"Here are the standard operating procedures for both the hat and the program," the HHMI scientist told the group pointing to the three-ring binder. "You simply need to follow the instructions step-by-step and you'll be able to run the experiment by yourself," he assured them. Phil and Ajay told Bob that they were proficient with computer programs and all they needed was a quick primer on how to start a new file to collect data.

As the students were listening to Bob's every word, Dr. Paolo was eyeing the vial labeled *RW88* that was to the left of the keyboard towards the back of the desk next to a cup of pens. He noticed hand-written notations on a second label on the vial but he could not decipher them from his vantage point. From experience he knew that the inscriptions could be the date the mixture was made, the initials of the formulator, the dose that should be used or an expiration date; it could also have a common warning: *For Experimental Use Only.*

The *William Tell Overture* barely had a chance to start when Bob answered the cell phone held firmly in his hand. It was his sister-in-law who said that she was taking her sister to the hospital because things were progressing rapidly and there was no time to spare. She told Bob that they'd meet him at the Labor and Delivery ward of University Hospital. The soon-to-be father ended the call and quickly showed Ajay and Phil how to start a new file. He also had the presence of mind to show them the commands needed to receive data from two hats simultaneously. As he reached for his jacket Bob told Dr. Paolo that the other wireless hat was in the large drawer in the *Control Room* and to call him if they needed anything. He also told them not to worry about locking up the lab when they left because he'd probably be back later in the day, and that security would secure the lab in any case. The students followed Bob from the small *Control Room* to the *Subject Room* where they wished him well.

"The other hat's in that big drawer," he said as the door closed behind him.

Suddenly finding himself alone in the *Control Room*, Dr. Paolo didn't hesitate to place vial *RW88* in the right pocket of his trousers. He then told the students that he was going to the men's room and instructed them to prepare to perform the experiment as discussed.

Dr. Paolo was the only person in the rather cool men's room on the second floor of Building 6. He entered the stall by the far wall then closed and latched the small door. In the dim light he read what was written on both labels on the vial. On one label, handwritten in black marker was *RW88*, and on the other label that wrapped to the back of the vial read *11/11/12, exp. 5/13, Animal Use Only, 0.02 ml/kg*. Dr. Paolo reached into his jacket pocket and retrieved a syringe he had taken from his own laboratory years ago. He plunged the needle of the 3cc syringe into the gray rubber septum of vial *RW88*, held the vial upright and withdrew just over 2 milliliters of the tracer. He then withdrew the syringe and slipped the vial back in his pants pocket. Carefully, Dr. Paolo recapped the syringe that now contained the deep pink fluorescent fluid and placed it back in its original wrapping, then into a clear plastic toothbrush holder. The holder containing the syringe fit snugly in the inside pocket of Dr. Paolo's overcoat.

Dr. Paolo purposefully removed his overcoat while striding across the *Subject Room* where everyone but Ajay was present.

"I'll hang up my coat and be right back," he told the students as he walked into the *Control Room* where he found Ajay seated in front of the computer console. Dr. Paolo put his coat on the hanger by the door, and placed the vial in his left hand. He then sat to Ajay's left, leaned on the table and, in a moment when Ajay was focused on the right computer monitor, returned the vial to its original place on the table next to the cup of pens.

"Were you able to start a new file?" Dr. Paolo asked as he nudged the binder of standard operating procedures to the back of the table making sure it knocked over the vial along with the cup of pens. Ajay, who had momentarily turned to his left to witness Dr. Paolo straightening up the vial and the rest of the fallen items, answered, "No problem. We're ready when you are."

Everyone agreed that Abby and Amy would be seated at the table in the *Subject Room* and that Abby would wear the blue hat. Dr. Paolo would don the gray-colored hat and be seated in the *Control Room* with Brad as his assistant; they would face away from the computer console and the one-way mirror. They would also not interact with Phil and Ajay who would monitor the computer program and the data collection.

As they had discussed a few days before arriving at MIT, Abby asked Ajay to have his computer program randomly generate then print two sets of twenty images, as he had done last semester. Ajay placed the images in two manila envelopes and taped them closed. With everyone in place and the wireless hats firmly on Dr. Paolo and Abby the experiment was ready to begin. Phil initiated the program. Silently, the two computer programmers watched as the right monitor showed an image of Abby's brain and the adjacent monitor pictured Dr. Paolo's brain. Activity was evident by the momentary flashes of white on one area of the brain that quickly moved to another region as if it was a game of cat and mouse except that the mouse was running in apparently random directions like a frightened rabbit.

The experiment was ready to begin although what Ajay and Phil had not realized was that the experiment had indeed already started but it had nothing to do with images on computer screens. After they slipped on their hats, Dr. Paolo and Abby opened one of the three little screw-capped collection tubes provided by Amy. Using the little scoop-like attachment that was on the inside of the cap, they scraped the inside of their own cheek with an up and down motion then secured the cap back onto the tube. Dr. Paolo handed the tube to Brad who labeled it "DP BEFORE" and Abby handed her tube to Amy who labeled it "AL BEFORE." Amy and Brad also recorded the time and date of the sample on the little vial and placed the tubes in a lunch bag that contained an ice pack. Cheek cells would be sampled two additional times over the next thirty minutes.

The telepathy experiment began in earnest when Ajay retrieved a manila envelope from his backpack, handed it to Brad then opened the door to the *Subject Room* to tell the women that the experiment was underway. At the minute mark, Brad removed an image from the manila envelope and handed it to Dr. Paolo who looked at it for approximately 10 seconds before closing his eyes to eliminate distractions. Within that same minute, in the soundproof room, Abby described to Amy the image transmitted by Dr. Paolo. Amy dutifully recorded the data in a bound notebook. Through the one-way mirror Ajay and Phil quietly observed Abby's mouth move and Amy recording the answer while keeping their eyes on the monitors; the little green light to the upper right part of the program window indicating that data collection was in progress.

The process was repeated nineteen more times with Brad handing Dr. Paolo a new image exactly on the minute mark. At the third minute of the experiment, Ajay had the idea of noting the elapsed time on the computer program when Abby gave her response; although they had not discussed this detail, he correctly thought that noting the time of this timing might be useful when they analyzed the data. He also noticed that Abby responded with remarkable regularity just before the half-minute mark as if she had no difficulties silently receiving the simple colorful images sent from Dr. Paolo's mind.

Nineteen minutes and thirty seconds after the experiment began, Amy wrote Abby's response, "red candle" in the notebook by the number 20, then gave the thumbs up signal to the reflective side of the one-way mirror to let Phil and Ajay know that they were done. Phil and Ajay waited 30 more seconds before they stopped collecting data and informed everyone that the experiment had ended.

The entire experiment was repeated but with Amy and Ajay seated in the *Subject Room* and Phil and Brad in the *Control Room*. Abby and Dr. Paolo were positioned at the computer console. Brad, who wore the blue hat, was to send telepathic messages to Ajay, who sported the gray hat. As had been done earlier, cheek cells from both participants were collected and placed in the cooler at timed intervals. A new set of simple, colorful images was produced and the experiment began with Phil showing the first image to Brad. Abby could not see the images, as she was watching the computer monitor that was dutifully collecting and displaying data transmitted from both hats, as it had done previously.

At the end of the second session, everyone gathered in the *Control Room* where Amy gave her notebook, with both Abby and Ajay's responses, to Dr. Paolo who had by this time gathered the manila envelopes that contained the now numbered images. As instructed, Amy had placed a number in the upper right hand corner of each picture to indicate the order in which they were shown.

"This is remarkable!" exclaimed Dr. Paolo as he made his way down Amy's list of Abby's responses while flipping through the images. "Perfect! Not one wrong, simply amazing."

"For me, it was easier this time," said Abby who was not at all surprised with the results.

"Why do you think it was easier," asked Phil who again recognized the subtle beauty in Abby's round face.

"I don't know...perhaps this is a more comfortable setting?"

"I felt more relaxed even with the strange hat on my head," said Dr. Paolo. "I think I was more focused this time too."

Dr. Paolo then reviewed Ajay's responses. Most were blank; not one was correct.

"I'm convinced," said Amy as she glanced over at the computer monitors. "Dr. Paolo you are one great transmitter and Abby, you're one hell of a receiver. And you two," she said pointing to both Brad and Ajay, "you two have some work to do." Everyone laughed as the computer program went into the automatic save and backup mode. The program then began to render the images into a continuous movie for playback analysis, a process that would take approximately eight hours according to the countdown time ticker. Ajay followed Amy's glance at the monitors and anticipated her question.

"The rendering will be completed about eight or nine tonight, and there is no way to review the data before the rendering and backup functions are complete. This part of the program is ironclad, it's critical, but I can tell you that there was quite a bit of activity from both Dr. Paolo and Abby during the experiment."

"Abby and I saw quite a bit of activity from you and Brad too," said Dr. Paolo who followed up with two quick questions. "Who will analyze the data once it's rendered? Will we need this special program?"

"The manual says that the rendering will save the data in a raw format that can be readily converted to many common video formats. But I think the best way to analyze the data is with Dr. Sukawa's program, at least that's what I understand," said Phil. "What would be ideal..."

But before Phil completed his sentence, the back door to the small *Control Room* abruptly swung open.

Jo Jung-Zoo was an unassuming graduate student in the Integrative Biology Department at MIT. His slender frame, well hidden in the oversized down-filled bright red winter jacket, made him look like the Michelin Man with an attitude. Jo was as startled to see the *Control Room* full of people as they were to see him. Through black, horn-rimmed glasses he surveyed each person in the small, padded room and focused his gaze on the group's elder.

"Hello, I'm Dante Paolo," said the professor as he extended his right hand to the young man. Jo bowed to Dr. Paolo as he extended his right hand in an awkward and weak effort to shake the stranger's hand.

"Aaa, my name is aaa... Jo, aaa... Jo Jung-Zoo," he replied in rapid, broken English. "I from... aaa ... Korea to aaa... study with Dr. Sukawa at MIT. Using his right hand's thumb to touch the same hand's pinky, then ring, middle and forefinger, Jo added, "I... aaa... at MIT four monts...aaa four monts tomorrow," as if the exact length of time that he's been at the institution was vital information to everyone's existence.

"Pleased to meet you Jo," said Dr. Paolo. "Let me introduce you to Abby, Amy, Brad, Ajay and Phil. We're friends of Dr. Sukawa and Bob...."

Jo nodded to each person then, with a look of relief at making a connection, said, "Aaa...Bob. Bob my boss. I work with Bob at MIT. Okay, Bob told me about...umm...friend Dr. Paolo. Aaa...okay, okay, I know. Now I know. Okay."

Seizing the opportunity to extract information that was missing from the standard operating procedures, Phil asked Jo, "Would you know if it's possible to access our data file remotely?"

Without removing his oversized red winter jacket, Jo took a seat in front of the computer and proceeded to describe how to access the files from anywhere in the world. Phil and Ajay followed Jo's quick maneuvers and they also made note of the long and convoluted username and password required for access. Jo also confirmed that Dr. Sukawa's program was needed to critically analyze the data but that the conversion of the rendered raw file to common movie formats would also allow for good qualitative evaluation of the data.

Following Jo's quick tutorial, the students and Dr. Paolo again found themselves back on Milky Way, headed for the subway, out of the city and home to Wilmington College. Dr. Paolo considered a return trip to the donut shop but then thought better of the idea when he suddenly began to feel nervous about the syringe in the toothbrush holder tucked in his coat pocket. As an adult he knew that he had committed a serious crime, but as a scientist Dante Paolo knew that it was much greater than a common theft. Removing potentially lethal biological or chemical substances from a research laboratory would trigger a Level 4 Emergency and Containment Response that would involve local, state, and federal authorities. He, the students along with Bob who was at that moment becoming a father, and Jo, who undoubtedly would still be dressed in his oversized, red winter jacket, would also be arrested and detained for questioning. And with Dr. Sukawa out of the country, the episode would quickly escalate to an international affair. Conspiracy theories would sprout quicker than mold in a spa. It would become a research institution's ultimate nightmare. Needless to say, using public transportation and running the risk of exposing large numbers of innocent people only doubled the jeopardy. Given the situation, Dr. Paolo wasn't thinking about coffee or donuts or lunch or even his cancer, he just wanted to get home safely and without incident.

———◦———

Dr. Benedetti stared out the large picture window in his living room. Perched on the backyard birdfeeder, the red male cardinal looked brilliant against the background of the evergreen pine trees whose branches were struggling to hold large clumps of wet white snow that fell from the mid-February gray skies.

"Green, white and red—*i colori dell'Italia,* he thought as his mind transported him back to the flag that hung in the corner of his Italian schoolroom where a nun taught religion, reading and writing and another woman, who was not a nun, came three times a week to teach English and mathematics. As he reflected on his childhood, his thoughts turned to his father and how fortunate he was to have been raised by those with a deep knowledge of nature; a type of understanding that extended well beyond what was needed simply to survive. Parents and grandparents challenged young Lorenzo to dig deeper, to ask questions no matter how basic they were and also, perhaps most importantly, they taught him to challenge answers too. Thoughts of his father led to memories of a hysterical scene seared into his young mind when news, delivered frantically by someone who burst into their small kitchen, of the death of his uncle—his father's brother—who was a reluctant soldier drafted to defend a crazed dictator.

The cardinal flitted away but Lorenzo Benedetti's thoughts remained in the Tuscan hillsides of his youth when life was rich, despite their humble existence and the ever-present uncertainties of life amid war. He remembered being content, not deprived or as poor as they really were, but satisfied with their simple ways. The few possessions he had, he treasured. They were small things like a magic propeller stick whittled by his grandfather from the branch of a chestnut tree, and a pet snake he caught in the woods, or new socks that were knitted in secrecy after he went to bed so they would be a surprise on his birthday; these items were his world.

Then, as abruptly as the cardinal's departure, he was back to snow-laden New England. He instantly felt lonely and old in his well-worn sweater, and when he felt this way—which became more frequent since the death of his companion—he would pour himself a second glass of red wine and write to his cousin in Tuscany. In the past their letters would be long and hand-written but now they corresponded by email because all of Italy, even it's most remote mountain villages like the one where Rosa lives, can access the Internet. Dr. Benedetti wrote:

> My dear cousin Rosa,
>
> I type these words on a dark, dismal cold and snowy Saturday in February feeling rather desolate. I long for your company and for the rejuvenating warmth of your Tuscan sun.

———•———

Dr. Paolo walked into an empty house and without removing his over-coat went directly upstairs to the comfortable family room that sported a large flat screen television, a leather sectional sofa and an outdated black Formica-topped bar. Feeling like the thief he was, he placed the tooth-brush holder containing the loaded syringe in the small freezer compartment inside the empty compact refrigerator tucked, unplugged, behind the bar. He didn't know the stability of *RW88* at room temperature or how long it would remain in this exact location, but he did know what it did to Cookie, and that's all the information he needed.

———•———

Because heat was included in the price of his monthly rent, Ajay's apartment was not just warm, it was downright steamy—just the way he liked it. In the midst of a snowstorm raging outside, the five seniors gathered at Ajay's place where they shared two pizzas, beers and each other's company. Even before the last slice was consumed, Ajay and Phil had logged onto Dr. Sukawa's lab computer using the username and password shared by Jo earlier that day. The MIT lab's computer was accessed without a hitch and they easily found their files.

"The rendering will be done in ten minutes," Ajay said to his guests.

"What's rendering? What's being rendered?" asked Abby.

"All of the recorded images of your brain are being stitched together to make a movie, a time-lapse movie. It should show what areas were active and when they were active," replied Phil.

"And Dr. Paolo's and Brad's and mine too," added Ajay.

Each minute of the rendering countdown to completion seemed like five minutes to the impatient audience. The only time Ajay and Phil left their seats in front of the monitor was to get another beer.

"It's done," Amy announced to no one in particular. "Look! It says it's done."

Everyone focused intently on the screen as the computer wizards charted their next move. After some discussion they figured out how to display two rendered movies simultaneously. They positioned the movie of Abby's brain images above those of Dr. Paolo's images and clicked on the right arrow to start each movie. Everyone watched the mostly gray translucent, nondescript images of the left side of the two brains appeared interspersed with sporadic and seemingly random flashes of white flashes that apparently signified neural activity.

"What are we looking for?" asked Ajay.

"I think we're looking for a pattern of alternating activity between the transmitter and the receiver," replied Brad who was intrigued by the images.

"Anyone see a pattern?" Ajay asked the audience while he kept focused on the screen.

"No, not me," replied Amy.

"Me neither," said Abby.

Disappointed, the students nevertheless also ran the rendered images of Brad and Ajay's brains. The results were the same. The activity in each brain appeared quite random and similar to each other.

"Perhaps we should call Dr. Paolo?" asked Phil. "Maybe he can give us some guidance?"

"That's not a good idea, not tonight," said Abby quickly. "He wasn't doing so well on the way back home. It looked like he needed to rest. Why don't I send him an email tomorrow and tell him what we learned. Let him get back to us on his own time."

"Works for me," said Phil who watched the monitor as both of the five-minute movies ended freezing the last frames in place. "It's amazing to me how two different people can have similar looking activity patterns."

"Perhaps we're more alike than we think," added Brad.

———•———

With the city sporting a fresh eight inches of heavy wet snow, Bob decided to walk home from the hospital at three in the morning rather than risk a ride in a taxi. Only six hours ago he watched helplessly as the woman he loved, the young bride he married not long ago, released a primal scream as she pushed an infant girl into the cold, but sure hands, of the OB/GYN who was strategically positioned in the bright, chaotic delivery room. Though he suffered not one contraction Bob was physically spent and emotionally drained. The snowflakes that instantly melted on his face on this dark winter morning felt refreshing and the journey home evoked a sense of survival as he trudged a mile or so to their two bedroom apartment.

By the time he arrived home he was so exhausted that, ironically enough, he was wide-awake. More out of routine than anything else, Bob opened his laptop and logged into the MIT email server. Even before the first message arrived he remembered that he had left Dr. Paolo and his students as they were beginning an experiment. A few keystrokes later he saw that Ajay and Phil followed his instructions perfectly and that the data had already been rendered. As the file came into focus his body was overtaken by a strong wave of exhaustion. He struggled to stay awake, but the new dad was able to tap a few keystrokes that initiated a cross-analysis auto script program on the student's data. He then logged off, closed the laptop, placed it gently on the cluttered wooden coffee table, and instantly passed out in place.

———•———

Dr. Paolo lay in bed curled-up like a freshwater shrimp as nausea repeatedly seized his intestines and twisted them tumultuously. Since he hadn't eaten anything that day the very motions of vomiting served only to coat his mouth and throat with acrid bile—a situation he fought to avoid. He tried to deflect his miserable state by thinking about the day at MIT but his thoughts were fleeting as his mind was overtaken with bouts of sharp violent pain. The last thing he thought of before falling asleep amid the pain was a specific something that he wanted to be sure to recall in the morning when he hopefully felt better.

"Don't forget, don't forget Cookie. Remember, remember images... don't forget...Cookie...don't."

The Plan

1

Dr. Paolo awoke early Monday morning feeling physically depleted but steadfastly determined not to waste another day in bed. At Laura's insistence he ate a slice of plain whole-wheat toast although he had no appetite whatsoever. The cup of hot black tea soothed him as the center of the two-day snowstorm headed east-northeast to the open Atlantic and onto Nova Scotia.

"This is my last winter," he said aloud to the empty house after Laura left for the hospital. The thought of not enduring another harsh winter didn't bother him as much as the thought that he'd probably never again taste wild blueberries that were ripe by mid-summer in New England. Thoughts of his pending death alternately depressed and motivated him but in a real effort to move forward the good professor took his cup of tea into the study and logged onto his computer.

Among the usual array of junk email from pseudo drug companies anxious to sell pills to enhance anything that needed enhancing were two emails of interest. One was from username <onalark>, it was From: Abby. Subject: Data. Date: February 18, 2012 11:21:15 PM EST and it was addressed

241

To: Dante Paolo and cc: Amy <a1616 >, Brad <b2930 >, Phil <p3014 >, Ajay <a1934>. It read:

> Dear Dr. Paolo,
>
> We wanted to let you know that we were able to access our data file at MIT. Ajay and Phil accessed the rendered movies and we were able to watch them simultaneously. However, we are not sure how to interpret the images. At first glance the patterns of activity seem to be random. We'd like to review these data with you. Please let us know when we can get together.
>
> Abby

The other email was from username Robert <rwyle >. The subject line was blank but the date that the email was sent was: February 19, 2012 11:50:15 AM EST, and it was sent only to Dr. Paolo. It read:

> I ran an analysis script on your experiment and there are some interesting patterns of activity in a unique part of the brain. This activity was seen with the person who wore the blue hat in experiment 1.
>
> Bob

Dr. Paolo read each email twice. Reviewing data is the lifeblood of scientists. It's what they live for, it's what motivates them, it's what makes them get out of a warm bed at all hours of the night because they know that the findings could lead to the next question or it could provide the final answer. Reading these emails was like looking at results through prosthetic eyes—there was something there but it was not at all in focus.

"Abby wore the blue hat," Dr. Paolo said to the monitor. "Abby wore the blue hat and I wore the gray one and what part of the brain are you talking about? What interesting patterns?" He thought for a moment, then responded:

From: Dante Paolo <dpaolo>. Subject: re: Data. Date: February 20, 2012 06:09:05 AM EST. His email addressed to: Abby <onalark >, Amy <a1616>, Brad <b2930>, Phil <p3014 >, Ajay <a1934>. It read:

> Dear All,
>
> Thanks for letting me know that you were able to access the data. I've just received an email from Bob Wyle who also reviewed the file. He saw some interesting patterns in a "unique part of the brain". I'm not sure what he meant but shortly I will send him an email to set up a time to discuss the results. Perhaps we should convene in one of the meeting rooms at the Wilmington College library. How's 4 p.m. Wednesday? If that's okay, then I'll ask Bob if he could call into the meeting to review the data. Let me know.
>
> Thanks again,
>
> Dr. Paolo

Everyone agreed to meet at the library on Wednesday afternoon at four thirty including Bob who would be video conferenced into the meeting. Dr. Paolo procured a small conference room at the library that was equipped with a computer terminal and Internet access. The firm midweek plans and the post-storm sunlight blasting through the clouds brightened the day and lifted Dante's somewhat sagging spirits. Reinvigorated, he returned to editing his manuscript.

———•———

The small rectangular, windowless meeting room in the library was designed and equipped for modern day functionality. On one long wall it had a whiteboard with felt pens and an eraser. It also had a computer and a monitor with Ethernet jacks on the wall for additional computer hookups if necessary. The indirect lighting was adjustable to allow for a better view of a presentation through the ceiling-mounted LCD projector. Ajay and Phil had already surveyed the equipment and brought an HDMI cable to maximize the resolution of the video projector. In a matter of minutes, they were able to display their data from the MIT computer through the room's computer to the projector and onto the whiteboard for all to see. They also were able to patch Ajay's laptop to a second video-in port on the projector so they could see Bob displayed in a picture-in-a-picture format on the same image. Bob initiated a video call with Ajay and almost instantly the new father's face could be seen in the upper right hand corner of the whiteboard overlaid on the rendered video images of Dr. Paolo and Abby's brain.

The meeting began promptly and without hesitation. Bob began by running the video images at high speed—five minutes were condensed into thirty seconds.

"Since I don't know who wore what hat, I'll just refer to them as the blue brain and the gray brain. Oh yeah, these data are from experiment one. When we run the video at condensed time, what we see are similarly chaotic activity patterns. That's not unusual since whatever both participants were doing, like breathing, hearing, scratching their head or whatever, obviously would involve neuronal activity. Now, if we expect activity to be confined to a specific region of the brain—like, for example, the occipital lobe if we're studying vision—we need to selectively eliminate the background activity bearing in mind that the pons may also be involved because it controls eye movement, got it?" Bob asked in a direct voice that didn't invite a response. "So, the genius behind Dr. Sukawa's program is that it can examine two brains simultaneously and pinpoint exactly where differences in activity are located."

The students and Dr. Paolo watched as Bob closed out the movie and opened another folder that contained several data files. The computer screen was filled with a checkerboard pattern of sixteen brain images. Bob explained that four rows of four timed shots per row progressed in chronological order from left to right.

"The program reviews the entire dataset and scans for areas of high activity. So, the person who wore the blue hat had peak activity in the limbic system, either the left or right parahippocampal gyrus, close to the innermost part of the brain. This is a new one for me. I've never seen activity in this part of the brain before."

"Isn't that also called the old mammalian region, somewhat primitive just above the reptilian region?" interjected Brad.

"Yup, that right," replied Bob. "Essentially it's involved with memory creation and recognition of visual scenes. It's probably how we initially imprint people like our mother on day one. Throughout our entire life this region of the brain helps us form very important associations; it distinguishes the good guys from the bad ones, recognizes those who would nurture us and those who would kill us. It's a region that drives human cognition. In essence, this region creates who we are. It's responsible for our very survival."

"Bob?" said Dr. Paolo but the slight delay in transmission did not reach MIT before Bob turned back to the data.

"And look here. I don't know what this means but the activity peaks almost exactly one minute apart," continued Bob as he highlighted the white area in each frame. "Did someone have a question?"

"Yes, I did, but you just answered it," said Dr. Paolo. "But now I have another. Was there activity in the same region for the other brain?"

"Hard to tell," replied Bob as he filled the screen with checkerboard images of the gray brain. "There was some activity in the limbic region here," he said pointing to the lower part of the image, "but the signal is weak, the gray hat is not as sensitive as the one used on the blue brain.

To know for sure if both persons had activity in the same area, the hats would need to be switched and the experiment repeated."

"Is there any other physiologic changes, like heart rate or overall neural transmission that could be derived from the data?" asked Amy.

"Heart rate, no; and overall neural activity is always consistently high, that's why we need to filter away most of the activity to find the peak area," offered Bob who moved quickly to make another point. "What's remarkable to me beside the location of the activity of the blue brain is the periodicity of the peak activity, how it occurred so regularly so when you graph the results on a linear time scale on the x-axis and activity on the y-axis, it looks like this." Bob opened a graph that covered most of the screen so that the brain images could be seen around the edges of the screen. The graph looked like a tidy row of silhouettes of perfect little Christmas trees without the jagged edges or the stumps. Lines of the graph rose up to a point from the left and back down to the bottom on the right. "To the best of my knowledge, this pattern has never been seen," declared Bob. "Oh, and another interesting thing. I ran the same analysis on experiment two and, well, I can only tell you that the results were very different compared with those from the first experiment. In essence there was no real activity difference in the limbic region. Both brains in experiment two looked like the activity of the gray brain in experiment one. I suggest you send these data to Dr. Sukawa. I'm sure he will also have some insights to share."

Everyone in the library room looked at each and nodded their approval.

Dr. Paolo quickly responded, "That's a great idea, Bob. Would you mind if I sent Dr. Sukawa an email with an outline of the experiment and, if you'd be so kind to package the data, I'll send it along as an attachment."

"Okay, but the only thing Dr. Sukawa will need is the file location because he can access the lab computer from anywhere. I'll send you the link by email," Bob replied.

"Thanks," said Dr. Paolo. "I'll send it out later this week."

"So here's my take," Bob said with conviction. "I'm blinded with respect to who wore what hat, but based on the data, I'd say that experiment one had the test subject in the blue hat and a control of sorts wore the gray hat. Whereas in experiment two, both participants were controls, like negative controls where nothing should work. Am I close?"

The small video camera on Ajay's laptop allowed Bob to view most, but not all of the room, but what he did see made him think he was correct. Those gathered in the library at Wilmington College had a wide grin; some in the room were shaking their heads in awe.

"Spot on," exclaimed Dr. Paolo. "That's exactly how it went."

"Nice," replied Bob. "Dr. Sukawa is going to love this. He's going to absolutely love this."

"Bob?" Abby began. "We were wondering how everything went the other night. Are you a new Dad?"

"Oh yes! Yes, I am. My wife and the baby came home yesterday, um, no Monday, Monday morning...."

"Does the baby have a name?" asked Abby.

"Erica. Seven pounds eight ounces and so far she's a great sleeper. I think she's the only one in our place getting sleep these days."

"Wonderful, congratulations," Dr. Paolo said before he offered Bob advice that he had wanted to give to himself. "Be careful not to let time with your daughter slip away, especially the first few years. They grow faster than you can imagine and before you know it she'll be leaving for college."

"Yeah, that's what I've heard," said Bob wearily as he was already feeling the strains of a new family that added to the ever-increasing demands of an academic researcher. "I took yesterday off just to be with her."

The teleconference session ended after Dr. Paolo reviewed the plan to send the data to Dr. Sukawa and after Ajay asked Bob a computer question relating to where the graphs would be filed.

"Well, I don't know about you, but I'm ecstatic!" said Dr. Paolo to the students. "I think this is great."

"Do you really think this is something new?" Amy asked.

"I'm not sure Amy, but if anyone could tell us the answer to that question, it'll be Dr. Sukawa. I'll get an email out to him by Friday. We should know more about these data by this time next week provided he has the time to review them."

While the others were chatting, Brad was at the computer. On the screen he projected an image of the human brain downloaded from the Internet.

"Here," he said, "pointing to the pink area on the schematic of the human brain. This is where the limbic system is located. It is also called the 'old mammalian system' because evolutionary it proceeded the neocortex or the 'new mammalian system' that is most of our brain. This diagram also shows the limbic system encompassing the so-called 'reptilian system' that controls our most basic, most vital functions. I didn't focus too much on this last semester but this primitive region is responsible for autonomic processes, things we don't think about like breathing, heartbeat, and body temperature control. The limbic region marks the beginning, at least as it relates to the brain, of our evolution as mammals with more highly developed thought processes."

"So what are you saying?" asked Phil. "Are you or are you not surprised that the activity in Abby's brain seems to have been located in the limbic region?"

"I don't know," replied Brad turning to face Dr. Paolo and the students. "On one hand, yes, since the limbic area is the cradle of our emotions and unconscious behaviors so Abby could be super sensitive and super responsive to other people right down to the level of their thoughts. On the other hand, one could make a plausible argument that the limbic region is too primitive to support such an advanced way of communicating. Such advanced processing would reside somewhere in the neocortex."

"Unless you consider verbal communication as devolutionary," offered Abby who had often considered but never before offered this potential explanation of her telepathic abilities.

"Backward evolution? More primitive?" asked Amy before the men in the room even had a chance to process the concept.

"Mmhmm," was Abby's tightlipped reply.

2

As he lay in bed in total darkness with the remnants of that day's energy, Dante tried to interpret the results Bob presented. But the cancer-induced nausea had returned and this time it meant business thanks to a belly full of celebratory pizza and beers he shared with the students after leaving the library. The violent eruptions of his gut-turned-volcano left him exhausted. He knew that this episode meant that he had eaten his last pizza—one of his all-time favorite foods and one he'd often made completely from scratch, baked on a stone then shared with friends.

His weakened state left him dizzy and unable to concentrate on the results so he redirected his mind to review the conversation that took place just a few hours ago with his students. They are so young with so much of their lives ahead of them, more tomorrows than yesterdays. They spoke apprehensively yet enthusiastically about college and how they were anxious about the fate of their application. Would they be accepted somewhere? Would it be their first choice? Second? Third? He wondered how each would handle the stress.

Ajay was quite confident that he would be accepted at MIT. His optimism was fueled not only by his near-perfect GPA, but also by "the pull" his father had with the MIT admissions officer as well as a prominent professor in the Computer Science department who virtually recruited Ajay when he was just a sophomore at Wilmington College.

And while Brad understood the advantages of "the pull" he didn't want to acknowledge the fact that his father had already made calls to Harvard and, in an attempt to peg one against the other, the Crimson's cross-region rival Yale, as well. Brad preferred the less pretentious but equally reputable Dartmouth or Brown as his top two regional choices for medical school and he also applied to the University of Minnesota Medical School mainly because Amy, who had cast her net of medical school applications much wider than did Brad, had checked off the Midwestern school on the list to receive her electronic application.

Brad and Amy rarely discussed medical school because they knew that the odds were better than even that they would soon be separated, a thought that did not appeal to either one of them. They spent long hours in each other's arms and spoke of how they'd cope apart now that their relationship had passed beyond the often-deceptive infatuation stage. Although they were eager to move onto the next chapter of their young lives with eyes wide open, they also sought to control its structure. The medical schools that accepted them, they knew, would write the first draft of their next paragraph.

Phil was outwardly envious of Ajay's certainty about heading to MIT. The prestigious school with the iconic Pantheon-like dome was Phil's first choice too although RPI in Troy, New York would also suffice. There were many fine universities that had stellar mathematics departments but few also had solid research programs. Because he desired to study applied mathematics, Phil sought a school with established mathematicians with robust research programs. And for Phil that meant only MIT or RPI. Attending any other school simply would not do.

Dr. Paolo was pleased to see how comfortable Abby had become in the presence of the others. Although still quite reserved, she was no longer the outsider. Abby applied to several schools including the local favorites, University of New Hampshire and the University of Massachusetts, as well as American University located in the nation's capital that also offered advanced degree programs in communication. Over pizza, Abby wanted to say that she would go to the school that offered her the best scholarship but decided against it as the others in the group did not speak a word about cost. "You're on your own kid," was the response from her father when he learned that his only daughter was applying to graduate school as if he had already spent his entire life savings on her education at Wilmington. "You should be done with school. Get a job and make some money. Get hitched. I'm sure someone will marry you. Why can't you just get a job, like me?" were his beer-laced words of wisdom that she promptly dismissed. Abby was too embarrassed to discuss her father, or her home life with anyone. If he came up in conversation, she would just change subjects. She knew that she'd find her way in the world and it would be on a path that led directly away from her father and his obnoxious family.

Thoughts of his students who had, in a way, become his surrogate children, relaxed Dr. Paolo's tense body. Brad was like a firstborn with his levelheaded and clear approach to solving problems. But with her self-assured confidence Amy could also have been his firstborn; she probably would have been a difficult infant and an overly independent toddler. Phil was clearly the middle child with a quick temper and an even quicker wit, and Abby would be the baby of the family, roundly adored and teased by the others but at the end of the day, she'd have the last word. Paternal thoughts of his imaginary children eased his pain stricken body to sleep.

Dr. Paolo awoke from a dreamless night with a dull pain towards the back of his head that forewarned of a full-fledged migraine if he didn't take immediate action. Two acetaminophen pills and an espresso later, he was back in bed waiting for the throbbing to subside; he needed a clear head to conceptualize, then to prioritize, how to make everything come together. The immediate task was to send Dr. Sukawa an email that described the experiment and the results; that task should be done by tomorrow if not by today. And now that they had completed one key experiment he also needed to think about the bigger picture but his mind, perhaps jittery from the higher than usual dose of caffeine, would not focus.

Were telepathy genes encoded and residing in the junk DNA? If so, are these genes expressed for only a short time during the telepathic episode, turned on then off like a light switch or are they always on, ready to go at a moment's notice? He wondered. Yes, these were important questions but he needed to formulate a grand plan and he needed to do it soon. Time was ebbing. It was already the end of February and he was feeling weaker with each passing day.

"The students spoke about graduate school. They'll be done soon," he said to an empty room. "Around the middle of May, that's not too far away. Then they'll be gone. And likely will I. I need a plan. I need to talk to Laura. Then I'll talk with Rob. That's it. First Laura then maybe Rob too." Dr. Paolo eased out of bed and made his way to the study where he grabbed a yellow pad and a pen. He then climbed back into bed to outline a strategy.

By early afternoon Dr. Paolo had it. He had completed the outline of his end game. It was how it had to be, and it was how it had to work. If he was going to do this right, to bring his last hypothesis to completion, and the end game, like the hypothesis itself, had to be well designed. It would take time. The process of the end game couldn't be rushed it had to be thorough and it had to be done in a particular sequence. There would be no retakes, no second chances.

This... he thought. *If this plan worked, it would be spectacular. I'd be the happiest person alive, or more likely I'd be a very content dead person. I wonder if it would matter if I'm content when I'm dead.*

———— · ————

"Where in the hell have you been?" asked the cheery caller whose voice Dante recognized immediately.

"Hey Rob, how are you? I haven't gone far. Where've you been? In fact, I was just thinking about you."

"I know, I know we've been on the go ever since winter break and the week in Cancún. I haven't spoken to you since we came back from that all-inclusive resort in Mexico, right?"

"No..."

"Well, it was awesome. Beverly's folks treated the whole gang to the trip in celebration of their fiftieth wedding anniversary. We did absolutely nothing for five straight days. The toughest part of each day was deciding what to drink. It was rough I'll tell you. We'll have to go with you and your better half someday, maybe next January? Then, when school started up all that relaxation went out the window and we're back to the daily grind. What's new with you?"

"Well, it's a long story and you probably shouldn't have asked," was Dr. Paolo's reply. "It's not..."

"What? What are you talking about? Listen, I hate to do this but I have to go. I have to get to my two-thirty class. Let's get together this weekend. You guys free Saturday night?"

"Yeah, probably. Well at least I am. I'll check with Laura and get back to you."

"Good. Ciao. See you soon, gotta run."

"Okay. Ciao. I'll let you know."

Dr. Paolo liked the timing of their tentative get together. He would chat with Laura tonight, review the plan with her, and then they could tell Rob and Beverly everything, or almost everything, when they were together. It would give him time to make adjustments to the plan in case Laura had any suggestions.

As the dinner hour approached, Dr. Paolo wanted to test a new risotto recipe that used saffron even though he was not overly fond of the exotic spice with the tangy scent and the beautiful deep orange color. But he became very tired as the hour approached 8 p.m. with no signs of his wife; the carefully measured Arborio rice was still dry as it waited to be placed in the pot of blended butter, olive oil and saffron. He knew better than to call or to worry about her and he knew that the window of opportunity to talk with her was now closed for the evening—she'll arrive home completely spent and in no mood for anything, least of all to discuss the details of his end game. Dejected, the good professor put the makings of the risotto in the refrigerator, turned off most all of the lights in the kitchen and made his way to bed. He even resisted the urge to check his email.

Dr. Paolo fell into a deep sleep almost immediately after his head lay on the pillow.

His mind saw a young lady with features that reminded him of Laura when they first met nearly 30 years ago. It seemed like she had something to say but there was nothing on her smooth face but a blend of sadness and longing, of anguish and confusion. She locked eyes with him in an obvious attempt to let him know, but he did not, would not, could not recognize her nor could he comprehend what she was trying to convey. And then, without reason, he looked at the darkness to the left of the young lady as if he anticipated the arrival of someone else. And there! There she was, his child-mother whom he had seen before in this strange place. But this time his child-mother ignored him. Instead she remained focused on the young lady, taking her gently by the shoulders and guiding her away. With the child-mother to her right, the young woman turned her head slowly to the left, as if she sought another private moment with him; her beautiful brown eyes projected a loving hello, and a wistful goodbye.

———•———

The subject line of Dr. Paolo's email to Dr. Sukawa and copied to the students served as an overt reminder that the attached data should not be shared with others. It read: Confidential. The text itself was short:

> Dear Dr. Sukawa,
>
> I hope this email finds you well. Please see the attached file.
> I look forward to your comments.
> Sincerely,
> Dante

Dr. Paolo wanted the message to intrigue. The attached word document described the details of the experiment and a link to the location of the exact data folder in the computer in his MIT laboratory. Bob Wyle had already deposited his own analyses of the rendered data in this folder so all of the information could be found in one place. Dr. Paolo anticipated a response within a week unless Dr. Sukawa was travelling and had no access to email.

Ever since the diagnosis, the mood most evenings at the Kean-Paolo home was quiet and rather dour. As a physician, Laura was resigned to her husband's fate but as a wife she did not want to acknowledge the inevitable outcome, especially after a long day at the clinic. She'd spoken privately with her colleague Dr. Kincade who thought that Dante was both unusual in refusing treatment and also wise to do so given the stage of his cancer. "He's right," said the congenial Dr. Kincade. "The quality of life during his final months will be better without chemo but he will experience a significant amount of pain. He will want to have some strong meds handy. But I'll admit it, forgoing treatment in his condition would be my choice too."

Laura just wanted to make sure that she wasn't missing anything—an experimental therapy, a clinical study—anything that could possibly be effective against this latter stage pancreatic cancer. There was none. Laura accommodated her husband when they were together but uncharacteristically and quite unconsciously she avoided him. She scheduled more patients and worked longer hours during the week and she found things to do out of the house on the weekends. Later that same summer, when she would find herself alone in the big house, Laura would reflect on the last few months of her husband's life and recognize what she had done. She'd reason that avoiding him was simply a coping mechanism, a deduction that relieved some of the self-imposed but not overbearing guilt. She rationalized that her behavior accommodated his preoccupation with the hypothesis project. She convinced herself that she did well to leave him to his own devices, and that his final time was of his design—as he so completely outlined it in what he referred to as "the death plan" on that Friday night sometime in February.

Composing the email to Dr. Sukawa was much easier than talking to Laura about the plan, what he lightheartedly dubbed "the death plan". He approached the matter over a Friday night meal of baked haddock with steamed asparagus tossed in chopped garlic and olive oil. A bottle of chardonnay was in the chiller on the table with several on standby in the refrigerator, ready if needed. On this night, Laura had neither the energy nor the desire to dodge the discussion, despite her deep distaste of the topic.

And Dr. Paolo did not hold back on details.

He began by telling her what she already knew; that he was getting progressively weaker and he felt that he was on the short end of the six-months-to-live-odds given to someone with stage IV pancreatic cancer.

"In other words, I've already celebrated my last Memorial Day," he added to punctuate the point. He then proceeded to tell her that he'd like to transform the first floor bedroom into a temporary hospital room. He'd need to rent a mechanical bed and an IV pole to hold bags of buffered saline and maybe nutrients too so he wouldn't dehydrate or starve to death.

Relocating to the first floor bedroom, also known as the guest room, would allow him to easily access the kitchen and the full bathroom that was also located on the main floor. He wanted to move everything needed, including his books, computer and printer from upstairs as soon as possible while he still had the strength to do it. Although Laura was somewhat surprised by the plan to convert the guest room into a hospital suite his next statement was not unexpected.

"And I'm ready for hospice," he said clearly while looking directly into the eyes of his wife. Laura took another sip of wine, pushed her plate away from and responded with learned professional stoicism.

"I agree," she responded blandly. "If you want I'll call Tom and ask him to write the order."

"No, it's my death, I'll do it my way. I need to tell him what traits I'm looking for in a hospice nurse. I'll need a young, extremely vivacious woman, a babe who's as horny as hell," he added with a smile to lighten the moment. "You know how sexy we dying old men are, don't you?" he added for good measure.

"Of course," offered Laura who was well versed at playing along with her husband's black humor. "I'll be sure to get you one of those sexy hospital gowns that'll turn anyone on, especially if they see you from behind," she added. "Would you like blue or white? Or how about one that dissolves away to nothing when you perspire?"

"Do they really make those?"

"No. Do you really think anyone would wear them?"

"Maybe. Especially those of us who like to die in our birthday suits."

Dr. Paolo again turned serious when he told his wife about how he would like his final day, his final hours, and his final moment to play out. He told her about the latest results of the telepathy experiment and of Bob Wyle's analyses. He omitted little as he recounted what he knew about the experiment with Cookie and of the promises of the *RW88* tracer. He told his wife that when he took his final breath he wanted her by his side for many reasons but mainly because he had specific things he wanted her to do. He also had a list of the people, other than her and the hospice nurse, he wanted present when he died, or at least around somewhere in the house. He also described each person's specific role.

Laura listened intently. She didn't say a word until after he described the retrieval of his body by the local funeral home for immediate cremation, a service that he would arrange and prepay in the coming days.

"And guess what? For an extra fifty bucks they'll dump or rather 'intern with loving care and respect' my ashes at the funeral home's Garden of Eternal Peace. Once I'm out the door, that'll be that."

"You've really thought this through, haven't you? Do you really think all of this will work?" Laura asked. "I mean you do appreciate the fact that the exact moment of death is really tough to nail? I've seen all sorts of situations where some people die unexpectedly or quickly while others hang on for a long, long time. No one can pin down exactly when the moment will arrive. Why do you think you'll be any different?"

Dr. Paolo was ready with an answer.

"It's simple, Laura," he said in a subdued soft voice that lacked any hint of humor. "Because I'm going to control my own destiny. I get only one shot at this and it has to be done exactly this way. Most people have little to no warning before they drop dead. My cancer has given me an opportunity that I don't want to blow. It has focused time. It'll bring me in for a rough landing but at least I'll know when I'm going down for good, and I know that there will be no smooth landing, not even a parachute. I'm going down hard. And it's not going to be pretty. My immune system is fighting a losing battle. I'll know when it's time to surrender, trust me I'll know. I just hope I've got the energy to do what I need to do before the final nose dive."

Later in the evening, Laura crawled into bed and snuggled up to her husband who was lying awake in the dark thinking about his plan. Silently, he put his arm around her shoulder and she placed her head on his bare chest. And as she listened to the tempo of his heavy heart, and as he smelled the familiar fragrance of her hair they were, for that brief moment, transported back in time when they were young lovers who enjoyed simple pleasures. Cuddling with Laura was among the most cherished moments of Dante's life. It comforted and assured him during times of stress and it made him feel needed when his strength was sought.

"You know that none of this will be easy for me," she said softly.

"I know but you'll do just fine. We'll be ready together."

"But what you want me to do is..."

"I know," he interrupted. "But I know that it'll work. I can feel it. I've never been so sure about anything before. It's almost like it's already happened. Like it's a play that has been written and we're just waiting for the cue to come on stage and begin the scene. Hey honey, that's an idea. I'll write a one-act play that starts with a death. Death as the starting point, I'll make it a comedy. Maybe a situational comedy, we'll call it 'The Last Laugh' and it'll be about..."

"Dante," Laura started with an understanding that someday soon she'd miss his spontaneous flights of fantasy. "I don't want you to write a play and this certainly isn't a comedy. I love you. I love you very much. I'll do what you want me to do but I think you're crazy but I also know that you're stubborn. I'll do it. I don't think it's right but I'll do it."

"Don't worry. It'll be okay," he said as he met her lips for a familiar kiss.

3

The text message Amy received from her father was direct:

>Call me when you can re: your samples.

Amy passed the phone to Brad who read the message then got out of bed and headed to the bathroom.

"Should I call him now?" she asked. But before he had a chance to answer she had already replied.

Dr. Ito told his daughter that he had completed sequencing the samples she had sent a couple of weeks ago. He had also probed the sequences using a proprietary label that showed something quite unexpected and he wondered if she would be able share the code with him so he can try to make sense of the findings. Amy told her father that she thought the professor would approve but she wanted to check to make sure. She also thought that Dr. Paolo would like to review the data. In reality Amy knew that Dr. Paolo would not object at all but she wanted to see the data first and thus she invented the precaution. Her father electronically sent the compressed data to her using a secured cloud folder they shared. Later that bright Sunday morning, Amy and Brad had their first look at the pattern of DNA extracted from Dr. Paolo, Abby, Brad and Ajay's cheek cells during the telepathy experiment.

Amy and Brad knew that scientists organize and analyze enormous amounts of data in different ways but they were astounded by the visual presentation of the DNA sequences. Each genome, with about six billion bits of information contained in the twenty-three pairs of chromosomes, was presented in a highly efficient manner with tiny numbers to the outside of the circular pattern. The instructions in the body of Dr. Ito's email stated simply to "tap on the middle to add more layers", a message that meant little to the young couple until they scrolled down to the second page of the file that contained the header "ALBEFORE" and a round colorful map with spikes of various lengths to the outside of the white circle that looked like the corona of the sun during a total eclipse. When Amy positioned the pointer to the center of the white circle and tapped the track pad, an additional layer of tiny square boxes lined the inside of the circle. Some of the boxes were completely red while others were only partially filled and still others were empty. Another tap produced a set of shaded rectangular tiles that formed little bridges between the outside ring with the numbers to the inside red squares, and a the third tap created a stunning pattern of curved lines of different colors that led from one part of the inside of the circle to another that made the circular genetic map resembled an elaborate, finely woven dream catcher.

"What the hell is all of this?" asked Brad.

"I have no idea," Amy said as she scrolled down to the next page labeled "AL20". "This must be the sample taken twenty minutes after the experiment started." Three taps later Brad and Amy saw essentially the same patterns as were seen on "ALBEFORE."

"There's no difference," said Amy.

"I don't see any differences either," replied Brad who left the room muttering, "the DNA part was a bust."

Amy scrolled down and examined "AL25", then "DPBEFORE," "DP22," and "DP27." The DNA patterns seemed virtually identical, including those from Brad and Ajay's cheek cells. Because there appeared to be no differences Amy didn't think anyone would mind if she told her father what the codes meant, and in any case, who could complain since he did sequence them for free.

"And it was my idea anyway," she rationalized aloud. Amy glanced at her phone; it was mid-morning in California.

"Hi Mom," she said to the familiar voice on the other end of the call. After a few minutes of ensuring her mother that she'd let them know immediately when she heard from medical schools, and also that information about graduation was now posted on the Wilmington College website, did she get to speak with her father.

"Hi Dad. Thanks for sending the sequences. I hope they weren't too much trouble."

"No, I used them to test out a different sequencing method and a new probe as well."

"That's great but I wish they showed some differences?"

"I don't know what you were looking for, where the samples came from or what even you were testing, but you couldn't ask for more differences—at least four of the samples were off the charts with the new probe compared with the other samples that ended in 'BEFORE.'"

"What? I didn't see any differences, at least nothing dramatic."

"Oh, it's about as dramatic as it gets," said Amy's father.

"I went through all three layers and..."

"There are four layers."

"Four, but I only saw..."

"Yes, the fourth layer shows the results obtained with our proprietary tracer. To see it you need to command-click in the center. Check it out and call me back, I'd like to get a run in before it rains. I'll be home the rest of the day. Call me back, okay? Bye."

Amy tossed her cell on the bed, opened her laptop and reexamined the pattern of each of the twelve DNA samples with the command-click layer.

"Holy cow," she said in a dead panned voice as she stared at the images on the screen. "Brad, check this out. You're not going to believe it."

———◆———

Laura answered the doorbell and welcomed their neighbors inside from the seasonably cool and starlit Saturday evening. When Dante emerged from the kitchen the eyes of his guests widened noticeably and what Rob said next would echo in Beverly's mind for years.

"Dante! What happened? You look terrible! You're so freaking thin. Are you on a diet?"

Dante anticipated this reaction as they hadn't seen each other for some time and he knew that he'd lost quite a bit of weight. He appreciated Rob's candor and that he didn't try to mask his emotions. The good professor walked over and gave Beverly a firm hug and, in an unusual move, he also gave Rob a hug as well. He then took a step back, and with Laura by his side he bluntly responded, "I have terminal cancer.

Pancreatic, stage IV." Then, in an effort to lighten the moment, he smiled and added, "Now are you ready for the bad news?"

"Wait, hold on here," said Rob. "You've got what? Pancreatic cancer? It's a treatable type of cancer, right? You've started chemo and that's why you've lost weight, right? You're going to beat this, right?"

"No I haven't and no I won't. I was diagnosed around the beginning of the year and it's been a tough couple of months. I'm terminal, well, we're all terminal but I just have a better idea of how terminal. And I decided to forego therapy in order to keep sane. I have a clear mind, and a few more things to accomplish before the summer. I'm in constant pain, I have no appetite and I generally feel like crap. Otherwise, it's just another day in paradise. But tonight I do have a bit of an appetite and I've made a nice meal and I want to hear about Mexico, so come in, can I get you a beer or a glass of wine?"

The evening went as well as could be expected given the shocking start. Rob and Beverly did their best to follow Dante's lead and to ignore the bad news, and Laura did her part to maintain a steady composure when what she really wanted to do was to lean on her neighbors—to share her anguish. Dante told his friends about his plan to transform the guest room in to a hospital ward and how he was getting his affairs in order. Lacking emotion, he told them that he was seeking hospice, and in the same breath, mentioned that he'd probably need a hand bringing some things down from the second floor. Rob readily agreed to help and he offered to do what ever was needed at anytime. Beverly looked at Laura and nodded, as if to say that she too was available.

Everyone did their best to eat dinner, to sustain a conversation and to look beyond the weight of the grim message, although everyone was clearly burdened by its gravity; everyone that is, except Dante who was rather upbeat and eager to make the most of the evening. Eventually the two bottles of Shiraz worked their ancient magic and by the time the yogurt parfaits were served everyone reverted back to a normal, or to a somewhat normal, level of socializing.

Sensing that it would be good for Laura to be alone with Rob and Beverly, Dante feigned fatigue and announced that it was time for him to head to bed. A few hugs later, he slowly made his way up the stairs to the master bedroom. As he drifted off to a dreamless sleep he could hear murmurs, chatters and a few sniffles coming from the kitchen below.

Now everyone that he cared about knew of his cancer. And for the first, and last time in his life, Dante was thankful that he was an only child, and also that he was childless.

4

Dr. Paolo had many collaborators during his long research career. As a graduate student he learned from his valued mentor that teaming up with experts in other fields created a deeper and more meaningful understanding of the questions you seek to answer. Most collaborators were skilled scientists who expertly filled gaps in your own knowledge that substantially improved the outcome of the study. However, not all interactions went as planned. More than once he'd waltzed into the collaboration gala with congenial and talented dancers who, late in the evening after the champagne bottles were empty, morphed into arrogant, egotistical ogres who abruptly left the good doctor alone on the crowded parquet with more questions and regrets, then answers and insights.

Immediately following the first online exchanges with Dr. Jin Sukawa and Dr. Jainbin Ito, Dante knew that his final professional collaborators would be among the best. Indeed, what Dr. Paolo could not have foreseen was how vital each expert would be to achieving the ultimate goal of his plan; they were skilled performers who would bravely complete the dance even in the absence of their lead dancer.

Dr. Sukawa apologized for his delayed email response citing several personal and business reasons why he had not replied sooner. He also admitted that he needed to check a couple of references to make sure that his feedback would be accurate. He wrote in the reply-all email:

> These data are unequivocally novel. I reviewed them and the experimental design and I agree with what Bob wrote in the notes that not only is it rare to measure activity in the phc gyrus but that the temporal aspect to the activity is unusual for any part of the brain let alone in one of the primitive regions. A hallmark of brain activity is its apparently random nature so the repeated sequential periodicity is absolutely unique. The only suggestion I can make at this juncture is to repeat the experiment at least one more time perhaps switching the blue cap to the transmitter.

Jin Sukawa ended the email from halfway around the world by instructing Bob Wyle to help Dr. Paolo in any way possible.

Dr. Paolo replied immediately. In the email he thanked Dr. Sukawa for taking the time to analyze the data and for providing valuable feedback and sound suggestions. He also promised to keep him informed of any additional data they generated. Dr. Paolo also made sure to restate the value of Bob's involvement in the project. The concise message ended by stating that he and his students were privileged to have the opportunity to work with such generous and gifted individuals. The email was copied to everyone on the team.

———•———

Amy spent over an hour on a video chat with her father reviewing the DNA sequence data sample-by-sample, layer-by-layer. Her father was a calm, unassuming man with a slight build, who usually displayed a steady and narrow range of emotions. But during the review of these data, Amy watched her father become uncharacteristically animated especially after she explained the nature of the experiments and the exact time when the cheek cells were obtained. His enthusiasm was infectious. It prompted Amy to act immediately. Without polling everyone's availability, she reserved a room at the library then called a meeting with Dr. Paolo and the others to share the sequence data and to describe and review her father's analyses.

Fortunately, Dr. Paolo was on his computer when Amy's email arrived and he replied before the others even had a chance to read it. He asked for the meeting to take place at his house on Wednesday evening rather than the library. Everyone agreed with the date and place.

Dr. Paolo's house would once again teem with youthful energy.

By the time the students arrived for dinner on Wednesday evening, Dr. Paolo had already started to transform the guest room into a hospital suite. The double bed had been removed and the computer desk, computer and printer were placed close to where the mechanical bed would be positioned upon arrival in a few days. Instead of preparing a meal, Dr. Paolo ordered takeout from a local restaurant that featured rotisserie chicken with French fries, rolls and a special sauce that was perfectly spiced and full of flavor; they also shared a large baby spinach salad. The group was eager to see the sequence data and to hear the details of Amy's chat with her dad.

"He was so excited that you'd think he'd discovered a new life form or something," Amy said of her father as Ajay connected her computer to his portable LCD projector. The vivid images of the different layers of the sequenced DNA looked like modern art on the off-white dining room wall.

The excitement in Amy's voice rose as she described with a mixture of both common language and molecular biology jargon what each layer of sequence data showed. She told her colleagues, who were beginning to coalesce into a small but formidable scientific team, that the most exciting results shown on the fourth layer of the DNA sequence data were obtained with a proprietary label; Amy did not know the molecular target of the novel label. By itself, this fact told Dr. Paolo that their study would generate even more interest among the greater scientific community because it could be the first study to describe the utility of a new DNA reagent. It would also invite more scrutiny, which is exactly what breakthrough discoveries attracted, and what Dr. Paolo sought.

"Amy, this is remarkable," said Dr. Paolo who couldn't believe what he was seeing. "I'm blown away. Thanks to your father and to you for analyzing the samples and for explaining these data. There is so much to say that I don't know where to begin but I don't want to forget to ask you to send your father's email address to me so I can thank him personally."

When discussion of the DNA results subsided, Dr. Paolo seized the opportunity and told his students about the plan.

"What I'm about to tell you needs to remain now and forever strictly confidential. You have a choice to participate, or not to participate, in what I plan to do with the rest of my life. Please let me know now if you are in or if you are out because once I say it I will assume that you will honor my wishes for privacy."

Dr. Paolo paused and looked around the table at their young fresh faces. Amy, Abby, Phil, Brad and Ajay remained still and seated. They were a team and he was their leader. They weren't going anywhere.

Dante repeated the details of his plan as he had described them to Laura. He left nothing out. He wanted them to know everything—the good, the bad, and the risky. He told them about what would automatically happen after he died and how he would ensure, as best he could, that everything was in place before then. He told them about the transformation of the guest room and about hospice. He again stated that their role in the plan was absolutely voluntary. He declared, rather convincingly, that he would be dead by the end of May given how his health was declining at an accelerated pace.

"Cancers will do that, you know," he said. "They'll outgrow your immune cells and just take you down. Cancer cells are relentless. Amazingly relentless."

Although Dr. Paolo was sounding solid and firm, Abby knew differently. His mind oscillated between calm and panic like a highly pulsed metronome desperately trying to maintain the manic maestro on measure. She was careful not to show what she sensed but inside Abby desperately wanted to throw her arms around her mentor—who meant more to her than did her own father—to give him a hug, to cry with him. She ached to tell him how much she admired his bravery and how he had given clarity and direction to her life, but instead, she sat silently like the others.

It was Amy's night and she assumed the role as the group's spokesperson.

"Dr. Paolo, I am committing myself to your plan and your final wishes."

Everyone seemed pleased that she spoke, as they were speechless. Amy not only committed herself but she also volunteered Brad to Dr. Paolo's plan then, without a second thought, she went a step further by offering to do whatever was needed to see that the plan was executed as outlined. The others followed Amy's lead and pledged their commitment. Phil leaned back in the dining room chair, stretched his arms over his head and lightheartedly added, "Yeah, count me in too Dr. Paolo, not much else to do. Senior year is full of waiting, whistling, and wishing. Waiting for some good news, whistling as if you're not waiting for news, and wishing that the waiting and the whistling would end."

5

Dr. Paolo's letter of resignation arrived on Dr. Holliday's desk on the Ides of March. It would be a day later, on the day before more than half of the student body and most of the college's faculty would be engrossed in green beer and corned beef, when President Holliday would share the news with Dean Benedetti. Two weeks later, on Good Friday, a day that haunted Dr. Benedetti since childhood when his grandmother told the impressionable child about the crucifixion and death of Jesus at exactly three o'clock in the afternoon on that hellish day centuries ago when the clouds turned black and the skies rioted in a full rage of thunder and lightning, on that perennially ominous anniversary, Lorenzo learned from Rob why Dante Paolo resigned. And like the puppet Pontius Pilot, the Dean of Academic Affairs felt unmistakably guilty, but held no remorse—after all he was a true Catholic. Later that evening Lorenzo sent a cryptically worded email to his cousin:

> Cara Rosa,
> Today, a great thorn has been removed from my side. The wound will heal. The thorn is now permanently dulled. It will no longer cause pain.

The Finale

1

Survival. It is the empowering sense of survival that embolden New Englanders to endure harsh winters, year after cold dark year. Survival, and the promise of better days heralded by the return of the white snow drops, the purple crocuses and the American robins that annually foreshadow a rebirth of sorts—the soothing warmth of springtime and the spectacular summer days that make this part of the world unique.

But this spring, as the Earth's tilt again favored North America and sun's light waxed into the early evening, Dante's energy waned; his body rapidly losing the fight and everything but his mind becoming progressively and visibly weaker. The makeshift hospital room was beginning to feel more like the holding cell it was. His mobility became increasingly limited. The bathroom, just a short few steps down the hall, seemed to be on the other side of the Atlantic. Laura would open the windows to freshen the room with new light and warm daffodil-scented air but the light did little to ease his discomfort, and the slight breeze only made him shiver. Nothing lessened the unadulterated pain wrought by the spread of the relentless cancer.

Dante was certain that he would not have survived to Mother's Day—a fabricated holiday not recognized in their house—if it were not for his clear mind, mineral and vitamin laced high-energy drinks, the letters and manuscripts he needed to complete, and a fireball named Jumpin' June.

June Kennedy was a bright, cute-as-a-button, energetic 20-year-old strawberry blonde whose heart teemed with compassion and endless empathy. She was a newly minted nurse's assistant who was trained and certified in home hospice and palliative care. She was a perpetually happy dynamo who approached most every issue like it was essentially irrelevant and of little consequence to the larger picture; a larger picture that in her youthful mind was not well defined.

"Little things don't bother me and since most big things can be broken down to little things, they don't bother me either," she said to Dr. Paolo when she interviewed for the position as his hospice care provider. Dante was instantly smitten with the life that June packed into her muscular five foot-two inch solid frame. She reminded him of one of those spring-loaded Olympic gymnasts with her shoulders back, chest out, bubble-butt posture, but besides her build, it was the pop in her step that led Dr. Paolo to give her a nickname she readily accepted and later would ask others to use.

Jumpin' June came by the house to tend to Dante first thing in the morning, usually by six, then at noon, and then again in the early evening; a flexible schedule that fit well with her current needs. Laura trimmed back her patient load so that she would arrive home earlier in the evening to take over the care of her husband. The addition of Jumpin' June to the daily household dynamics perfectly accommodated Laura's need to be out of the house first thing in the morning to attend rounds at the hospital.

April was the month when Dante Paolo's scale of health tipped decidedly and permanently to one side. The nausea was constant as was the ever-present pain, a potent blend that all but eliminated his appetite; the downward spiral was accelerating. Only his hypothesis, and now Jumpin' June, made the month of April tolerable. Barely.

———•———

No one likes rejection but at some point everyone experiences its potent sting. Odds were high that one of Dr. Paolo's students would receive a letter of rejection since graduate schools accept only three percent of all applications they receive. With the exception of Brad and Ajay everyone received a rejection letter from at least one school. While Abby entertained the possibility of rejection, and was thus prepared to handle the disappointment, Amy was distraught by the rebuff not only from Harvard, but also from Yale and Columbia. Her grades were near perfect, MCAT scores within the top five percentile and her application was packed with many achievements and accolades.

"I'm too damn Asian," she would cry to Brad. "It's discrimination at its best!" And while she didn't fault Brad for being accepted into "every goddamned medical school" where he had applied, they both knew that it had more to do with his upper crust heritage than with anything else.

"You didn't get a single goddamned rejection!" she'd scream in disbelief. "Not one!"

As it turned out, Amy received and quickly accepted a placement offer from the University of Minnesota Medical School in Duluth, which in her own words was: "Located in the middle of the country, between Boston and nowhere."

In one way Brad also had no choice. He had no choice but to accept Harvard's offer, it was virtually a directive from his parents. And with their scholastic fates sealed, Brad and Amy realized that the thousand miles that separated Boston from Duluth would be the first real test of their young relationship. They also knew that if they emerged as a couple after this episode in their lives—as they would—that they would be able to overcome the certain divorce infection that plagued most medical students who got married while in school, or after graduation when they would labor as an intern, or a resident, in a hospital.

Ajay would not be denied. He quickly accepted the offer of a full scholarship to MIT and he also signed up immediately for the summer graduate student prep course, an eight-week intensive review of mathematics, applied sciences, natural sciences, computer programming, anthropology, and artificial intelligence. He was as content as a skier in the Alps.

It was a youthful faculty that persuaded Phil to accept RPI's offer to join its School of Advanced Mathematics.

"Have you ever even heard of the Hudson River?" Phil asked Ajay who wanted to know more about RPI.

"No," replied Ajay.

"Well RPI's in Troy, New York. It's on the Hudson River. Troy is famous for almost nothing but it is near a town called Whitehall that is the 'Birthplace of the U.S. Navy'. Whitehall is about 150 miles from the Atlantic Ocean, go figure. Best thing about Troy is that it's close to the Adirondacks, which is like Maine except it has more people and fewer blueberries. Ajay, you don't have a clue what I'm talking about do you?" Phil asked. Indeed the newly minted MIT graduate student had no clue what Phil was saying as Ajay hadn't stepped foot outside the state of Massachusetts since he arrived at the academy four years ago.

Abby's road to graduate school rested solely on American University where she was placed on a waitlist; all other schools rejected her outright.

When Dr. Paolo learned of Abby's waitlisted status—which is a dedicated student's highest form of torture—he took matters into his own hands. The ailing professor sent an unsolicited email to American University's Dean of Admissions that read:

> Abigail Lark is a highly motivated, thoughtful and gifted individual who will become one of your prized graduate students. She promises to be a leader among her peers, an innovative and driven researcher, and a dedicated academic and teacher. Abby is easily in the top one percent of the students I've encountered over a quarter century of teaching at Harvard. It is without hesitation or reservation that I strongly encourage you to accept her into your graduate program in the School of Advanced Communications.

Dr. Paolo ended the email by stating that Abby did not seek his help with her application nor did she ask him to send this endorsement. Thirty-six hours later Abby received an email from the Dean of Admissions who informally congratulated her on being accepted into the doctorate program of Advanced Communication at American University. The email also stated that a formal letter of acceptance should be received within a week and that the University would appreciate a response with her decision to accept or decline the position within ten days of receiving the letter.

Abby did not wait for the formal letter to arrive. During a direct call to the Dean, she accepted the position as well as the offer of a teaching assistant position that provided a nominal but reasonable stipend, along with a full tuition wavier. But the first thing she did after receiving the congratulatory email was to phone Dr. Paolo to share the good news. The excitement in her voice was undeniable and during that brief call the professor was, for a moment, pleased and cheery. Shortly after the call ended, however, the broken man broke down; his days of doing good things and helping others were rapidly drawing to a close.

Abby would never learn of Dr. Paolo's intervention.

———•———

He cried often and openly on his deathbed, in his prison cell hospital room, alone in the empty house during that chasm of time between Jumpin' June's late afternoon departure and Laura's early evening arrival. Since the diagnosis, Dante accepted his disease but now he had to accept his death. And sleep, or what masqueraded as sleep being only brief periods of insentience, offered only a temporary reprieve from the constant pain; the pain, the pain, the ruthless pain that radiated throughout his body in all directions with no particular point of origin or purpose.

This time there was no child-mother nor auntie Kay, nor his father nor anyone else, just the beautiful young woman who reminded him of Laura and the young man. They were standing together side by side. They looked directly at him. Ever so slightly they, in near unison, nodded. They were ready for him.

2

Cara Rosa,

On this first day of May I should be focusing all of my energies on preparations for graduation and rejoicing that we are near the end of another school year. However, yesterday I learned that the thorn I had referred to so coarsely in my last email is closer to death than I thought. He has refused treatments and all medications. I've known him only for a short time and yet his pending death haunts me as if I am the one who seeded his cancer. I must release these worthless concerns and focus on the graduation ceremonies, which are only four days away. Please write soon. I long to read your voice.

Abbracci,
Lorenzo

———•———

Laura arrived home an hour later than usual on May Day and despite her decades of experience with patients who were close to death, she was taken aback by how rapidly her husband had deteriorated in just twelve hours. His skin was decidedly more gaunt and yellow, his breathing was shallow and labored, and his heart rate had accelerated; he was becoming dehydrated and delirious. As discussed previously Laura inserted an IV line in her husband's right arm and started hydration fluids at a slow drip rate. She then called her office manager and informed her to cancel her appointments for the rest of the week. All but certain that her husband had only days to live she would nevertheless wait until the morning to initiate her husband's plan. She needed to be absolutely sure.

3

Graduation is the time of the year when academic institutions shine. Buildings get a fresh coat of paint, steps leading to ornate buildings and statues of founders and past presidents are power-washed clean. It's a time when lawns are manicured, landscape mulched and trees and bushes are trimmed or replaced. The all out effort is designed to impress visiting parents, invited dignitaries, and the soon to be, newly minted alumni. And nothing pleases the master of ceremonies or the president of the institution more than to hold commencement exercises outside in perfect weather of blue skies with high, puffy white, cumulus clouds, warm temperatures and a light southerly breeze.

The cool, overcast start to the day of Wilmington College's one hundred and thirty seventh commencement ceremony, held on Saturday the fifth of May, did not foretell the almost perfect weather that lay ahead. The chillier than average temperatures pleased the graduates and professors who wore the traditional caps and gowns, and the fathers and grandfathers who wore suits to the formality, whereas most of the mothers and grandmothers would have preferred the temperature about ten degrees warmer. The refreshing air also helped the graduates recover from a final night of partying after the customary dinner with family and friends who travelled great distances to witness the lofty achievement of earning an undergraduate degree.

And with taut white tall tents and strategically positioned loudspeakers, the orchestra performing classical and modern music along with original scores by the students and professors, and vendors stationed to the perimeter of the school grounds selling food and drink and trinkets, the atmosphere was more circus then cerebral, more jocular than practical. And at Wilmington College, like at all other institutions of higher learning across the nation, there were rules to follow before, during and after the ceremonies. For one last time the College would impart their way on the young adults who would, by the end of the afternoon, be released to the greater world. For most of them this day would mark the end of their education while others will arrive at a new academic start line.

No alcohol, no sandals, no funny sunglasses or hats, no yelling or screaming, and definitely no profanity. Stand in line with your class, follow the instructions, listen politely to the Commencement day speaker, then walk briskly on stage to receive your leather bifold that will one day hold a real diploma after the bills have been paid in full. Stand still for the official picture that will be taken by the official photographer, then walk back to your lawn chair and be seated. And one more thing, enjoy the day; after all, it is your day.

It was nearly high noon and the processional was about to begin as signaled by the call to attention by the long-held note emanating from a single trumpet that echoed from the speakers located throughout the grounds. During the middle of the amplified note Abby, who was standing in line next to someone from her class she hardly knew, felt her cellphone vibrate in the back pocket of her black slacks under her thin black graduation robe.

———•———

Two o'clock Saturday morning and the dark, night air outside his window was eerily still. Dante Paolo could not sleep through the pain that traversed his cancer-controlled body, which perhaps was a good thing because he knew that this day, this Saturday, would be different than any other he'd experienced in his life. Through the agony, his memory treated him to one last bit of ecstasy, music. His mind played a two-piano, four-hand rendition of Lecuona's *Malagueña*. The tempo started slowly with purpose that he had always associated with vicious perseverance, but as the movement climbed to the ever-rising crescendo what he clearly hears—what he had never heard before this moment—was that the crescendo was a tender, resolute declaration of submission despite its tenacious façade. As the melody played, he wept.

It was unfortunate that today was a Saturday. Throughout his life, this weekend day had been his favorite one of the entire week. As a child he eagerly anticipated the parade of Saturday morning cartoons that began precisely at seven o'clock when the stations began to broadcast programs after the national anthem ended. As a teenager he would drag his sorry self out of bed early on the first weekend morning not to watch cartoons that were now shown in vivid Technicolor, but rather to deliver the morning paper along his neighborhood route—a job that taught him the value of a dollar. As a young man in his twenties he could hardly contain his desires to see his girlfriend on Saturday evening despite having had worked all day at the local bakery. Her perfume imbued on his dress shirt would linger into Sunday, a scent that would make him explode in a renewed sense of sexual passion, like a Pavlovian dog on steroids. Saturdays during the past few decades were filled with the routine seasonal chores associated with the pride of home ownership.

If he could, he would record in writing the historical significance of this day as he had done just a handful of times in the past, for he knew it would be his last. Through the darkness of the room his imagination saw the stagehand grabbing the heavy rope that would lower the curtain on his final scene. He also heard Laura lightly snoring on the couch in the living room adjacent to his medical room prison cell.

At least those on death row know exactly when they are going to die, he thought to himself. *That's got to be better than this.*

He wanted to again find a way through the pain's maze, but he could do so no longer. He was becoming delusional, his mind vacillating between lucid and lost, with the latter gaining on the former. He'd thought about this moment, his death, in the past during many walks in the woods, during sleepless nights; he wondered how it would be. He no longer had to wonder. It felt final. Bewildering.

So this is how it ends, the finale. Taken down by cancer. I...

Then he remembered.

The plan. His carefully laid out plan now had to advance on its own inertia. He could no longer stoke its fading embers. He just needed to make sure that his final entry; his last experiment was initiated as planned.

As planned...

As planned...

As planned...

Focus on breathing, he pouted soundlessly like a goldfish gasping outside its glass bowl on the cold, dry nightstand.

Fuck you pain! Fuck you cancer! He screamed in his head.

Remain calm. Relax. Don't lose it. Soon it will be light and...

Adrenalin shot through Laura's body as she processed the first rays of Saturday morning's sunlight. She tilted her head to expose both ears; she tried to listen. She lay very still. Not a sound emanated from the converted guest bedroom. She leapt to her feet tossing the blanket aside and, with heart pounding, braced to see her husband dead.

He was as still as a boulder in a dried riverbed, but he was not dead. The early morning's chalky light was just enough for her to see his chest expanding and contracting ever so slowly and shallowly. His eyes were closed and his head was turned to his left towards the windows.

He was quiet but his skin was a shade of yellow that she had never before seen on a human being. It looked almost translucent as if illuminated by an internal oil lamp. His body was shutting down and she knew that he wouldn't make it through the day. He was in liver failure and probably he was now in kidney failure too.

She thought about the plan.

"Do I really have to do this crazy plan?" she questioned aloud hoping that Dante would reply.

There was no answer.

Laura opened the dresser drawer and pulled out the blue cap Bob Wyle had dropped off earlier in the week. Her husband did not seem to notice as she placed the snug-fitting hat on his head. Then, as detailed in the plan, she concealed the blue hat with a black and gold Boston Bruins winter cap.

There, she thought to herself. *At least you won't be chilly.*

Slowly, Dante Paolo turned his head and faced his beautiful wife who was so healthy and so full of life. Their eyes met. They conveyed a reciprocated message of enduring love and of fading hope. Nothing needed to be said. It was over and they both knew it.

"Help me," he whispered through labored breath. "Help me write a great ending."

"I will," she sighed. "I promise, I will."

4

Jumpin' June stood in the doorway of the makeshift hospital room and stared at Dr. Paolo for a moment before turning back to the living room where Laura was seated on the couch. The young nurse had never experienced someone actually dying and although her training should have prepared her for that event the only thing she could do was to break down and take comfort in Laura's arms.

"Oh my God, he looks so bad," she wailed. "He changed so much since yesterday...from just yesterday! What happened?" What Laura had at her ready disposal was a medical explanation of what had occurred and what was about to occur but she said nothing because she knew that the young woman neither sought nor needed a lecture at this moment.

"I don't want to see him suffer," said the young nurse between sobs. "I should go get him some morphine patches. They'll put him at ease. I'm licensed to carry them."

"He specifically rejected the use of pain killers and he's managed well to this point," offered Laura. "So I don't think they'll be needed."

"I'll bring some back when I return around noon, just in case."

"Okay, that'll be fine," said Laura just to appease her.

Jumpin' June left the house by 9:00 a.m. with a promise to return by noon with the high strength morphine patches.

———•———

The text message on Abby's phone was simple: The time is near.

Laura had no idea where Abby was or what she was doing when she sent the text message. She was just following the plan. Immediately after sending the message, Laura gathered the items as detailed in Dante's plan and placed them under his bed and out of sight, hidden by the overhang of the white mattress cover.

Abby's eyes widened and her heart rate surged as she again read the four-word message on the small screen. In an instant she forwarded it to the group that had been preprogramed in her phone then calmly broke out of line and walked towards the student parking lot.

The processional and the line of students marched forward as Abby stopped to slip out of her graduation robe and to take off her cap; she did not want to look like a bride leaving the alter on her wedding day. With her robe draped around her arm, she turned to the left and saw Amy and Brad sprinting hand-in-hand towards her like newlyweds fleeing a shower of birdseed and rice. Phil jumped in Brad's Audi whose exact location in the parking lot was relayed by Abby and the four almost-graduates were on their way to be with their beloved professor for one last time.

"Oh, my fucking word. I am so fucked!" said Phil as Brad left the congested campus and entered the highway. "My parents are going to absolutely kill me. Great fucking timing, Dr. Paolo!"

"Yup," replied Brad with a deep sigh. "I don't want to even think about the consequences."

Abby and Amy sat in silence. They wondered to themselves what they were doing and what they were about to find when they arrived.

Both Jumpin' June and Laura were unprepared for the sudden arrival of the students, some of whom were still in their solid black graduation robes.

"Don't tell me you graduated today," Laura said upon seeing Brad, Phil and Amy in their robes.

"Well, technically not yet," replied Phil who walked past Laura eager to get to his station. "That will take place in about fifteen minutes," he added glancing at his watch as he made his way to the now familiar kitchen.

Abby was shaking when she hugged Laura. At that moment, it was uncertain who was soothing whom but both women appreciated each other's firm, comforting embrace. When the hug ended, Abby went and sat in the living room couch and helped herself to a tissue to wipe her tears.

Amy sought to keep her emotions in check but fell apart once she saw the stream of tears on Laura's face. Before heading to the kitchen to join Phil as per protocol Brad placed his hand on Laura's shoulder while she and Amy hugged.

"These are Dante's students," Laura said in a raspy, cracked voice to Jumpin' June who had just emerged from Dr. Paolo's makeshift hospital room. "This is Amy, that's Abby over there, and Phil and Brad are in the kitchen. June Kennedy is Dante's hospice care provider."

Jumpin' June quickly shook the hands of the women but didn't bother to make her way to the kitchen to meet the men because she had an urgent message for Laura.

"He asked for you."

———•———

Jan Heilman strode across the stage, stole a glance out to the audience where she spotted her younger sister standing on a metal fold-down chair beside her father waving her arms wildly. Jan then shook hands with President Holliday, then Dean Benedetti before finally receiving the rectangular blue leather bifold with the Wilmington College insignia emblazed in gold on the cover from a Chancellor of the College.

"Phillip J. Hess," the loudspeaker blared.

Lisa Jackson, the next person in line, did a stutter step as she started to make her way across the stage only to be halted by the Registrar. Lorenzo Benedetti looked down the line of graduates. Not only did he not spot Phil, but also could not see Abigail Lark nor Bradford MacIntyre, who should have been within sight of the stage. By the time Henry Yott, the last person to receive a degree from the college that year crossed the stage, the total number of absentees numbered exactly four—Hess, Ito, Lark, and MacIntyre.

The Dean made the connection immediately and thought: *That bastard! What in hell is he up to now?*

5

Laura turned the knob and slowly opened the door to the converted guest bedroom. She paused momentarily to look back at the living room where Amy, Abby and Jumpin' Jane were seated on the couch chatting softly to each other, then entered the room that had become heavy with the fetid air of pending death. She closed the door behind her.

For the moment he was relaxed and he was not moaning in pain, which was a good thing because Laura absolutely hated to hear people moan. She leaned across her husband's torso to hear him say in a shallow voice, "I've always loved you. Thank you for all you've done for me and... and for what you are about to do. I am at peace. Are they here?"

"Yes," she replied.

"Good," he uttered through pulsated breaths. "Tell them I'm at peace. Please don't make this...please don't make this drag on...now's the time honey. Do it."

"Honey," Laura said with bloodshot eyes swollen with tears. "One thing I've never told you...that I now want you to know, is that when we lost the baby..." Laura paused then closed her eyes tight to hold back a flood of tears, "we actually lost two of them, twins... a boy and a girl... they told me that you had left the room after the first one was delivered, the second one had died about a week earlier and was delivered along with the placenta ... I didn't see the point of telling you, of adding to your pain.... to our pain," she added as she put her head down on her husband's sunken chest and sobbed openly releasing decades of pent-up agony.

"Got it," Phil said to Brad as he pointed to the screen on the laptop that was on the kitchen's granite counter. "The hat is transmitting perfectly. Recording."

Laura's words were difficult for Dr. Paolo to comprehend. The pain had paralyzed his mind. He was numb. He'd trained himself to focus exclusively on the plan. Laura was still until her husband uttered his final words:

"Do it now!" he demanded with as much energy and conviction as his feeble body could muster.

Reviewing this exact moment in her mind many times over the past week did little to prepare Laura for the flood of emotions she now experienced. They clutched her throat like the grip of a raptor's talons and her knees quivered uncontrollably. Drawing on the strength of her husband's panicked voice she reached under the bed and retrieved the small syringe filled with the fluorescent pink fluid. Dante knew that within seconds of injecting the fluid into his IV line, the toxic fluid would enter his brain, which would likely be as lethal for him as it had been for Cookie. He also predicted, based on what Cookie's handlers witnessed, that the tracer would cause him tremendous pain, an event that would be in direct violation to the famous oath Laura pledged to uphold when she graduated from medical school. Yet her actions were swift and sure. She twisted off the luer-locked needle at the base where it attached to the syringe, then tightened it onto the extra port of the IV line. Like she'd done millions of times before when injecting her patients with life-saving vaccines or antibiotics, she pushed steadily on the plunger with her thumb until the contents of the syringe were emptied into her husband's circulatory system.

The tears that rolled down Laura's face had not reached her blouse before his back arched violently upward as every muscle in his body constricted in acute pain. His elbows and forearms were flat on the bed, his head had angled backwards and his pelvis thrust upwards towards the ceiling—every muscle was in spasm. Through a clenched jaw escaped only muted sounds of deep agony as the chemical dye burned its way through his veins and arteries destroying their fragile inner walls as the tracer travelled the multi-branched highway that led from one cancer-riddled organ to the other. But it was when *RW88* reached the usually impermeable blood-brain barrier did Dante Paolo's eyes popped open, his clenched jaw tried to force out a scream but one never materialized.

The pain's intensity was unimaginable as the chemical shot up through his cranium and down his spinal cord.

With purpose, Laura removed the syringe that carried the dye and attached a new syringe full of sterile saline. She plunged the saline through the port to clear the IV line of the pink tracer and then she refilled the syringe with dark red blood by pulling back on the plunger. Before it had a chance to clot, the blood was injected into a tube of the solution her husband had prepared to immediately stop all cellular processes including DNA replication. Laura removed a sterile cotton swab and she tried not to think twice about plunging it into the now slack mouth of her pain-encased husband, who had been transformed in a matter of seconds into a test subject of his own making. The cotton swab containing the dying man's cheek cells was placed in a special tube and capped tightly. Both tubes—one containing Dr. Paolo's blood and the other containing his cheek cells—were placed in insulated container with ice packs and stored in the bedroom closet as instructed.

She then placed her warm forefinger on his right wrist. Dr. Laura Kean felt no pulse.

With steadfast efficiency, she removed both hats and quietly placed them in the closet next to the insulated container. She then closed her husband's eyelids and instead of trying to close his jaw, she just covered his entire head with the white bed sheet.

Laura was emotionally spent.

She opened the door and faced the young ladies who were still seated on the couch and said simply, "He's gone, one oh-seven p.m. I've stopped the IV."

Instantly, Abby rose from the couch and cupped the new widow's face with her young hands. Staring directly into the physician's eyes Abby softly whispered, "Thank you. It's awesome. You *still* are my joy, my world."

Upon hearing these words Laura embraced Abby tightly and wept openly.

June wasn't use to any of this and she really didn't want to go into the room to confirm that Dr. Paolo had in fact died. Although she violated protocol, she also trusted the physician's assessment. Desperate for a cigarette, June asked Laura if it was okay if she went outside to call the ambulance.

Laura nodded in approval.

What transpired in a matter of seconds made Brad and Phil recoil. From the laptop's screen Dr. Paolo's brain looked like an exploding star, a supernova. It appeared as if every possible neuron in his brain fired simultaneously, an event that created a brilliant explosion of pure white. After that instant, what would later be coined as the "STAB moment", the neural activity monitor went dark leaving just the outlined image of Dante Paolo's braincase, until that too faded to black.

———•———

The Moment of Absolute Clarity was coupled with a complete reconciliation of all aspects and conditions of human existence.

Dante felt no pain after he saw the intense light; a swirling array of white that he had hoped triggered a response he'd pre-programmed into his subconscious. The response, the last signal sent from his human brain, was a single-worded message to Lorenzo Benedetti.

The pain dissipated. He was now in a place never before described. The place had no bounds, no time, nor friction. He recognized his counterparts from the other verses. They were there, all of them. They communicated with no words or actions but effortlessly by thought alone as the wind speaks to the sky, the stars to the moon, a different language altogether. They knew each other without pretense or question and they acknowledged and welcomed his energy into this dimension that revealed a simple and logical transition.

He also recognized the child-mother and the man, the young woman who looked like Laura and the young man. And others too, including auntie Kay.

Could it be this simple?

Yes, it is always been simple, easy but you've been blind. Cloaked in denial.

Now you are complete.

Now you understand.

Now you too have been reconciled.

———◦———

Within fifteen minutes of having received June's call, two EMTs from the town's ambulance service rolled a gurney into the living room and carefully placed the flaccid body of Dante Paolo onto it. Laura, June and the students did not watch. They were in the kitchen consoling each other. After loading the body into the ambulance, the two EMTs came in with some paperwork that released the body to them and with instructions to transport it directly to the crematorium in nearby North Woodland. Laura signed the paper as the next of kin and then June attested to have witnessed Dante Paolo's death. She also noted the exact time Dante was pronounced dead. The official cause of death simply read: Complications of pancreatic cancer. The ambulance drove away quietly without sirens or flashing lights; the emergency vehicle didn't need to get anywhere in a hurry—it was no longer a matter of life or death.

6

Dr. Benedetti arrived home in the early evening with plenty of time to enjoy the fading light of the setting sun. The traditional post-commencement dinner with Jean and some of the college's Trustees went smoothly, but he felt impatient and distracted unlike past years when he unwound at this end of the academic year celebration. *Perhaps*, he thought to himself, *it's time to retire*. And in keeping with another long held and more private end of the year ritual Lorenzo Benedetti poured himself a glass of Vin Santo effectively emptying the bottle he had carried back from Italy years ago. *Empty. How apropos.*

He placed his glass of the sweet wine on the table next to the base of the computer's monitor and began to compose an email.

> Cara Rosa,
> Today we graduated the one hundred and thirty-seventh class from the college. It was a beautiful warm day and one to remember.

Dr. Benedetti completed typing the sentence then reached for the glass on the desk and took a small sip of wine. He returned the glass to the table having thought of the next sentence and placed his hands on the home position on the keyboard when he noticed an error on the last sentence. It read:

> It was a beautiful warm day and one to reconcile.

Without much thought Lorenzo replaced "reconcile" with "remember" and continued typing when the word instantly reverted back to "reconcile." "What's this? It must be some auto-correct problem or something," he reasoned aloud. He overcame the apparent software problem by simply ending the sentence with "cherish" and continued to compose his email.

> Cara Rosa,
> Today we graduated the one hundred and thirty-seventh class from the college. It was a beautiful warm day and one to cherish. For me it was remarkable how little enjoyment I

felt presiding over the ceremonies compared to past years, perhaps I am ready to leave this position and this way of life. Are you ready for me?

Dr. Benedetti smiled at the question and the thought of spending his days with his sweet cousin as he looked down at the keyboard. But what he saw when he looked up at the screen startled him.

> Cara Rosa,
> Today we graduated the one hundred and thirty-seventh class from the college. It was a beautiful warm day and one to cherish. For me it was reconciled how little enjoyment I felt presiding over the ceremonies compared to past years, perhaps I am reconciled to leave this position and this way of life. Are you reconciled for me?

He retyped "ready" and it immediately reverted back to "reconciled". Then, ever the experimentalist, he typed "recognize" and it too changed to "reconciled"; "remarkable", "reconfigure", "recoil", and "remade" all changed immediately to "reconciled". Indeed, every word he typed that began with "re" became "reconciled".

In sheer frustration from what the Dean assumed was a glitch in the software, he pushed and held the power button on his computer until the computer turned off; the monitor went black. In one harsh gulp he finished the remaining Vin Santo and retired for the evening.

———·———

Dante Paolo's body arrived at the crematorium with one hour to spare before the burners were turned off for the day. In keeping with the crematorium's protocol, the director called Laura as the next of kin to confirm that Dante Paolo's body had, in fact, been sent by ambulance to their facility for immediate cremation as instructed in the prepaid plan purchased a few months ago. Laura confirmed the director's statements. She also declined the option to witness the initiation of the cremation process, which was usually reserved for short memorial services. The last item on the director's checklist was final approval from the next of kin to have the ashes interred in the Eternal Garden, which was, according to their website: A lovely, peaceful and professionally landscaped garden located behind the crematorium where remains are placed in a dignified manner to be forever reconnected with the blessed earth.

Laura approved, and the call ended.

Since it was the last burn of the day, the operator of the cremator—a young man in his late 20s—decided to manually override the automated cremation program and allow the bone fragments and ashes to cool slowly overnight instead of rapidly using an energy-consuming cooling system.

The next day, a Sunday, the young man returned to the crematorium just after sunrise. He transferred Dante Paolo's chunky, chalk-like remains from the large burn tray into a well-worn metal bucket.

The dense growth in the wetlands behind the crematorium sieved the sun's shallow, but intense early morning rays, as the young man still groggy with sleep, left the rear of the building with the well-worn metal bucket in hand and walked the short distance to the Eternal Garden whose entrance was marked with a green granite post. He made his way beyond the professionally landscaped section that featured a small stone bench and a dry birdbath to a recently dug dirt pit. With the metal bucket's handle in his left hand the young man used his right hand to tip and empty the container of its familiar looking contents.

As the cooled remains fell into the pit, a slight ground-level breeze lifted a single fleck of gray-colored ash skyward. It drifted aimlessly pass the edge of the Eternal Garden to a wooded area beyond the wetlands.

The light fleck of Dante Paolo's carbonaceous essence—tossed higgle-dy-piggledy by the whims of the playful breezes—silently landed atop the edge of a slate-colored, veil-thin, newborn flesh of a *Craterellus cornuco-pioides*, the Black Trumpet of Death, the fungal delicacy that had success-fully eluded both the professor's plate and palate.

The Manuscript

1

The anger and disappointment displayed by the parents of the missing graduates was appropriately substantial. There were no text messages or phone calls. There was nothing but total communication blackouts. No one knew why the four graduates would leave their moment of glory— their day in the spotlight, their day to dance across on the main stage. But most troubling to the parents and family members alike was that no one knew their whereabouts; they'd simply disappeared. Even the campus police were of little help. All they could do was to keep everyone calm and gather the necessary information.

The only person who had an idea of what might have happened was Dean Benedetti. He knew that there was a connection between the four missing students and the ailing Dr. Paolo but he had no way of communicating this information to the parents of the missing graduates. And with his cell phone sitting idle in his apartment during graduation ceremonies, Ajay did not read the text at all. He suspected that he knew what had happened to his friends, but he too kept quiet.

By midafternoon Saturday, when the four mutineers arrived back on campus, the party was clearly over. The circus atmosphere had diminished to the point that the cleanup crews had already begun to pick up discarded programs and shreds of burst balloons. Trash bins were being emptied and folding chairs collected and packed into crates on their way to storage.

And except for Abby, whose father had left campus for the tavern long ago, the others had no trouble locating their respective families on the vast green lawn. The MacIntyre clan, which included second cousins some of whom were only toddlers, was huddled with Amy's parents as the two families had met the evening prior in a get-to-know-the-parents-of-the-girlfriend luncheon. The Hess family was off alone under a large tree looking around as if they had missed something larger than the commencement exercise itself.

Phil noticed that Abby's father was not present and he asked her to stay with him for support as he faced his family. He reasoned that they wouldn't explode too loudly if they thought that Abby was his girlfriend, and for the most part, the scheme worked.

For consistency and in solidarity, they all vowed to use the same excuse: "It was his dying wish that we all be together and we didn't want to let him down. We just reacted to the situation and we did what we thought was the right thing to do, just as you taught us." And although some of the anger subsided when told of the passing of their much-respected professor, not everyone was pleased with the excuse; it made them feel second-rate to someone whom they hardly knew.

None of the four students, now officially Wilmington College alumni, nor Dr. Ito, uttered a word about Dr. Paolo's experiments.

Brad looked across the lawn at the others and saw an opportunity. Knowing that his father was always prepared for the unexpected, Brad asked if there was room at the party for Abby, Phil and Phil's parents. To celebrate the day and to boastfully announce their son's acceptance to

Harvard Medical School, the MacIntyre's had reserved the entire banquet room at *Ship-to-Shore*. They even hired a string quartet to entertain the family and friends invited to the early evening event. Seating for seventy-five would accommodate the MacIntyre's out of town friends and family, including Amy's family who had been invited during the previous day's luncheon, a few fellow college trustees and, of course, President Holliday. Brad was roundly assured that there would be plenty of room for the Hess family and for Abby as well.

For her part, Abby let her father know that she was fine and that she would be home later. She made no attempt to add that Mr. MacIntyre had also invited him to the party because she knew that he would not care to mix with this crowd.

———•———

The news of Dr. Paolo's passing spread quickly.

Although most everyone knew that he had end-stage cancer and was in hospice care, the news still struck his neighbors, friends, and fellow faculty members oddly for three reasons: how rapidly the disease had progressed, because he was in good physical health before the diagnosis, and because he was relatively young.

Robert Pierce received the tell-all text message on his smartphone from Beverly who detailed the activities in the neighborhood including the sighting of Brad's Audi and the arrival and departure of the slow-moving ambulance with its sirens and strobe lights off. Compared to the early part of the message, the last line seemed rather crude: EMTs removed body.

But as sour as the message was Rob got the point and he somberly shared it with President Holliday when he spotted her shortly after commencement ceremonies ended. Rob pieced together the circumstance surrounding the disappearance of the four graduates, inferences he also shared with his boss.

With the sad information Jean Holliday did as she always did—she sought to make things better. She thought to recreate the commencement ceremony at the celebration gathering at *Ship-to-Shore* later that evening for Brad, but what she could not have known at that time was that all four absent students would be at the celebration. So later that evening when Dr. Holliday called each student up to the front of the banquet room to receive their diploma, they in fact were handed the same, re-circulated leather bifold emblazed in gold with the Wilmington College insignia—a move that worked perfectly to the delight of each attendee as well as to the respective family's amateur photographer. The private commencement scene was one of those unscripted moments in life that came as no surprise to Brad, who had witnessed several of them in his young life, but one that made Amy, Phil and Abby shake their head in disbelief.

The graduates raised a glass of champagne and toasted each other, and Dr. Paolo too. They marveled at how well, against all odds, their roller-coaster day had turned out. They were together at the start of a new chapter in their lives, a chapter created by Dr. Paolo during his life, and forged forever by his death.

2

Lorenzo Benedetti learned about Dante Paolo's passing not from Jean Holliday but from his administrative secretary when he arrived at his office the Monday following Commencement.

"It was inevitable," was the only comment the Dean could muster as he collected his mail, entered his office, and closed the door behind him. On the top of the pile was a large brown envelope bearing his name not typed, but handwritten. He sat in his large black leather chair, turned the envelope over, undid the clasp and removed its contents: a plain white envelope and a letter dated April twentieth.

Dear Dr. Benedetti,

I know you. I know who you are. I know what you thought yesterday and what you are thinking right now. Don't bother asking Rosa because she won't know. Only I know and shortly you will know too. Surprised? Well, frankly, so am I. Not because I have entered your mind but because how simple it was. I've RECONCILED the universal truth. For all of your research in neuroscience (and I read all of your papers, even those that are complete BS) you didn't even come close, not even remotely close, to discovering this truth. But, to your credit, you didn't let failure stand in your way and you did develop some important tools and, while you did some interesting things, you completely missed the big picture. You see Lorenzo, skeptics and critics like you can drive science forward or you can drive scientists mad. And sometimes you can accomplish both at the same time and, right, you guessed it, I'm one of those scientists whom you drove mad. In fact, in my current state, I remain a madman even now that I've proven a hypothesis that will RECONCILE every aspect of human existence. The results that you are about to witness will irrevocably show that my students and I have RECONCILED three areas of science that others thought were IRRECONCILABLE. It is Nature's one and only Holy Grail. It RECONCILES many fields including neurobiology and biology, genetics and epigenetics, physics and metaphysics. It is the answer to all of the unanswered questions posed by humans since the spark of their primitive first thought. It will define our very existence and you, Lorenzo, will use your pathetically attained stature in the scientific arena to shepherd this manuscript to the public for the benefit of all mankind. And yes, you have no option but to follow the instructions written on the paper contained in the enclosed white envelope. By the fact that you recognize the bolded words above demonstrates that I have your mind. Should you fail to follow these instructions, I will be your personal plague, your eternal scourge. So I suggest that you take this matter seriously. Don't test me Lorenzo for you will not like the consequences.

Dante Paolo's signature was on the bottom of the letter with the date written in the European-standard style of day, month and year, printed directly across his last name, a method used by many scientists to prevent forgery.

Dr. Benedetti leaned back in his chair and stared directly ahead, uncertain of his next move. He reread the letter and asked himself several questions. *No one at the college knows about Rosa, no one. How would he have known about Rosa? Did he hack into my email account? I guess that's possible but then the word "reconcile"? Is this simply a coincidence? Yes, yes probably so,* he reasoned.

Quickly he picked up his iPad and started a new Note. He tapped the letters: b-o-y and the word "boy" became visible on the note. On the next line he tapped: s-c-h-o-o-l and "school" appeared. Tapped: r-e-p-o-r-t and "reconciled" appeared; r-e-p-a-i-r-e-d and "reconciled" appeared.

Dr. Benedetti quit the application and stared straight ahead. He leapt out of his chair and, taking the iPad with him, went outside his office to the startled secretary.

"Here take this and type a Note," he demanded in a hurried voice.

"I've never used one of these things," replied the elderly secretary.

Dr. Benedetti took the iPad back and started a fresh Note by tapping the plus sign in the upper right hand corner of the app, a move that also prompted the keyboard to pop up from the bottom of the screen.

He handed the tablet back to the secretary and commanded, "Type the word 'girl'". The secretary, who had never before typed on a flat surface awkwardly found the home hand position and rapidly typed g-i-r-l and "girl", appeared. She looked up at Dr. Benedetti who then bellowed, "Type 'violin'," he said and instantly the word "violin" appeared on the yellow, lined screen. "Now, 'refrain'" he barked. And, just as the secretary expected, the word "refrain" appeared on the line next to the words "girl" and "violin". After seeing the results, Dr. Benedetti took the iPad from the bewildered woman's hands, closed the cover that effectively put the tablet to sleep, and returned to his office closing the door behind him. At his desk, Dean Benedetti opened the cover of the iPad and the electronic yellow Note instantly appeared. Typed on the page were the words "girl" next to "violin" followed by the word "reconciled".

He closed the iPad's cover, placed it on the desk and picked up a yellow notepad and a fine-point Parker pen. His cursive handwriting had lost some of the perfection that had been drilled into him by the nuns who were his elementary school teachers but it was nonetheless superior to most men his age and readily legible. He carefully wrote the word "violin" with the familiar motions of his thumb and forefinger that grip the pen that created the letters of the word in sharp black ink. This simple result pleased Dr. Benedetti and with that little victory he moved on to the deciding part of the exercise. On the next line his fingers led the pen in the dance that began with a left-to-right upward sweep that formed the lower case "r" followed by a swoop back down to the solid line briefly as the pen was led upwards again to produce a small loop that was the letter "e". The next set of pen strokes should have fashioned the letters of rest of the word, "-member", that Dr. Benedetti had intended to write, but his hand was abruptly and decidedly appropriated and to his stunned disbelief the pen was instead guided to shape the word, "reconciled".

He did not repeat this test. His hand had encountered a force similar to the rubbery energy felt when one tries to bring the same pole ends of two strong magnets together. It was the oddest sensation he'd ever felt in his long life.

The Parker pen landed with a thud on the yellow pad as he again recoiled in disbelief. He then picked up Dr. Paolo's letter and reread the last line:

> Don't test me Lorenzo for you will not like the consequences.

Dr. Benedetti told his secretary that he would be working from home for the rest of the day and promptly made his way out of the building and off campus. In the solitude of his home, Lorenzo Benedetti tried to gather his thoughts, to prepare himself for what may be contained in the still sealed white envelope. He had no idea what to expect but the strange events that transpired last evening and again this morning had him on edge. He could feel his heart racing. Perhaps a shot of brandy was needed to calm his nerves but he decided against it given the mid-morning hour.

Sitting at his home desk, he used a solid brass letter opener to create a clean slit on the top of the envelope. Inside he found a single item. It was a small translucent plastic container that snugly held a thin SD card. The 1G printed on the tiny data storage disc indicated that it could hold up to one gigabyte of data. With shaky hands, Dr. Benedetti opened the container and pulled out the SD card and held it by the edges to avoid touching the gold-plated contacts. He noticed that the little slide on the side of the card was in the locked position, a precaution designed to ensure that no one accidently overwrote its data. He located an SD slot under a plastic flap in the front of his desktop computer just below the never used floppy disk drive. He carefully inserted the card then turned on the same PC that had annoyed him to no end just twelve hours earlier. A few minutes later, when the computer had completed it startup cycle, Dr. Benedetti clicked the SD card icon that was labeled "The Last Hypothesis" and opened it to see that it contained another folder with the same name. But when he clicked on this second folder a text box appeared that prompted the user for a password.

A password? Did I miss something in the envelope? He wondered. But after another look inside both the white, and the larger brown envelope, he was convinced that he had not missed anything so he decided to try the label of the SD card because it seemed like an obvious password but when he typed t-h-e-l-a-s-t-h-y-p-o-t-h-e-s-i-s the message on the screen read: Incorrect password.

As he leaned back in his chair to contemplate his next move, his eyes spotted the empty glass of Vin Santo from last evening. He picked up the glass and smelled the sweet aroma of liquor that had dried at the bottom of the glass and, in that instant, a Pavlovian-trigger was pulled and the password came to him clearly. He pulled himself towards the keyboard and typed r-e-c-o-n-c-i-l-e, but, to his dismay, the incorrect password message appeared with an added message that asked: Hint? Dr. Benedetti clicked on the word "hint" and the short cryptic phrase read: past tense. The elderly scientist stared at the clue then back to the glass, then back to the clue and thought for a moment before he pounced on the keyboard and typed r-e-c-o-n-c-i-l-e-d. The folder now opened readily. Inside it listed two folders and one document file in alphabetical order.

The folders were color-coded. The green folder was labeled "Data", the blue folder was labeled "Manuscript" and the document file was a simple titled: Read First. Lorenzo double-clicked on the document file and a three-page letter appeared on the screen. The letter contained a pointed and sharply worded set of instructions that prepared him for what he was about to read in the "Manuscript in Preparation" document that would be found in the blue folder and the experimental results presented in detail in the green folder.

The three-page letter explained the entire story beginning with how he generated The Last Hypothesis following the classroom research conducted by Amy, Brad, Abby and Phil. In truth, Dr. Benedetti could only recall Abby's telepathy presentation at the seminar program, not for the data she described, but because he marked that moment as the beginning of the end of Dante Paolo's short tenure at the college. The letter continued, without verbosity, to describe the key experiments performed with Dr. Bob Wyle who worked in Dr. Jin Sukawa's lab at MIT, and Dr. Ito's contributions in sequencing and analyzing DNA.

In the middle of the second page, Dr. Paolo described his merciful, and simultaneously meaningful, suicide. In haunting detail he described the clever way he self-injected RW88 into the IV drip line without anyone's knowledge; not even those individuals that he assumed would be present. The exact methods would be revealed only to the readers of the manuscript. In fact, Dr. Paolo stated that the only way to know if the final experiment was executed would be when Dr. Benedetti received emails from Ito, and Wyle or Sukawa. It was anticipated that Dr. Wyle would be the first to contact him, probably within a week, with the results of the final experiment followed by emails from Dr. Ito within a month or so. Dr. Paolo explained that he anticipated the results of the final experiments and therefore took the liberty to include the presumed results in the draft manuscript.

The letter gave Dr. Benedetti low-level authority to revise the manuscript, but it also stated that The Last Hypothesis must be supported, or nullified, by final experiments. The Last Hypothesis was either right or wrong, it must not, under any circumstances, be altered to conform to other data. Furthermore, given their superior understanding of both the technology and of the scientific principals being tested, Drs. Ito, Wyle and Sukawa must have the final word on how the methods are presented, and how the data are described and discussed, in the manuscript.

Dante Paolo's instructions ended with a detailed plan of how the manuscript should be submitted and the list of authors. With scientific publications, the position of a person in the list of authors denotes one of two things: the relative intellectual contribution to the project, and the head of the laboratory from where the work originated or was conducted. The latter spot was traditionally reserved at the end of the list:

> The author list shall be written as follows and without exception, Phillip Hess*, Abigail Lark*, Bradford MacIntyre*, Amy Ito*, Robert Wyle[1], Jainbin Ito[2], Jin Sukawa[1,3], and Dante Paolo[4].

The asterisks denoted that each person contributed equally to the project; the superscripts 1 and 2 referred to their respective academic affiliation that was printed in tiny font at the bottom of the first page. Superscript 3 identified the corresponding author, the person who is the contact person for the publishers and the media.

Only a month prior to his death, Dr. Paolo aggressively recruited Dr. Sukawa to agree to hold this most valuable and visible of academic assignments. The elder scientist acquiesced given Dante's failing health and also because of the "profound findings of the telepathy experiments", data that would be eclipsed in importance by the newer results of Dr. Paolo's final experiment. Superscript 4 pointed to a single word in the footnote: deceased.

The acknowledgements section of a scientific publication is where the source of funding is presented, and also where minor contributions of others are listed. Before computers and word processors the typist, and the person who drew the figures by hand, would be listed in the acknowledgements section. For most individuals it would be the only time in their lives that their name would appear in print; it amounted to fourteen and a half of their allotted fifteen minutes of fame.

The letter also indicated that the manuscript already contained a completed acknowledgements section. Only two names were listed.

> We thank Ajay Adani for technical input and Lorenzo Benedetti for assistance with the final preparation of the manuscript.

The letter was signed and dated by Dante Paolo and included two short postscripts. One postscript read that Abby Lark was the student contact on the project and that he should send her an email soon to verify his involvement. And the other postscript described a way to get the manuscript—which was sure to be controversial—published.

All this work for an acknowledgement? Lorenzo thought to himself before even taking a look at the manuscript. *What a waste of time. I don't need this!* But no sooner did he formulate those thoughts when his right hand, his strong sure dominant hand, was invisibly drawn, with the accelerating attractive force of the opposite poles of two magnets, to the white paper dated April twentieth that was laying on his desk. The fingers of his right hand picked up the bottom of the letter and, without Dr. Benedetti's deliberate assistance, tilted it upward. With a sudden twist of his right wrist, the letter angled slightly upwards to align with the neuroscientist's ever-widening eyes that clearly focused the last line:

Don't test me Lorenzo for you will not like the consequences.

Like a manual transmission unable to shift out of neutral, the Monday after graduation is a strange day stuck somewhere between anticipation and initiation; a fleeting moment of blissful limbo. The groggy graduate is no longer a structured student burdened with the constant demands of the academic think-day nor has he or she stepped foot on life's conveyer belt that forever grinds to adulthood complete with permanent problems and persistent payments. And to make it all the sweeter it was the dreaded first day of the work week when the conveyer belt that carried the rest of society could clearly be heard churning in the background.

The sunlight that entered Abby's bedroom brought with it decidedly warmer breezes that entered through the east facing window. Lying on her side Abby raised her arms as she twisted to lie on her back. She opened her fisted hands allowing the digits to spread wide open in a manner that seemed to mimic the motions of the pink perennial primrose that blossomed in the empty lot adjacent to her house. The morning stretch combined with the lingering memory of Phil's surprising passionate kiss after Brad's party caused her nipples to harden and her areolae to crinkle tight under her well-worn cotton tee shirt that doubled as her nightgown. Allowing herself a moment of indulgence, Abby cupped her firm left breast with her right hand and slowly brought its forefinger and thumb together on the hardened point squeezing harder and harder all the while imagining that it was Phil's hand. Her invigorated left hand found its way under her shirt to the soft supple skin of her round belly and downwards to the top of her warmed panties. Bringing her legs together while allowing her imagination and her hands to take control made the graduate moan quietly as she shivered in delightful self-gratification.

She then laid there alone amongst her tousled bed sheets and allowed herself to go back to a dreamy state of quasi-sleep where she reviewed in her mind the highs and lows of the past few days. She wondered whether such a convoluted day, like last Saturday, would happen again, for in her young lifetime it had already happened twice and both involved the death of someone she loved. She wondered if perhaps the ability to navigate life's peaks and valleys—to endure loss—was the key to long-term survival. Abruptly, Abby snapped out of her languid state when she thought of the possibility that Phil may have sent her an email that sat in her cyberspace inbox unopened, ignored. And while her inbox did indeed have an email awaiting her attention, it was not from Phil, but from that last person she expected.

The email was from username dpaolo that came from an organization's server: posthumo(r)usly dot org. Typed in the subject line was: The Last Hypothesis and it was dated: May 7, 2012. It was sent at precisely 12:00:01 AM EST. It was addressed to: Abby using her username: onalark, and the attachment line read: thelasthypothesis.doc. The strange email read:

> Dear Abby,
> I found this online organization that will store and then send an email to anyone I wish at the time I choose after they get the official word from the coroner's office that I've passed. Do you like the name of the organization? It only cost $5 and there are no annual fees! Ha!
> I'm writing to you (and only to you because I know you can handle it) about The Last Hypothesis. I've assigned the responsibility to shepherd the manuscript of our findings to Dr. Benedetti. If everything goes as planned he should have received a copy of the manuscript I drafted and instructions on how to proceed. Dr. Benedetti has been instructed to reach out to you, as a coauthor on the manuscript and as the student point person, as needed. He should try to contact you as shortly; he has your email address. I hope this is

okay with you. I've also left a hardcopy of the manuscript as well as an electronic copy of the manuscript and all of the data with Laura. She'll give it to you when you are ready. And don't worry; this is the last email I've written to you.

I wish you all the best, my dear Abby.

The email was simply signed: Dante, but it did contain a postscript:

PS: If Dr. Benedetti ever gives you (or anyone) any trouble, repeat these words to him verbatim: Don't test me Lorenzo for you will not like the consequences.

Abby read and reread the email. She wasn't sure whether she should laugh or cry, so she did both but not in that order. She wiped away tears as she chuckled over the part about not being too expensive and how there were no fees. She felt honored that he trusted her even though she wasn't the brightest one in his class. Yet sitting there, in her room, on the beautiful summer-like day her thoughts turned to last Saturday and to Laura. Abby picked up her cell phone and return dialed the number to Laura's phone. As Laura's phone rang Abby realized that she had never before spoken to her on the phone and she wasn't sure what exactly to say or how to address the widowed physician.

"Hello, this is Laura, is this Abby?"

"Um, yes...yes, Dr. Kean it's me Abby..."

"Please, it's Laura, and I'm so glad you called, Abby. It's been a blur since Saturday and I was just thinking about how remarkable it was that you..." Laura paused as her voice began to quiver with the memory of the students entering her house dressed neatly, some still in their graduation robes. Laura had recounted those moments repeatedly with several friends starting on Saturday evening when Rob and Beverly arrived unannounced carrying a loaf of crusty French bread, an antipasto platter and two bottles of wine. Laura was delighted to see them as she described the events of the day beginning with Dante's rapid downward spiral that began early in the morning, the compassion of Jumpin' June and the arrival of the students. Rob told her about graduation ceremonies and of the missing students. "I had no idea they were at graduation," Laura admitted to her neighbors.

"Oh God, Abby," Laura continued, "I hope your parents forgave you and what about the others? Oh, I just feel terrible, I didn't know you were graduating or else I wouldn't have texted you."

"It turned out just fine," replied Abby who was not prepared to hear an apology. Abby then told Laura how the rest of graduation day unfolded. She told about the scene back at the college, the spontaneous invitation, and the lavish dinner party hosted by the MacIntyre's. She described how they received their diplomas from President Holliday at the restaurant recycling the same diploma in the presence of their families. Abby skipped the detail that her father was not present.

"But I called not only to see how you're doing but also to tell you that I received an email from your husband..."

"Yes! Yes! I received one too!" Laura interrupted ecstatically. "From some weird website that sends emails postmortem? I was stunned to see this. He didn't tell me about this beforehand and as I read the rather short message it made me laugh and cry at the same time. It mentioned you and that you might call about a manuscript. I was really taken aback to see it on my computer but I have to admit that I'm thankful to have received it and also that he wrote only one. I don't think I can handle getting these every day. And do you know how he ended the email?"

"Do you mean the email he sent to me?"

"No, mine."

"No, I don't."

"He wrote, and I'm going to quote directly, 'Thank you. It's awesome. You still are my joy, my world'. Abby, did you get that? He wrote the same words in the email that you whispered to me after he died but he must have composed the email some time ago. Did he ask you to say those words?"

"No, they just came to me. I remember that I simply walked up to you and cradled your face in my hands and repeated words that entered my mind. Obviously those words were from him and..." Abby hesitated as tears swelled in her eyes and her voice quivered, "...and it was just this morning that I remembered that I used to cup my mother's face with my chubby little hands when I was a toddler, at least I've seen pictures of me doing that to her. I haven't done that to anyone since."

"Oh Abby, how sweet. And do you know how I know those words came from Dante. Abby, do you know?"

"No."

"Because after our first night together, after we made love for the very first time, afterwards he held my face in his hands and said, 'you are my joy, my world'. They were deeply moving words to me because no one had ever said anything like that to me before. They were truly private and quite personal, words that Dante used to confirm his love when I was his girlfriend, then when I was his fiancé and then as his wife. After each and every time we'd made love he'd say those words to me in the utmost sincerely and loving way. Do you believe that, Abby?"

"Yes I do, Laura. Yes, I do."

———•———

The whistle on the teakettle reached its highest pitch before it broke Dr. Benedetti's trance-like stare at the knot on the giant beech tree in his backyard; two dry teabags had already been placed in the cream colored ceramic pot. A proper British woman taught him that once the boiling water was added, the lid was to be placed atop the teapot immediately. The teapot then was to be encased with an insulated cover that matched perfectly the contours of the vessel in order to maintain the heat while the teabags steeped for five minutes after which time they were removed and the dark steaming liquid stirred once. The small amount of milk placed in the cup was almost at room temperature before Lorenzo added the scalding tea. At the computer with a cup of the perfect caramel-colored tea, he was now prepared to read Dr. Paolo's manuscript. He wasn't sure what he would find but his expectations were quite low based on what he saw and heard from Dr. Paolo's students in Anderson Auditorium last December. *Surely there was no story worth publishing*, he thought as he moved the arrow cursor to the folder labeled "Manuscript" and clicked twice. Inside the electronic folder was a single document.

The first page stated the manuscript's title. On the top of the page printed in boldfaced capital letters was the boldest, most audacious title Lorenzo had ever read: *Neurogenetic Transformations at the Moment of Death*. Besides the fact that it bordered on plain silliness, it also failed to describe the findings, which is what titles of scientific papers should convey. "Is this science fact or science fiction?" he said aloud as he re-read the first page.

In few words, the manuscript's Abstract section described the problem, the methods used to solve the problem, the results, and no more than two sentences to describe the significance of the results. The Abstract occupied about one-half page. The grammatically polished sentences were double-spaced, like the entire manuscript, but unlike most scientific articles that were dry and boring, this Abstract was beautifully written; its words grabbed the reader's attention and conveyed the message with unmatched clarity and purpose. There was no doubt that Dr.

Paolo's intent was to be understood by professionals and the general public alike.

Dr. Benedetti read the Abstract three times then leaned back in his chair exasperated. While the writing itself was clear, the science behind the words was completely unconventional. It was like describing the light bulb to those who had only candles, or like telling Galileo that men walked on his beloved moon. It was like reading fiction as it morphed into fact.

And although he knew essentially nothing about parallel universes or telepathy he did know something about DNA and he was certainly knowledgeable in neurobiology, thus he flipped to the sections of the manuscript that dealt with these topics. Reading this part of the manuscript is where he found the next surprise of the day.

Lorenzo Benedetti knew of Jin Sukawa and of his longtime efforts to map the functions of the human brain but he had no idea that he was collaborating with Dr. Paolo. His inability to remember that Brad had mentioned Dr. Sukawa in his December seminar meant that he was either not paying attention, or that his short term memory was beginning to fail. It was, in fact, a combination of both deficiencies that were becoming more frequent after the tired Dean turned 70 but on this spring-like day his focus was clear and his memory vivid as he read the sections of the manuscript related to research on the brain. Reading the detailed methods section that described the gray and blue hats containing probes and transmitters and how they sent brain activity wirelessly to a computer for processing, and the corresponding findings of the telepathy experiments complete with the time-lapse video of Dante Paolo's and Abby Lark's brains stirred within him long silenced passions of scientific inquiry and experimentation. The results of these experiments were clear to Dr. Benedetti: there was a direct cause and effect between the telepathic transmission of information and activity in the parahippocampal gyrus region of their brains. There was no doubt in Dr. Benedetti's mind that they had found the area of the brain responsible for nonverbal communication, a finding that he knew would immediately open up new branches of brain research. But he also knew that while these results were groundbreaking, they did not by themselves constitute a paradigm-shifting manuscript. That, experience taught him, would require a deeper understanding of the process. How was it controlled? How did it evolve? Why doesn't everyone communicate that way? How do you turn it on and off? These questions swirled in Dr. Benedetti's head when he came upon a gap in the results section of the manuscript.

He refilled his teacup and read the electronic yellow note that floated along side the blank part of the page. It read: "See Last Experiments addendum. Insert results here—brain." Dr. Benedetti scrolled towards the end of the manuscript file were he found a section labeled: "Last Experiments." This section was its own mini manuscript complete with Methods, Results and Discussion sections. It also contained a rather lengthy electronic yellow note. The note described the plan in detail and why the last experiments were performed. In the note, Dr. Paolo confessed to having borrowed *RW88* without the knowledge of his MIT collaborators. He also described how he planned to self-inject the tracer and how he expected it to end his cancer-filled life. The note went on to say that he asked Laura to collect cheek and blood cells at the moment of his passing for DNA analysis that would be conducted in Dr. Jainbin Ito's lab. Dante Paolo reiterated his hypothesis that most of the brain functioned to transform Earthly Energy to Universal Energy and that the code for this elaborate but virtually instantaneous process was embedded in the so-called noncoding regions of our DNA. The newly released Universal Energy is then able to interact with Self Universal Energy from other parallel universes. Dr. Paolo predicted that the tracer would show all of the functions of the higher brain firing in unison with simultaneous transcription and processing of the heretofore-silent DNA. Dr. Paolo wrote:

> After this occurs, the vessel of the human body is spent.
> It is worthless other than the organic parts valued only by
> plants, scavengers and parasites.

The note indicated that he should expect the results of the last experiments from Dr. Ito and from the MIT lab within weeks. They should be inserted in the manuscript at the position of the placeholders.

As it would eventually turn out, Dr. Paolo also correctly anticipated the responses of the critics, especially with regard to the final moment when his own brain's activity is visualized with the experimental tracer.

> They will no doubt want to know if this is a repeatable find-
> ing and that answer is: yes. In fact, the initial results with
> *RW88* were obtained in a nonhuman primate named Cookie
> and the data can be found in the final moments of Cookie's
> life. Dr. Bob Wyle or Dr. Sukawa will find the corroborat-
> ing nonhuman primate data in the file labeled 2012.01.02.
> *Cookie.* They now have this information and I'm sure that
> they'll use these findings as further proof of the tracer's
> ability to visualize higher brain function at the moment of
> death.

The lengthy note ended with a hopeful desire that Dante's final plan was indeed executed as scripted because by the time these words are read it would be too late for him to do anything about it. If so executed then the results will not only have been repeated, but also revolutionary and reconciliatory as well.

———•———

The demands of being a new parent while trying to maintain a world-class research program were having a visible toll on Bob Wyle as he shuffled unenthusiastically into his decidedly more disheveled office that had become a refuge from the chaos created by the colicky child, her sleep-deprived mother, and his ever-present, over-bearing and "under-appreciated" mother-in-law. And to add insult to injury, it was Monday, the day of the week when everyone in the lab had some problem that arose over the weekend that needed his immediate attention. And so with one hand gripping a large coffee, Bob jiggled the mouse and woke the computer from hibernation to check his email with subject lines that amounted to a "whine" list. But there was one email with "Personal" in the subject line that caught his immediate attention.

It was from dpaolo from an oddly named organizational server. It was dated: May 7, 2012 12:00:01 AM EST.

Dear Bob,

Depending on circumstances impossible to predict, when you read this email you may or may not have heard of my passing. This email should be delivered to you within 48 hours after my death from a web-based group called Posthumo(r)usly. I wrote this email in April to let you know what I plan to do with RW88. I plan to use your sensitive tracer to image my own brain's activity at the moment of my death. I plan to self-administer approximately 1.8 mL of RW88 I.V. as my final physical act at the moment of my death. I was wearing the blue hat. I procured RW88 during my last visit to MIT without your knowledge or anyone else's knowledge or anyone's help. I acted completely alone. If all went as planned, there should be a new folder with data from the moment of my death on your server. Not only do I hope the experiment worked but that the results corroborate those you obtained with Cookie (see the final minute of that experiment!) and also that they fit The Last Hypothesis, a project that you will learn more about in the coming weeks. With luck, this effort will make you and your tracer (even more) famous. Thank you for sharing your expertise.

Sincerely,

Dante

Bob read the letter three times before he searched the obituaries in the *Boston Globe* to confirm that Dante Paolo of Andover, Massachusetts had indeed died of pancreatic cancer on the prior Saturday at the age of 52. Bob slowly rose from his desk and closed his office door, just as Jo appeared hoping to get a few minutes with his boss before heading out to the animal room.

But "Aaa..." was as much information Jo would be able to divulge before Bob bellowed, "Not now!" as the office door slammed shut. He went back to his computer and accessed the folder containing Dr. Paolo's experiments. To his disbelief a new data file had indeed been generated on the previous Saturday.

Did he really inject himself with *RW88*? Bob wondered as he opened the file. His heart rate markedly increased as the checkerboard pattern of sixteen brain images populated the screen. His eyes examined each chronologically ordered image as it appeared. He was terrified, and he began to perspire profusely. This was the first time that anything Bob made in the laboratory was used in a human being. He knew that most lab animals, even nonhuman primates, are poor predictors of what might happen in humans so what he was viewing on his computer was unchartered territory in human brain research. As Bob felt the full gravity of the moment he became nauseous.

The quality of the images was superb but the first sixteen were unremarkable with only the expected amount of background activity visible. Bob advanced the program to show the next set of images that loaded one-by-one, from left to right on the screen.

Nothing, he thought to himself. *Maybe he didn't do it. Maybe he changed his mind.* Images 10...11...12...13, were not impressive, just random activity but as image 14 loaded Bob's eyes widened. It showed diffuse activity throughout the entire brain like the dim glow of a cold fluorescent tube. Images 15 and 16, the last image of that panel, were unlike anything Bob had ever seen. Image 16 was as blinding as noontime sunlight on new snow. Dr. Paolo's entire brain was alive with activity. Every region was virtually pure white—from the frontal lobe to the cerebellum, the temporal lobe to the occipital lobe—neurons from every crevice, every fold, every twist and turn were in a rapid fire mode like the release of hundreds of thousands of million blinding white fireworks that exploded just above Boston's Esplanade on the Fourth of July that turned that piece of earth from night to day.

"Unfuckingbelievable," Bob murmured as his eyes darted between images 14, 15 and 16. "What a progression!"

He again advanced to the next set of images.

Image number 1 filled its space in the grid. It looked diffuse like image 14 in the previous panel, and then image number 2 filled its spot on the grid. It showed no activity at all. None. The only thing Bob could see was the light gray outline of the brain cavity. Not even random sparks like those seen at the end of a hand-held sparkler as it exhausts the final few specks of metallic aluminum powder.

Just gray.

Image 3, 4, 5, 6, 7, and all the way to the last image on that panel, image 16, was gray. Bob advanced to the next set of images only to see that all of the images to image number 10, when the transmission ended, were also gray.

Dr. Paolo's brain was active no longer.

Seconds after being deprived of life-carrying blood, the brain, like the rest of the body, begins to decompose. The ultimate organ that was more powerful than anything man had yet created, that held more information than all of the world's computers combined, and that contained the greatest mysteries of our time, was starting to turn into an amorphous jelly-like liquid with no structural integrity, no meaning and no purpose.

Bob instructed the program to render the images to a movie then turned back to his list of emails. Further up the list were the emails that were sent more recently, including one from Phil Hess. The email from Phil was brief and its message would have been obscure had Bob not opened Dr. Paolo's email first.

You'll find a new file in our folder.

4

Dr. Jainbin Ito loved the outdoors and he enjoyed spending quality time with close friends. So on the Monday after graduation, he was particularly pleased to be spending one-on-one time with an old friend he hadn't seen often enough over the years; the hiking trip was an unexpected bonus.

Henry Kelly, who made a fortune by launching two successful surgical device companies around Boston, met Jainbin Ito during MIT's orientation back in 1982 when they both entered the graduate program in engineering. As a way to nurture cross-culture experiences, MIT paired individuals from different backgrounds as roommates and the differences, at least physically, could not have been greater between Henry and Jainbin. The powerfully built young man with reddish-brown hair from New England's Irish-Catholic heritage shared a room with the thin, if not frail looking, foreign student from Japan who had only read about Boston and its famed MIT from books, journals and university catalogs before actually arriving in Cambridge. They began their improbable friendship as an odd couple back then, but now, some 30 years later on their drive north on interstate 93 to the White Mountains to see what remained of the Old Man of the Mountains, they laughed at how little they'd changed.

"Henry, you could say that both of us look better than the Old Man himself," commented Jainbin in reference to the recent collapse of the naturally formed Great Stone Face of Conway granite, the long-standing symbol of New Hampshire.

"Can't argue with you there," was Henry's reply.

Neither man complained about their physically demanding, round trip hike to the summit of scenic Cannon Mountain. The day bordered on perfect with mild, summer-like temperatures, blue skies, no crowds, and most importantly, no black flies. By luck, they picked one of only four days in the New England spring when nighttime temperatures were just below freezing thus curtailing the daytime hatching of the king of outdoor pests.

The two friends were halfway down the mountain when they were brought back to reality—a world they had successfully escaped for most of the day. The call on Jainbin's cellphone was from his laboratory in California. They had just received an overnight shipment from Massachusetts addressed to him and they wanted to know what they should do with the samples.

"Are they from Dr. Kean?" he asked. "They are? Okay, great. Please process them immediately and let me know when you have the data."

———•———

Bob reread the part of Dr. Paolo's email that mentioned Cookie.

"See the final minute of that experiment," he whispered to the monitor quoting directly from the email. He wasn't sure what Dr. Paolo meant by this parenthetical statement because he routinely reviewed all data gathered from an animal experiment.

"Did I miss something?" he wondered as he searched the lab's data files for the *RW88* experiment with Cookie.

Inside the *RW88* folder Bob found the electronic file and instead of looking at the panels of images, Bob opened the movie file created with those images and forwarded to the final few minutes of the experiment. He watched intently as the movie played at twice the normal speed, the rate used last time it was viewed. The grayish images of Cookie's brain alive with white flashes of activity that passed quickly then, abruptly, they were punctuated by diffuse white, like the dim glow of sheet lightening before the monkey's images turned gray and the movie then ended. Bob moved the cursor back to two minutes from the end and adjusted the playback speed to normal.

"It's here!" Cookie's brain activity changed momentarily from diffuse white lightening to a brilliant clapping bolt before it faded to gray. Bob exited the movie version and examined the still images.

"Here," Bob said to his cluttered office pointing at image 2012.01.02. *Cookie.00:16:15*, "diffuse without focus...but here, at 16:30, it explodes with activity just before..." he whispered as he moved along to 16:45 and 17:00 "all activity stops, just like what happened to Dr. Paolo. Incredible! Wow! But what the hell does that mean? What happened?"

He needed to go for a walk to clear his head and to think. What were the ramifications of losing track of an experimental substance—a substance that was known to be lethal—that was subsequently used in a human? Should it have been in a locked cabinet? When would Dr. Paolo have taken *RW88*? Could he tell Dr. Sukawa about the new Dr. Paolo data without including the part about *RW88*? The questions came to him in rapid succession and none of them had easy answers. He correctly concluded that Dr. Sukawa would want to know immediately that Dr. Paolo had stolen, and then self-administered, *RW88*. He had no other choice because the images were exquisitely detailed, the tracer worked perfectly. Perhaps he should start by simply forwarding Dr. Paolo's strange pre-death-written-post-death-delivered email then admit the truth about his innocence related to the theft of *RW88*. He would then follow up with a second email that described the data of Dr. Paolo's brain obtained at the moment of death, and in that same email he could also include an analysis on the reexamination of Cookie's data file.

By the time he circled back to drab Building 6 on Milky Way, Bob Wyle had a plan as well as a new acronym. In the lengthy email he composed to Dr. Sukawa, Bob included Dr. Paolo's final email as well as a description of the final explosion seen with Cookie and then with Dante Paolo at the time of their respective deaths. He coined this final Synchronized Total Activity of the Brain, the STAB moment.

Creating an abbreviation is the easy part, Bob thought to himself. *Figuring out why the STAB moment happens and what it means is the real challenge.*

—————◆—————

Dr. Benedetti was unaccustomed to feeling indecisive and hesitant, but he was unsure how to handle the manuscript. Admittedly, Dr. Paolo's clear warnings were highly effective. The Dean was genuinely frightened; actually he was shaken to the core by the thought of the ramifications associated with not making the right decision. Although he didn't feel possessed on a moment-by-moment basis, he did not want to endure any other strange experiences, as if he was indeed being manipulated by Dante Paolo from the beyond.

In due time Dr. Benedetti would reluctantly fulfill his role in submitting the manuscript for publication, but it wouldn't be done today, this week, or even this month. The entire process would take time and he needed to be patient and careful. He correctly thought: *The rest of the manuscript will come to me and I will do my part as instructed.*

———•———

Abby read the entire draft of the manuscript in a single sitting. Although she didn't understand everything Dr. Paolo had written, she sensed from the last section where the relevance of the findings were discussed in more general terms that the work would be of high importance not just to scientists, but to everyone. She was both shocked and nervous to have her name among the list of authors on the title page because she was unsure of the associated responsibilities. If it were published, would there be media attention? Would she have to defend the data in a public forum? And if that were the case, how would she handle it?

Following a short bout of trepidation, she decided to let the others know about the draft manuscript and maybe about Dr. Paolo's email too. Her text to Amy, Brad, Phil and Ajay included a request for them to meet at *Toast of the Town* for happy hour at 5 p.m. to discuss the manuscript. Everyone but Ajay was able to attend.

———•———

The first day of the workweek was always slow at *Toast of the Town* but it was virtually empty on the Monday after graduation, as most of the students had already left campus for the summer. Abby purposely arrived early and chose the table in the back corner away from the centrally located bar, and the entrance to the kitchen. She smiled when Phil arrived and she was pleasantly surprised when he gave her a quick kiss on her cheek, a gesture that made her feel absolutely wonderful and alive. They chatted about the upcoming summer and by the time Amy and Brad arrived they were well into their first beer. Abby didn't need telepathy to know that the new medical students had just climbed out of the shower; their wet hair still emitted the odor of passion fruit-scented shampoo revealed that story.

Abby patiently waited until they had ordered something to eat before retrieving a hardcopy of the email and the manuscript from her backpack.

"This is probably going to freak all of you out but this morning I received an email from Dr. Paolo," she said as she simultaneously raised her right hand to prevent Amy, who was seated to her right, from asking the obvious question. "I know what you're going to say, Amy so hang on. Dr. Paolo wrote the email weeks ago and sent it to an online company called 'posthumo(r)usly dot org' that apparently stores emails then sends them out on your behalf after you've died."

"That's clever," said Phil. "Got to love these out of the box, no wait; out of the coffin ideas," he added to a round of moans.

"I think it's kind of creepy, getting an email from someone who's dead. It gives me the chills," said Amy who raised her shoulders and tucked her elbows to her side in a childlike display of fright. "I hope he didn't send one to me."

"Really, it's very clever and it's a great way of having the last word. Everyone wants to have the last word, right? I love it. I'm going to sign up," remarked Phil.

"What'd it say Ab?" asked Brad who sat directly across from her.

"To tell you the truth, when I saw it in my inbox, it frightened me too but then as I read it I heard his voice in my head, you know how that happens? Then, I found it quite comforting." Amy shivered again.

Instead of following her initial plan to paraphrase the letter, Abby decided to simply read it aloud verbatim. She skipped the personal ending as well as the postscript instruction relating to Dr. Benedetti. Abby then returned the hardcopy of the email to her backpack and pulled out the manuscript.

"So Dean Benedetti's in charge?" asked Amy.

"I guess so," replied Abby.

"Something doesn't seem right here. Were they tight? Dr. Paolo and Benedetti, were they close?" asked Brad. Does Benedetti know what's going on?"

"I agree, something doesn't sound right. Dr. Paolo never mentioned him at any of our meetings," said Phil just as their meals arrived along with a second round of beers for everyone except Amy who would not even finish half of the first one.

"I don't know what Benedetti knew before, but he sure knows about it now and Dr. Paolo must think he can pull it all together and get it published, I mean none of us know anything about publishing research, right?" asked Abby.

"My dad's published," replied Amy. "But I have no idea how he did it."

"Well, I checked out Dr. Benedetti and he's published over 500 articles in his day. I really didn't know that he had this whole other life as a researcher," said Abby.

"Really?" questioned Phil, "I thought he was born a Dean."

"He was a neuroscientist, a successful researcher at Rockefeller University in New York. Perhaps that's why Dr. Paolo chose him," Abby said then quickly added. "He can probably use his past experience and contacts to make sure the paper is submitted and whatever needs to be done to get it published. In any case, what I thought I'd do is to send him an email to let him know that I'll coordinate the communications between the five of us, okay? So please don't disappear on me. Let me know when you're leaving town and your new email address."

"I think the Wilmington College email address is ours forever," offered Phil who had heard that other schools offered this benefit to their graduates. "Right?"

"Maybe, but it probably depends on your level of donation," Brad said in jest. "So cough it up man, you're an alumnus now."

"Not while I'm in grad school, no way. They'll have to put me on their deadbeat list or something until I make some cash," said Phil.

"Hey, wait!" said Amy with that burst of enthusiasm that comes with a good idea. "We should arrange a meeting with my dad and Dr. Benedetti and maybe even Bob Wyle before my dad leaves this Friday. That way everyone will be able to meet everyone else in person. What do you guys think?"

"Yeah, I think that's a great idea," said Brad. "That'll bring Benedetti into the circle and maybe we'll learn the latest from Dr. Wyle and from your dad too. Should I try to reserve the library room for Wednesday night, say seven?"

"Sounds good to me. I'll send out emails to Benedetti and Wyle," said Abby.

"I'll make sure my dad is available," replied Amy who recalled that her father had just met everyone the other night at Brad's bash.

"And what if Benedetti can't make it?" asked Phil. "Shouldn't we first find out if he's available?"

"Oh he'll make it," replied Abby. "I know he will."

5

Extended time away from the daily grind as the Director of his company's Research and Development division proved to be highly therapeutic for

Dr. Ito. Hiking and fishing in the White Mountains of New Hampshire with his buddy, early evening walks with his wife on the sandy shores of the Atlantic made him consider, for the first time, the virtues of retirement. Less and less time was spent checking in on his lab to make sure that there were no major problems that required his immediate attention, and fortunately, all was quiet on the West coast. With each passing day in New England he began to realize that there were other avenues to explore in life and perhaps now, with Amy well on her way, was the time to transition to retirement, a concept that was foreign to his forefathers.

Amid thoughts of retirement, Dr. Jainbin Ito logged onto his work email to again check in on his group. Among the ever-growing list of company announcements and invitations to meetings was a message sent Tuesday afternoon from his lab. The message from his head technician was clear:

> We've completed sequencing the DNA samples sent by Dr. Kean but we're planning to rerun the activation profiles on some of the segments because the results were strange despite the fact that both the positive and negative controls worked perfectly.

The short email described the experiments they planned to run overnight and that he should expect another email with the new results tomorrow.

That would be today, thought Dr. Ito.

———•———

The new alumni felt oddly out of place as they strolled into the familiar library for the first time since graduation. The building that was usually bustling with activity was so quiet that the low hum of its large air handler could be heard emanating from high above the ceiling. And no one, not even the sole librarian, seemed to care that Amy was signing in a guest or that Phil was toting a backpack containing his laptop computer; the place was essentially empty this week before the start of the summer adult education classes.

The meeting, like the library itself was quiet and cordial, and unlike prior meetings held in that same room, it would be brief. Abby presided. She opened by introducing everyone, including Bob Wyle, who participated via teleconference, and Dean Benedetti, who seemed more interested in being with Dr. Ito, whom he perceived as an equal, than anyone else in the room.

Abby's goal was to keep the objectives of the meeting simple and focused. She began by reviewing the structure of Dr. Paolo's course, the projects that student each had chosen, their reports to the class, then to the greater college. She recalled Dr. Paolo's hypothesis that had been generated from their research, the plan and the experiments, and the current status of the manuscript. She ended the brief overview by describing in general terms the studies that were underway as well as her understanding of how information would flow. Data from Dr. Ito, Dr. Sukawa, and Dr. Wyle would be sent to Dr. Benedetti for insertion into the manuscript and then the more complete version of the manuscript would be reviewed by everyone prior to submission of the final version by Dr. Benedetti.

Dr. Benedetti listened stoically and apparently absorbed every word of her scripted instructions. He waited a few moments after Abby ended to see if anyone had anything to add before he started. No one did. Clearly it was his turn.

"Well that's all well and good, Abby, but Dr. Paolo left me with the arduous assignment of trying to get this manuscript published. In fact, not only did he leave me with the latest version, but with all of the data as well. I've spent a considerable amount of time this past week reviewing both the raw and the processed data and I must say, and with all due respect to my departed colleague, that I am not convinced that this research rises to the distinction of publication, at least not in the mainstream journals that serve to bring cutting edge science to the learned world. Moreover, I am not convinced of the connection..."

The small voice from the slight, neatly dressed man seated in the corner of the table started low but rose steadily until it overtook, then interrupted, Dr. Benedetti's diatribe. Everyone present in the room, as well as Bob whose entire face filled the wall-mounted monitor, turned to Dr. Jainbin Ito who, until that point, was engrossed at the screen of his small laptop.

"I suggest," Dr. Ito stated with indifference to the more senior scientist, "that judgment be reserved on what may or may not be worthy of publication until all of the data are collected and examined, as Abby aptly stated." Dr. Ito set the laptop on the table, faced Dr. Benedetti directly and added, "Based on the data I've reviewed with DNA samples submitted from the telepathy experiment and especially the activation data I've just received from my lab with DNA obtained from Dr. Paolo at the moment of his death, if confirmed, and let me emphasize, if confirmed, will be described by others as either 'paradigm shifting' or 'paradigm expanding'. These data alone, Dr. Benedetti, in the absence of any other, will be so distinctive, so exceptional, and so radical that they will mark the beginning of an entirely new field of exploration in human molecular biology. I say that with over four decades of experience examining human DNA sequences."

The room was silent.

Dr. Benedetti was blindsided by the rebuke from the small, slightly built Asian but he instantly realized that he badly underestimated Dr. Ito's intellect. And before Dr. Benedetti was able to form a response, Bob Wyle chimed in with the latest information from MIT.

"Dr. Sukawa is cutting his sabbatical short. He'll be back next week to personally oversee the follow-up experiments with *RW88*," Bob stated with a mixed look of surprise and relief. "Both of us reviewed the neuroactivity data with *RW88* recorded at the time of Dr. Paolo's death and we independently arrived at the same conclusion. The results are either an artifact induced by the tracer, or well, quite frankly, it is a finding that would immediately cause, as you said, a paradigm shift in the field. If confirmed, it would be so novel that it would eclipse all other discoveries made in our field over the past 50 years. In fact, it could become its own field and Dr. Sukawa is coming back to focus solely on this research."

"But it's only a single experiment," blasted Dr. Benedetti who was feeling outmaneuvered. "One experiment by itself means very little!"

"That's just it," replied Bob as quickly as the video transmission would allow. "The results of the monkey data with *RW88* at the time of his death were identical to those obtained with Dr. Paolo. The patterns were essentially identical and we would have missed it if it weren't for Dr. Paolo. No one ever thought to explore that exact moment of time, the moment of death."

"But what does it mean?" asked Dr. Benedetti whose body stiffened and whose language sounded more agitated and defensive. "All of this could be nonsense!"

"I assure you Dr. Benedetti," countered Dr. Ito, "the DNA aspect of this work is not to be trivialized and, if I understand the larger picture, if I can comprehend its full meaning, if I can see the completed picture when all of these pieces are assembled, then we are not just at the cutting edge of science and discovery, we are well beyond it. We're in a discovery goldmine. Dr. Paolo will have united at least three vastly disparate fields of science into one unifying concept so encompassing, so immense and so elegant that it will instantly convert current theories to fact while creating entirely new ones to study. Together as a team we should move to embrace this moment and to finish the work he started."

The graduates sat transfixed by the exchanges between the three professionals. Amy jotted some key words in a small notepad to help her recall the discussion while Abby struggled to keep her composure in the face of Dr. Benedetti's obstructionist attitude.

"I refuse to participate in this exercise in futility," said Dr. Benedetti defiantly. "To be involved with this infantile project would be a waste of time and energy and it could damage my hard-earned reputation in the field. These experiments were not performed with the type of rigor necessary to..."

Abby had heard enough.

Drawing power from the fact that Dr. Benedetti was no longer her Dean, she rose from her chair, looked directly at him and said in a voice that was deep and stern, "Dr. Benedetti, I am not sure why Dr. Paolo chose to engage you with this project but I'm sure he had sound reasons for doing so. I do not profess to be the smartest person in this room but from what I've heard it seems to me that we've started a journey from which there is no turning back; a journey that could be important..."

Dr. Benedetti was not having any of Abby's challenge. "Spare me the lecture," he said slowly and without breaking eye contact with her.

Abby's demeanor stiffened. She turned ferociously intense. Her eyes widened and her eyebrow tightened to a focus aimed squarely at the Dean. She was unaware of anyone else's presence when she said in a low guttural voice, "Don't test me Lorenzo for you will not like the consequences."

Dr. Benedetti's hands were folded serenely on the table when Abby voiced the declarative threat. Then abruptly and with a sudden jerk, the left hand broke free from the other and headed towards the wireless keyboard on the table directly in front of him. It was clear from the stunned look on Dr. Benedetti's speechless face that the movements were involuntary, not of his own doing. Everyone in the room, including Bob via the video feed, watched silently as the index finger of the jerky left hand extended towards the center of the keyboard then smoothly landed on the letter Y before it rose slightly and moved to the left—tap, then down a row—tap.

The prompt on the wall mounted computer screen below the projection of Bob Wyle's face was Dr. Benedetti's neatly typed response: yes.

The Submission

1

Summer is usually a time for students to relax, have some fun, earn some money and to recharge their batteries for the fall semester. But the summer after graduation from Wilmington College was a decidedly awkward time for Dr. Paolo's former students.

Ajay's initial eagerness to attend MIT's summer graduate student prep course was tempered after only the third day when he felt like he had entered some intellectual hazing camp. There was no end to the assignments, no end to the reading, and definitely no down time. Welcome to MIT. Where You Arrive Thinking That You're Smart and Leave Smarter Than You Think, read the new banner at the campus's main entrance. As the summer temperatures rose and the evenings invited long strolls on the beach and sailboat outings on the Charles River, Ajay wondered to himself whether he was actually smart to choose the demanding school in the first place. He didn't have a break all summer; not until the Saturday of the Labor Day weekend, a day when he slept until two in the afternoon then awoke startled by a dream that he missed class only to realize that it was the start of the three-day holiday before the beginning of the fall term.

———•———

Phil never imagined that Abby's seemingly innocent invitation to her house after the meeting at Toast of the Town at the beginning of the summer would lead to an afternoon of wild, uninhibited sex. From the first time he met her on the first day of *Teach the Professor* right up to his third mind-altering orgasm of their first daytime romp, Phil seriously misjudged the telepath. Abby unleashed on the unsuspecting, self-proclaimed math nerd, several year's worth of raw, pent-up hunger for uninhibited sex. By the end of that afternoon, and well before Abby's dad arrived home from the pub, the college-bound couple agreed to have a monogamous fun-loving, sex-filled summer. Their oft-repeated motto was: "No commitment—no disease." Phil loved the fact that he could just think it and she'd understand, and with him, Abby was refreshingly free. As the summer progressed, their friendship grew beyond spontaneous physical escapades, and the sweat-soaked cotton sheets to the point that they cautiously, and ever so slowly, began to care for each other. Abby even helped Phil find a place to live in Troy; a one bedroom flat above a bakery with a view of the Hudson River to the east and a short walk to the RPI campus to the west.

"You know, I'm going to miss you someday," Phil said to Abby as they dined at a Thai restaurant in Albany after he paid the security deposit and first month's rent on Flatbread, the nickname they gave to his new apartment.

"Yeah, sure you will. You'll just miss my body," she responded slyly.

"No...well yeah, I'll miss that but I'll also miss your mind."

"It's all about keeping a sound mind and body, right? Which one would you like to start with?"

"Your mind."

"Liar!" she exclaimed teasingly.

Phil wanted to reciprocate and help Abby transition to D.C. but she did not need to find a Flatbread. She was required to live on campus; it was a part of the deal when she accepted the teaching assistant position in return for free tuition. She told him that the University had living facilities for graduates that accommodated both singles and married couples. From what she gathered from the University's website, the living arrangements seemed quite nice.

"Plus, I couldn't afford D.C.," she said. "It's one of the most expensive places to live in the country."

"I've never been there but I heard it's a great city, especially if you like government, or museums or history," Phil replied.

"You know something? I'm going to be spending quite a bit of time in D.C. and I've never been there either. I applied online, and then I just had a phone conversation with someone in admissions. All I know is that I'll be in the doctorate program in Advanced Communications. I don't even know who my advisor will be, nothing!"

"Sounds like a road trip to me," said Phil rather impulsively.

"Road trip? We're already on a road trip."

"Okay then, road trip part two. On to D.C.! It's only like six hours from here. I say we do it. I don't have to get back for any particular reason, do you?"

Three months later, when she stepped off the train at Union Station alone with an oversized suitcase and a laptop, Abby would appreciate Phil's spontaneous road trip. Although not a world traveler by any measure, Phil nonetheless realized the importance of familiarity when moving to a new town and so he made it a point during their two-day whirlwind tour around the nation's capital to visit the famous train station and to ride the Metro as much as possible.

Taking the train to D.C. from Boston's South Station was a great way to leave her dad who hated to pay for parking more than he disliked driving in the city. He simply dropped Abby off at the ornate building and didn't even get out of the car for a farewell hug. The goodbye and good luck was short and sweet, just as she had hoped it would be.

The ride from Boston to D.C. was slow but sure. It was a wonderful way to start her new life of independence as it gave her time to take in the moment. And as the Metro wound its way to Tenleytown/AU her new home stop, she recalled with delight the fulfilling sex she enjoyed with Phil in their relatively inexpensive room at a motel close to the University just a few short weeks ago.

The small rectangular dorm room with its white concrete block interior, and small wooden bookshelf and dresser easily accommodated Abby's meager belongings. Lying on the newly made bed weary from the trip, Abby's thoughts began to drift. She wondered how Laura was faring without her husband, how Amy and Brad's separation went, if Ajay now ruled MIT, and what Phil was doing in Flatbread in Troy, New York. She also wondered if she would again be as happy as she was during the "no commitment, no disease" summer before graduate school.

————•————

Amy was indifferent to the University of Minnesota Medical School located in Duluth near the tip of a lake somewhere towards the middle of the country. "This place is nothing more than a safety net," she thought during her visit there in the middle of the frigid winter. She was all but certain that other, more attractive places, to attend medical school would accept her. But as the summer solstice morphed into the fourth of July and Amy stood in front of Brad—her backside pressed tightly against him, his arms wrapped tightly around her—on Boston's Esplanade to again listen to the familiar melodies of the Boston Pops

Orchestra and to watch fireworks, she tried not to think about the fourth of August when she would head west to Minnesota. The Californian thought she'd visit the east coast for four years to please her dad and then hustle back to the warmth of the southern Pacific coast. She wasn't supposed to fall in love with New England nor meet the man whom she would eventually marry. Her plans were to be single until she completed medical school and had a career as a practicing physician. She sought to be an independent, career woman. At least those were her ideals four short years ago, when she was younger and more naïve.

On that same Fourth of July, Brad thought little about Harvard Medical School just down the road from the Esplanade. He simply sought to savor the scene, to take in the warm, slightly humid, summer air filled with excitement, music, and forthright patriotism. He wanted to savor this moment with Amy, someone he had come to treasure more and more with each passing moment. He too tried not to think about their upcoming separation, a time he knew would test their commitment, their love. He wondered whether their relationship was like an ill-timed firework that brilliantly lit the sky only to fade to nothing or perhaps their separation would serve to forever strengthen their young bond. Surrounded by tens of thousands of strangers he sought to displace these thoughts and to live the moment, to hug her even tighter to him, to feel her hard body, to enjoy the sweet smell of her hair.

Their time on the Esplanade would be but a fleeting moment that each would recall as they sat at orientation on the first day at their new institution of highest learning, separated by one-half the distance of a great land. Their minds were filled with excitement while their hearts were empty. The test of their commitment had begun in earnest.

Laura Kean had always been her own person and an independent soul, so the transformation from wife to widow was somewhat seamless. Her marriage to Dante was more convenience and admiration than need and devotion and while his absence left an appreciable void in her life, it did not create crazed chaos.

Dante's death did give Laura a fresh perspective on time and of her own mortality, however. She decided to make changes in her life especially if she was going to explore Italy as she and Dante had once planned to do together in retirement. Towards that end, Laura's new mantra was: simplify, simplify, simplify and she began by placing her house on the market.

Just days after her husband's cancer-consumed body was wheeled out through the same threshold that decades earlier he carried her in when they purchased their one and only home, the house that was supposed to be filled with two if not three children, the building that had welcomed guests and parents alike, the house that always remained too big for two people, was sold by the end of the summer to a young couple with a toddler and another child on the way. By Labor Day, Laura had emptied most of the house of the once-treasured belongings that instantly became meaningless after Dante's death.

Jumpin' June helped Laura disassemble the makeshift hospital room. She even found a new home for the IV pole and the fancy, semi-electric bed. To repay the young nurse—who insisted that Laura continue to address her by the nickname bestowed by her very first hospice patient—for her friendship and extraordinary kindness to Dante, Laura gave her the guest bedroom furnishings including the solid cherry bedframe with the little-used mattress and bedspring, matching armoire and twin nightstands, and lamps. The young provider—who would eventually leave hospice care to become an emergency room nurse where the pace of perpetually panicked activity matched her end-less, ever-youthful energy—was overjoyed with the first pieces of qual-ity furnishings. Jumpin' June's relationship with Laura would always be quite special.

Laura paid cash for a one-bedroom luxury condominium conve-niently located within a short walk to the hospital. She even took the bold move of parting ways with her car, as well as Dante's trusty Volvo, and relied solely on public transportation and instantly available rental cars for outings to the city or to the mountains.

Her new condo was sparsely furnished, neat and tidy. Her new life, she decided, would be easy and efficient.

2

Dr. Benedetti never quite recovered from the bizarre events that trans-pired in the library at Wilmington College. Badly shaken by the incident, the aging Dean abruptly left the meeting as soon as he regained control of his hand. He uttered not a word; there was nothing more for him to say. He would simply await their orders and submit the completed man-uscript as per Dr. Paolo's instructions. That's all he would do, no more, no less.

Ironically, the shocking events at the library also provided Lorenzo with needed clarity. That evening, alone in his empty house, he decided to resign as Dean of Academic Affairs at Wilmington College. *Jean will have to find a new intellectual gatekeeper for the Institution*, he thought. He offered to initiate the search for his replacement but he didn't plan to be around when the students returned in the fall. If necessary, they'd have to find an interim Dean as his decision to leave was steadfast; he was ready to retire in Tuscany and to spend time with his dear cousin Rosa, who eagerly awaited his return. In essence, Lorenzo sought to return to his childhood, to harvest chestnuts, grapes and olives, he wanted to make wines and oils and to once again cherish the fruits of the earth before he became a permanent part of it.

So Dr. Benedetti, like Laura Kean, also spent the summer selling belongings including his home. His collection of out-of-date textbooks was donated to the local high school and his vast collection of fine literature was accepted by the town's library. He shipped a few of the books he had edited during the peak of his academic career, as well as novels signed by their authors, to Rosa who had already made room in her house to accommodate the arrival of her cousin and his belongings.

Between launching a search for his replacement, cleaning out his office, and preparing his house for sale, Lorenzo Benedetti had little time to worry about Dante Paolo's manuscript.

3

Dr. Jin Sukawa returned to Boston to focus solely on Dr. Paolo's findings.

For much of his research life Dr. Sukawa had secretly and quite discretely studied the electrochemical potential of the brain at the time of death. He reasoned that there was too much information stored in the brain for it to simply vanish. And unlike the relatively simple heart, the brain isn't a muscle; it is an elaborate, constantly active and highly functioning interconnected network of electronic pulses. Dr. Sukawa sought to answer a simple question: He wanted to know if the human brain was associated with a larger, more encompassing network. Mice and monkeys would only take the science so far and thus he knew that one day he'd have to explore the human brain to make significant and lasting progress.

Sketching experiments on paper was simple—actually doing them was virtually impossible because to capture the precise moment of death he'd have to induce it. Dr. Sukawa didn't think there would be a problem recruiting terminally ill patients that would volunteer to die in the name of science but the MIT legal team told him that the ethical and legal challenges of doing this type of study without the use of painkillers such as morphine—that would confound the results—were insurmountable. So as he grew older, Dr. Sukawa reluctantly accepted the fact that the study would probably never be done in his lifetime. The best he could do was to provide the theoretical framework to test his hypotheses and hope that future scientists will pick up where he left off.

Now all of that changed because of one brave scientist, Dante Paolo.

With Dr. Ito's blessing and cooperation, Dr. Sukawa took charge of the project. Each knew little of the other's field of study but they readily understood their relative importance to the project. They needed each other's expertise in order to make the story whole and since they were beyond the age when one tries to get ahead by putting others down, the collaboration worked smoothly. They agreed to be co-senior authors and co-corresponding authors on the manuscript, a decision that also showed solidarity in their findings and conclusions.

Dr. Ito's laboratory had indeed repeated the experiment with Dr. Paolo's DNA and the results were identical to those they had obtained initially; Dante's DNA was completely unmethylated at the moment of his death. Dr. Ito explained these findings in an email to everyone involved with the project:

These methyl groups control gene activation. When bases of the DNA have methyl groups they are not activated but rather they are silent. Ninety-one percent of the DNA from Dr. Paolo taken a week before he died was methylated, that means that most of his genes were not activated, a result well within the normal range. However, at the moment of his death, his entire DNA was unmethylated which means that all of his genes were being transcribed at that time. Remarkably, every single region of his DNA was activated. This result was completely unexpected. It is as novel as it is confounding.

Dr. Ito went on to describe brand new data his lab obtained with DNA from other animals including ten mice, a minute before, and then just as they were sacrificed. As with Dr. Paolo's DNA, the DNA purified from mouse cells at the exact point of death was completely unmethylated compared to just a minute before they died. DNA from each of the ten individual mice showed the same results—a rapid reversal from methylated to unmethylated states. The results were identical for other laboratory animals including pigs, hamsters, rats, and even old world monkeys.

We know that this process is not simply a consequence of cell death because we were able to measure residual cellular enzymatic activity at the same time that the DNA became unmethylated. In other words, the DNA actively shed all of its methyl groups while other cellular activity was occurring. Total gene activation appeared to be a preprogramed and a deliberate move by the cell. How this happens, why this happens and what purpose it serves may well take several generations to understand fully.

———•———

At MIT, Dr. Sukawa knew that he had to directly confront the administration on the potentially damaging fallout from having a laboratory reagent not only stolen but also then used by a dying man in what would be considered an unauthorized and unapproved clinical experiment. He arranged a meeting with the Provost, the Dean of Research, and the Head of Research Compliance who, at Dr. Sukawa's request, brought a member of the university's legal counsel.

During the two-hour closed door meeting Dr. Sukawa and Bob Wyle described a timeline of events beginning with Brad's email. It documented each visit by Dr. Paolo and his students and what activity they performed during each visit. They described the formulation of *RW88*, its safe use in mice as well as its fatal effect as a neural tracer in Cookie. They also showed pictures of where *RW88* was stored in the laboratory.

Dr. Sukawa used a draft of the manuscript to describe in detail what had transpired with Dr. Paolo. He told the group that neither he nor Bob had any indication that some of the tracer had been removed from the lab. They made sure not to use the word 'stole' or 'stolen' or 'theft' or 'thief' when they described events or Dr. Paolo. They had no idea when the experimental tracer was taken, who took it, and they certainly had no idea that Dr. Paolo was planning to use it on anyone, let alone on himself. As far as they knew, there was no conspiracy, nor any illegal activities committed either by them, by members of their laboratory, or by anyone else associated with Dr. Paolo at any time.

"Yes," Dr. Sukawa admitted to the small group, "I did allow them access to our brain imaging equipment. And yes, I did authorize Dr. Wyle to help them with these experiments, and yes, based on their interesting initial results I did allow Dr. Paolo's students to borrow the blue cap, but I did not know how or when or where it would be used. I would assume, and this is purely speculation on my part, that Dr. Paolo was truthful when he stated in the email, posthumously sent to Bob on May 7, 2012 at 12:00:01 AM EST, that he acted alone. I'd like to end my overview by saying that the data generated by Dr. Paolo using *RW88*, combined with results from the telepathy and other experiments are nothing short of astounding. I can go into more detail if you like but suffice it to say that the publication of these data will have a dramatic and lasting impact on science and on mankind. The value of these findings will extend far beyond the immediate scientific community."

The small group was silent. It was as if they didn't know where to start or who among them should start the discussion. Here before them was a world-class neuroscientist, an MIT professor who had started his stellar career a decade before the most senior among them—the Provost—had even stepped foot on campus. His research had spun off several companies that were some of the most successful businesses in the Commonwealth and annual donations to the University from these grateful businessmen were in the tens of millions.

"So," started Ms. Legal Counsel, an athletically built woman in her mid-40s, "is there any proof that *RW88* was actually injected by Dr. Paolo?"

"All we know is what he wrote in the email," replied Bob Wyle.

"That's circumstantial evidence. Was an autopsy done on Dr. Paolo?"

"Not that I'm aware..."

"Was there anyone present when he passed?"

"Yes, his wife," replied Dr. Sukawa. "As I understand, at her husband's request she took a sample of cheek cells for DNA analysis when she thought he was at the point of death. She's a physician, so I guess she knew the moment when she saw it."

"From my perspective," continued the attorney, "the use of *RW88*, if in fact it was used by Dr. Paolo, is the main issue here because the telepathy experiments were non-invasive and altogether not dangerous. If we're investigated by the government we'll probably get a small fine, a slap on the wrist for not having approval to do the study but that's about it. So what it really comes down to is *RW88*. Was it really injected?"

"I guess they could exhume Dr. Paolo's body, right?" asked the Research Compliance officer.

"He was cremated," said Bob.

"That's even better," replied Ms. Legal Counsel. "So there's no real evidence that he actually used it other then what he wrote in the email?"

"And the data," Dr. Sukawa said pointing out the obvious. "The email stated that he planned to use it, the data confirmed its use and the manuscript states he used it. There is no way that these images could have been obtained with any other chemical. They are absolutely clear and highly detailed."

"But there is no physical proof, correct? There is really no evidence that the tracer killed Dr. Paolo, right?" the attorney asked.

"He had advanced pancreatic cancer," Bob said. "That's all I know."

"Is his widow pursuing any legal action against us? Or anyone?"

"Not that I'm aware of," said Dr. Sukawa stoically. Bob just shrugged his shoulders indicating that he also didn't know.

The Provost had heard enough.

She thanked Dr. Sukawa and Dr. Wyle for coming forward and disclosing the information about *RW88* and the experiments. She asked Dr. Sukawa for a remedial plan to secure experimental solutions as well as a timeline of when he thought the manuscript would be submitted. She then asked the attorney to recommend an action plan on how to proceed on the premise that Dr. Sukawa will submit the work for publication that will include details of the use in a human of *RW88* without a clinical trial approval. She explicitly wanted to know whether they should be proactive and deflect potential problems or should they be reactive to them, when or if, problems arose.

Within a week of the meeting Dr. Sukawa submitted a standard procedure for securing not only experimental solutions but also all laboratory chemicals using a key and a number lock system. He also made sure that his laboratory participated in special training to ensure that everyone understood the safety and security regulations.

Legal counsel spent two weeks weighing all of their options. At the end they concluded that they should prepare a reactive response, a strong defense. The decision, which was accepted by the Provost, hinged on the premise that Dr. Sukawa was correct in predicting the impact of the research on the greater public. Positive acceptance of the findings by the public would outweigh any potential reprimand issued by federal or state regulatory agencies. Such actions would then be considered petty and a waste of taxpayer's money.

"Who," asked the attorney, "but a minority of absolutists would rail against scientists who risked everything for the benefit of mankind? It may turn out that Dr. Paolo will be celebrated as one of the greatest thinkers of all time, and if that's the case, then there will be no reprimand whatsoever. The case would be closed even before it could be considered reasonable enough to open."

4

By mid-September, Amy, Abby, Brad, Phil and Ajay were beginning to feel the all-out reality of postgraduate life while Drs. Sukawa and Ito completed revisions to the manuscript Dr. Paolo had originally drafted. The almost-final version contained results from the additional tests and experiments that supported, and expanded, Dr. Paolo's initial results and overall hypothesis.

The manuscript not only detailed the specific region of the brain responsible for nonverbal communication but also the location in the DNA of genes responsible for this trait. It also explained, backed by an exhaustive array of data, the remarkable and virtually simultaneous events of the activation of every gene, including what was located in the soon to be renamed "junk DNA," and the firing of every neuron in the brain at the moment of death—the so-called STAB moment. The manuscript boldly proposed that this synchronized final act, one that would eventually be shown to occur in all living creatures, might be involved with self-preservation; exactly how this occurs and precisely what is preserved remained a mystery.

The final version of the manuscript was reviewed and approved by everyone then sent to Lorenzo Benedetti for submission precisely as instructed by Dr. Paolo. Why Dr. Paolo assigned this important task to an apparent antagonist, the one person who was the least supportive of the project, and someone who did not contribute at all to the study was puzzling. Dr. Sukawa would have preferred to submit the manuscript himself as he had done for decades but true to his honest and forthright nature, the MIT professor simply did as instructed.

Dr. Sukawa hand-delivered the manuscript to Dr. Benedetti. The two men met for lunch in Winchester at a simple yet elegant café in the center of town not far from the train depot on a sunny, unseasonably mild, mid-September day—the sort of day when it felt like summer would not yield to fall. It was the first, and the last time, these neuroscientists would be together. Their shared interest in neurobiology and in the findings described in the manuscript served to keep the conversation flowing smoothly and effortlessly throughout the protracted meal. They spoke about the early days of neurology and how rudimentary the tools were back then compared with those available today. Dr. Sukawa described some of his latest intellectual pursuits but admitted, for the first time, that his sabbatical made him think more about retirement and returning to his ancestral roots than continuing to do research.

"Lorenzo, there always will be interesting questions to answer," Dr. Sukawa started to say in his soft but strong and sure voice. "And while I've asked many in my life I won't be the one asking them in the future.

Science is perpetual but I am not. I am ready to let the Earth spin as it will without my meager influences."

Dr. Sukawa's words resonated with Dr. Benedetti who, in a rare move for the fiercely private Dean, shared his future plans with the MIT professor. Before this moment, Dr. Benedetti had revealed his retirement plans solely to President Holliday and to Rosa; he knew that no one else would care. At least Dr. Sukawa faced the same kind of retirement-type ideals. It was the type of conversation Dr. Benedetti needed—before he left America for the last time—to reaffirm in his heart the value of the individual. In Dr. Jin Sukawa he saw a productive, thoughtful and hard-working immigrant with malice towards no one, someone who freely shared his intellect and inventions, indeed his very life, with the world without hesitation or reservation.

"Did you know Dante Paolo?" Dr. Benedetti asked pointedly.

Dr. Sukawa looked down at his empty plate, thought about the question for a moment then said, "No, I never had the chance to meet him. But I wish I had."

"Why?"

Again Dr. Sukawa paused. He chose his words carefully. "Because I would like to know how he developed such a unifying, encompassing hypothesis. Where did he find the inspiration? That's what I want to know. From what I learned searching online, Dr. Paolo had a productive, somewhat average, scientific career at Harvard. He was mainly a bacteriologist and an immunologist who developed vaccines. So, I'm curious to know how someone who studied very small things and focused on essentially one field of biology came to think on a broader, larger scale about vastly different fields of science."

Lorenzo Benedetti let his colleague's words dissipate and rest before he offered a truthful response. "I was there when he came to Wilmington College. He sought a new direction in life and he found it at the College.

He wanted to teach a course that neither he nor anyone else had ever taught before and he wanted it to be as informative to him as it was to the small number of seniors who signed up to take it. I openly belittled the course from the beginning because I doubted its value, but he persevered—which, as you know, is the hallmark of a good scientist. He ended up with a group of motivated students who learned a great deal from him and, as it turned out, he from them. I believe that's when he started to think differently."

"So he was able to explore freely, outside the confines of the laboratory and inside the minds of young, agile thinkers."

"Exactly. Dante Paolo was unburdened from the demands of the institution and program constraints. He was free to take risks with his thoughts and ideas. In many ways, he was like early scientists—Pasteur, Koch, and Fleming—who thought deeply and tinkered endlessly, someone who discussed and defended their findings with other solid thinkers. He was like fearless scientists who learned to question everything and, perhaps most importantly, who were not afraid to fail. In his class, Dante didn't just listen to his student's questions and comments, he heard them as well."

After the coffee was served and the lunch was approaching a natural end, Dr. Sukawa reached into his brown leather satchel and retrieved a white Tyvek envelope that contained two hardcopies of the final manuscript as well as a softcopy on a CD.

"Lorenzo," Dr. Sukawa said as he handed the envelope to the Dean. "I am as poor at predicting the future as I am predicting what will happen tomorrow, but if this manuscript is my last then I will have left the field on a very high note. Mankind will have a timeless treasure. I want to thank you in advance for doing your important part. Let's stay in touch, shall we?"

"Indeed," Dr. Benedetti replied as he accepted the envelope.

The two men stood and together they walked out of the now empty café towards the train station. There, in the long rays of sun that found their way through the maze of red brick buildings, the two men faced each other, shook hands and went their separate ways. The torch of responsibility of getting the manuscript to the scientific community, then out to the world, had successfully been passed.

5

During the peak of his research career, airplanes were his second home but Dr. Benedetti was uncharacteristically anxious as he boarded the Boeing 787 wide-body at Boston's Logan airport. Other than an occasional trip to Italy to visit Rosa, his time in the air had lessened sharply since becoming Dean and thus he lost the mental mindset of a world traveler. The special attention from the cute stewardess, first class pampering and a halfway decent, airplane-size bottle of merlot soothed his nerves.

He also knew that this would be his last flight from the United States—his time in America had come to an end.

During the first two hours of the overseas Icelandair flight he re-lived the past few months—the sale of his home and most of his belongings, the search for his replacement at the college and the farewell celebration, and the shipments of a few of his personal items to Rosa, who at that very moment, was busy sprucing up their home in anticipation of his arrival. Lorenzo Benedetti's chores were completed with relative ease compared with what he needed to do to submit the manuscript for publication.

The most respected scientific journals in the world used a two-tiered review process whereby an associate editor acts as a manuscript's initial screener. With good reason, but also sometimes quite arbitrarily, these editors reject manuscripts based on nothing more than his or her own whims and personal bias. When this happened with Dr. Paolo's manuscript, Dr. Benedetti had neither the patience nor the tolerance for such games; a message he took directly to the journal's head editor.

The head editor of any journal was no match for a riled Dr. Benedetti and, in short order, the relatively younger scientist-editor agreed to allow the manuscript to go out for peer review but promised nothing else beyond that point in the process. This conciliatory move was acceptable to Dr. Benedetti because he knew that the scientist-editor would take the path of least resistance and send the manuscript to two of the four scientists listed in the manuscript's cover letter as potential reviewers. Dr. Sukawa and Dr. Ito carefully chose their esteemed colleagues as "having the expertise required to review the scientific content and merit of the manuscript."

As the Dreamliner gradually descended on the relatively small international airport north of Stockholm, Dr. Benedetti was glad he spent the extra money on a first class ticket. He felt rested and ready for the emotional challenges that lay ahead.

———•———

It was the simple yet awkward act of putting button studs and cufflinks on his tuxedo shirt that ignited memories of his sole term as President of the European Society for Neurosciences. Those five years were the most productive, rewarding and, in retrospect, the most exciting time of his career. He was at the highpoint of his game with a well-funded laboratory brimming with gifted scientists, invitations to the major cities in Europe—Paris, London, St. Petersburg, Madrid, Amsterdam, Prague, Zurich, Berlin as well as Florence, Siena and Rome—where he presided over a meeting, or presented his latest research findings. He was in high demand as a lecturer and he loved the attention, the glory, and the power. His vast intellect combined with his tasteful wit and proper charm endeared Dr. Benedetti to scientists and dignitaries alike and as such, he was invited to attend events that were increasingly more lavish, and more formal, less science but more politics. He found these events to be both entertaining and challenging: he was amused by the various masks worn by those in attendance and challenged by the game of finding the one or two true intellects in the room, who were easily identifiable by their look of profound boredom.

It was though a life-long comrade, a Professor Emeritus at the University of Lund, that Dr. Benedetti procured an invitation to the Nobel Award Ceremony and Banquet in Stockholm. The invitation to the highly anticipated annual event was granted due to a serendipitous yet ironic occurrence. It was announced just a few weeks prior, in November, that the Nobel Prize for Medicine and Physiology was awarded to Professor Richard Johnson from Johns Hopkins University who adapted and modified a single-protein domain labeling technology initially developed by Dr. Benedetti to study the nervous system. The innovative adaption allowed the Hopkins researcher, and countless others after him, to study in fine detail how infectious agents trafficked through vectors to hosts, like the malaria virus passing through the mosquito to humans. The findings exposed an Achilles heel to many deadly viral infections—a clever shuttle mechanism used by viruses to get into insects so that they could disperse widely, then out of the flying vector to start the final infectious process in the unassuming human host. As it turned out, the mechanism was a near-universal process that led to the discovery of a new class of highly effective antibiotics, a discovery that saved millions of lives and made millions for the small company founded by Professor Johnson.

Had Dr. Benedetti been a decade, or even a half-decade, younger the award would have driven him mad with envy. But he had already come to terms with how narrow the claims of the patent issued on this labeling technology were written; the overly concise claims opened the way for others to easily modify them, thus making them brand new inventions. Dr. Benedetti's lawyers advised him not to sue for patent infringement because no one, in their opinion, stole the claims listed in his breakthrough patent.

The bastards can't see beyond today's headlines, he thought of the Nobel committee as he left his hotel room for short walk to the Stockholm Concert Hall.

The evening was an amalgamation of pageantry, royalty, and formality performed with the precision of a fine Swiss watch. With the King, Queen and lovely Princess of Sweden seated on stage opposite the Nobel laureates, the traditional opening welcome delivered by the Society's Secretary General morphed into a short but meaningful lecture on Alfred Nobel, the Society's founder, sole benefactor and pacifist inventor of explosive materials and devices.

Dr. Benedetti sat quietly in his seat in the vast, ornate auditorium with the Royal Orchestra perched high above the main stage to the left of the central podium where the King would eventually hand each honoree the esteemed gold medal and certificate. As he scanned the audience he realized how little had changed since he attended such highbrow events so many years ago. There were the very old white-haired men in their rented and rigidly starched tuxedos graced with their own medals of achievement worn around their thinning necks nodding off only to be awoken by the periodic polite clapping of the crowd. Some gents, seated next to their tiara sporting, silver-haired spouse or young mistress who pretended to be intellectually engaged in the events when, in fact, they too were beginning to feel weary. Indeed, the musical interludes were highly effective in keeping most of the attendees attentive during the two-hour private ceremony. There also were those who pretended to comprehend the 500-word synopsis of the life work of the laureates contained in the gold-emblazed booklet that also had the day's schedule of events. And then there were others in attendance who just happened to be born into wealth, without a clue as to how money is earned; they were in the grand hall simply because it was their birthright to be seen by millions at the nation's annual, early winter, hallmark event.

This, I do not miss, Dr. Benedetti thought to himself as his gaze returned back to his own booklet. The banquet, which featured short presentations by the ten new awardees, was scheduled to begin immediately after the medal ceremony with cocktails and light hors d'oeuvres.

Impatiently, the former Dean glanced at his watch.

Dr. Benedetti waited for the right moment to complete his mission. He stood alone amid the crowd in the glass-enclosed foyer outside the banquet hall where a line of white-gloved waiters waited for the cue to serve dinner.

"Good evening, Herr Doktor," was how Dr. Benedetti greeted the famed German neurologist, Franz Albracht, who was the current Secretary General of the Nobel Committee.

"Why, Lorenzo! I was pleasantly surprised to see your name on the list of attendees. How have you been? It's been such a long time and to be honest, I cannot remember the last time we were together," replied the Secretary General.

"I believe it was in Vienna perhaps 15 years ago? But time takes on a new meaning at our age, wouldn't you agree? It becomes, well, shall we say, irrelevant?"

"Agreed," chuckled the affable Dr. Albracht.

"I know you are a busy man in high demand this evening, but I wanted to make sure to give you this," Dr. Benedetti said firmly as he reached into the inner pocket of his tuxedo jacket. "Inside is a tiny disk that contains a manuscript that reconciles what was once thought to be irreconcilable. It will set into motion new fields of studies and limitless opportunities for mankind. I wanted you, my friend, to have this before the world learns about it next month, in the New Year. It has been accepted for publication in a special edition of *Nature*." Dr. Benedetti handed the Secretary General a small, sealed envelope containing a SD card.

The Secretary General looked at the small, tan unmarked envelope then slipped it into the inner pocket of his tuxedo jacket. He was about to ask a question when an aide approached and informed him that he was needed in the banquet hall. The two old friends took each other's hands in a firm grasp and bowed their heads towards each other in a sign of deep mutual respect.

Dr. Benedetti looked directly into the tired eyes of his colleague and said, "Remember what we used to say when we were young, 'life is just a hypothesis'? Be well my friend."

As the crowd slowly began to make its way into the vast banquet hall where an elaborate dinner would be served, Dr. Benedetti lagged behind and again glanced at his watch. In his mind he quickly reviewed what would transpire over dinner: idle chat with someone he barely knew, then the speeches during an overly rich dessert served with fine coffee or tea, followed by a champagne toast to the new laureates and calls for a better tomorrow through continued donations to the organization.

Dr. Benedetti placed his goblet, half-empty of red wine, on a nearby table, turned and walked out into the cold Swedish night. Outside, in front of the majestic Hall, a young man dressed in a black tuxedo approached from his left. He walked quickly towards him with purpose as if it was a matter of some urgency.

"Pardon sir?" the young man said with a British accent. "Are you not Dr. Benedetti?"

"Yes, I am. And who might you be?"

"Michael, sir. Michael Beal," he replied as he extended his hand. "I recently completed a postdoc with Dr. Johnson and I now have a faculty appointment at Oxford. My lab is focused on the evolution of neuronal activity in the absence of overt stimuli. I've read all of your works." As he realized the gravity of the private moment with his idol, the young scientist groped for the proper words to express his thoughts. "I simply want to thank you for creating such a solid foundation."

A local limousine driver approached and asked them if they needed his service. Dr. Benedetti waved him off then turned his attention back to Michael Beal.

"Thank you. You're very kind. Today must be a special day for you."

"That it is. But to be truthful, the main reason I accepted Dr. Johnson's invitation to come to Stockholm today was the possibility that you would attend. I wanted to extend my gratitude to you directly, in person."

Moments ago, inside the Grand Hall, the past parted with the past. Here, outside in the dim glow of the interior lights and under the watchful eye of the full moon, the past met the future.

The neuroscientist-turned-Dean had received from the young man a gift rarely given: a validation that one person's life positively influenced that of another. "I wish you all the best—both inside the laboratory and with your personal life. Find the balance and you'll find success," Dr.

Benedetti told the young man as they again shook hands before going their separate ways.

Dr. Benedetti briskly walked back to the hotel. He went directly to his room and silently packed his bags for an earlier than originally planned morning flight.

6

The small twin-engine plane was in the air about one hour, almost half way to Milan, before Dr. Benedetti summoned the courage to open his iPad. He was heading home with the satisfaction that he had completed the job of publishing the manuscript and also in having planted a seed. He was now ready to move on, to live a simple life in Tuscany, in his childhood village with his dear cousin Rosa. He wanted his remaining days to be worry-free with no regrets or concerns.

The temporary glossy keyboard popped up from the bottom of the yellow electronic notepad awaiting his slight touch. The seat on the half-full plane to his left was not occupied so there was no concern of anyone sneaking a peek, and the flight attendant seemed content to sit and do nothing the rest of the trip so he was, for all practical purposes, alone. Tentatively, he touched the "r" key, and then the "e" key followed by "m-a-r-k-a-b-l-e" then closed his eyes for a mid-air minute. Despite the low frequency hum of the engines he could feel his heart thumping inside his chest and he also could feel the palm of his hands become moist. When he looked down at his iPad, the only word on the yellow electronic notepad was: remarkable.

He stared at the word for a moment then typed the word "rekindle"; the word "rekindle" appeared as if his former secretary had typed it for him. Satisfied, Lorenzo Benedetti closed the black leather cover to the mobile device, put his head back and smiled.

Epilogue

1

Cold, nearly frozen raindrops landed in the Hudson River in Troy, New York but in Flatbread, the New Years Eve celebration was hot and steamy. It was that misty time after sex—when physical expressions are often and effectively transformed into verbal ones—that Phil asked Abby details about her telepathic ability. The more time he spent with her, the more he became intrigued with the efficiency and utility of telepathy. Abby read Phil's mind with little effort, it was as natural as taking a breath.

"What do you have to do to read my mind?" Phil asked, as he lay naked next to her, his right hand resting under the sheets on her upper left thigh.

"What do you mean?"

"Do you have to think, 'Okay now I'm going to read Phil's mind and find out what's going on in there' or does it work some other way?"

"Sometimes it's like that, like when we did the experiments with Dr. Paolo, or when I walked into class that day and tuned into what each of you were thinking. But most of the time it's not that way. They're just there, drifting in the air, like music from a radio.

"Oh yeah, I've always wanted to know, what were Dr. Paolo's thoughts that day? I mean, you did look fucking foxy and these babies were right out there, front and center," he said as he turned on his side and cupped her breasts for emphasis.

"I don't remember," she lied.

"Bullshit! I don't believe you. Come on tell me, he won't know."

"How do you know that?"

"What do you mean, 'how do you know that'? Do the deceased communicate with us?"

"They try to but..." her voice trailed off as she wondered if it was going to sound too strange to say aloud but to her surprise, he accurately completed her sentence.

"They're shut out! Only those with telepathic abilities can communicate, right? Am I right?" Phil twisted again so he was lying on his belly. He looked Abby squarely in her eyes and asked again, "Am I right?"

"Yes and no."

"What do you mean?"

"You don't have to be a telepath, anyone can do it. It's like learning a new language. Anyone can do it, you just have to work at it."

"So will you teach me how?"

"No. I mean, well, maybe someday. Trust me, it's not for everyone. Most people won't know how to handle it."

"Why? Sounds kind of cool to me. Where do I start?"

"You start by capturing a specific time."

"Specific times? Like midnight or noon?" Phil asked as he rolled onto his back.

Abby propped herself up on her left elbow to face Phil. "There are only certain times when channels are open. You have to capture those times or it won't work. Phil, I don't think you're ready to hear this."

"But I am. It could be very cool to think about this other, whatever you call it, 'dimension' mathematically. And in order for me to do this I'll need to understand it better. I'll need to experience it."

"Okay, listen. There is a time when you're going to sleep or just waking up, a fraction of a second between when you're conscious and when you're asleep or essentially unconscious. That's the time, that's the window you have to go through."

"But that's impossible. Since I was a kid I've just pass out when my head hits the pillow. I'm out like a light. I totally shutdown."

"No you don't," Abby said as she lay back drawing the blankets up to cover her neck. "Your senses wind down gradually. One second your brain is churning, thinking about something and you can still hear sounds, then the next second you're asleep, you're not thinking about anything and you don't hear anything. By that time you've moved beyond the communication window, it happens instantly. Then, when you wake up, the same thing happens but in reverse. When you come out of your sleep you gradually start to hear sounds, right? And your brain boots up and you start to process those sounds and you create thoughts. By the time you realize that you're awake, it's too late, the communication window is closed."

"I get it. I'll work on it. I can do that," Phil said with a bit of trepidation. "But then what do you do when you freeze that moment? What do you see? What do you do?"

"That's when things get interesting and ... well ... it could be dangerous too," warned Abby. "Once you develop this skill there is no going back. Phil, trust me, you probably won't like what you learn. Don't do it. Trust me."

———————

Although it left his earthly vessel, the essence of Dr. Paolo's core, his Universal Energy was re-condensed and full of unbridled power without intellectual or spatial boundaries. It was ready for the next adventure. It was as alive today as it's been for billions of years but no longer confined to the profound limitations of the human form—where it resided for a mere celestial second—his unique Universal Energy was once again free to traverse the other verses amidst the vast expanse of the Omniverse. Dr. Paolo's Universal Energy was and it still is, thought in its purest form.

It quickly visited other familiar Energies; those of his earthly mother, father, aunts, uncles and his two children. But very little time was spent in their presence, as each knew all about the other, and like other Energies, they effortlessly resumed their place in the highly unstructured and, for the most part, asynchronous space.

2

Abby listened to Phil's deep breathing as he lay close to her warm body. She knew that he wouldn't be able to capture the communication window tonight, not after the high level of physical energy he'd just expended. Wearily, she lay on her back and focused on her own body at rest. With her heart rate slowing, and her breathing becoming more and more shallow, Abby easily found the familiar window. The message from her former mentor could not have been clearer:

The last hypothesis was only the beginning.

The End.

I'd like to extend a heartfelt thanks to family and friends who took time to read early drafts of this novel. Their feedback, advice and encouragements were greatly appreciated.

www.ingramcontent.com/pod-product-compliance
Lightning Source LLC
Chambersburg PA
CBHW031116210626
46816CB00016B/1498